After the explosive events of *The Lion Li*
normal for burly fisherman Robin Shipp
the ancient Moth & Moon approaches h
and an unexpected arrival brings some sl
on a perilous journey alone.

While he's away, his lover, Edwin, anxiously prepares for the birth of his first child with his friend, Iris. Her wife, Lady Eva, must travel to Blackrabbit Island for a showdown over the future of the family business. Meanwhile, Duncan nurses an injured man back to health but as the two grow close, the island's new schoolmaster makes his amorous intentions clear.

Robin's search for answers to the questions that have haunted his entire life will take him away from everyone he knows, across a dangerous ocean, and into the very heart of a floating pirate stronghold. Pushed to his limits, Robin's one last chance at finding the truth will cost him more than he ever imagined.

WE CRY THE SEA

The Moth and Moon, Book Three

Glenn Quigley

A NineStar Press Publication

Published by NineStar Press
P.O. Box 91792,
Albuquerque, New Mexico, 87199 USA.
www.ninestarpress.com

We Cry the Sea

Printed in the USA
First Edition
March, 2021

Print ISBN: 978-1-64890-234-5

Also available in eBook, ISBN: 978-1-64890-233-8

Content Warning: This book contains depictions of the death/deceased family member, death of a secondary character, graphic violence, murder, and mention of trauma.

To Mark. None of this would exist without you.

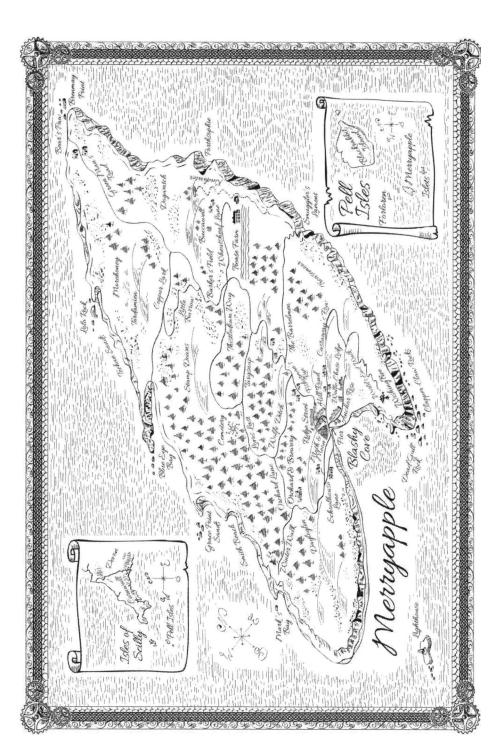

FIFTY-ONE YEARS AGO

In the village of Blashy Cove, the infant Robin Shipp is found aboard a boat named *Bucca's Call*. His father will raise the boy alone.

FORTY-ONE YEARS AGO

His father's best friend is apparently murdered on the same night his father leaves the island under mysterious circumstances. Soon after, his father dies at sea. Robin, declared the son of a murderer, is shunned by the community at large and believes himself an orphan. He works alone as a fisherman on his father's boat.

LAST SUMMER

A hurricane strikes the island and changes the course of Robin's life. It leads him to reconcile with his former partner after years of estrangement, to find love in the arms of his best friend, to prove his late father's innocence, and to discover his mother living in the very same village.

LAST WINTER

Robin and his friends travel to Blackrabbit Island. There, Robin's lover, Edwin, finds his own mother living in a shanty town of people made homeless by the hurricane. While on the island, Edwin is asked to father a child with his friend, Iris. He says yes. Together with Robin's new-found half-brother, they help foil a plot to overthrow the ruling council of the island. In the battle, Robin's hand is badly injured.

NOW

It's September, 1781.

Chapter One

Finding a gull in one's bathroom has a way of bringing into sharp focus just what massive beasts they truly are. They certainly appear large when harassing people at the seafront, or circling overhead, but coming face to face with one in a domestic setting really shows them in a whole new light. It wasn't actually using the privy, of course, though its demeanour suggested it could have if it wanted to. Rather, it seemed content to simply sit there and wait out the bad weather.

It wasn't until Robin Shipp approached that it began to caw and squawk furiously, flapping its wings with an air of indignity, as if protesting at him having the temerity to walk in without first knocking. Which, in all fairness to the gull, he had done, but then it was his lavatory and up till that point he'd never known it to be frequented by any type of wildlife whatsoever.

Despite his name, Robin had little affinity for, or interest in, birds. Especially gulls. He found them pests, for the most part. He was a fisherman and spent more time than he'd like trying to shoo them away from his catch. This one in particular was known to him as the Admiral, one of a pair of seagulls who fought a never-ending battle for supremacy of the harbour. Robin stood there, in the whitewashed room, shouting at the bird to leave for a good five minutes before accepting it wasn't going to be quite so easy.

He slowly slipped off his woollen overcoat and held it open, advancing as cautiously as his enormous frame would allow, then flung it quickly over the toilet. The gull was not amused, nor was it shy in expressing as much. After some kerfuffle, Robin managed to bundle it up in his coat, fearful the whole time of injuring its wings. He didn't like gulls, but he'd never be needlessly cruel or violent towards them either.

He wrestled the creature out of the room, across the narrow hall, and into his bedroom. The doors to his balcony were open. The method of admission, he suspected. He shook his coat open and the gull tumbled out, mewing loudly, before plodding to the balcony and flying away into the rain. It looked back to squawk at him one last time. An insult, Robin was certain. He shut the doors and sighed. He was late.

He pulled closed the front door of his tall, thin house and trudged down towards the harbour. He tugged his flat cap low over his eyes though the weather was already beginning to ease. With his meaty thumb, he rubbed the palm of his left hand. Injured the previous year, on the night of the winter solstice, it had never properly healed. His hand was always stiff now, with a deep ache and a white, weblike scar. Rubbing helped as he found it seized up if he neglected it too long, especially in cold weather. He'd been advised by the local doctor to keep rubbing it as often as possible as it kept the blood flowing, or some such.

Robin didn't really understand the mechanics of it. He'd been eager to resume fishing after the worst of the winter season had passed but quickly discovered his efforts hampered by his injury. He tried to pass it off as a minor inconvenience, but deep down he knew it was serious. He'd been a fisherman all his adult life, and before. He'd started when he was a young boy after his father had died and he couldn't imagine any other way of living, didn't want to imagine it, even. The hurricane of the previous summer, just over a year ago, had turned his whole world upside down and while he couldn't have been happier about it, the upheaval had been daunting. What he craved now more than anything was some peace and quiet.

With his bull neck, jug ears, and hooded eyes, Robin had never considered himself an especially attractive man, so quite what the undeniably handsome Edwin Farriner saw in him, he couldn't rightly say. Yet there Edwin was, sheltering from the rain against a market hall pillar, waiting for him. He was tall, though not as tall as Robin, in his early forties, so ten years Robin's junior, with receding and close-shaved ginger hair. His smile never failed to light up Robin's heart.

"You're late," Edwin said. "He won't be happy."

"Ho ho! When is 'e ever 'appy?"

The rain stopped and the clouds broke. They stood gazing at the roof of the Moth & Moon, shielding their eyes from the midday sun. Atop the enormous inn, workers hammered nails and sawed wood. A framework was coming together—six sided and spacious enough to comfortably fit ten men. Robin pulled his cap lower and cupped a hand around his mouth.

"Oi! Duncan!" His deep voice carried clear across the little harbour. "Time to eat! Come on!"

From the rooftop, Duncan Hunger waved and began to climb down the many ladders strapped to the rain-slick tiles. The Moth & Moon was expansive and ever-changing. A hunk of wood, glass, and lime wash, which seemed to regularly sprout fresh bay windows, bud whole new rooms, and blossom balconies. Its roof, or rather roofs, rose and fell like the sea—a tiled wave here, a slate swell there—and took some skill to navigate. Duncan grasped one of the numerous chimney stacks and used it to swing himself around to firmer footing. When his boots finally touched the ground, he shook raindrops from his coat.

"You're late," he said.

"Only a little!" Robin said. "I 'ad a visit from the Admiral."

"It's all well and good for you two to swan up whenever the mood strikes you," Duncan said, "but some of us have work to be getting on with."

Robin chuckled again. Duncan's natural state was irked, and he never needed a particular reason to complain. He cleaned all the lenses in his unique spectacles with a handkerchief. Small, round, and fixed with multiple thin armatures, they were of Duncan's own design. He was forever fiddling with them, setting first one lens in place and then another. Robin wondered if Duncan would be forced to add even more arms with even more lenses as he grew older. Duncan was Edwin's age but a couple of heads shorter. He was squat, burly, with wavy black hair, long sideburns, and an expression that indicated he had somewhere more important to be, so if you wanted him to stay, you'd better make it worth his while.

"'Ow's it goin'?" Robin asked, pointing upwards.

"Slowly," Duncan said, fixing the spectacles back into place on his button nose. "We should have been finished with the basic frame by now. The others are dragging their heels."

"Nothing to do with you resetting the wood every ten minutes and telling everyone they're doing it all wrong?" Edwin asked.

"Whoever could have told you such a thing?" Duncan asked. "It's a gross exaggeration and a terrible slight on my good name. Can I help it if I'm a perfectionist? I want this new bell tower to stand the test of time, to be..."

Duncan trailed off and pointed out to sea. "That boat's coming in a bit fast, isn't it?"

Robin turned and squinted before reaching into the pocket of his long, navy-coloured overcoat from which he produced a battered copper spyglass. He extended it to its full length. The glass was a touch foggy, but it was enough to determine a single occupant at the helm of the lugger.

"Can you see who it is?" Edwin asked.

"No," Robin said. "I can't see 'is face. But whoever 'e is, 'e needs to slow down or 'e'll run aground."

Robin ambled down to the pier, quickly overtaken by the much sprightlier Edwin and Duncan. All three men frantically waved their arms and shouted, trying to alert the sailor to the danger. The sailboat began to turn, taking it away from the harbour and straight towards the headland. Straight towards the rocks.

With a terrifying crack that landed like a lightning strike, the boat splintered against rocky outcrops, and its occupant was flung into the water. Without a moment's thought, Robin ditched his cap, overcoat, and jumper. He hopped around, pulling off his boots, before diving into the sea. Edwin followed suit. They splashed about in the choppy waters, unable to find the man.

"Robin!" Duncan said. "Over there! To your right! No, the other way... Starboard, man! Starboard!"

Robin kicked his massive legs furiously to avoid being dashed against the rocks himself. With one deep breath, he dived beneath the surface to search where Duncan had indicated, but there was no sign. Underwater, Edwin was pointing furiously. Robin turned to find the figure of a man floating limply. Together, he and Edwin grabbed the victim and brought him to the surface. Robin's lungs were burning, and he gasped for air.

Once ashore, they lay the drowning man on his back. He was breathing and coughed up some seawater. Blood poured from his left eye, dying part of his white beard crimson. He was huge, as big as Robin himself. A crowd gathered around them. Robin brushed the man's lank hair away from the wound.

"Easy, easy," Robin said. "You're safe now. What... Wait. *Vince?*"

"Hello, brother," Vince said. His usually growling voice was weak and cracked.

"Let's get him to the inn," Edwin said.

"No," Vince said, grabbing firmly onto Robin's arm. "Too many people."

"We'll take you to my 'ouse, then," Robin said. "It's not far."

They loaded Vince onto a borrowed cart and took him up the steep slope of Anchor Rise. He placed one huge arm across Edwin's shoulders, the other across Robin's, and together they all sidled through the blue front door of Robin's home. Scarlet dots gathered on the black and white tiles of the hallway floor as blood dripped from Vince's eye, yet still he stared at the oil painting on the upstairs landing. Once inside Robin's front room, they put him by the fireplace and wrapped bandages around his head and leg. They would have to do until Doctor Greenaway could be summoned.

"I didn't recognise you under all the hair," Duncan said.

"Haven't had much chance to get it cut," Vince said. "Been busy."

"Too busy to visit us, like you said you would."

"Here now, aren't I?"

Edwin handed him a mug of water and Vince sipped it, then pawed at his throat, obviously in some discomfort.

"How did you end up running aground?" Duncan asked.

Vince sipped his drink again but said nothing.

Robin frowned. "Vince? Did you 'ear 'im? What—"

Edwin coughed and placed his hand on Robin's arm. "Let's just give him time to get his head clear. He's obviously had a terrible shock."

Robin had only met Vince once before, around the same time he'd injured his hand. Before then, he didn't even know he had a brother. They'd promised to stay in touch, and they did, after a fashion. A couple of short letters had been exchanged but nothing more.

"Well, you can stay 'ere as long as you like, of course," he said. "My 'ome is your 'ome."

"How's he going to manage all those stairs with his leg the way it is?" Duncan asked. "You'd be better off staying with me, I suppose."

Vince growled something approaching gratitude. "Help me up," he said.

"You don't 'ave to go right now," Robin said, as he once more he let Vince lean on him.

"Hallway," Vince said.

Robin guided him back out onto the black and white tiles. Vince pointed at the painting upstairs.

"Who's he?"

"Oh, right, you never met 'im. It's our dad, Captain Erasmus Shipp," Robin said. "It were painted a few years before 'e died."

Vince shook his head. "Can't be Dad."

"Why not?"

"Because just this morning, I saw that man in Wolfe-Chase Asylum."

Chapter Two

Duncan cleared away his carvings and drawings to make room for his guest. He was a toymaker by trade and often spent his nights in front of the fire, whittling away at blocks of wood or sketching up plans for his next project.

Robin helped Vince into the living room, bumping into a table and chair as he went. Robin was taller than anyone else in the village and broader too. Vince was similar in stature—stout and brawny—though Robin's round belly eclipsed Vince's own. Robin set Vince down as carefully as he could, which meant he landed with a thud on the sofa. It creaked under his heft, much like the floorboards beneath Robin's feet. Duncan's little blue house on the hill wasn't designed to accommodate two giants at once.

"Doctor Greenway will be along to see you soon," Robin said. "'E's out at the Trease farm, but 'e's been sent for."

Vince nodded, then grimaced and held his head. Bramble, Duncan's cat, sauntered into the room, tail curled round the door as though he were trying to pull it closed behind him. He rubbed first against Robin's leg and then Edwin's. He stopped when he spotted Vince and hissed before running out of the room. Robin cleared his throat and put his hands in his pockets.

"Now," he said, in a tone of voice completely unfamiliar to Duncan, "what's all this about you seein' Dad?"

"Lady Wolfe-Chase has started moving people from Blackrabbit Gaol to the asylum," Vince said. "People who need looking after, not punished. One of them is a thewy man with long white hair and bright-blue eyes. Gotta be in his seventies at least, but big, like us. Strong. Been imprisoned for about a year, maybe less. Never says a word but keeps drawin' these symbols over and over. Anchors wound with snakes. It reminded me of somethin' but took a while to put my finger on it—the pendant on your cap. And my tattoo."

"Dad's sigil," Robin said.

"Didn't think much of it, till I saw the paintin' in your house. He's listed at the asylum under the name Bill Barrow but it's him. I'm sure of it."

Robin was silent for a good long while. Duncan shuffled about uneasily. The death of Robin's father had a profound impact, not simply on Robin, but on the whole village. Everyone had thought Captain Erasmus Shipp murdered his closest friend, Barnabas Whitewater, and fled the island only to die on a whaling ship shortly after.

The truth had come out in the aftermath of the hurricane the previous summer. Barnabas Whitewater died in an accident the same night Erasmus Shipp left to protect the village from an old enemy of his. If Erasmus Shipp was still alive, it meant he'd stayed away from the village—from Robin—for forty years. Duncan couldn't begin to imagine what thoughts must be going through Robin's head.

"Well, there's nothing we can do today," Edwin said. "Why don't we leave you to get settled? We've brought you some of Robin's clothes. You're both around the same size; he's bound to have something to fit you. At least they'll be dry."

Duncan saw them to the door, where Edwin leaned in close and whispered, "Are you sure? Just the two of you alone here? He's a dangerous man. I wouldn't like to see him in a bad mood."

"He's not as bad as he used to be, I think," Duncan said. "It'll be fine."

Robin grabbed him by the shoulder and squeezed a bit too tightly. "Thanks for doin' this, Duncan."

Edwin took the reins of the horse as Robin hopped onto the back of the trap, causing it to rock under his considerable weight. Duncan closed the door and went out to his workshop. There he rummaged around amongst his tools and offcuts until he found what he was looking for.

He returned to his front room to find Vince leaning against the fireplace, stripped entirely naked save for the blanket across his broad shoulders. His burly, heavily tattooed body was covered in bruises and scars—some old, some new. He had the distinctive mark of a gunshot wound in his side. Duncan had been present for that one. Indeed, it had been Duncan's own former lover, Baxbary Mudge, who had inflicted it.

On Vince's hefty upper arm was a tattoo of the same unusual anchor adorning Robin's cap, with its spindle of rope held in its crown. The symbol used by Robin and Vince's father. Across the rest of his powerful body were ships, mermaids, and all manner of animals. One could spend all day reading his skin. And what a pleasant day it would be.

"Didn't know where else to put them," Vince said of his clothes.

Duncan made no effort to avert his gaze. "That's perfectly fine, don't worry. Here, I thought you could use this."

He handed over a walking stick carved from ash wood. The grip was made of silver and shaped like an octopus, with tentacles curling down and around the shaft.

"Pull the top," Duncan said.

Vince tugged at the bulbous head which came away to reveal a long-bladed dagger. "Didn't realise life here was so dangerous."

"It isn't," Duncan said. "Which is why it didn't sell, I suppose. I made this one too long for a normal person anyway, but it might be right for you."

"Aren't I normal, then?"

"Not in the least," Duncan said.

Vince turned the blade over, examining its edge. Standing there naked, wounded, bathed in firelight and brandishing a knife, he looked savage, powerful, *primal.* Duncan's throat fluttered; his heart pounded in his ears. He scooped up the wet garments.

"I'll fetch you some more blankets. Why don't you go and lie down? You should probably be resting after your ordeal. You can take my bed."

Vince slotted the knife back into the walking stick and leaned on it, trying it for size. "You goin' to ask me what happened?"

"Not unless you want me to," Duncan said. "Do you need some help?"

Vince grunted as he limped to the bedroom, but it might have been a laugh, Duncan wasn't sure.

Upon leaving Duncan's house, Robin and Edwin returned the borrowed horse and trap to the stables of the Moth & Moon. They knew the village would be full of speculation about Vince, so Robin suggested they stop in for a drink and a chat with the chief gossip—his mother, Morwenna Whitewater.

They found her in her usual spot at the large round table close to the main fireplace. She was in her early seventies, with sharp features entirely unlike Robin's, and was rarely seen without her red shawl. She was attended, as usual, by some of the elder men and women of the village. Her circle of Tweed Knights, as they were lovingly called, were joined for the evening by the sailor with the scarred eye, Mr. Penny, and the jack-a-dandy, Mr. Kind.

"She wants me to stay home with the baby," Mr. Kind said. "Can you imagine? These clothes covered in...*spit*...and who knows what else?"

"She wants you where she can see you," Mr. Penny said. "She knows you too well."

"Mum," Robin said as he leaned down to kiss her on the cheek.

His mother shooed away some young children from their seats to make room for Robin and Edwin.

"What's happening?" asked Mrs. Hanniti Kind, without looking up from her knitting.

"Who was on the boat?" asked Mrs. Greenaway.

"How did he run into the rocks?"

"Was he injured?"

"Is it serious?"

"Will he die?"

Robin held up his hands and chuckled. "Wait, wait," he said. "The man was Mr. Vince Knight, from Blackrabbit. My brother. Well, 'alf-brother, strictly speakin'."

"Oh," said his mother. "*Him.*"

She hadn't taken the news of Vince's existence tremendously well. Robin was himself a product of an affair, as his parents had never been handfasted, but there'd been no hint of Erasmus Shipp having fathered other children. His mother had bristled when he had told her about Vince. She had said she was happy for him, of course. For someone who had thought himself an orphan, finding more family was never going to be a problem in Robin's eyes, but still in her words there had been the lingering hint of, what, betrayal? Loss? A longing for what might have been?

"He was badly injured," Edwin said. "He's recovering at Duncan Hunger's house."

Robin appreciated Edwin's tact. He wasn't sure exactly how Vince had received his injuries, but he suspected they weren't all caused by his accident. He thought it best also not to say anything about the patient at the asylum until he had the chance to speak to his mother in private.

"Really?" said Mrs. Kind. "How very thoughtful of Mr. Hunger. Tending to the man in his hour of need. I'm told there's a strong family resemblance between you two, Mr. Shipp."

"I'm not sure what you're gettin' at..." Robin said.

"I'm not getting at anything, Mr. Shipp. After all, Mr. Hunger is well known for his hospitality and warm demeanour."

"I 'ope you're not suggestin' Duncan has any...*intentions*...towards Vince?"

"I would never suggest anything of the sort," Mrs. Kind said as she raised an eyebrow and carried on knitting.

Robin's mother tapped her cane on the wooden floor as she often did when peeved. Beside her, the dishevelled sailor, Mr. Penny, was speaking to his friend, the always immaculate Mr. Kind.

"We were there when Mr. Shipp pulled him ashore," said Mr. Kind. "We actually met him once already. Last Midwinter, in Port Knot. We didn't realise who he was then."

"The infamous Vince Knight," Mr. Penny said, raising his eyebrows.

"Infamous?" Robin's mother asked.

"Vince is notorious in Port Knot," said Mr. Penny. "The red hand gripping the town by the throat. Every stream of criminality runs through him. You daren't so much as pick a pocket there without getting his permission first. Ah, not that I would, of course."

"Of course," said his mother.

"I'm surprised at you associating with his sort, Mr. Shipp," Mr. Kind said.

"'E's family," said Robin.

"Well, yes, quite, of course, of course," said Mr. Kind. "Didn't Mr. Shipp tell you about him, Mrs. Whitewater?"

Robin's mother tapped her cane sharply again. "He told me some things," she said, "but it appears he left out some of the more salacious details."

"Keep an eye on him, Mrs. Whitewater," said Mr. Penny. "Family or not, he's trouble."

Robin wanted to object but even he had to concede Mr. Penny wasn't wrong. Vince used to be everything Mr. Penny said he was. He was a ruthless, violent criminal at the very top of the pecking order. By the time

Robin first met him, he was already trying to turn over a new leaf, but they'd had little contact since then. What if Vince hadn't been true to his word? What if he'd gone back to his old ways? Perhaps those injuries he suffered had been at the hands of a rival gang, or even the Port Knot watchmen? He had more questions than answers.

He took some solace in the fact Duncan seemed to trust Vince, at least to a certain extent. They'd known each other for years, albeit not well, from the time Duncan had spent living on Blackrabbit Island. One had to earn Duncan's trust; it wasn't given lightly. Robin hoped on this occasion it wasn't misplaced.

Mr. George Reed, the innkeeper, arrived with drinks and put them on the table before turning away, coughing into a handkerchief. He was a personable man in his sixties, short—shorter than Duncan, even—with neat grey hair and beard and kind eyes.

"That sounds nasty," Robin said.

"I'll be fine. Don't worry," George said. "It's just something doing the rounds. Oh, actually, I need to speak to you—when you get a minute?"

"I'm free now," Robin said.

"You're certain? May we talk in private?"

Robin followed George through the bar area, under some staircases sprinkled with paintings, down some steps and up some others. They travelled along curving hallways—some carpeted, some bare—and through rooms Robin would swear he'd never seen before in all his years visiting the inn. A room filled with maps led to one stuffed with chairs, which in turn led to one filled with nothing but dolls. Undiscovered rooms were something of a hallmark of the inn, along with staircases, numerous and varied in style, that almost never took you where you wanted to go. The simple act of getting from the ground to the top floor might require navigating a dozen or more of them. The shortest distance between two points may be a straight line but in the Moth & Moon the line was likely to be twisted into a fisherman's knot.

"Somethin' on your mind, George?" Robin asked.

"I was going to ask you the same thing," George said. "You're very quiet."

"Got a lot to think about," Robin said.

"I'm sure you have. Between Edwin's child coming, your brother arriving the way he did, and your hand."

Robin frowned.

"There's nothin' wrong with my 'and," he said.

"Then why have your catches been so light lately? And why have you been rubbing it for the past few minutes?"

Robin looked down and sure enough he was massaging his palm again. He hadn't realised he was doing it. "I didn't think anyone would notice."

"Well, your friends have noticed. And we're worried about you."

"I'll be fine. I'll work somethin' out. You know me," Robin said, forcing a smile. "What did you want to talk to me about?"

"You'll see," George said with a little cough.

They went around a corner, up some flights of stairs, and down a wallpapered hallway until they stopped at a sash window. George heaved it open and climbed out onto a flat part of the roof. Perplexed, Robin followed, finding the window much more of a tight squeeze than the diminutive George had done. Across the rooftop he was amazed to find a door.

"Where are we?" he said. "You can't even see the bell tower from 'ere."

"The Moth has lots of hidden places like this," George said as he undid the bolt.

He stepped inside to a shallow, bright room containing a writing desk and a large porthole window overlooking the sea. Robin was flabbergasted.

"The only way in 'ere is across the roof? What is this place?" Robin asked.

"It's my writing room," George said. "You can't see the window from outside because of how the roof is arranged. I only discovered it a few years ago, if you can believe it. I think it was originally meant to be a temporary storeroom when this section of the inn was being built. The Moth guards his secrets well."

"His?"

"Oh yes. The Moth & Moon feels like a man, don't you think? Ever-spreading waistline, craggy features, filled with ale?"

"I suppose 'e does, now you mention it," Robin said, chuckling.

He pawed at the stack of papers on the desk. A quill rested beside them.

"What are you workin' on?" he asked.

"I've been writing down everything I know about the island. All the history of the village, of its people. All of our stories."

"Ghost stories an' all?"

"Especially those—they're my favourites."

Robin lifted a page and slowly read aloud. *"The old gods returned to their forests and deserts, their mountains and streams, their 'omes and 'earths. Spirits of air and land and sea. Woden and Frig, The Wild 'Unt and the Buccca, piskies and mermaids, the Green Man and the wights, all were changed, made kinder and gentler by their brief exile."*

He turned more sheets over in his hands. "I didn't realise you were writin' the 'istory of the world."

"Just a bit of context, is all."

Robin didn't entirely understand what he meant by that.

"People did return to worshipping the old gods for a little while, after the Romans fell, though less fervently," George said. "I think it's poetic to imagine those evicted deities returning to the fields, climbing under the hills, settling in lakes and forests again. Grateful to be remembered. But after a while, people realised they no longer needed them. They were a childhood fantasy we outgrew. I shudder to think what the world would be like if we hadn't."

"I should give you my dad's journal to read, there's some of my family 'istory in there. Plenty o' tall tales too."

"That would be helpful, thank you. Nobody has written the history of the island before and I've been privy to plenty of it over the years. I don't want our stories to be lost. After all, I won't be around forever."

"You're soundin' a bit ominous now. You feelin' your age, Georgie-boy?" Robin said with a laugh.

George sat in the room's only chair. "In a manner of speaking," he said. "I've had several long discussions with our good Doctor Greenaway, and I'll spare you the grisly details, but the long and short of it is... Well... I've got only a handful of years left. If I'm careful. If I'm lucky."

Robin's face dropped. He thought he'd fall over, and he steadied himself with a hand on the cold stone wall. "Oh, George..." he said, removing his cap as a mark of respect. "I'm so sorry."

"It's fine, it's fine. I've made my peace with it. But it has rather set the clock on things."

"Is that why you've been coughin'? Mum's been doin' it too, is she...?"

"No, no, the cough is something new. Mr. Penny already had it and made a full recovery; we will too. No, my illness has been with me for a while."

"You never said anythin'.'"

"Not in my nature. You know me. This is why I wanted to talk to you. I need to know the Moth & Moon is in good hands once I'm gone. I don't have children, none of the staff are in a position to take over, nor do they want to, truth be told. The Moth is a commitment. A lifelong commitment. It takes time to run. And money."

"An' I 'ave both."

"And you have both."

"Not enough to buy the place though."

"I'm not selling it. I'm giving it to you. Well, leaving it to you."

Robin was stunned at the offer. Never in his wildest dreams had he imagined such a thing. The Moth & Moon was an institution, the heart and soul of the village. It was like being offered the sea, or the sky. "It would be...a massive 'onour."

"It would be a massive responsibility. During the hurricane, Lady Wolfe-Chase made me see how running the Moth is also being custodian of the whole village. The Moth needs to be placed in a safe pair of hands. And I can't think of a safer pair than yours, Robin."

"Even now?" Robin said, holding up his scarred palm.

"Even now," George said.

Robin welled up. From the news or the offer, he couldn't say. George hugged him tightly.

"I know it's a bit overwhelming. I probably should have waited to ask you, but time isn't really on my side."

"No, no, don't worry," Robin said. "I'm just... I'm thinkin' about all the times you were there for me over the years. When most of the village shunned me, you always stuck up for me."

"I did more than that for you," George said with a wink.

"True, true," Robin said, laughing. "You know, Edwin asked me recently why you and I never courted."

"Hah! Can you imagine?" George asked. "With me as grumpy and foul-tempered as I used to be and you always so jolly. It never would have worked."

"A lot's changed this past year," Robin said.

George's pale-blue eyes sparkled in the moonlight. When he smiled, his eyebrows slanted upwards and the lines around his eyes deepened. His whole face lit up and his kindness shone through.

"Why did you never settle down with anyone, George?"

"Amazing as it may seem, there isn't a great demand for stumpy, grumpy old men."

"You weren't always old," Robin said with a grin.

"Running the Moth didn't leave much time for courting. And I never had any real interest in it to begin with. The odd bit of fun with a stout sailor or a charming fisherman is enough for me, always has been. And I've never been short on companionship." He spread his arms as wide as he could. "I've got the whole village in my home most nights! Now, if you're agreeable, I'll make the announcement in public, so it's all nice and legal."

"Just...let me talk to Edwin first," Robin said.

"Of course, of course," George said. He lightly squeezed Robin's elbow. "You've no idea what a relief this is. It's a weight off my shoulders."

Robin put his cap back on. He didn't have the heart to tell George how uncomfortable the idea made him. Not only mentally but physically too. He had to duck to pass through every doorway in the place and he wasn't a graceful man. He lumbered around, knocking into people, dropping things, breaking them—and that was when he was concentrating. He wasn't built to be indoors—he needed the sea, the air, the space. The thought of being cooped up indoors all day, surrounded by glasses and chairs and other easily broken objects filled him with a cold fear.

"What are you going to call it?" he asked. "Your book?"

"You know," George said, "I'm not sure."

The copper pipes carrying hot water around Robin's tall, thin house rattled and banged, as they usually did. The invention of small, affordable clockwork pumping systems had revolutionised how people washed in their homes, but if you wanted quiet, efficient plumbing, you needed to head to the mainland, to the big cities.

Robin didn't mind. Noisy as it was, it was preferable to a tin bath in front of the fireplace. Robin lay in the water with his arms and legs hung over the edges of the tub. There wasn't a bath on any island in which he could comfortably fit. His round belly rose above the waterline and a wooden toy replica of his beloved boat, *Bucca's Call,* floated between his beefy thighs. His cap hung on a hook on the wall facing him and he stared at it, unblinking. He might as well have been a thousand miles away, so lost was he in his own thoughts. Edwin stood in the doorway with his arms folded.

"You've been very quiet since you got back," Edwin said. "Do you think it's true? About your dad?"

"Maybe. I don't know," Robin said.

He lifted a wet hand to his face and rubbed it across his bald head, stopping to twirl his fingers through the solitary tuffet of short, white hair above his forehead.

"It's too much to 'ope for, isn't it? I mean, I always dreamed of findin' 'im and now there's actually a chance, it's too much to take in."

"You sound more excited than you look," Edwin said.

Robin chuckled a little. "I am. I really am. I might finally get to find out why 'e left. No more second-guessin'."

"Robin," Edwin said. "I'm happy for you, but please, just...be careful."

"What do you mean? Careful about what?"

Edwin sat on the edge of the bath and took him by the hand. "I... Vince hit his head, so he might not be thinking clearly."

"I know."

"The man in the asylum might not be your dad at all."

"I know, Edwin. I'm bein' sensible, I promise. I've been thinkin' about what Vince said. Before the asylum, Dad—"

"Or Bill Barrow."

"Yes, fine, whoever 'e is, 'e were only in Blackrabbit Gaol for less than a year. So where were 'e before then? If 'e weren't dead and 'e weren't imprisoned, why didn't 'e come 'ome? Why didn't 'e come back to me? To Mum?"

"I've been thinking about it too. And...there's no easy way to put this, but what if he didn't come back because, well, because he simply didn't want to?"

"What a terrible thing to say," Robin said as he gently pulled his hand away.

"I didn't mean it to sound so harsh, but... Look, your father was a pirate. We know as much from his own journal. Then he moved back here, had you, became a fisherman, but from what your mother had told us, he never sounded particularly happy."

Robin plucked the little model of *Bucca's Call* from the water and fussed with its sails. "'E weren't 'appy because 'e couldn't be with Mum because she were married to Barnabas Whitewater," he said.

"I know, I know," Edwin said. "But your dad may have been content to let everyone think he was dead so he could...I don't know...go back to being a pirate again, perhaps."

"You think 'e were 'appier without me in 'is life? Without Mum?"

"I wouldn't put it in those words."

"You sort of just did," Robin said as he rested the toy boat on his belly.

"You used to idolise your dad," Edwin said, "and I know finding out about his pirate life was hard for you, but I worry you're desperately hoping for some noble justification for his actions when there might not be one. I don't want you to get hurt, Robin."

"I know you don't," Robin said. His brow furrowed and his lip pouted a tad. The model of *Bucca's Call* slipped from his stomach and fell into the water, tipping over as he sighed and sank lower into the bath.

"Forty years is a long time," Edwin said. "A lifetime. Just...try not to pin all your hopes on him."

Robin forced a smile. "I won't."

"You probably will though," Edwin said with a sigh.

"I'll try not to?"

"That's all I ask," Edwin said, leaning in to kiss him on his forehead.

Chapter Three

Robin awoke to find himself alone in the blue, empty stillness before dawn. He clambered out of bed and lifted a clockwork striker-lantern. He turned the key on top of the little brass lamp and a shower of sparks ignited the candle within. He quickly dressed, then plodded downstairs and found Edwin in the kitchen, wrapping some ham and bread. He was bathed in warm candlelight and Robin couldn't help but wrap his arms around Edwin's waist and kiss him. They stood there for a few minutes, holding each other. Robin felt calm in his arms, felt the chaotic world settle into place. A calm soon disturbed by a knock on the front door. Duncan had arrived.

"Vince is still asleep," he said. "I thought I'd pop round so I could say mean things about him before you left. Are you all set?"

Robin laughed and grabbed his bag from the hall.

"Ready when you are."

Edwin closed the door behind them and all three men made their way down the steep, cobbled road named Anchor Rise. Duncan's lantern swung as he walked, casting dancing shadows on the whitewashed houses. He spoke in hushed tones about how much food Vince was eating and how much space he was taking up.

"There's somethin' I've been wantin' to say to you both," Robin said. "I think... I think I'm goin' to 'ave to give up fishin'."

Duncan raised his eyebrows and stopped dead in his tracks. "I never thought I'd hear you say those words."

Edwin took Robin's injured hand. "It's this, isn't it?" he said, lightly tracing the cobweb scar with his finger. "It's worse than you've been letting on."

Robin nodded sheepishly. "I 'aven't been tryin' to 'ide it. I promise. I wouldn't lie to you about it. I were tryin' to work through it, is all. I thought it were only a matter of gettin' used to it, of findin' some way to cope with it, but..."

"It's slowing you down," Edwin said.

"A lot more'n I thought it would," Robin said. "An' I'm not gettin' any younger. I'm already older than most fishermen out there. My joints are goin' too, and it's only goin' to get worse."

"It'll be hard not to think of you as a fisherman any more," Edwin said. "It's part and parcel of who you are."

"I know, an' I feel the same way. I don't want to give it up, but things change, don't they? This past year, everythin's changed for me. I suppose it makes sense for this to change too."

"Well, I'll be honest: I'll feel a lot better in some ways," Edwin said. "I always worried about you out at sea, all alone. Anything could happen." Robin motioned to object but Edwin held up his hands. "I know, I know, you've been sailing since before I was born and you're better at it than anyone in the village. Doesn't stop me worrying."

"You don't actually need to work, though, do you?" Duncan said. "Not like the rest of us. You have the money your father left to you."

"'E left me enough to get by, but I need to keep busy."

They arrived at the pier, where *Bucca's Call* was moored. Robin threw his bag down into her.

"What will you do instead?" Duncan said.

"I 'aven't decided yet, but George has made a proposition."

"Doesn't he know you're with Edwin now?" Duncan said.

Robin made a face. "Not that sort of proposition, you smutty dog," he said. "George, well, 'e wants me to take over the runnin' of the Moth & Moon."

Edwin was shocked. Duncan looked confused.

"When?" Edwin said.

"Soon as possible, I think. Don't tell 'im I said, but...'e's not well. I don't know the particulars, but 'e's makin' plans for when 'e...for the future. I'm in two minds about it; I don't know if it's a good idea."

"It isn't," Duncan said. "I'm not being cruel, but let's be honest, Robin, you can barely get through breakfast without smashing a cup or a plate. How are you going to cope with the hundreds of glasses in the bar? Will you even fit behind there? Didn't George have the floor raised because he's so short?"

"The floor can be lowered again. And there's more to the inn than serving behind the bar," Edwin said.

"Oh yes, I can just picture you changing bedclothes and emptying chamber pots, Robin."

"The Moth is the heart of the village," Edwin said. "It's where handfastings, funerals, and everything in between happens. It needs someone strong and dependable at the helm. Someone the people trust. I think George chose the very best person."

"Well, you would think so," Duncan said, rolling his eyes.

Robin and Edwin carefully picked their way down the slick stone steps to the water's edge and climbed aboard *Bucca's Call.*

"Whatever I decide," Robin said, "there's somethin' I need to know first."

"Your dad," Edwin said.

"My dad. I need to know so I can put that night behind me, once and for all. The night he disappeared."

"Interesting timing on George's offer," Duncan said as he undid the mooring line and threw it down to Robin.

"In what way?" Robin asked.

"Well, Edwin has worked hard lately to give up drinking and you start running a tavern."

"Oh!" Robin said, turning to Edwin. "I 'adn't thought of it like that! I won't do it if it makes you un'appy."

Edwin smiled and held Robin's hand again. "Don't be silly," he said, "It's fine. I'm fine. Duncan is just being Duncan."

He made a face in Duncan's direction before laughing. Robin hoisted the sails, and they began to gently drift away from the pier.

"So, when you get back and start pouring ale, are you going to scuttle *Bucca's Call*?" Duncan called after them.

"Never!" Robin said forcefully. "'Ow dare you even suggest such a thing!"

"You could hang her from the ceiling in the Moth," Duncan said.

"No," Robin said.

"She'd make a nice decoration."

"Stop."

"You could fill her with plants."

"Duncan."

"Or use her for firewood."

"*Duncan!*"

Bucca's Call was a scarlet-hulled, two-masted lugger, easily big enough for them both and more besides. Still, Edwin did his best to stay out of Robin's way as he deftly guided them across the sea between Merryapple and Blackrabbit. Edwin clasped the neck of the whiskey bottle kept tucked under a thwart for emergencies, turning it round and round.

"What's up with you?" Robin asked as he slipped his meaty hands around Edwin's waist and hugged him tightly.

"What makes you think anything's up?" Edwin said.

"The look on your face," Robin said. "You're 'ere but your mind is someplace else. You thinkin' about 'avin' a drink?"

"Hmm? Oh, this," Edwin said, lifting the bottle. "No, no it was something to keep my hands busy. If I was going to drink, it would be scrumpy, anyway."

Robin leaned forward and kissed the back of Edwin's lightly freckled neck. It made Edwin close his eyes and sigh. It always did.

"It's getting close," he said.

"Ho ho, what, already?" Robin said.

"Not that," Edwin said, turning on his seat so they were face to face. "The baby. It's almost here and I'm almost a... I'm not ready."

"Is anyone ever ready?"

"I don't know, I suppose not? But I still feel... I don't know."

A gull screeched overhead, marking the break of dawn. A blaze of orange blossomed into the purple sky.

"You feel like inside you're still the same young tearaway who got drunk every night and climbed trees naked?"

"They weren't always trees," Edwin said, "but yes, I suppose. It's such an enormous responsibility. Sometimes, I wish they'd asked you to be the father."

"Why me?"

"Because you're so much more...settled than I am. More mature and I don't mean your age—I mean inside."

Robin chuckled, his round belly bobbing up and down.

"*Mature*," he said. "I'll let you in on a little secret. Doesn't matter what I look like on the outside, because inside I'm still a ten-year-old boy who just found out 'is father died. I'm still the boy who woke up one day and found out 'e were all alone in the world. Should I live to be an 'undred, I don't think I'll ever be anythin' else."

"But you've done so much, survived so much."

"So 'ave you. You're stronger than you know."

"It's... I look at Duncan and what happened with his dad and I worry."

"You could never be like 'is dad. You could never be violent."

Edwin stood and grasped some line or other. He was sure Robin had told him the name of it a dozen times or more, but he couldn't remember what it was called if his life depended on it.

"I'm not saying I would be, but I can't help but worry. Then there's you and your dad."

"My dad never laid a finger on me."

"No, no, I didn't mean... Ah, I'm sorry, I'm not explaining myself properly. Look, on the one hand you have Duncan who hates his father and on the other there's you, who idolizes yours. Or you used to, at any rate. Maybe you always will, a bit. I don't think I could cope with either scenario. And what if something bad happens to me and I end up scarring my child for life, like your dad did to you?"

"Isn't it somethin' every parent thinks about?" Robin said. "And aren't you forgettin' somethin'?"

"What?"

"Well, on the one 'and there's me, on the other 'and there's Duncan, and in the middle, there's you."

"The middle hand?"

"Forget the 'ands!" Robin said, laughing again. "I'm talkin' about your own dad. Didn't you ever speak to 'im about all this?"

"Sort of. A bit. I tried to ask him how he'd felt before Ambrose was born, but he simply shrugged and said he didn't think much about it. He said it would be like worrying whether or not the sun was going to rise tomorrow. It was a part of life."

"That were Nathaniel all over," Robin said. "Kept 'is 'ead down and got on with what needed doin'."

"He said the same about when I was born too. It's like everything in his life was sort of...planned out in advance. Fated to be. He'd gotten married, had children, ran the bakery, passed it on to me, all according to plan. He didn't make waves; he didn't fight back. He was carried along on life's tide, right from the moment he was born till the moment he died."

"Maybe there's somethin' to be said for 'is approach to life," Robin said. "Takin' each day as it comes."

Edwin didn't find the idea particularly comforting. He'd found his father sleeping, or so he'd thought, by the fireplace barely two months earlier. He tried to rouse him, but when he touched the icy cold skin of his hand, he knew there was nothing to be done.

Nathaniel Farriner was buried in the island's cemetery—a wild-flower meadow with a single yew tree in the centre. His gravestone read "Father & Baker." He'd left instructions that Edwin's mother, Sylvia, wasn't to be mentioned on it. Edwin had travelled to Blackrabbit shortly after, to the asylum, to tell her about his death, but she hadn't understood him, hadn't reacted at all. Edwin wasn't sure if that was a kindness or the most upsetting thing he could think of. The woman who had tormented his father for their entire marriage now seemed not to remember him at all. No one in the village spoke of his own late brother, Ambrose, any more. Perhaps it was the destiny of all Farriner men to slip away and be forgotten.

Robin slid the boat past the far larger merchant ships and through to the busy harbour of Port Knot. There they hired a carriage and were soon travelling out of town along the leafy green laneways leading to Wolfe-Chase Asylum. Sunlight dappled the lush, plum-coloured velvet interior of the carriage. Being the size he was, Robin needed a seat all to himself and was sitting with his husky hands pressed between his knees, staring out the window.

Edwin sat facing him, watching shadows from the sun-splashed trees dancing across his pleasant, round face. He wasn't very difficult to read. Edwin could always tell when Robin was sliding into sadness, when he needed a gentle nudge to bring him back. He also knew when to leave him alone with his thoughts.

When they arrived at the asylum, they disgorged themselves from the carriage and paid the driver. Edwin took Robin by the hand and squeezed. He was forcing him to pause and take a breath, stopping him from blundering headlong into the unknown.

Ahead was the imposing edifice of Wolfe-Chase Asylum, formerly known as Chase Manor. It extended into the distance on either side of them and was built of a pale stone the colour of fog. High above the entrance, Edwin could just make out the glinting front of Moonwatch, the elegant dining room, with its wall and ceiling made of glass held in place by a metal framework shaped like a ship's wheel with a letter *C* in the centre. Edwin thought it too grand to be used by just the staff for their meals and wondered if it was also where they fed the patients.

"Are you ready?" he asked.

Robin exhaled loudly and tipped his cap back. "I think so. I 'ope so."

Their heavy black boots crunched on the gravelled courtyard as they walked up the wide granite steps to the oak front doors, which they were surprised to find already open.

"Hullo?" Edwin called.

His voice echoed in the clean, marble tiled hallway. Ahead was the main staircase, a richly carpeted affair which rose to a landing, then split in two. The landing still held the enormous taxidermy wolf which had disturbed Edwin when he first saw it last winter. A commotion could be heard coming from the east wing, so they headed towards it. Fearing the worst, Robin beckoned Edwin to stay close to the tiled wall. He leaned round a corner to where a heavily bearded man brandishing a cutlass was threatening a kneeling nurse.

"Tell me!" the bearded man said.

The nurse pointed a shaking finger to a room in an adjacent corridor. Several other people opened it and in seconds ushered out a very tall, thickset man with a blanket covering his head. They kept him ducked low and guided him through a broken window to freedom. The rest of the asylum staff were being held at musket point by a slight man who kept nervously looking about. All the attackers were dressed in baggy, unwashed clothes. Some wore headscarves. There was only one thing they could be.

"Pirates!" Robin said.

He dashed forward and grabbed the bearded man's arm to stop him from using his sword. The man yelled out in pain. Edwin helped the nurse to his feet and guided him away to safety. About them, half a dozen more pirates swarmed, cutlasses drawn.

"Let him go," the skinny man said in a Dutch accent.

Without warning, the bearded pirate punched Robin in the nose, causing him to stagger back momentarily and loosen his grip. The pirates then ran to the window and leapt out. The skinny man with the musket was the last to leave, and he kept his weapon trained on Robin the entire time. When they'd gone, Robin and Edwin leaned out the window as the pirates made their escape through the grounds of the asylum. Mrs. Honor Knight, the fearsome warden of Wolfe-Chase Asylum, barked orders at her staff to check on the other patients.

"There's a little beach about a mile over there," said Mrs. Knight. "They've probably got a longboat waiting for them. What are you two doing here, anyway? Well? Are you going to answer me or stand there gawping?"

Edwin's heart was thumping so hard in his chest, he could hardly think straight.

"We, well..." Robin said. "We were... You see... Vince said..."

"Vince!" Mrs. Knight said. "Have you seen him? My son? Where is he?"

"He's fine," Edwin said. "He came to us in Blashy Cove."

Mrs. Knight held her hand over her chest and exhaled. "Nobody's seen him since the hullabaloo yesterday. What happened to him?"

"He looked like he'd been attacked."

"Yes, that sounds about right. He was supposed to be working out in the old groundkeeper's cottage. There had definitely been some fighting in there as well. One of the pirates talked about something happening 'too early.' Clearly they wanted Vince out the way before the raid."

"Were they really pirates?" Edwin asked. "What did they want?"

"They came to free one of their own, from the looks of things," Mrs. Knight said. "I suppose they sent someone after Vince first to get him out of the way."

"Who did they take with them?" Robin asked.

"An elderly man recently sent here from gaol," Mrs. Knight said. "Mr. Bill Barrow. Why?"

Edwin and Robin exchanged glances. Edwin felt a cold dread creep over him. "He's someone you know. We believe—Vince believes—this Bill Barrow person might actually be Captain Erasmus Shipp."

"Ridiculous," Mrs. Knight said, folding her arms. "Don't you think I'd have recognised him? The father of my only son?"

"Would you, though? It's been, what, fifty years, give or take, since you last saw him? And Vince said he has long hair now and wears a beard."

Mrs. Knight thought about it for a moment. "He wasn't here long," she said. "And he kept avoiding me, turning away from me. I never heard him speak. I mean, I suppose it could be him. But I thought he was dead?"

"We all did," Robin said, quietly. He tipped his cap to Mrs. Knight, turned on his heels and marched out.

"Robin, wait!" Edwin said.

"No time. I've got to get after them," Robin said.

He hurried as quickly as he could out of the asylum. He wasn't built for speed, and Edwin caught up with him easily and ran on ahead.

"Wait for me!" Robin called after him. "We don't know what them pirates will do if they get you."

Together they rushed through the gardens and across the fields beyond. A copse of sweet chestnut trees stood between them and the small, rocky beach. In the distance, Robin spotted a longboat. He pulled out his spyglass.

"Well, is it him?" Edwin asked.

"Can't make 'im out," Robin said.

Farther out, in deep water, sat a brigantine with a distinctive masthead in the shape of a charging bull.

"There's their ship," Robin said. "It's not flying any colours."

They hastened back to the asylum courtyard and Robin climbed, panting, into the waiting carriage in the courtyard.

He bellowed at the driver. "The 'arbour! Quick as you can!"

Edwin jumped in and sat facing him as the carriage rumbled across the loose gravel. "What are you going to do?"

Robin was struggling to catch his breath. "I'm gettin' *Bucca,* and I'm goin' after 'em."

"And then what? What if they're already underway by the time you reach them?"

"I dunno, I'll 'ave to follow 'em, I suppose."

"For how long? You don't even know where they're going! This is madness; please, Robin, wait and—"

"*No!*" Robin said with a force Edwin hadn't experienced before. "No, Edwin, I'm sorry, but no. I'm done waitin'. I'll not lose 'im a second time."

"Then I'm coming too."

Robin leaned forward and clasped Edwin's knee. "No, you're not, my darlin'. You've got the bakery to think about. Iris, the baby. And you're no sailor. I can't be out there worrin' about you on top of tryin' to find Dad."

Edwin wanted to argue, but he knew Robin was right.

"Please," he said, "if you don't know how long you'll be out there, at least get some supplies first. Food, water. You'll need them, won't you?"

Robin and Edwin walked the busy harbour, hand in hand, doing their best to ignore the hustle and bustle of the busy port around them. Each time Edwin visited, he said he thought it more raucous, more chaotic, more dangerous. It felt as though a fistfight could break out among the quarrelsome dock workers at any moment. It wasn't unusual to see someone discovering they'd been pickpocketed or suffering in the aftermath of a more violent robbery.

Edwin tried to convince Robin to hire a larger boat, fearing *Bucca's Call* was too small for the task. Robin, of course, would have none of it.

"She'll look after me," he said, running his hand along the scarlet hull. "She always does."

Bucca's Call was open-decked so the only storage was in compartments beneath the seats which spanned her width. However, her bow was presently covered by the detachable platform Robin had made years earlier so he'd have somewhere to lie out under the stars with Duncan, and now with Edwin. He'd forgotten to remove it before they left Blashy Cove. He stored some small barrels of fresh water beneath it and flung some bags of food into a hatch midship, beneath a thwart.

"Please be careful," Edwin said.

Robin's eyes stung with bridled tears. He wanted to be strong for Edwin. "I will," he said, cupping the side of Edwin's beautiful face. "I've got too much to lose now."

Edwin slipped a letter into Robin's pocket and spoke in a low, warm voice. "Don't open it yet," he said. "Save it until you really need it."

"Do me a favour?" Robin asked. "Give my dad's journal to George Reed. And tell 'im I'm flattered, but it 'as to be no. Tell 'im 'e'd be better off findin' someone else to take over the Moth."

"He'll be disappointed."

"I know, and I 'ate to let 'im down, but it'll be for the best in the long run. I can keep fishin' for a while longer."

Robin leaned down and they kissed. He basked in the warmth of Edwin's body, telling himself to remember every moment, every sensation. He hoped the memory would keep him warm during cold nights at sea. He unfurled *Bucca's* pristine white sails and guided her away from the pier, waving. He didn't know if he was doing the right thing, but he was doing the necessary thing. And that would have to be good enough.

Chapter Four

Vince slept clear through the night and most of the following morning. When he woke, he found Duncan standing over him, carrying a bottle and a glass tumbler on a tray.

"Oh, sorry, I didn't mean to wake you," Duncan said. "I've brought you some water."

His hands were shaking a touch and the items rattled as he set them on the bedside table. He was nervous. Vince was used to having that effect on people but he didn't know Duncan felt the same way around him. He'd always liked Duncan, though they'd spent little time together. He appreciated Duncan's fire, his willingness to fight back against the world. A short man with a short fuse. A lot of spirit in such a small package. Vince pawed at the fresh bandage over his own left eye.

"Ah, I wouldn't do that," Duncan said softly. "I'm sorry, but Doctor Greenaway said...well..."

"Spit it out, man," Vince said.

"He saved the eye but not your sight. I'm sorry, Vince."

Vince growled and exhaled sharply, as if he'd taken a sudden punch to the gut. He knew the damage was severe, but he thought he'd reached help in time. He grabbed a fistful of blanket and twisted it.

"I tried to wash and mend your clothes," Duncan said, "but most of them were ruined, apart from your overcoat."

He opened the curtains and hovered by the window, fussing with the tie-backs or some such. Vince couldn't see what exactly he was doing, and he didn't really care. It was obvious Duncan was building up the courage to speak.

"Do you want to tell me what happened?" Duncan asked, at last. "Those bruises on your body—they weren't all from the wreck, were they?"

"Penhallow and Palk," Vince said with a sigh.

"Those two louts who used to work for you?"

"Worked for Mudge, you mean."

Mr. Baxbary Mudge had been Vince's employer and, years earlier, Duncan's abusive lover. Last winter he'd attempted to blow up a stage containing the ruling council of Blackrabbit and seize control of the island himself. Vince had helped thwart his scheme, with help from Duncan, Edwin, and Robin. He'd received a gunshot wound to his side for his trouble.

"As did you," Duncan said. "You all worked for him, but Penhallow and Palk answered to you. How did they escape gaol?"

"Never got sent there in the first place," Vince said. "After what happened last winter, they escaped, been in hiding till yesterday. Wanted revenge for me turning on them. Was clearing out a cottage on the grounds of the asylum, and they jumped me. Penhallow, Palk, and two others I'd never seen before. Swear they looked like pirates. Pushed me inside and locked the door. Started to kick and beat me. Got one of them on the floor straight away, out cold. Smashed his head open. The other three, though"—he held his hand over his eye—"did this. Palk was the real threat. Huge, strong, young. Weak jaw though. Went straight for it. All my focus on one point. Got him down. In a headlock. Threatened to snap his neck if the other two didn't back off. They did, surprisingly. Swear I saw actual concern on Penhallow's ugly face, even if only for a minute."

"What happened? Did you..."

"No. Penhallow made a deal. Either I kill Palk and they kill me, or I let Palk go and I leave Blackrabbit for good. Got Penhallow to give me his knife and marched Palk to the shore. Let him go when I found a boat. Made for the only place I knew I'd find a friendly face."

"Here," Duncan said.

"Could barely think straight after the beating. Couldn't see where I was going properly because of this." He gestured towards his ruined eye again. "Ended up running aground in the cove."

"Aren't you worried what they'll do now you've gone? Your mother, the asylum?"

"Penhallow and Palk are wanted men. They won't last long on Blackrabbit. They won't get anywhere near Mum. If they've any sense, they're on the way to the mainland by now. Land in Cornwall, head north. Disappear."

"And if they haven't any sense? If they come after you again?"

Vince touched the bandage over his eye.

"Then I'll make them pay."

Edwin's stomach was in knots when he knocked on the door of Morwenna Whitewater's cottage. It was the first time he'd ever been there without Robin. He got along well with Morwenna, but they were rarely in each other's company without someone else present. He fixed his shirt while he waited for her to answer the door.

"This is a surprise," she said. "Are you alone? Come in, come in."

He followed her inside and sat in the cramped kitchen. The walls were festooned with paintings made by her late husband, the very talented Barnabas Whitewater.

"I need to talk to you," Edwin said as she filled a teapot. "Robin won't be home for a while."

"Whyever not?" she asked.

"We went to Blackrabbit this morning. Actually, I think you should sit down. Please."

Morwenna sat in her favourite chair and wrapped her red shawl tightly around her shoulders. Her face was pale, her mouth open. "You're worrying me, Edwin."

"Robin didn't want to say anything to you until he was sure, but Vince...well, he thinks he saw someone at the asylum in Port Knot."

"Who? Who has he seen?"

"Captain Erasmus Shipp."

Morwenna laughed. It was a short, sharp, nervous reaction. She tapped her cane over and over on the stone tiles by the fireplace, striking the air with sharp notes. She scanned his face, looking for some trace of the joke, some hint of a lie.

"Vince said this man had been in gaol for about six months before being moved to the asylum," Edwin said. "We went to see him but when we arrived the asylum was under attack. By pirates. They escaped with the man who may or may not be Erasmus Shipp. Robin went after them."

"What do you mean, *went after them?*" she asked, her hand at her throat.

"He took *Bucca* and chased after them. I couldn't stop him, and he wouldn't take me with him."

She sank into her chair, looking all around as if searching for an answer or a way for it not to be true. "What's he going to do when he catches them?"

"I don't know. I hope he's going to find out who the man is and return home, with or without him."

"They're pirates!" Morwenna said. "Who's to say they won't simply kill him?"

"They've no reason to. Robin's not a threat to anyone." He dearly hoped he was right. Pirates had a reputation, certainly, but didn't they also live by a code, by a set of rules? Robin wasn't after their ships, their money, or their lives. He just wanted answers. "Besides, if it is his dad, he won't hurt him."

"Did you see the man?" she asked. "Do you think it's really him?"

Edwin shook his head. "It all happened too fast," he said. "I thought it was far-fetched, but the fact it was pirates who came to rescue him..."

Morwenna was quiet for a minute or so. She seemed to drift away into her memories. Her eyes, so unlike Robin's, darted from side to side. "I don't know if I want it to be true," she said. "Isn't that terrible?"

"Erasmus's death must have been a terrible shock, especially coming so soon after your husband's."

"The grief was so wretched I thought I'd lose my mind," she said.

"Both of the men you loved were gone. And your motherhood was a secret known only to yourself."

"I don't want to think he's either been imprisoned all these years," she said with a sigh, "or has simply chosen to stay away. Both options are horrible."

Edwin poured the tea and handed a cup and saucer to her. "Have you spoken with Vince?"

"Not yet. I've been hearing about some of the things he's done. He sounds perfectly nefarious. Why didn't Robin tell me about him? About the kind of man he is?"

"It's not that he didn't tell you about him," Edwin said. "He merely let off a few of the details."

"You think him being the master of Blackrabbit's criminal underbelly is a detail?" she asked. "You think a legion of vicious gangs under his thumb is a detail? Those people are all violent thugs, and they're all *afraid* of him."

"I'm sure he told you Vince wasn't exactly an upstanding citizen. But Vince said he's trying to start over. Duncan said the same about him. Robin thought it wasn't fair to colour your opinion of him before you'd even met. Didn't you always hate when people round here did the same to Robin? Tell all and sundry what a terrible man he was, before they'd even met him?"

Morwenna shifted about in her seat and stabbed her cane at the floor. "A low blow, Edwin," she said.

"Worked, though, didn't it?" Edwin said, grinning. "Robin will be fine. He's big enough to take care of himself. He'll be back in no time. You'll see."

Chapter Five

Mr. Nick Babbage stood at the head of the cramped classroom before the children of the village. Eight, in all. He was told the numbers would vary, depending on the tides, the harvest, and the time of year. Some children had other responsibilities at home. He was warned such would be the case in these remote communities. Indeed, it had been the case all over the country until relatively recently. People were finally beginning to understand the importance of a formal, structured education.

He was well-dressed, forty, boxy-framed, with a full, tawny beard and moustache. He'd often been told his resting appearance was of a man who was deciding whether or not to punch someone on the nose, though he wasn't the sort to engage in violence of any kind.

He'd arrived on the island during the commotion surrounding the shipwreck, and no one had paid him much attention. He'd had his belongings delivered to his lodgings on Ridge Street, which to his dismay was located at the very top of the steep hill dividing the village in two. The schoolhouse was situated further down the slope of a hill to the west of the village. Or was it the same hill? He wasn't sure. Whatever the case, the cove was ringed by enormously inconvenient obstacles he supposed he'd spend most of his time either climbing up or sliding down. The schoolhouse stood alone but for one little blue house further up, with what looked like a workshop of some kind attached to it.

Nick had found in the desk drawer a note from the previous schoolmistress, one Mrs. Amity Cardew. She had left instructions on where various keys could be located, the lessons she had already covered, and a list of troublemakers to look out for. He wasn't clear on why Mrs. Cardew had left her post and hoped to find out later when he spoke to his uncle.

"Now, children," he said, "my name is Mr. Babbage. I'll be your new schoolmaster and—"

"You're the doctor's nephew, aren't you?" one young girl asked.

"I am," he said, slightly taken aback. "How did—"

"Everyone's been talking about you for days," she said. "Mr. Dominic Babbage, from London, if you don't mind."

"I'm not sure—"

"Come to take over the school because he couldn't cope with life in the city."

Nick's eyes narrowed, and he cleared his throat. "What is your name, Miss?"

"May Bell, sir."

The name at the top of Mrs. Cardew's list of troublemakers.

"I'm the apprentice to Mr. Farriner at his bakery," she said with obvious pride. "He insisted I take one day a week to attend lessons. I don't see the point, honestly. I can learn everything I need from Mr. Farriner. And Mr. Reed. And my mother. And anyone, really."

"Yes, well, I think we've heard enough out of you for now, Ms. Bell. Today's lesson is—"

"Ah, here you are!" came a voice from the doorway. "So sorry I'm late."

Doctor Mark Greenaway let himself in and greeted his nephew with a warm handshake. It had been a decade or more since they had last met. His uncle had grown wider around the waist and greyer in the moustache. His monocle dangled, as ever, from a gold chain. The canary yellow waistcoat he wore was borderline garish, but Nick supposed fashion wasn't much of a consideration on the island.

"I trust your journey was uneventful?" his uncle asked, his baritone voice warm as ever.

"Yes, yes," Nick said, "Though my arrival rather more so. There was a shipwreck? An injured survivor?"

"Oh yes, I know about all it. I've just been tending to him. I wanted to stop by and make sure you were settling in. I can see you have your hands full. I'll come by later and take you for supper in the Moth & Moon and tell you all about the wreck."

Without another word, his uncle was gone, leaving Nick a tad flustered.

"Take me where?" he asked.

Lady Eva Wolfe-Chase sat in her study and scribbled some notes on a shipping manifest. Since handing the day-to-day running of her family company off to her cousin, she'd tried to become less involved, tried to make more time for her wife, Iris, but every now and then something would cross her desk and demand her attention.

The room in which she worked was bright and airy, painted duck-egg blue and had a tall arched window overlooking the headland and down to the cove. She'd filled the room with cabinets to store documents and plans but she never quite had enough space for them all. Boxes filled with paper rested on almost every surface.

On the very highest shelves were scrolls rescued from her family home, Chase Manor, before its conversion into an asylum. The scrolls dated back to the birth of the Chase Trading Company and she wanted to ensure they were safe. Thickly bound identical books marked with years and months lined the lower shelves. Several quills and inkpots littered her desk, along with an astrolabe and broken sextant. A small fireplace stood empty under a lavish painting of Iris's parents.

"This would be a perfect spot for a cradle," Iris said.

Eva set her quill down. Iris stood in the doorway, her red curls tumbling down onto her gown, a viridian robe volante.

"I hardly think so," Eva said. "How could I be expected to work with a mewling infant in my office?"

Iris didn't rise to the bait. She almost never did. "They will of course be *your* mewling infant, my love. Not a stray we drag in off the street."

Iris was running her hand across some old books and she pulled one from a pile. "Look," she said, "you've even made a start on some reading materials for the baby. *The Dancing Princess*."

Eva rose from her leather chair and kissed Iris on the cheek. She took the book from her hands.

"My favourite story as a child," she said.

"Now, whatever could have drawn you to the story of a princess sneaking away to dance with a beautiful, flame-haired girl?" Iris asked.

"I need peace and quiet to work," Eva said, returning the book to its proper place. "The lodge has many other suitable rooms. Anyway, shouldn't a nursery be in the attic?"

"It's too stuffy up there. Besides, this is the closest room to ours," Iris said, gazing out of the window. "And the view is quite special..."

"Never mind the view; you should be resting." Eva took her wife by the shoulders and guided her to a sofa.

"I don't need any more rest," Iris said. "I need a change of scenery. Take me to the Moth & Moon later."

"No," Eva said.

"Oh, please, Eva, only for a little while!" She stamped her feet on the fuchsia rug. It was an imitation of a tantrum, a feint meant to emphasise her point. Iris wasn't truly given to such hysterics.

"No," Eva said, "it's too noisy, too dirty and too filled with hazards. What if you were to trip on the lopsided floor or some drunken lout were to bump into you?"

"I promise to avoid all lopsided louts and drunken floors. Or whatever it was you said."

Eva glared at her.

"I'm going with or without you," Iris said, as she slowly stood, holding her belly and trying not to let the effort show.

"So you can come and keep an eye on me or you can stay here and worry."

Nick Babbage was staggered by the sheer size of the inn. Four storeys high, or was it five? The irregular construction, the hodgepodge of styles, the seemingly random placement of windows all made it hard to be sure. There wasn't a straight wall in the place. One could barely walk ten paces without descending or ascending some apparently superfluous steps or swerving to avoid a support column. Staircases, spiral or otherwise, could be found in the most unexpected of spots, creating a seemingly unending amount of quiet little alcoves. The floor rose and fell like the sea with steps leading down to furnished pits and others leading up to platforms ringed with railings.

The area in front of the main bar was the most uncluttered, the most spacious. It was open to the upper floor, creating a gallery which seemed to Nick to be not only the heart of the inn but of the village itself. Patrons leaned on bannisters, shouting at each other in mostly good-natured ways. Beer swished from tankards, cider dripped onto clothes, and a platoon of apron-clad servants carried trays laden with food, drinks, or empty plates. Uncle Mark led him to a table near the colossal fireplace and motioned to one of the servants.

"Two scrumpies and two crab pies, if you would."

"This inn," Nick said, "I've never seen the like. Where does it end?"

Uncle Mark placed his thumbs in his pockets and beamed proudly. "It doesn't! The Moth & Moon is eternal, dear boy! And getting larger."

"Yes, all the banging and those men on the roof, what are they doing?"

"They're building the quite excellent suggestion of our own Mr. Shipp. A bell tower, to warn against another hurricane."

"Isn't the hurricane the reason Mrs. Cardew left?"

"Blackrabbit suffered a lot worse than we did," his uncle said. "One of the schoolhouses over there was completely flattened by it. Mrs. Cardew was asked to go over and help run its replacement. It has more pupils and pays more money. I can't say I blame her for leaving. Education is so terribly important. Do you know there are places on the mainland where people still cannot read nor write?"

"It's more common than you think." Nick examined a niche in the wall behind him, one of dozens.

"The walls here are home to all manner of trinkets," his uncle said. "It's the custom for visiting crews to leave a gimcrack of some sort in one of those nooks. Over there, statuettes of strange creatures carved in faraway lands, over here some jewellery, above your head are colourful exotic bottles, from the looks of it. There are a thousand other curios scattered about. One could spend a year searching and never find them all."

Nick lifted some dusty coins. He held one up to the light. It was six-sided and with a square hole in the centre. "I've only ever seen these in books!" he said. "There're really very old. Do you think the innkeeper will sell them to me?"

"I'm sure he would, but whyever would you want some old coins?"

"For my collection," he said and immediately wished he hadn't.

His uncle's bushy eyebrows arched in exactly the same way everyone's did when he told them of his pastime. The reaction went as follows—surprise, disappointment, embarrassment, usually followed by a hasty change of subject, which wasn't required in this instance as the server arrived with their order. Steam rose from the crab pies, and Nick's mouth watered. He hadn't eaten since very early that morning. He eyed the golden liquid in the tankards with some suspicion.

"What is this?" he asked, lifting the drink and sniffing it.

"Scrumpy," Uncle Mark said, as if he was supposed to know what it meant. "Cider, my boy, cider! A local speciality. You'll need to develop the taste if you're going to fit in around here."

Nick sipped it cautiously and found it sharp and bitter. He made a face and set the tankard down.

"Well, maybe it will grow on me," he said. "Or *in* me."

"Excuse me," came a voice from behind, "I'm terribly sorry to interrupt."

Nick turned to find a dark-haired woman exquisitely dressed in a striped polonaise. He rose to his feet as she held out a hand to him.

"Lady Eva Wolfe-Chase," she said. "I'm so sorry to disturb you."

"Not at all," Nick said. It had been some years since he'd been in the presence of actual aristocracy. He didn't even know there were any on the island. It didn't seem the type of place for it.

"I actually wished to speak to the good doctor," said Lady Wolfe-Chase.

Uncle Mark wiped the scrumpy foam from his curved moustache with just a hint of weariness, Nick thought.

"Of course, Lady Wolfe-Chase," his uncle said. "At your service, as always. I assume this is about your wife?"

"She isn't eating properly, and I was wondering if you could take a quick look at her? We're sitting over there by the window; it shan't take a moment."

Uncle Mark followed Lady Wolfe-Chase without enthusiasm. Nick remained standing, unsure if he should follow or resume his meal. His uncle spoke to a heavily pregnant red-haired woman in a nearby booth.

"I hear you're not eating, Lady Wolfe-Chase," he said.

The red-haired woman shook her head. "I'm not bleddy eating because I'm not bleddy hungry!" she said loudly.

"But Iris, my dear, you must keep your strength up," Lady Eva said.

"I cannot eat all hours of the day and night! Honestly, Eva, you won't be satisfied until I'm the size of a house!"

"I'm merely trying to–"

"I know what you're trying to do, but–"

Uncle Mark spoke some quiet words which calmed the atmosphere. He returned to Nick and resumed his meal.

"Expectant parents," he said. "It's always the same. Fussing over nothing. I'm rather surprised at Lady Eva, though. She always seemed the level-headed one, but I swear she's panicking over the slightest little thing. I've seen more of those two these past few months than my own wife."

"When is she due?" Nick asked.

"Oh, not for a little while yet."

He set his knife down and ran his thumb across his fingertips. "Speaking of parents, how is my dear sister?"

"Mother is well, thank you," Nick said.

His uncle coughed and appeared distinctly uncomfortable. "And your father? You know, you and I have never spoken about what he did, and may I say how profoundly–"

Nick held up his hand and swallowed a mouthful of the freshest and most delicious crab he'd ever eaten. "There is no need," he said. "It's done. There's little sense in dwelling on things we cannot change."

Chapter Six

Duncan opened the door of his little blue house to find Edwin standing with a fresh loaf of bread in his hand.

"How's the patient?" Edwin asked, handing him the loaf.

Duncan shushed him and ushered him into the living room, where he whispered like a conspirator. "He's outside in the garden."

Edwin leaned to peer out the window. Vince stood with his wide back to the house, leaning on a cane.

"It's the first time he's been outside since he got here," Duncan said.

"Truly? I didn't think his injuries would keep him bedbound?"

"They don't, not really. His leg is sore, granted, but I think…" Duncan glanced out the window to make sure he wasn't overheard. "I think he's scared."

"*Scared?*" Edwin said, much too loudly.

Duncan grimaced and slapped Edwin's arm. "Keep your voice down, you idiot! I don't want him to hear!"

"What's he got to be scared about? Look at him: he's immense."

"Ever since he was attacked, I think… I don't know, I think it's done something to him. Inside. His confidence is gone. I think he's feeling… I don't know…*humiliated*, I suppose."

"Has he said as much? Are you sure he isn't just sulking?"

"No, of course not; he's not much of a talker. He's a bit like Robin used to be, in that respect. Must be a family trait. I thought he'd want to head back home by now, but he's just moping about the place, taking up a *lot* of room."

"Be fair. He only arrived yesterday. I could try having a word with him, if you think it'll help?"

"You–" Duncan stopped when the back door slammed closed.

Vince stomped into the living room, tapping his walking stick on the stone floor. "Edwin," he said with a nod.

"Vince, good to see you up and about," Edwin said. "Sorry I've not been over sooner, but I've been to Blackrabbit."

"Where's Robin?" Duncan asked.

"Well, that's what I came to tell you. May I?" he said, gesturing towards a chair.

Duncan bade him to sit. "You know you don't have to ask."

"The man who may or not be Erasmus Shipp," Edwin said, "was liberated from the asylum by a gang of pirates, who, we think, orchestrated the attack on you to keep you from interfering, and Robin has set off after them."

"*What?*" Vince said.

"That's a lot of information in one sentence..." Duncan said.

"Stupid bleddy fool," Vince said. "Why didn't he wait for me?"

"He didn't want to lose the trail, and you wouldn't be much good to him," Edwin said.

"Oi, *watch it,*" Vince said with a snarl.

"I meant you'd be very little use on a boat like *Bucca's Call* with a busted eye and a battered leg."

Vince hung his head low and slumped into a chair. Its legs creaked under the strain.

"I'm sure Vince didn't mean to snap at you," Duncan said.

"I know," Edwin said, forcing a smile. "It's just your way, isn't it? We all have our own ways."

"So, Robin's going after a gang of vicious pirates on his own?" Duncan asked.

"Hopefully, his father will stop them from hurting him," Edwin said.

"If it even is his father."

The silence which followed was excruciating.

"How did you get home from Blackrabbit?" Duncan asked.

"After I went back to visit Mum in the asylum, I tagged along on a Chase Trading Company ship. One of the perks of being close with the owners."

"*Close,*" Duncan said. "A funny way of saying you're fathering the heir to the Chase family fortune."

Edwin laughed and Duncan was glad to hear it. Still, there was something in the way he avoided eye contact, the slight strain in his voice. Edwin always played his cards close to his chest, but Duncan could tell he was worried. He was going to have to do his bit to keep Edwin's spirits up until Robin returned.

"Did you see your mum while you were there?" he asked. "How is she?"

"Much the same," Edwin said. "She wasn't aware of any trouble, or of anything else, really. She doesn't seem to notice me when I'm there any more. It's probably for the best. I hope Duncan is taking good care of you, Vince. Oh, we spoke to your mother, told her you were safe here with us. She was worried about you."

"That'll be the day," Vince said with a snort. "Hope she isn't expecting me back any time soon."

"Oh, are you staying long?" he asked.

"Thought I might, for a little while."

This was news to Duncan, who crossed his arms.

"If it's not a bother?" Vince asked.

"No bother, no bother at all," Duncan said.

It very much was a bother, but he didn't feel as though he was being given much of a say in the matter. He couldn't very well turf an injured man out onto the street.

"Has Duncan offered to show you the woods?" Edwin asked. "Or take you fishing?"

Vince growled indistinctly under his breath, and Edwin shifted about on his feet.

"Oh, um, yes, yes I suppose we could," Duncan said. "Go fishing, I mean."

"Let yourself into Robin's house: he'll have all the gear you'll need."

"You got a key?" Vince asked.

"For what?"

"Robin's house."

"Won't need one," Edwin said. "We don't lock our doors in Blashy Cove. There's no need."

"Got nothing worth taking, I suppose," Vince said.

Duncan sprang to his feet. "How very thoughtful, thank you," he said, ushering Edwin to the door. "We'll pop round tomorrow. Goodnight." He closed the door and took a deep breath. "You could make more of an effort to be civil, you know."

Vince adjusted his position in the chair. "Not easy for me, all this," he said softly.

"Edwin's done nothing but be kind to you. At the very least, try not to be overtly mean to him. He's a decent man; he doesn't deserve it."

Vince squirmed in his seat. If Duncan didn't know any better, he'd say Vince looked a trifle ashamed. "Don't like fishing," Vince said.

"No one in their right mind likes fishing. It's boring but it puts food on the table. And it will let you be seen by the village, let them get used to you being here. Look, when I first moved here, I wasn't exactly welcomed with open arms. I came here from Blackrabbit, which meant I wasn't to be trusted. You know the animosity between the islands. Stupid, but ancient. Anyway, when I first started courting Robin, he suggested taking me fishing. He said it was a good way to let the villagers get used to seeing me around, and it showed I was making an effort to fit in. But you can't go looking the way you do."

"What's wrong with the way I look?" Vince asked.

Vince's lank silvery hair hung over his eyes. His beard was bushy and unkempt. Back when he was the most feared criminal on Blackrabbit he'd kept it all short and tidy, though he'd never struck Duncan as the vain sort. Duncan beckoned him to the kitchen and prepared a bowl of hot water. From a cupboard, he produced a set of clippers fitted with a clockwork mechanism which kept the blades moving at a fast yet steady pace. He wound the little key and the device clicked to life.

"Take your shirt off and sit," Duncan said, pointing to a stool.

Vince did as he was told, dropping his linen overshirt on the table. Duncan put a cloth around his beefy, bare shoulders, covering up a tattoo of a portly nude man astride a barrel of rum. Duncan started to remove the grubby bandage from Vince's eye. Suddenly, Vince grabbed his wrist, hard. Duncan winced.

"Don't," Vince said. "Don't want you to see..."

They were so close to each other, Duncan could feel Vince's warm breath on his skin.

"It's fine," Duncan said softly. "You can trust me."

Vince relaxed his grip, and Duncan unwound the wrapping. The eye, formerly icy blue, was as grey as a heavy winter sky and it moved, sightless. The eyelids remained but were cut, bruised and swollen.

"How bad is it?" Vince asked.

"You haven't checked?"

Vince shook his head.

"Honestly? It's bad but not as bad as you probably think. You'll be scarred, but the skin will heal."

"So, I'm still beautiful, then?"

It was the first time Duncan had heard Vince make a joke, and he blurted out a laugh which was louder than necessary.

"Hah! As beautiful as the first time I saw you."

He prepared a fresh bandage and instructed Vince to hold it in place over his eye, to keep any stray hairs from entering the cuts. He lifted a handful of Vince's silvery hair and set the clippers to work.

The blades sliced and chopped, littering the kitchen floor with little hairy nests. After a few minutes work, Duncan ran his hand across Vince's big head, brushing away loose strands. Vince closed his eyes and exhaled deeply. Duncan gently blew on Vince's neck to dislodge more cuttings, and he thought he heard Vince utter a deep, rumbling purr. It caused him to pause for a moment before getting to work on Vince's beard. He set the clippers to a slower speed. The cold steel brushed against Vince's cheek, his throat, but he didn't flinch. He merely fixed Duncan with an inscrutable stare which caused Duncan's mouth to run dry.

When he was done, he again rubbed away any loose hair. He ran his stubby fingers through the beard, across Vince's strong jaw, over his uncoloured lips. He stepped back to admire his handiwork; then, from a drawer, he produced a small leather item.

"I almost forgot," he said. "Doctor Greenaway gave me this."

"What is it?"

"Close your eyes," Duncan said with a grin.

Vince did as he was told and Duncan set the object in place, then held up a small mirror.

"You can look," he said.

Vince took the mirror and examined the small oval covering his injured left eye.

"An eyepatch," he said.

"You don't have to wear it, but the doctor thought it might be useful."

Vince flipped it up, inspecting the damaged flesh beneath.

"I think you should use it, if only to prevent you from scaring children the way Mr. Penny does."

Vince stroked his beard, checking his reflection. "Longer than I usually wear it," he said. "Hair too."

"I thought it looked a tad more distinguished," Duncan said. "Not that the shorter style didn't suit you, but it did have a touch of the street brawler about it."

"More practical," Vince said, still checking the mirror.

"In what way?" Duncan asked.

"Meant an opponent had nothing to grab in a fight," Vince said.

"Well, hopefully, your fighting days are over."

Vince just grunted.

Chapter Seven

Robin had failed to catch up to the pirates' rowboat before it reached their ship. The brigantine with the bull masthead was already underway by the time he'd left Port Knot harbour. He'd spent all day and night trying to catch it, but the distance was now too great. The best he could do was try to keep it in sight and hope they made landfall soon. He checked his charts and reasoned their most likely destination was the Azores, a group of islands in the Atlantic Ocean. The westerlies carried ships right past them and made them a perfect spot for pirates to raid.

They were roughly nine days sailing away. He had enough provisions to last the journey. If he was careful. The pirate ship was far larger and slow enough for him to keep pace in spite of their head start, but it also meant they were capable of storing plenty of supplies. Robin had no real idea how long he'd be at sea and had stocked *Bucca* as best he could, but if he was forced to make land to resupply he risked losing the pirates altogether.

He held a spyglass to his eye and scanned the horizon, coming to rest on a blurry haze in the distance. He squinted and could make out one mast. No, wait, two. It was the pirate ship, for certain. He adjusted his course, making a note of the heading. He thought it best to keep far enough away to avoid raising suspicion but close enough so he didn't lose sight of them in case they changed direction. He hoped they weren't paying too much attention, or at the very least didn't consider his little fishing lugger to be a threat. After all, what if it wasn't his father on board? He'd be easy prey for pirates. Mind you, he had nothing of value worth taking save for the sovereign coin holder Edwin had given him last Midwinter.

Alone on *Bucca's Call*, his thoughts turned to his childhood, as they so often did. Ten years he'd spent with his father. Just the two of them in their tall, thin house on Anchor Rise. Every boy sees their father as a giant but in Robin's case it was close to the truth. His father was the biggest man on the island. Broad, brawny, and quick with his fists. He was perhaps the most well-known too. Notorious, even.

Robin could no longer be entirely sure how much of his memory of his father was based on their time together and how much was based on stories he'd heard over the years. If there was a fight to be had, his father was either in the middle of it or the one to put a stop to it. He was famous for being unbeatable in arm-wrestling and savoured the chance to demonstrate his prowess with the sailors who docked at the island. He was also famous for gloating. Sometimes, his lack of magnanimity in victory irked his opponents and a scrap would ensue. His father would always throw his punches with a grin on his face.

Robin remembered being loved, which was a lot more than some people could say. Life on the island was hard, at times. They were isolated in the winter months. Blashy Cove was a fishing village and in winter there was no fishing to be done. Cooped up for weeks and months in the Moth & Moon or in their homes, tensions among the villagers could easily flare. The smallest of slights could take on exaggerated meaning. Feuds lasting whole generations often had their origins in a frosty, dark, drunken evening in the tavern.

His father had been quick to anger yet quick to apologise. Whenever he snapped or yelled, he'd slump his shoulders and put his hand on Robin's arm, a look of genuine anguish on his face. He tried. That was what Robin remembered the most. He tried to be better than his nature, better than his upbringing.

Robin had learned about his own grandfather only through stories his mother told him and the notes in his father's journal. His grandfather had been a hard-hearted man who feared nothing more than being left destitute and so would not allow the lighting of a fire in the hearth except during the very coldest of nights. A captain himself, he'd put Robin's father to work at an early age, repairing boats in the harbour and then serving on board his ship. He'd died from a musket shot. No matter how frosty their relationship, it must have been a difficult thing for his father to witness. Robin supposed this harsh start in life had left its mark on his father and made him determined to give Robin a better childhood than he'd experienced himself.

There was a single line in his father's journal which leaped out at Robin when he first read it— "*It was all for my son.*" Everything his father had been through, the piracy, the life at sea, building *Bucca's Call*, learning the fishing trade, it had all been for Robin's sake. He'd done it all so Robin wouldn't have to face the same hardship. He wondered if he'd ever have the opportunity to thank him.

Chapter Eight

Duncan and Vince sat side by side on the end of the pier, fishing rods in hand. Neither had spoken for a good ten minutes. Duncan had felt uncomfortable at first, exposed, even. He wondered what people would say about him spending so much time alone with Robin's brother. There was a time, not so very long ago, when he couldn't have cared less about the opinions of others. *That's Robin bleddy Shipp's fault,* he thought. *Making me soft.*

It was a bright, clear morning, and they weren't alone on the pier. Two women sat closer to shore, teaching their son how to bait a hook.

"Must have been nice to grow up in a place like this," Vince said.

"I suppose so. Nicer than the farm I grew up on, which admittedly isn't saying much. You were in an orphanage, weren't you?"

"Did I tell you about it?"

"You mentioned it once before," Duncan said.

"Horrible place," Vince said. "Dad left Mum pregnant with me. She was working in Chase Manor as a lady's maid. She couldn't stay on there and raise me alone. So she made a choice. She put her position and the Chase family above me. Dropped me off at the orphanage. Let them take care of me. Every once in a while she'd visit. Sit with me for an hour or two. Then leave and go back to her life."

"It must have been very upsetting."

"You'd think so, but for the longest time I didn't know anything was wrong. Thought it was how every child lived. Was surrounded by children in the same position, but some didn't ever get visits. If anything, I thought I was the lucky one. As I got older, I started to realise what was actually happening. Would cry for Mum to take me with her. When I was ten years old, she took me out of the orphanage. Put me to work in the kitchens at Chase Manor. Did that for a few years. Worked under the watchful eye of the cook, Mrs. Tressloggett. Don't think I ever saw any of the Chase family."

"Did you live at the Manor?"

"In servant's quarters. Big dorm room. Bit like the orphanage, I suppose. Me and a handful of other children. Cleaning ovens. Sweeping chimneys. Mopping floors. Then I moved to working in the stables. Was outside more. Liked that. Didn't like the horses much. Or they didn't like me. But the work was better. Had my first boxing match there. Me and another stable hand didn't see eye to eye. The stable master suggested a bout to settle it. Lad was a couple of years younger than me. Shorter too."

"I bet you were tall as a boy."

"Taller than everyone. Was confident I'd clean his clock. He knocked me flat on my arse in under a minute. Taught me humility, it did. Worked harder. Got stronger. Next time we fought I knocked him out cold. A visitor to the stable saw; he was impressed. Offered me money to join him. To become a fighter. So I did."

Vince's fishing line danced in the water. He didn't attend to it.

"Spent years boxing in clubs and streets. Legal and otherwise. Won fights. Lost fights. Always got stronger for it. My new employer, Jack Kneebone, was a crook. Started using me as his enforcer. As a debt collector. Had me rough up some of his enemies. And some of his friends. Turns out I had a knack for it. Because I didn't care who I hurt. Not really. The money was good. Fell in with a gang of people who all worked for him—Fred, Tamsyn, Hector, and Jasper. We were thick as thieves."

"Literally," Duncan said.

There was a smile on Vince's face, only a small one, but it was there. "We drank in all the worst pubs. Gambled. Pinched whatever wasn't nailed down. We were notorious. The Pebbleshoe Runners, we called ourselves. After the lane we had our hideout on. We were feared. And respected. Mostly." He took off his tricorne cap and scratched his head.

"Other gangs would try to take us down a notch every once in a while. Sometimes we'd win, sometimes we wouldn't. But we stuck up for each other. Anybody who so much as looked at one of us the wrong way got a beating from the rest. We believed in each other, you know? Believed together we'd all make it out of the muck. Only Fred did, though. Wrangled his way into a job at Port Knot bank. Kept his nose clean. Worked hard. Bought a fancy house on Barley Hill. Settled down. Raised a family. Tamsyn drank herself to death before her twenty-second year. Hector, well, I was in love with him but didn't know how to tell him. Wasn't much of a talker back then."

"How you've changed," Duncan said.

He meant it as a joke but he didn't think he'd ever heard Vince talk so much before and certainly never about his past.

"Consoled myself in the arms of anyone else who'd have me. Got more than one girl pregnant."

"Children?" Duncan said.

He was amazed at how casually Vince announced this fact. He'd never even hinted as much before.

"Assuming they're still alive," Vince said. "Their mothers didn't want anything to do with me. Who can blame them? Was at the dog races with Jasper when I found out he and Hector were courting. He knew how I felt about Hector. He'd tried to hide it from me. He looked terrified. Took a swig of my ale and gave him a slap on the back. Wished them well. They were my friends. What else could I do?"

"What happened to them?"

"Jasper and Hector? They started running a market stall. Selling stolen goods at first, but they saved money. Went legitimate. We lost touch. Think it was deliberate on their part. Couldn't be seen mixing with the likes of me any more. Crossed the road if they saw me coming. Hurt me, it did. The lack of loyalty.

"By then, I was the oldest of Kneebone's charges, as he called us. Gangs from all over Port Knot united by him and kept in line by me. One day, years later this was, Kneebone had me knock on the door of a tenement. One of his debtors hadn't paid in months. Owed a fortune. Kicked the door in, found Jasper cowering on the floor. Hector had died weeks earlier in an opium den. Jasper didn't have the money. No way to get it. We took his market stall, whatever goods he had left. Took everything. He couldn't pay his landlord. Ended up on the streets. Got word they found him a month later. Frozen to death in a shop doorway."

"Vince..."

"Not proud of it, but what could I do? It was business. Jasper should have known better than to borrow money from Kneebone. Should have come to me for help. But he didn't. Stupid bleddy fool. Anyway, it went on for a few years, made a name for myself. People were scared of me. Used to avoid looking me in the eye. Would stop talking when I entered a room. Could make a grown man quiver and sweat simply by looking at him. Liked it. Liked the respect."

Duncan's line twitched, and he pulled in a decent-sized pollack, knocking it on the edge of the pier and tossing it into a crate. He did it all in one fluid motion, the result of spending far too much time with Robin. Vince watched him intently.

"Ask me," Vince said.

"Ask you what?"

"What you've wanted to ask me from the first time we met," Vince said.

Duncan finished rebaiting his hook and cast the line back into the water. "Have you ever taken a life?"

"Started getting offers from other criminals. Doing jobs on the side. Jack Kneebone found out about it. He didn't like it. Tried to teach me a lesson with a very sharp knife. We fought and I killed him with it. Like to say I didn't mean to, but I didn't try very hard to stop myself. He was the first. Weren't many more after him, and they were all crooks who were trying to do away with me or someone I cared about."

"Someone like Martin, you mean?"

Vince twitched where he sat, adjusting his weight. Duncan was well aware he was on dangerous ground talking about Vince's late husband, and he tread as carefully as he could, but he had to confront the simple fact that he didn't really know this man at all. This thug by his side. This killer in his home.

"Once Kneebone was dead, I took over his business dealings. His games. His schemes. Suddenly, I was a significant figure in the criminal underbelly. Didn't take long for me to scare off any rivals. Then Baxbary Mudge came on the scene."

"Oh," Duncan said. "*Him.*"

Even the mention of his former lover's name was enough to cause a sting in his belly. The embarrassment, the regret, and the tinge of fear.

"Ambitious. Smart. A charmer. Wanted my help eliminating rivals to his family's mining company. Offered me a lot of money. More than I'd ever seen. So I ran his competitors off. Mudge suggested a partnership. Of sorts. Could see the benefits. He had clout with the magistrates. And the watchmen. Needed my contacts. We worked together for years.

"Somewhere along the line, I started letting him take over more and more. Maybe I was getting tired of it. Don't know. It was around then he got involved with someone. A brash farm lad from the mainland. Too good for Mudge, but he didn't realise it. He was tough. Quick wit. Sharp tongue. Would shout down anyone who gave him lip. Fearless. Didn't have much contact with him though. Mudge kept him under lock and key."

It was nice to hear how highly Vince thought of him. Usually, Duncan didn't like to dwell on that time on his life. He'd loved Baxbary Mudge, at first. Loved the lifestyle, the money. Back then, Vince had been a somewhat shadowy figure, always lurking in the background.

"Did you know how badly he was treating me?" Duncan asked.

"No. Not entirely," Vince said, running his bulky hand across his own jaw. "Knew he wasn't good to you. Knew he wasn't kind."

"But you never said anything?"

"Wasn't any of my business. For all I knew, it was how you liked it."

Duncan's cheeks flushed, and he sat up straight. He slammed the fishing rod down.

"Don't get shirty with me," Vince said sternly. "Didn't see you very often. Mudge didn't talk about you. The odd word here and there, maybe. Met some very unusual people over the years. People who like to be treated all sorts of ways. Knew some folk who paid good money for courtesans to treat them like animals. Beaten, whipped, branded. All sorts."

Duncan sank into himself and crossed his arms. He knew Vince was right. It wasn't fair to blame him. Vince's fishing line twitched again.

"The hurricane," Vince said. "Last summer. It was the start of the end. It flattened one of the arcades in Port Knot, along with the tavern I used as my base. The Dogtooth, it was called. You probably remember it."

"Mudge took me there once. Awful place, with those horrid mustard colour tiles and the ingrained stench of who-knows-what."

"Killed a lot of my men when it came down. Had to dig my way out of the rubble. It let Penhallow and Palk rise in the ranks. Wish they'd been in the damn place when it came down. Was clear right from the start they were gunning for me. Winter solstice, last year, was my way out. Mudge ended up behind bars for trying to kill you and the council. Penhallow and Palk were set to join him, or so I thought.

"Mum had me back working at Chase Manor again, after thirty-odd years. Of course, it's Wolfe-Chase Asylum now. Was working as a porter, mostly. Lugging equipment and boxes around. Think Mum wants me there to keep the more unruly patients in line. And to keep me out of trouble. It worked. Until a couple of days ago. Penhallow and Palk came for me. And I ended up here with bruised ribs, battered leg, and a busted eye."

Vince's fishing line jerked wildly.

"Steady!" Duncan said. "Tease it out, side to side, there you go. Now, start reeling in. Smooth but fast. That's it, you've got it!"

Dangling at the end of Vince's line, tail flapping wildly, was a wide, flat ray.

"You're a natural!" Duncan said. "You Shipps were made to be fishermen."

"Not a Shipp, remember?"

"You should have been," Duncan said. "If your dad had been more responsible..."

"And what, married my mum?"

"Maybe. Or taken care of you when she couldn't. He could have raised you here."

Vince turned to gaze across the harbour with his one remaining eye.

"This could have been my home," he said. "In another life."

He didn't say a word during the entire walk home.

Archibald Kind swiped at some tall grass as he sauntered along the sandy trail to Porthsophie, a secluded beach on the eastern side of the island.

"The thing is," he said over his shoulder, "I'm just not the stay-at-home type. I need to be out there, in the world, seeing all it has to offer."

"And being seen in return?"

His companion, Mr. Penny, was smirking.

"Well, yes, quite," Archibald said, fixing his flaxen hair into place. "Arminell is a sweet girl, truly the most wonderful wife a chap could ask for, but surely she can understand I'm ill-suited to the task of—"

"Staying home and raising your son?"

"When you say it in such a tone you make me sound unreasonable. Where are you going?"

Mr. Penny scrambled down the sandy hillside to a small, ash-grey sailboat with no nameplate or identifying marks whatsoever.

"Not one of the island fleet," he said. "If anything, it looks as though it came from Blackrabbit."

Two sets of footprints led from the craft to the hill.

"Why wouldn't they use the harbour?"

"Whenever I sail into a little beach like this, it's because I don't want to be seen."

"Smugglers, do you think?" Archibald asked.

Mr. Penny was crouching down for a closer look. He found another set of prints. Paw prints.

"Why would smugglers need a dog?" he asked.

"Somebody out for a sailing trip, then," Mr. Kind said. "They've probably gone for a walk inland."

"Perhaps, perhaps not."

"Not everyone shares your devious mind or intentions."

"But some do," said Mr. Penny. "Some do."

Chapter Nine

A gentle knocking on her study door roused Eva from her trance. She'd been flipping through some Chase Trading Company documents and had drifted away on a daydream.

"Yes, Drake," she said. "What is it?"

The lodge's footman lingered in the doorway. His gaze remained fixed on the far wall, and he sighed heavily before speaking.

"There's a Ms. Stability Popplestone to see you, ma'am," he said. "She's waiting in the hall."

"Drake," Eva said, "when I converted Chase Manor into Wolfe-Chase Asylum I gave you the option to either continue working there or to come and work here at the lodge. Are you unhappy with your choice?"

"No, ma'am."

"Then perhaps a little less ennui in your voice is warranted, yes?"

"Yes, ma'am."

He returned moments later with a broadly smiling young woman dressed in a modest bonnet and shawl who quickly introduced herself and sat bolt upright in her chair.

"You come very highly recommended," Eva said. "I understand you worked for my cousin, Dorothea?"

"I did," she said. "Such a stimulating woman. So vibrant."

Eva had always thought her cousin somewhat dull but saw no reason to be disagreeable just then.

"My wife and I are expecting our first child and require a nanny. Do you have any questions?" she asked.

"How many people are living here at the lodge?"

"Myself, Lady Iris, the baby—when it arrives—a footman, and a cook."

"Very good," Ms. Popplestone said.

Her voice was high and sweet. Eva thought it a contrivance. She also spoke quickly, as if she was trying to get all her words out before being interrupted.

"I like to keep the numbers to a minimum in the first few weeks. Less disturbance, you see. I shall expect visitors from outside the family to be kept at bay for the first month, at least."

"Why so?" Eva asked.

"For the well-being of the child," she said as though it was painfully obvious. "Unfamiliar voices can disquiet a baby and leave them in a nervous position which can last a lifetime."

Eva cocked her eyebrow. It didn't sound at all likely, but she knew nothing of childcare.

"I hope you don't mind me saying, but you don't strike me as being the most motherly of women," Ms. Popplestone said.

Eva sat back in her chair. The expensive leather creaked exactly as she hoped it would, puncturing the air with opulent authority.

"And you can tell as much from this one meeting with me?" she asked.

"I've done my research. I always do, before speaking to a potential employer, especially one as important as yourself. You have no other children, and I can't recall you spending any time with Dorothea Chase's offspring while I was there."

Eva tapped her finger on the desk. While she always respected someone who was forthright, she was irritated at the sharpness and truth of Ms. Popplestone's remarks. She wasn't very motherly—it was true—and she didn't particularly like children although she'd heard many times it was different when they were one's own. She hoped desperately it was true.

"Lady Wolfe-Chase," Ms. Popplestone said, "I have many years of experience with the best families on Blackrabbit, and if I am going to work for you, I need you to trust me, and you can trust me. Implicitly so. You have only one sister, correct? Is she likely to visit often?"

Eva leaned forward and crossed her hands. "No, not very likely. I haven't seen her since she was five years old."

"And I understand your mother died when you were young? And your father wasn't given to spending much time with you?"

"Is there a point to this, Ms. Popplestone?"

"I only mean to say you were likely taken care of by a nanny, were you not? And you grew up to be a four-square woman of business. Our ways may seem strange but they do work. You yourself are testament to the fact."

Eva folded her arms. "Flattery will not work on me, Ms. Popplestone. Nonetheless, there is some urgency at play, and my options are somewhat limited as not everyone is willing to move to this island. I must travel to Blackrabbit in the afternoon. I shall return in two days' time though I am loath to leave Iris in her condition. As such, you will be expected to commence your duties immediately. Is this agreeable to you?"

"Very," said Ms. Popplestone.

"Good. For now, your only role is to prepare for the arrival of the child. A room in the attic has been cleared for a nursery. You shall have the room next door. Please purchase whatever you think is necessary for both. My wife is not to be disturbed unduly. If you have questions, you may direct them to Drake or to Mrs. Roscrow, the cook. I hope you will enjoy your time here at Wolfe-Chase Lodge."

One could not in good conscience call the Moth & Moon a beautiful building. It was a tad too sloppy for such a description. In its four hundred year history it had been expanded with an eye to efficiency, not to aesthetics. An extra room was needed so one was added. A balcony seemed like a useful idea, so one was added. Another floor would be advantageous, so one was added.

Neither was much consideration given to longevity, and so the Moth was in a near constant state of repair. Over time, entire wings of the inn had needed to be demolished and entirely rebuilt, such was their state of dilapidation. It was not uncommon to see one of the many staff members with a hammer or pot of paint in hand. Employment at the Moth & Moon meant accepting that in a single day one could be server, washer, baker, carpenter and stable hand.

Given the wide-ranging and random assortment of items left in its niches, it was possible the Moth & Moon held pilfered items of cultural significance or, indeed, actual treasures. Most likely, it was simply stuffed with flotsam and jetsam the crews didn't want to be stuck with, but it was the brimming potential contained within each item which excited the imagination of George Reed. As the innkeeper of the Moth & Moon, he had a story for them all and delighted in telling them. From the mermaid's comb, with its ability to confer great beauty on whoever used it during the summer equinox, to the giant's plough which once furrowed the clouds themselves, George had stories to spare.

Even still, the Moth held its secrets well. He'd taken over the running of the place after his fathers had both passed away many years earlier and even though he'd grown up there, he found he could still be surprised by an unexpected discovery.

He was presently mopping up one sadly unsurprising discovery. One which came all too often with the territory. Every once in a while, someone would have too much ale and find some dark corner to be sick in.

"Mr. Reed?"

George turned to find Arminell Pinch standing with her hands clasped. She was a young woman in her twenties, with a wide face, sleepy eyes, and clad in a green cotton-twill dress. She had been a server at the tavern until recently.

"Ms. Pinch," George said. "How lovely to see you. All is well, I trust? Your child?"

"Hale and hearty, Mr. Reed, thank you," she said. "Although it's Mrs. Kind now. Well, Arminell, to you, of course."

George apologised, saying his mind was elsewhere. He had performed their handfasting himself, in the springtime.

"I wanted to combine our last names," she said. "To become Mr and Mrs Kindpinch but Archie's family were most insistent on keeping the name as it is. Tradition matters they said. I don't agree, but what can I do?"

"The Kinds were among those shipwrecked here on the *Eclipse*," George said. "They were some of the first settlers, helped build the village. If any family was going to be mired in tradition, it would be them."

The island had been uninhabited until a storm blew a ship onto the rocks some centuries earlier. Many sailors who survived chose to settle there and their descendants took great pains to remind everyone else of their seniority. Arminell dropped her hands as she spoke, her shoulders slumped. She appeared utterly deflated.

"I have to be honest, Mr. Reed; I'll go mad if I have to stay at home any more. I was hoping you might be open to the idea of my returning to work?"

"May I ask why? It's no secret you didn't like working here. I thought you were glad to be out of this place?"

"Archie needs something to keep him tethered. Some time at home will do him the world of good."

Archibald Kind was the village fop. A roguish charmer who was very popular with women. Arminell had been the first to tame him, the first to make him chase after her, seek her approval and, more often than not, her forgiveness. George failed to disguise the look of incredulity on his face.

"Mr. Kind is going to stay home?" he asked. "To take care of your son?"

"I know," she said, "but he's better at it than you might think. I think Archie would enjoy looking after him, if he'd just calm down a bit and spend some time with him. If I'm here then he'll have no choice. Just let me work a few hours a week, just until I find something else."

"Just until you find something better?"

"Yes. No! I didn't mean it like that, Mr. Reed."

"I know. I'm just teasing. Of course you can come back. Your mother was the best worker I ever had, and I made her a promise that there would always be a place for her family here. You can start by washing these floors." He handed her the mop and directed her to the pile of fresh vomit in the corner.

"I immediately regret this," she said, gagging.

There are certain tasks we must perform that we will avoid at all costs, be it through prioritising other duties or simple procrastination. For George, it was the two large, adjoining rooms on the second floor of the inn. Whatever their original function—ballroom? meeting place?— they'd been used for nothing but storage for as long as George could remember. Everything without an immediate use was shoved inside and the doors hastily closed. No longer. His diagnosis had lit a fire within him and he was determined to do all the little jobs he'd been putting off for years.

He heaved a box full of empty bottles, kicking up a cloud of dust. He coughed and coughed and had to sit down to regain his breath. As if his existing malady wasn't enough, he had to contend with the coughing sickness passing through the village. More and more people were coming down with it every day. The dust didn't help either, mind you.

Well, there simply wasn't time to be ill. He slapped his thighs, set his jaw, and forced himself to his feet. There was always work to be done in the Moth. Behind the box of bottles were long obsolete maps, wound tightly and brittle at the edges. Under them, jar after jar filled with buttons. Big, small, shiny, dull, every colour one could imagine.

From beneath an old saddle, he drew a rusted sickle. It was the one used in the murder of a farmhand in the early 1600's. On Treasemoor, two men had gotten into a fight over a woman and it ended in tragedy. George's mother had removed it from the bar, declaring it far too grisly to be on display. She had always been squeamish about such things and hated the sight of blood, didn't even like hearing about it. She'd hold his hand whenever talk in the bar turned too lurid. When he was very young, she'd often dragged him away, claiming the stories too violent for a child to hear.

George shook his head as if to shoo away the fog of memories. If every object he found was going to spark old memories to life, then clearing the space was going to be a longer and tougher job than he anticipated.

A rapid tapping of shoes in the hallway signalled the arrival of young May Bell. She always ran, no matter how many times she was warned not to. The floors of the Moth were unpredictable, and she could easily trip, though she never did. She navigated the inn with an ease second only to George himself. She ran into the room and straight into his arms, hugging him tightly.

"I've been looking all over for you!" she said.

"Hullo, May," he said. "Shouldn't you be working at the bakery? Or at school?"

She shrugged as she often did when asked a question she had no intention of answering. "It's very dusty in here," she said, wiping a box with her dress.

She climbed onto it and swung her legs, banging her heels against the side. A rhythmic thump-thump-thump filling the room. She stared at George in an odd way.

"What is it?" he asked.

Thump-thump-thump. She twirled her hair. "Mr Reed, why don't you have a husband? Or a wife?"

George stopped what he was doing and sat down. He thought about his answer for a moment.

"I never wanted either," he said. "I'm happier with my own company. Took me a while to realise as much, mind you."

May furrowed her brow.

"Not everyone needs to be paired off, you know," he said.

"That's not what my mummy says."

George raised his eyebrows and bit his tongue. May's mother was becoming every bit as interfering as Mrs. Whitewater's Tweed Knights, whose greatest pleasure in life was partnering up people in the village. Indeed, they had tried to do as much for him many years ago. He'd been a different man then. Sullen, withdrawn. He hadn't taken their meddling well and briefly considered banning them from the tavern, though a riot would likely ensue. When it came to carnal matters, he preferred the company of men although there hadn't been many. Robin Shipp was one though the last time had been some years earlier. George had always appreciated Robin's discretion in the matter. Robin had been lonely yet never clung to George, never mistook their time together for anything more than it was.

When George was younger he'd had a number of sailors fall in love with him and shower him with affection whenever they were in port, though he'd never been able to reciprocate. He'd tried to explain to them how he simply didn't experience the need to be with anyone in a romantic sense, but they each took it badly, seeing it as personal rejection. He'd been hurt by their reactions. More than he let on.

"Is that all you came to ask me?"

"I wanted to know, is all," she said, nodding.

"Are you going to help me here or are you going to go back to work?" he asked.

May gave the box one final thump with her heel before jumping off.

"I'd better go back to the bakery," she said. "Mr. Farriner can't cope for long without me."

She ran off at full tilt, leaving George alone in his room full of old memories.

Chapter Ten

Duncan hung his midnight-blue overcoat by the door and joined Edwin in their usual booth. The Moth & Moon was busy and noisy with it. Clouds of pipe smoke drifted past. A band of musicians played in a corner by the fireplace and a table of old men were singing along as best they could.

"Where's Vince?" Edwin asked.

"He's not coming," Duncan said. "I know, I know, I tried to persuade him, but he was having none of it."

"Is it me?"

"Is what you?" Duncan asked.

"The reason he won't come out. Does he not like me?"

"I know you need everyone to like you but don't worry, it's not you. Like I said the other day, I think it's his confidence. He's used to being the scariest man in town, of everyone being afraid of him and jumping when he snaps his fingers. He's... I don't know...brooding? Sulking?"

"He's had a setback, and he's feeling sorry for himself," Edwin said. "Now, who does that remind me of?"

"Another Shipp family trait."

"Robin takes everything to heart and sometimes it overwhelms him. Where's he sleeping? Vince, I mean?"

"In my bedroom," Duncan said.

Edwin arched an eyebrow and smirked.

"It's not like that," Duncan said. "He's too large for the settee and there's not enough space on the living room floor, what with all my furniture and bits and bobs, so he's sleeping on my bedroom floor. I offered him my bed–"

"I'm sure you did," Edwin said.

"–but he gave it up after a couple of nights," Duncan said, shooting daggers at Edwin. "He said it was too soft."

"I bet he snores," Edwin said. "He looks like a snorer."

"He doesn't, actually," Duncan said. "It took me a while to get used to him being there. He's so quiet for a man of his size. It's unnerving."

"You're taking a risk with him, you know."

"How do you mean?"

"He was the biggest, meanest criminal in the biggest, meanest town on these islands."

"Was. Past tense. He's changed."

"Has he?" Edwin asked.

"Look, you didn't know him way back when. The Vince you met over the winter solstice—the Vince sleeping on my bedroom floor—he's a pussycat compared to the one I knew when I lived on Blackrabbit. I wouldn't have let *that* Vince anywhere near me, let alone have him in my home. He was ferocious."

"And all his anger disappeared overnight did it?"

"No, not overnight, but... Just trust me. Vince is different."

"If you say so."

"He's a very light sleeper. The slightest noise wakens him."

"I suppose in his line of work it pays to sleep with one eye open," Edwin said.

"Not exactly an option for him any more..." Duncan said. He chewed his lower lip and drummed his fingers on the table.

"What is it?" Edwin asked. "What's on your mind?"

"There was a moment the other day. Between me and Vince."

"What kind of moment?"

"You know, the bated-breath kind. The eye-contact-held-for-a-bit-too-long kind. The heart-skipping-a-beat kind."

"Oh! Oh. You're not going to pursue it, are you? Please tell me you're not."

"I don't know, I think... I mean, don't you think he's sort of...you know...attractive?"

"For starters, he is the brother of—and looks a lot like—your former lover, which makes it very odd."

"Ah, you keep saying that but I don't see the resemblance between him and Robin at all. Robin is jolly and sweet, Vince...isn't."

"Secondly, I think he's dangerous. This is a terrible idea."

Their food arrived. Steaming hot fish pie and potatoes. Duncan immediately tucked in—he was famished. Edwin didn't touch his plate.

"What?" Duncan asked between chews.

"You want to do it even more now, don't you?"

"No. What? No, I don't."

"Hah, yes you do!" Edwin said. "I can see the glint in your eye! You hate being told what to do, or what not to do, so of course now you're going to jump in feet first. I'm telling you, though, as your friend, if you do this you're going to end up getting hurt. And you're going to hurt other people."

"Like who?" Duncan asked.

"Robin, for one."

"Ah, he won't care."

"He might. You know how sensitive he can be."

"He's a grown man, and so am I, and so is Vince. I don't need Robin's permission. Or yours, come to think of it."

"Then why did you tell me?"

"Because...I just... Shut up."

"Ah, *shut up*. Excellent badinage. I can see why Vince is unable to resist your charms."

Duncan flicked a piece of pie crust at him and laughed.

"Still playing with your food at your age?" Lady Iris Wolfe-Chase had arrived unnoticed and alone. "Room for two more?" she asked, holding her belly.

"Iris!" Edwin said. "Of course, please join us."

"Should we push the table back a bit? Or have the seat reinforced?" Duncan said.

"You know, Mr. Hunger, I am a Lady," Iris said as she struggled into place. "With a capital *L*. I'm sure I could have you exiled or imprisoned or the like."

"Shouldn't you be resting?" Edwin asked.

"Edwin!" she said. "Please don't start. I was going out of my mind at home. Our new nanny has been keeping everyone away."

"I know, I tried to visit yesterday, and she wouldn't let me past the front door," Duncan said.

"I'm going to have Eva speak to her," Iris said. "Anyway, talk to me about the world, about the village, about anything other than the baby. How are you coping without Robin?"

"I'm fine," Edwin said with a smile. "It's only been a couple of days."

"Edwin," she said. "You're among friends. No one else can hear us. How are you really coping?"

He ran his hand across the back of his head. "We haven't been apart since we've been courting. I keep imagining all the things that could go wrong."

"Ah, yes," she said. "The Catalogue of Imagined Tragedies, I know it well. I flick through its pages every time Eva travels for work. My staple is a boom swinging around, hitting her in the back of the head, knocking her overboard into the sea, whereupon she becomes caught up in the folds of her gown and drowns. What's your current imagined crisis?"

"Shark attack," he said. "But the sharks manage to jump out of the water and attack him on the boat."

She gently squeezed his sinewy, freckled forearm. "Edwin," she said in her softest, warmest tone, "that's ridiculous. You're an idiot."

He laughed heartily and it was good to hear. Duncan had wanted to broach the subject but hadn't wanted to upset him. He and Iris were friends of old, Duncan should have known she'd be looking out for him too.

"I know, I know. He'll be fine."

"There you are!" Eva said, as she charged across the tavern floor towards them. "I was worried sick."

"I told you I was coming here, with or without you," Iris said.

"How did you manage to get past Ms. Popplestone?" Eva asked.

"It wasn't easy. I had to get Drake to distract her, which he did not want to do. You know, I don't think he's entirely happy working for us?"

"Never mind him, are you quite comfortable, my dear?" Eva asked. "Shall I have them bring you a cushion? Or a footstool?"

"No, Eva, I'm perfectly fine," Iris said.

Duncan thought he could hear a little strain in her voice.

"Although I have forgotten my gloves. Do you think you could run out to my carriage and fetch them for me?"

"No need, I'll have one of the staff go." Eva raised her hand to summon a waiter but Iris grabbed it.

"Please, I honestly would rather you went yourself. They were a gift from you, and I'd hate for anything to happen to them." She gently kissed Eva's hand and smiled sweetly at her.

"I'll be back momentarily," Eva said. She rose from her chair, her satin gown rustling. When she had moved out of earshot, Iris slumped back in her chair.

"Gentlemen," she said, "Please take me to a boat and sail me away until this baby arrives or I fear my dear wife may not live to see the winter."

"Oh dear," Edwin said with a laugh. "Has it really come to this?"

"I thought she would have calmed down by now, but her constant worrying is as exhausting as it is endearing." Iris rubbed her temples as she spoke. "And as we approach the final few months, her fussing has intensified. She seems certain every cobble, every floorboard, and every breeze contains mortal peril only she can save me from."

"She's merely being careful," Edwin said.

"And I understand—I do, but it's stifling. I swear she won't be happy until she can put the baby in a full suit of armour."

"That's quite a sweet idea," Duncan said. "You could get your uncle to make one at the forge."

This idea was met with a withering stare from Iris.

"No? A little helmet? Little breastplate? Little mace to smack away other, more evil babies? No?"

"Why don't you make yourself useful and go fetch me a drink of water, please, Mr. Hunger?" Iris asked.

Her tone was stern, but Duncan knew she was joking, mostly. Nevertheless, he did as he was told, slipping past her and making his way through the crowd to the bar. His thoughts turned, as they so often did recently, to Vince. He didn't know what to do about him. Was he honestly attracted to the man or was it nothing more than a passing infatuation? Vince was menacing; he prowled around like a caged tiger; he was rude, surly and very, very alluring. And in all fairness, where was the harm in pursuing a little fun with him? He wasn't suggesting marriage, but merely passing the time in the way two men with similar proclivities are wont to do.

Robin wouldn't mind, Duncan was certain. Well, mostly certain. Surely Robin would see the situation from Duncan's point of view? It's not as if he was spoiled for choice when it came to lovers. Eligible bachelors on the island were few and far between.

No, the main sticking point, as Duncan saw it, was the fact he and Vince were under the same roof. Close quarters had a way of skewing perspective. After all, he'd be lying if he said he'd given Vince much thought since their last meeting over the winter solstice. Perhaps what was truly getting to Duncan was simply their proximity. The musk of the man, the heat from his body when he stood near. The way he rubbed his meat-pie-like hands over his own soft, silvery beard. His heavy brow silhouetted against the candlelight... Coupled with the fact it had been some months since Duncan had last lain with anyone, it was no wonder he was beginning to feel lascivious. If things between them did progress but turn sour, Vince could always move into Robin's house, now he was mobile again. Or even in with Edwin. Or he could simply go back home to Blackrabbit.

And on that note, how long was Vince going to stay? Duncan had thought once his injuries were healed Vince would want to return home but apparently he was content to remain on Merryapple. Perhaps he was waiting for Robin to return? But then Vince didn't actually know Robin very well. The first time they'd met had been only months earlier. Vince had promised to visit then, though not under these circumstances. When he thought about it, Duncan realised he was likely the only person on the island Vince had actually known before coming here. Given the way things had gone for Vince on Blackrabbit, Duncan may well be the only friend Vince had in the world. So there was something else for Duncan to worry about.

He nodded to Hamilton Bounsell, the village butcher, who was deep in conversation with the ruddy-faced farmer Mr. Trease.

"It's very odd," Mr. Trease said. "Why would anyone take paintings all the way up to my farm for no other reason than to burn them?"

"Nobody's used those outbuildings for years," Hamilton said. "I remember sneaking up there with my Fanny when we were courting for a bit of privacy..."

"You what?" Mr. Trease said.

Hamilton's ruddy face burned even redder and he swallowed hard.

"I... Everyone does it. A nice set of unused huts, tucked away near the woods... I thought you knew?"

"No, I didn't," Mr. Trease said. "And I'll tell you another thing, my bucca statuette has gone missing."

"The one your wife made for you?" Hamilton asked.

"The very same. Vanished into thin air. She's beside herself; nobody knows what's happened. I suspect one of the children has broken it and won't own up."

While he waited to be served, Duncan became aware he was under intense scrutiny. A man was staring at him from behind a pillar. A good-looking, boxy, bearded man around his own age, with peaked hair, a long nose and a wide jaw. He didn't recognise him and considered the overt attention a little odd but thought no more of it. Many strangers from passing ships could be found in the Moth & Moon on most nights, some of them a good deal stranger than others. He lifted the jug of water Mr. Reed had placed in front of him and returned to the booth to find Eva had taken his spot on the bench.

"I hope you don't mind?" she said.

Duncan slumped into a chair with wobbly arms. "Not at all," he said.

"One belly is enough in that seat," Edwin said, pointing to Duncan's stomach. "When is yours due, by the way?"

Duncan glared at him and was about to reply when Doctor Greenaway arrived with a companion.

"Ladies," the doctor said in a curiously boisterous fashion, "I didn't get a chance to introduce my nephew earlier."

The other man stepped forward. It was the man from the pillar, the one who was staring. "This is Mr. Dominic Babbage, the new schoolmaster."

Introductions were made to everyone at the table, though Duncan felt Mr. Babbage's bright eyes never strayed too far from his own.

"And this is Mr. Hunger," Doctor Greenaway said. "A talented toymaker and carpenter."

"A delight to meet you, Mr. Hunger," Mr. Babbage said, beaming from ear to ear. "I'm Dominic, well, Nick, really, Nick will do fine. I noticed you earlier but I wasn't sure if I should introduce myself. I didn't want to seem untoward."

Duncan stood and shook Mr. Babbage's outstretched hand. He found it a touch sweaty. Doctor Greenaway and his nephew continued on their introductory tour of the tavern while Duncan returned to his chair.

"I suppose I better be getting back to Vince," he said. "I left him some food but..." he trailed off when he realised everyone at the table was staring at him with odd grins on their faces. "What?" he asked. "*What?*"

Vince closed the front door of Duncan's house. He moved to lock it before remembering that Duncan never did. Bramble the cat lay on a windowsill, staring maliciously.

"What are you looking at?" Vince asked.

He held out his hand to stroke the cat's head but Bramble flicked the paw of his stunted leg at him, scraping his finger. Vince growled and walked away, sucking the wound. He plodded down the little hedged laneway from Duncan's house to Winter Walk and paused at the foot of the hill. He had an unobstructed view down to the harbour, to the Moth & Moon. He considered turning back, then chastised himself for being so weak. He couldn't face one meal with his brother's lover? With Duncan? But it wasn't them, it was everyone else. All there, in one place, under one roof. Well, roofs. How many did the inn have? So many peaks and troughs, it was impossible to tell. It was almost a village in itself.

On he strode, across the harbour, his jaw set. Upon passing a stack of lobster pots encrusted with ruddy dried seaweed, he heard a friendly voice call out.

"Hullo there!"

He turned to find a kindly looking woman crossing the road to greet him. She carried a basket of vegetables. He nodded and grunted and made to carry on his journey but she moved in front of him.

"You're Mr. Shipp's brother, aren't you? But you're not a Shipp, are you? You're..."

He was about to speak but she shushed him.

"It'll come to me..." she said, brow furrowed in thought. "Knight! That's it, isn't it? Mr. Invincible Knight. Such a name! Oh, I've heard all about you, Mr. Knight, you're a bad egg, aren't you? Port Knot's worst criminal, so I'm told! A thief, a ruffian, a proper blackguard, by all accounts. You don't look so scary to me, though. Well, maybe a bit. I think it's the eyepatch. And the beard. The whole village is talking about you," she said with a smirk.

Vince had no idea how to respond. Was she warning him? Threatening him?

"Mr. Shipp is often a talking point of late," she said. "We only recently discovered his mother was one of us and now we find he has a brother, too! Well, a half-brother, at least. It doesn't surprise me, I must say. Captain Shipp was quite the Lothario. I remember him well."

"You remember my father?"

"I do, I do. He tried it on with me once, but I said no. I was in love with my Trevor, for all the good it did me. He was a fisherman, was Trevor, never caught much and drowned at twenty-seven. Not at sea, mind you, in Kindwater stream, up by the farm. Fell in, drunk. I always did wonder, mind you, what would have happened if I'd taken your father up on his offer. He weren't short of a bob or two, your dad. It would have been handy. Terrible how he ended up, at the bottom of the sea. Terrible. But then he was a pirate, so I suppose it was bound to happen eventually. I hope you're not a pirate too! We'll have no trouble here, Mr. Knight!" she said, poking him in the stomach.

Was it playful? He still had no idea. Flustered, he rushed off back the way he came, back towards Duncan's house, without saying a word.

"Hope it wasn't something I said!" the woman called after him.

Chapter Eleven

The following afternoon, Nick Babbage walked down narrow Hill Road, garbed in his finest feathered hat, teal coat, and knee breeches. As he wandered through the village, he started to feel somewhat overdressed. The locals were garbed a good deal more simply. Shawls were the thing for ladies, loose fitting trousers for the men. These were, he realised, working folk, with little need for silks and shiny shoe buckles. Nonetheless, he smiled and nodded at passers-by and tried not to pay too much attention to their stares.

He was surprised at how many shops the tiny village had. He passed a bakery, a haberdashery of some kind, a chandler selling all manner of tools and paint and there was even a toyshop, of all things. The sign above read *D. Hunger Toys & Games*. He straightened his cravat, removed his round-brimmed hat, and fixed his chestnut hair into place before opening the door.

The shop was crammed full of colourful toys. Overhead, a small wooden goose tethered to the ceiling flapped its wings as it flew in circles, forcing him to duck and dodge his way past it.

"Be with you in a minute!" a voice called out from the back room.

"No hurry, Mr. Hunger," Nick called back.

A black-and-white cat with a stunted paw lay stretched out on a table, warming itself in a sunbeam. Nick stroked its head with the back of his finger and it purred without opening its eyes.

"Ah, hullo," Mr. Hunger said, wiping his hands on a cloth. "What can I do for you?"

Nick cleared his throat a little and stood up straighter. "I'm not sure if you remember me. We met last night. I'm Nick Babbage."

He held out his hand, but Mr. Hunger showed his were covered in blue paint.

"Sorry, I'm working on a piece," he said. "Yes, I remember you. The doctor's nephew."

He couldn't be entirely sure, but Nick thought Mr. Hunger a touch irked by his presence.

"I'm taking over the schoolhouse," he said, "and I wondered, since you were a carpenter—"

"Toymaker."

"Yes, toymaker. Yes," Nick said, his back growing damp with sweat. "But a carpenter also, I gather? Are you not working on the inn's belfry? Why does an inn need a belfry, in any case?"

"It's more than a mere inn," Mr. Hunger said.

Nick coughed again. He moved to loosen his collar a touch. Did Mr. Hunger's eyes have to be so expressive and inviting? "Well, yes, you see I was hoping to enlist your aid at the schoolhouse. There are some minor changes I would like to make, and I was hoping you might assist me."

"Assist you? So, you'd be doing most of the work, and I'd be helping?" Mr. Hunger asked.

Nick thought he saw a little twinge at the corner of Mr. Hunger's increasingly kissable mouth. A suppressed smile. Nick crossed his own arms and laughed. "No, I suppose not. You'd be doing the work—you're the expert, after all. I mostly saw myself in more of a supervisory capacity."

"Telling me what to do and the like."

"Precisely. You seem the type to need constant oversight."

That got a grin out of Mr. Hunger. His plump lips parted, revealing pretty white teeth. Nick thought he saw a sparkle in those hazel eyes too.

"I am quite busy," Mr. Hunger said. "Between work here and at the belfry..."

"It wouldn't take long. A day, at most. I don't have much money, I'm afraid, but I could provide you with ale and bread. Cheese. Maybe even some grapes, if you're very well behaved."

A proper laugh this time. Mr. Hunger's whole face seemed to change. His eyes crinkled at the edges and his belly shook, just a touch.

"Well," he said, "how could I say no to such an offer?"

"Wonderful!" Nick said, clasping his hands together. "Would tomorrow suit?"

"Tomorrow! You don't hang about, Mr. Babbage."

"We're given so little time, Mr. Hunger. It's an awful shame to waste it."

Morwenna Whitewater sat by the fireplace in the Moth & Moon with a ball of wool in her hands, turning it over and over. Since Robin had left, she had been too distracted to work on anything. Some of the Tweed Knights were gathered about her, dissecting the business of the day. Top of the agenda remained the pregnancy of Lady Iris Wolfe-Chase.

"Having children at their age," said Hanniti Kind. "It's ridiculous. And it's a risk. Lady Iris will be lucky if she survives. I've seen women half her age succumb to the ravages of childbirth."

"They have the very best doctors from Blackrabbit. I'm sure she'll be fine," said Morwenna.

Mrs. Greenaway sniffed and turned away. "My husband's medical knowledge used to be good enough for the Wolfe family," she said. "Now she's aristocracy, suddenly she needs outside help."

"And what about us?" Hanniti asked. "Morwenna and I have delivered most of the babies in this village. Midwives with unparalleled experience! But no need for us, not with Doctor Cranch around."

"To be fair," Morwenna said, "Doctor Cranch's involvement is more to do with the nature of her work."

"Yes, what was it they called it?" Mrs. Greenaway asked. "*Romantic Medicine?* All that business with syringes and whatnot. I don't see the need for it. Why Lady Iris and Mr. Farriner couldn't simply conceive a baby in the usual way is beyond me. Haven't they lain with both women and men before?"

"I suspect her wife and my Robin might have had something to do with it," Morwenna said.

"Speaking of great beasts, have you heard? There's been sightings of a wild dog," Mrs. Greenaway said. "Bleddy hefty thing, it is. It savaged some of the Caddy's rabbits."

"I heard it was black as night, with red eyes," said George Reed as he placed some drinks on the table.

"Don't start with the stories, you," said Mrs. Greenaway. "You'll have turned it into a ten-foot-high monster who breathes fire before long."

George laughed as he went about his work. He never could resist a tall tale and Morwenna was certain he'd have concocted a new one by the time the next ship full of gullible and entertainment-starved sailors arrived in port.

"Where did the dog come from?" she asked.

"Must have sneaked off a boat," Hanniti said. "Likely the crew didn't notice till they'd left."

"Well I hope they come back for it," Mrs. Greenaway said. "Before it does any real damage."

Chapter Twelve

The bright, airy draughting office of the Chase Trading Company was the envy of shipwrights the world over. It was topped with a barrel-vaulted dome ceiling and set with many large windows which filtered in light only from the north, eliminating shadows and creating a smooth, even illumination throughout the day. Eva stood pouring over the plans for a new ship.

"It seems a little extravagant," she said.

The engineer wrinkled her brow. "I was told money was no object."

"Oh, were you?" Eva said. "Who could possibly tell you such a blatant mistruth? My cousin, no doubt. Well, I spent the morning going over our books and I'm sorry to say money very much is an object. I see no reason why a schooner, of all things, should be fitted with such—"

"Are you still complaining, my dear?" came a voice from behind.

Eva turned, ready to snap. Instead she flung her arms wide and laughed. The figure in the doorway was dressed head to toe in white silk embroidered with bronze thread. Half her face was covered by an animal mask made of russet-coloured feathers.

"Darling!" Eva said. "Whatever brings you here? Official council business?"

Ms. Clementine Frost took her by the hands. "Oh, no, this?" she said, taking off her mask. "I only wore it to annoy the bankers on my way here. Can you believe they refused to finance the rebuilding of my tearoom last year? When I was appointed to the position of Fox, however, they began falling over themselves to get in my good books. Best of luck to them, I say."

The engineer scooped up her plans and excused herself as Eva and Clementine retired to a smaller, wood-panelled office upstairs.

"I heard word the great Lady Wolfe-Chase was in town, and so I dashed right over," Clementine said. "Very naughty of you not to let me know yourself."

"I wanted to, believe me," Eva said. "But I've been so busy since I arrived. Dorothea's out of control. She's spending money like it's about to turn stale."

"She isn't doing very well on the council, either," Clementine said. "I've finally managed to convince her to allow her committee to make most of the decisions."

Dorothea Chase had been appointed as the new Swan of Blackrabbit Council around the same time Clementine had been made Fox. While Clementine had settled into her role as the official contrarian and voice for the voiceless, Dorothea had struggled under her new responsibilities as the Minister for Shipping.

"Thank you so much for looking out for her," Eva said.

"Since you're here, you absolutely must attend the grand reopening of my tearoom on Friday."

"I couldn't possibly. I have to get back to Iris."

"Iris is weeks away from her due date, and you deserve a little fun. Look at those bags under your eyes."

"I beg your pardon?"

"Well, maybe not bags, but pockets, at least. You, my dearest, are stressed. I know the signs. I know you better than anyone. I was going to send an invitation, but I didn't think you'd leave your little rock to attend. But since you're here anyway, it is no hardship. Oh, please come." Clementine lightly gripped Eva's arm, as if to literally twist it.

"I haven't brought anything to wear," Eva said.

"This is Port Knot! Go out and buy something; there's plenty of time to have it altered. Or, no! Better yet, I'll have a gown sent over." She clapped her hands as she always did when excited.

"I've the perfect gown in mind—it arrived only last week. I shan't hear another word on the matter; it's settled."

Eva threw her head back and groaned. Her trip was taking longer than expected. She'd be at least another day or two looking through the company books and supposed an extra night wouldn't kill her.

"Fine," she said. "I know when I'm beaten. I suppose the council is invited?"

"Yes, sadly," Clementine said, slumping back in her seat. "Such a bore but we do what we must. I was hoping Dorothea, at least, would decline, but—"

"Oh, here she is now," Eva said loudly, hoping to spare Clementine the embarrassment. "Cousin!"

After the death of her father, Lord Marley Chase, control of the family company had passed to Eva, who had in turn appointed Dorothea as director. Eva kept an eye on proceedings from Merryapple as best she could, although it had proved more difficult than she had anticipated. Dorothea greeted them and sat in a chair, looking tired. Generally a quiet, unassuming person, she could nonetheless vacillate between timid and volatile, capable of sudden fiery outbursts. Eva had taken it as a sign that somewhere inside there lurked a confident and forthright woman striving to be set free. She hoped to be the one to bring it out of her. So far, no luck.

"What did you think of the new ships?" Dorothea asked.

Eva stood with her hands behind her back. "They seem a tad...indulgent."

"I thought they looked nice..."

"Yes, well, niceness comes at a price, and I'm uncertain it's strictly necessary in our business."

Dorothea adjusted the fold of her dress and turned away. She produced from a pocket a small note which she handed over.

"What does it say?" Clementine asked.

"Apparently some pirates from Driftwood are planning to raid one of our convoys," Eva said.

"What's Driftwood?"

"It's a pirate fable," Eva said, "a supposed colony where they all live in peace and harmony. It's not real."

"Sounds like it might be. I bet you a bottle of something grotesquely expensive it exists!"

"You're on."

Clementine giggled and adjusted her stole. "So, you think the note is a lie, then?"

"Oh no, the raid will be very real. They use the threat of Driftwood to scare us. We daren't attack them lest we enrage an entire island of their kind into retaliation. It's a freebooter fairy tale. Do we have time to arrange an escort?"

"No," Dorothea said. "Our ships are already underway."

"Then the best we can do is dispatch a patrol to deal with the raiders," Eva said.

"I'm not prepared to risk our forces," Dorothea said. "We're still recovering from the damage caused by the hurricane and are far from full strength. It's why I've commissioned those new ships..."

"So, we let the pirates attack our ships?" Eva asked. She couldn't believe what she was hearing. The weakness of the woman was infuriating.

"It's an occupational hazard," Dorothea said. "Besides, we have them insured. The crews have all been warned not to put up a fight unless they're absolutely certain they can win. We know from experience that if they cooperate with the pirates, they won't be harmed."

"Where did the note come from?" Eva asked.

Dorothea sniffed and turned away once more. "It was delivered a couple of days ago," she said, "by a very fragrant woman named Troke."

"And you're only showing it to me *now?*"

"I have been somewhat busy," Dorothea said.

Eva paced the floor, slamming her hand on the table. "We will dispatch a patrol to intercept the raiders."

"We will do no such thing," Dorothea said, rising from her chair. "The woman who brought the note was herself a pirate."

"Why would she warn us, then?" Eva asked.

"She must not be part of the raid," Clementine said. "She means to have you do away with her comrades."

"Or her competition," Eva said.

"How ruthless."

"Precisely," Dorothea said. "And I will not be manipulated by the likes of her."

"You would stand by and do nothing?" Eva asked. "You would lose our goods, our ships, potentially the lives of our crew for what? A point of principle?"

"I will not be a damned pawn in the game of pirates!"

She had approached Eva with chin held high and fists clenched. She wasn't quite as tall as Eva, her clothes not quite as expensive, her eyes not quite as sharp. Yet here, at last, was the fire Eva had sensed in her, here was the defiance beneath the meekness, the lion in the mouse. It was a shame to have to stamp upon it.

"You would make widows and orphans for the sake of your pride?" Eva asked.

"If need be," Dorothea said.

"This remains my company," Eva said softly. "And a patrol will be sent, Dorothea. I insist."

George thought he was going to break a rib. He was doubled over, his whole body shaking with the force of his coughing. Saliva dripped from the corners of his mouth as he fumbled in the pocket of his waistcoat for a handkerchief. One appeared before him, held by Arminell Kind. He gratefully took it and dabbed his mouth, drying his neat, grey beard. Farther down the hall lay a bundle of bedclothes. She must have dropped them and come running. Was he really in such dire straits? She placed a hand on his back.

"It's fine, it's fine," he said. His voice was hoarse and weak, and his legs wobbled as he steadied himself against a wall. He was light-headed and little dancing blobs of colour gathered at the edges of his vision.

"It's not fine," she said. "You've got what Mrs. Whitewater has. You should rest."

"No time," George said. "The Moth waits for no man."

"Can I help, at least? What are all these boxes?"

"I'm moving them out of these storage rooms. I need to go through them and throw out anything damaged or damp or useless."

She picked up a seashell comb. "What, like this?"

"Well, no, not that," George said. "That belonged to Mrs. Cecilia Barker; she wore it to the opening of the Painted Mermaid Museum. They're all gone now, the Barkers. One of the first families to settle on the island, they were. She was the last of them."

"So what? It's just a ratty old comb; why keep it?"

"It's a part of village history, of our heritage. This very comb is in the painting on the third-floor landing. Well, one of the third-floor landings..."

"Oh, so it is," she said. "I thought it looked familiar. How did it end up here?"

"The Moth & Moon is a tidal pool for the village's flotsam and jetsam. All sorts of things get washed up here. Not all of it important though," George said. "Which is why I'm clearing it out. Give those linens to the washers and then come back up here. You can help me with the rest of the boxes. If you want to. I know it's more than you signed on for."

"No, it's fine," Arminell said, turning the comb over in her hands. "I want to."

Chapter Thirteen

The framework for the bell tower's roof was complete. The workers who assembled it said as much. They stood back and admired their handiwork, congratulating themselves on a job well done. Duncan, to no one's surprise, disagreed. The east corner was off by more than a few degrees and the support strut on the south corner was thinner than the rest.

"It shouldn't be perfect!" said Mr. Trescothick. "It wouldn't look right!"

Duncan sighed and tapped his own forehead, trying his very best to stay calm. "It wouldn't look right if it was perfect? And how, if I may ask, did you come by this frankly startling opinion?"

"Look around you!" said Mr. Trescothick. "Nothing about the Moth & Moon is perfect. Everything's off, everything's slanted or crooked."

"Only because it was all built before *I* got here," Duncan said through gritted teeth. He had always been bothered by the inn's lopsided corners and uneven walls. How hard was it to get it right?

"Well, I think it looks fine and Mr. Reed put *me* in charge of the tower," said Mr. Trescothick.

"For now," Duncan said.

Silently fuming, he navigated his way across the landscape of roofs and ladders until he reached the ground. He stood by the front doors to the Moth & Moon, dusting himself off. Nearby the gull named the Admiral was fighting for food against his fierce rival, Captain Tom. They kicked up a flurry of dust over a bread crust until the young Peter Underton ran past and scared them both off.

"What's that meant to be?" came a voice from behind.

Vince stood, leaning on his cane, and staring at the inn's clockwork sign.

"It's a moth circling a crescent moon," said Duncan.

"Can see that," Vince said, "What's around the outside of it?"

"Leaves and branches. It's supposed to be as if you're looking out through a wood or some bushes at the cove."

Vince scanned the harbour. "There aren't any bushes down here."

"Well, not now," Duncan said. "But there may well have been when the sign was made."

"Old then? The sign?"

"Very," Duncan said. "Wasn't always clockwork, of course. The moth didn't always move."

"Did the moon always look like Mr. Reed?" Vince asked.

Duncan tilted his head and examined the face on the moon. Bearded and with a little flat nose, it did, in fact, resemble George Reed quite a bit.

"Huh. I never really noticed before," he said.

Vince just grunted. "How's the belfry coming along?"

"Quickly," Duncan said. "Far too bleddy quickly. If they'd only take their time, it would be better. If they'd listen to me—"

"Why won't they listen to you?"

"Probably because I'm still the Blackrabbit blow-in. Things might have changed for the better round here, but I swear, these islands will never get over their stupid rivalry."

"Here," Vince said, "it's not stupid. It's ancient."

"Can't it be both?" Duncan asked.

"They're nice enough to me."

"Of course they are, you're Robin's brother. And they're too frightened to get on your bad side."

"Hang about, you're not from Blackrabbit," Vince said. "You're from Cornwall."

"Originally, yes, but I moved from Blackrabbit to here. More than enough for some people to take umbrage."

"Want me to have a word with them?" Vince puffed out his impressive chest and balled his gargantuan fists.

"Not necessary," Duncan said, admiring Vince's physique. "Once Robin gets back, I'll get him to put me in charge."

"How?"

"Oh, don't you know? Mr. Reed is leaving the inn to Robin."

Vince tilted his head back as if trying to take in the entire building in one glance. "What does Robin know about running an inn?"

"Absolutely nothing," Duncan said. "But he's spent more time in there than anyone, apart from Mr. Reed himself."

"Used to work behind the bar in the Dogtooth every now and then..."

"Hey, there's an idea!" Duncan said. "You could work here! In the Moth!"

"No..."

"Yes! It's perfect! You don't like working at the asylum, and I'm sure Robin would be delighted," Duncan said, placing his hand on the small of Vince's back and gesturing towards the colossal inn. "The brothers Shipp, side by side in the Moth & Moon!"

"Keep telling you, I'm not a Shipp."

"Ah, details, details!"

"Don't actually like, you know, *people*," Vince said. "Not one for talking and the like."

"And therein lies the beauty of it: you wouldn't have to! Robin could talk the hind leg off a donkey; you could leave the hospitality side of things to him! Can't you see it though? You taking orders behind the bar, keeping the rowdy sailors in line, Robin charming the customers with tales of the high seas. You could live upstairs. You'd have everything you need here. Gainful employment. Family. Friends."

Vince was silent for a moment. The waves crashed against the harbour. Gulls screeched overhead. "Do I have friends here?"

Duncan stood facing him, gazing up into his ice-blue eye. "You have at least one."

Spots of rain freckled the window panes as Nick pushed the last desk to the back of the classroom. He'd already swept the floor twice and considered doing it once more when there came a knocking. He fixed his hair into place and straightened his cravat before he opened the door to Mr. Hunger, who stood in the school's little porch, sheltering from the drizzle.

"Come in, come in," Nick said. "The weather turned quickly, didn't it?"

"Rain is never very far from here," Mr. Hunger said, taking off his midnight-blue overcoat and hanging it on a hook. "It's how it got its name."

"I don't follow."

"Blashy Cove, "Mr. Hunger said. "Blashy. It means rainy."

"Oh!" Nick said. "I never thought about it. I assumed it was someone's name."

Mr. Hunger let himself through the entrance hall to the school's only classroom.

"Were you educated here?" Nick asked.

"Oh no, the school has only been here for a few years. And I'm not from the island—I was born and raised in Cornwall."

"Oh really," Nick said. "I confess I cannot say your accent sounds any different from the others I've heard here."

"Wait till you meet Robin," Mr. Hunger said, smiling.

"A friend of yours?"

"A very dear friend. He's away dealing with...family troubles. Now, what is it you needed me for?"

"Well," Nick said. "I've had a bit of an idea. It came to me in a dream actually. I had this sourced from someone in the village." He pulled at some linen to reveal a very large, smooth piece of slate. "I was wondering if you could build a frame for it and hang it on the wall at the front of the classroom? Maybe add a little lip at the bottom for my chalk?"

Mr. Hunger ran his stubby fingers across the slate. Nick found himself gazing at the hair sprouting from the back of Mr. Hunger's hand, following it to his thick wrists and watching it disappear under the cuffs of his cream-coloured shirt. He found Mr. Hunger's somewhat stumpy arms to be quite endearing and imagined them wrapped around his waist. They wouldn't stretch all the way round, of course. Nick had put on some weight in recent years and found he quite liked it. He felt more like himself, in a sense.

"What's it for?" Mr. Hunger asked, snapping him back to the moment. "Surely you're not going to get the children to all write on the same slate?"

"No, no, not at all," Nick said, slightly flustered. "It's for me. I can write my lessons on it and the whole class will be able to see."

"Huh," Mr. Hunger said.

He looked impressed. Nick hoped he was. Mr. Hunger went back outside to retrieve some wood and tools from a covered cart. For the next hour or two, Nick did his best to stay out of the way as Mr. Hunger measured, cut and sanded his way through several long planks.

He admired the skill on display, of course, but also the way Mr. Hunger carried himself, the way he'd rub his husky hands over the wood, the wisps of black hair escaping from his collar and reaching up towards his throat. He was shorter than Nick by a head or more and his braces sat on square shoulders, framing his belly. He was portly as a rum barrel, with robust thighs and a plump rear end Nick did his absolute very best not to stare at.

They stopped a couple of times for refreshments which Nick had prepared. The ale loosened Mr. Hunger's tongue.

"I must say, I'm surprised an island this small having a schoolhouse at all," Nick said.

"Not to mention all those shops."

"We're very lucky," Mr. Hunger said. "Port Knot, over on Blackrabbit, is the busiest harbour on these islands, but success costs money. Traders who want to dock there have to pay harbour fees and there're taxes on goods brought in, on sales made. Not here. Here you can come, set up a stall on market day, and keep whatever you make. People come from far and wide to get a good deal. While they're here, they'll have something to eat and drink in the Moth. And where does the Moth get its supplies from? Us. The villagers. The islanders."

"From very far and wide, judging by the old coins I found in the tavern walls. Mr. Reed was kind enough to give them to me. I wanted to pay for them but he insisted. A way of welcoming me to the island, he told me."

"Sounds like our George," Mr. Hunger said. "Why did you want them?"

Nick hesitated, unsure if he should say anything. "They're, ah, they're for my collection. I like coins, you see. I...um...I think they're sort of...fascinating."

"Oh really?" There was mild eyebrow raising, but no hint of disappointment. "Don't they call it the hobby of kings?" Mr. Hunger asked.

"They do! It used to be only the very wealthy could afford to do it. Did you know people used to cut pennies into halves and quarters to make small change? A quarter was called a *fourthing* which is where we get our word *farthing* from."

"I did not know that."

"I was worried about coming here," Nick said, "but there's more than I expected. A lot more."

Mr. Hunger paused mid-chew and Nick thought he saw a colour rise in his cheeks. "You are very forward, Mr. Babbage."

"I don't like wasting time. And the children call me Mr. Babbage. I should like it very much if you would call me Nick."

"If you insist, Nick. But you should know my last experience with a forward gentleman did not end well."

"What happened?"

"I almost died in an explosion he caused."

"*What?*"

"Him and a former lover of mine were part of a conspiracy to overthrow the council on Blackrabbit."

Nick almost jumped out of his chair. "Last Midwinter!" he said. "At the solstice celebrations on Blackrabbit! I read about it in the papers!"

"Did you? I didn't think anyone on the mainland paid much attention to what happened here on the Pell Islands."

"In fairness, apart from being home to the Chase Trading Company, nothing interesting has ever happened here before," Nick said. "You were truly there?"

"I was nearly all over there."

Nick was amazed to hear him be so flippant about such a horrible experience. The story had been widely reported in the London newspapers, though details were scant, and it was difficult to tell what was truth and what was journalistic hyperbole. As he poured more ale, Mr. Hunger shared the whole story with him.

"My word, you've had a time of it," Nick said.

Mr. Hunger raised his eyebrows and nodded. "So, you can see," he said, "why I might be a tad *apprehensive* about leaping into—"

"Bed?"

"A relationship! Honestly, Mr. Babbage, are all the men in London like you?"

"No, there's only one of me, I'm afraid," Nick said, smiling broadly.

He couldn't help himself. "You're not used to being on the receiving end are you? I've seen you about; you're usually the one with the sharp tongue."

"Never mind your tongue. Can you give me a hand?"

Mr. Hunger gripped one edge of the now-framed slate while Nick took the other. Together they heaved it to the front of the classroom. Then Mr. Hunger took a chair and set it against the wall. "You probably won't need one," he said. "You're one of those lucky tall people."

"I'm not so tall," Nick said.

"Compared to me, everyone is. The only person shorter is George Reed." Mr. Hunger grunted as he spoke; then he carefully rolled up the sleeves of his shirt, revealing meaty forearms covered in black hair which Nick did his best not to stare at. His absolute very best. "When you're ready."

Nick hadn't noticed Mr. Hunger taking hold of the slate once more.

"Right. Sorry."

Nick took the other edge and together they lifted the heavy slate up to the hook Mr. Hunger had earlier fixed to the wall. It took some careful manoeuvring and once it was up they fixed it into place.

"Solid as a rock, Nick."

"And perfectly level," Nick said, holding out his hand. "Well done, Mr. Hunger."

Unlike their first encounter at the toyshop, there was no reason for Mr. Hunger not to shake it and he did so slowly, deliberately. His grip was firm, his palm warm and rough, etched with a lifetime of toil.

"Duncan," he said. "Call me Duncan."

Chapter Fourteen

The winds had died away, leaving Robin adrift. It had been a day since he'd lost sight of the pirate ship. A full day of nothing but sea and sun. He checked his compass and chart over and over, making absolutely certain he was heading in the right direction.

"There's nothin' out 'ere, *Bucca*," he said. "Nothin' at all."

With no option but to wait for the winds to pick up, his mind wandered home, to the warmth of Edwin's bed. He reached into his coat and drew the letter Edwin had thrust into his hand before leaving. With sore fingers, he tore at the wax seal, unfolded the page and slowly read.

> *My dearest Robin,*
>
> *As I write, you are haggling with a shopkeeper in Port Knot over the price of supplies for your journey. I wish you would wait until we can find someone to accompany you; however, I understand why you will not.*
>
> *Your father's disappearance has been an open wound in your soul for as long as I have known you. I do not know if he is alive or dead, but whatever the case, I hope with all my heart you find the answers you are searching for. I hope they bring you the peace you deserve, and most of all, I hope when you return, you will do me the honour of becoming my husband.*
>
> *Forever yours,*
>
> *Edwin*

Tears welling in his eyes, Robin clasped the letter to his chest. Not being the most confident reader, he scanned the letter again and again, saying the words out loud to make absolutely sure he'd understood what Edwin was saying. He'd long ago put thoughts of marriage out of his mind, decided it simply wasn't for him. He'd almost proposed to Duncan once, had it all planned out, but just before he asked, they started arguing about something minor, as they always did. Just as well, really. It would never have lasted.

With his thick, square-edged finger, he traced over Edwin's name. His husband-to-be's name. He considered turning *Bucca* around, returning to Merryapple there and then, but that would accomplish nothing. The niggling doubt in his mind would never go away. He wouldn't find the answers he needed at home. The wind picked up again, filling *Bucca's* sails. With renewed determination, Robin took to his feet and tended the line.

"Onwards," he said.

Chapter Fifteen

Duncan and Vince sat in the Moth & Moon, waiting for Edwin to arrive. It had taken some coaxing to get Vince out of the house. He really didn't appreciate the genial nature of the villagers. More than once Duncan had to intervene when someone came up to make friendly small talk which Vince appeared to take as some kind of attack. To be fair, Duncan also found it a tad suspicious. The people had never been this friendly to Blackrabbit folk in the past. He suspected a lot of it was down to Vince being Robin's brother, but then he had noticed a shift in attitudes in the past year. Ever since the hurricane, the villagers had been a touch more open, more welcoming, even to Blackrabbit natives.

The rivalry between the islands was ancient, its origin lost in the mists of time. Not even the village's great sage, the innkeeper Mr. Reed, knew its roots. The feud peaked every year at the height of summer when a boat race took place between the island residents. Anyone with a boat could enter and play for their island's pride. The contestants started at the harbour in Port Knot and raced clockwise around the islands. Sailors from Blackrabbit had won the past three years in a row. Robin usually entered in *Bucca's Call* and made good time, but he had declined to participate that year. He said he was too busy, but Duncan suspected his injured hand had more to do with it. It was affecting his sailing, no matter how much he denied it.

Duncan suggested Vince sit in the corner of the booth, with his damaged eye to the wall. It calmed him a bit, as Duncan suspected.

"You're like a wounded dog," he said. "Snapping at anyone coming at you from your blind side."

Vince took a drink of whiskey but said nothing.

"I was talking to Edwin about you," Duncan said. "I was telling him about how much you've changed."

Vince lowered his head and frowned. Duncan hadn't expected such a simple remark to sting him.

"Not in a bad way," Duncan said. "For the better. You're not the angry, violent thug you used to be."

"Half the man I used to be," Vince said in a low voice.

"Now, come on, Penhallow and Palk didn't—"

"Not them," Vince said. "Martin."

It was the first time Vince had mentioned his late husband unprovoked.

"Beautiful, he was. Long dark hair. Twinkly eyes. A gambler, fixed card games, dice games, whatever he could. Fastest hands on Blackrabbit. We were handfasted within a year of meeting. Always listened. Understood me. We were happy."

"I remember," Duncan said. "I was still with Baxbary Mudge at the time. The effect Martin had on you was clear, even to me. You weren't quite so angry all the time. What happened to him?"

He held his breath, unsure of how Vince would react to the question.

"Ms. Mellicent Auger arrived," Vince said. "Bigwig from Devon, she was. Smuggler, mostly. Not above a bit of extortion and murder as well. She wanted Port Knot. Thought it was ideal to run her empire from. Wanted me to work for her. I refused. She had Martin drowned. To teach me a lesson. So I killed her. And every one of her people on Blackrabbit. Over the course of a week. I hunted them down and slit their throats."

Duncan said nothing but his stomach clenched. There, in the candlelight, Vince took on a bizarre *otherness*. He seemed suddenly to be out of place, aggressively alien to his surroundings.

"Nothing fancy," Vince said. "Nothing noisy. Wanted revenge. Deserved revenge. Once it was done, so was I. Had a skinful of that life. But I was stuck. Needed the protection afforded to me by Mudge, by my position in his schemes. But it was the start of it, I think. When I knew the life had beaten me. Started looking for a way out but couldn't find one. Until the winter solstice. You three showed up. Helped expose Baxbary Mudge."

"To be fair, it was mostly Robin and Edwin," Duncan said. "I spent most of the time in a cell or tied up in a barrel."

"But I didn't know them. It was you I... You don't know what it meant to see a friendly face."

"My face has been described as 'scowling,' 'bothered,' and 'like thunder' but rarely 'friendly,'" Duncan said.

"Then we have something in common. Besides wanting to kill Baxbary Mudge."

"I never—"

"You held a pistol to his head."

It was true. Duncan had once held a musket in his hand, had it levelled at Baxbary. It would have been so easy to do it. Robin had talked him out of it.

"I just wanted to scare him," Duncan said. "I was never going to pull the trigger. It's not who I am."

He meant it. He hated Mudge more than anyone alive, but Duncan didn't have it in him to kill someone.

"Just as well," Vince said. "It's a slippery slope."

"What do you mean?"

"Once you break the seal, it's done. Once you take one life, you've done the worst thing you'll ever do. You're ruined. So you might as well take another. And then what's three? Four?"

His voice, already so dispassionate, was thoroughly monotone now. His eye wasn't focusing on anything; he didn't move, not a muscle, not an inch. A single movement would spoil the moment, ruin whatever connection was running between his mouth and this truth in his head.

"You really think you're ruined?" Duncan asked.

Vince said nothing. He was still as a rock save for his eye, which widened. Duncan couldn't help but lean over and lay his hand upon Vince's.

"I'd say feeling the way you do means you're far from ruined. There's hope for you yet, Vince."

Edwin had remarked more than once how similar Vince and Robin were, but right then Duncan thought they couldn't have been more different. They'd both been victims of circumstance, both suffered, but in very different ways—Robin at the hands of the villagers, Vince at his upbringing, his choices. Duncan wondered how long Vince had wanted to say these things. How long he'd waited to find someone who would understand.

"Why are you telling me all this now?" Duncan asked.

"Thought it was time. You've been...good to me. These past few days."

Duncan's stomach tightened again but not in the same way. Vince held his gaze for a moment longer than he usually did. His one uncovered eye was an icy blue and it saw right through to the heart of Duncan.

"You don't have to go back, you know," Duncan said.

Vince tilted his head.

"To Blackrabbit, I mean," Duncan said. "Even if you don't want to work in the Moth with Robin, you can stay here. With me. With us, I mean. All of us."

"You honestly think Robin would want me here?"

"Robin would be over the moon."

"At having his criminal half-brother hanging about?"

"I can promise you, Robin doesn't care about your past," Duncan said. "And he won't hold it against you. When he gets back, you need to spend some time with him, just the two of you. Trust me. You'll see."

Vince clasped Duncan's hand and squeezed, gently.

"This all looks terribly serious," Edwin said as he approached the booth.

Duncan and Vince both quickly pulled their hands apart. Edwin sat beside Duncan and set a mug of coffee on the table.

"Edwin doesn't drink," Duncan explained to Vince. "Because he's boring."

"I've done plenty of drinking in my time," Edwin said. "I'm happy to give it a miss now. Coffee or tea is all I need."

"Very wise," Vince said, swirling whiskey around in his glass. "Wish I could give it up. Causes me nothing but trouble, normally. 'Course, that's usually because I've been smuggling it into town..."

"You're a smuggler?" Edwin asked.

"Among other things," Vince said. "Not any more though."

"What will the people of Blackrabbit do without you?" Duncan said, laughing.

"Someone else will take over. They always do. Where there's opportunity, there's someone waiting to pounce on it. Should have seen the state of the town when I left."

"What happened?" Edwin asked.

"Port Knot went bad pretty quickly after Baxbary Mudge was imprisoned and I...retired," Vince said.

"Bad?" Duncan asked. "You mean it got even worse?"

"Without me and my gang around to keep the criminal element in check, the streets became even more dangerous. Pickpockets turned to outright armed robbers. The bank was raided in broad daylight. It's virtually impossible to take a coach out into the countryside without encountering highwaymen. Surprised you didn't run into any on the way to the asylum."

"I have noticed a change in the place since I started visiting Mum," Edwin said. "The harbour in particular is getting rougher every month. It's like there's an undercurrent running through it now. A quiet war."

Vince picked at his own stubby fingernails as he spoke.

"There's a hierarchy to the underworld," he said. "A pecking order. You don't simply show up, start robbing houses. Mugging people. Criminals are very territorial. All of Blackrabbit was my territory. Port Knot, especially. Now all the budding young crime lords are trying to take my place. Which is why the head of the island's ruling council called me in to see her a few weeks ago."

"You met with Rabbit?" Duncan asked.

The council of Blackrabbit all had animal names instead of titles. An ancient custom and one taken quite seriously.

"She knew with me and Baxbary Mudge gone there'd be a power vacuum," Vince said. "Certain factions would start vying for control of Port Knot's underworld. She knew there'd be violence. With all of her attention on the new council, she wanted someone who knew the lay of the land, as it were. Wanted my help sorting the mess out. Turned her down, though. Can you really see me on the side of the law?"

"She wanted you to join the watch?"

Duncan found it very hard to imagine anyone going to Vince when they needed protection from criminals. He looked more likely to help the villain than the victim.

"The watchmen are supposed to keep the peace," Vince said, "but they're just a bunch of nose breakers and skull crackers on the council pay. Some of them used to be in the gangs. They still are, I suppose. An official one."

"You wanted a fresh start, didn't you?" Edwin asked. "A chance to change your ways? What better way to show it than by helping to clean up the town you once terrorised?"

"Sounds reasonable when you say it," Vince said.

"He's always doing that," Duncan said, slurring his words a little. "Making you see how you've been wrong all along. I hate it."

"You love it," Edwin said. "Without me to set you right you'd give in to your every terrible instinct and who knows where you'd end up? Who knows what damage you'd cause?"

Vince slid out of the booth and made for the water closet. Duncan's gaze followed him. When he turned his attention back to the table, he found Edwin staring at him.

"What?" he asked.

"Stop," Edwin said.

"Stop what?"

"Do you think I didn't notice your eyes following Vince's bum out of the room?"

"I can't help it, it's a very fine bum!"

Edwin shook his head and laughed. "This is a terrible idea," he said.

"Hush up, you boring old tuss," Duncan said with a laugh. "Drink your coffee."

Duncan climbed into bed. His head was swimming. He'd had a lot to drink, more than he'd usually have. He, Edwin, and Vince had talked for hours. It had been a wonderful night. A single candle flickered on the nightstand. He lifted a snuffer and extinguished the light.

This is a terrible idea.

"Vince," he said softly. "Come to bed."

There was no response. In the emptiness of the night, the only sound was his own heartbeat. Then Vince stood, naked, his ice-blue eye catching the shaft of moonlight from between the curtains. He moved slowly from his bundle of blankets on the floor towards the bed. Duncan pulled back the covers. Vince hesitated, but only for a moment, before climbing in. Duncan was instantly engulfed in the heat coming from Vince's massive, powerful frame. Vince propped himself up on one arm and with the other he ran his hand through Duncan's black chest hair then up to the side of his face. Duncan's breathing became faster. That hand could crush his skull, but the touch was so gentle.

This is a terrible idea.

Vince leaned down and kissed him. It was fierce and rough and clumsy, but his lips were soft. Duncan stroked his silvery beard, the way he'd wanted to since the night he'd trimmed it. Vince was kissing his neck now, and Duncan moaned with pleasure. In the back of his head, he again heard Edwin's words.

This is a terrible idea.
He didn't listen.
Morning came slowly.

Chapter Sixteen

Vince woke to the gentle touch of sunlight on his face. He stirred, his head throbbing from last night's whiskey. He was alone in Duncan's bed. Duncan had lain in his arms for most of the night, resting his head on Vince's chest. It had been...pleasant. The warmth. The comfort. The affection. What's more, it had actually *meant* something. Duncan was intrepid, spirited, and he never held his tongue—all qualities Vince greatly admired, though he suspected they were also the qualities which would come to grate on his nerves after a while.

He turned over to look at where Duncan had slept. Was he falling for Duncan? Surely not. His brother's former lover? A bit too close to home, no? Then again, while Robin was his brother, he hardly knew the man. How would he react when he found out? Would Vince be forced to choose between them? Was Robin that sort of person? He didn't think so, but when it comes to affairs of the heart, who can really say how anyone will react?

He rubbed his face and clambered out of bed. His leg was healing but he still needed the cane to make any significant journeys. He never wore anything to bed and saw no reason to cover up, especially not after last night. There was no sign of Duncan anywhere in the little blue house. He had most probably gone to his toyshop in the village. Had he sneaked away, ashamed to face Vince after what happened? Or had Vince merely been sleeping too deeply to notice him leave?

He removed his eyepatch and splashed some cold water on his face, under his arms, between his legs. He opened the kitchen door and stood in the yard at the back of the cottage, breathing the cold morning air. He was being foolish. He'd had a drink and felt vulnerable, but he'd never admit it out loud. Whiskey always made him wistful. No, no, he was getting it all mixed up—Duncan had shown him kindness, not tenderness. Comfort, not affection. He wasn't falling in love; he was responding to the goodwill Duncan had shown while nursing him back to health. They'd gone to bed as friends and woken up the same.

That was all. Yes, that was all.

Vince finally dressed in the afternoon, and only because he was expecting company. He opened the door to Edwin Farriner and invited him in. They sat facing one another by the fireplace. Vince handed him a tumbler of whiskey which Edwin politely declined.

"Oh, forgot you don't drink," Vince said. He downed the contents of the glass before lifting his own.

"This is the first chance we've had to talk," said Edwin. "Just the two of us."

People on the island loved to talk, Vince had come to realise. He'd found Edwin difficult to fathom. They'd spoken a handful of times but always in the presence of Robin or Duncan. He was handsome, certainly. Square jawed and well built. Charming, too, in his own way. But quiet. Vince had taken it to mean he was hiding a darker side. Perhaps a mean streak or a hidden resentment, though he'd yet found no evidence of either.

"I was going to invite you to my home above the bakery," Edwin said, "but I didn't think you'd appreciate climbing stairs in your condition. How is your work going at the asylum? What has your mother got you doing there?"

"Lugging heavy boxes about, mostly. Keeping rowdy patients in line. Mum tells them stories about me. The terrible things I'll do to them if they don't behave. Doctor Cranch told her not to. She said it isn't necessary to frighten them like that. The asylum keeps me busy. There's always work needs doing. Wanted to come here, to the island. Wanted to see Robin, see Duncan, but it was hard to find the time. Hard to get away."

He adjusted his eyepatch slightly.

"How's it healing?" Edwin asked.

"Slowly. Still wish Robin had waited for me."

"Don't worry, he'll be fine."

"Know why you didn't go, but why didn't Duncan?"

"Duncan's no sailor; he'd be more of a hindrance than a help. Would you have stayed here in the village if Duncan had gone with Robin?"

Vince turned the glass in his hand. "Probably not," he said. "Wouldn't feel right here without him."

"I didn't know you and Duncan were so close."

"Closer than we ever were. Especially now."

"Why especially...? Oh," Edwin said. "You two have...?"

"Is it a problem?"

"Not for me, no. I just... I thought he would have told me, is all."

"Give him a chance. Only happened last night."

"You know he used to be involved with your brother?"

"So?"

"Don't you think it's a little... I don't know...close to home?"

Vince supressed a snarl. No one likes hearing their own doubts echoed back at them. "No," he said. "Known Duncan a lot longer than I've known Robin."

"Are you two courting then?"

Vince frowned and shook his head.

"Was only some fun on a drunken night," he said. "Something we needed to do to..."

"Get it out of the way?"

"Exactly."

The idea brightened Vince's mood a touch. He hadn't been able to put into words exactly how he felt, but Edwin had helped put it into perspective for him.

"You talking from experience?" Vince asked.

"Oh yes," Edwin said, scratching his jaw with his thumb. "Plenty of it. There was a time I couldn't be in the company of someone I fancied without flirting, without ending up in bed. Once that was done, it was like I could properly see them, you know? Lust was always a barrier I had to burst through before I could relax and get to know someone."

"Same thing happened with Robin?"

"Oh, no, no. This was a long time before I knew him. I'm glad, actually. If we'd met back then, things could have gone very differently between us. I wasn't the same man back in those days."

"Were you a fisherman too? Or a sailor?"

"I've always been a baker, like my father and grandmother before me."

"So, you've spent your whole life in a kitchen just baking bread?" Vince asked.

"Well, not only bread…"

He wondered what it was Edwin and Robin had in common. Robin had spent his life outside, on the sea, not stuck indoors. Perhaps Edwin had hidden depths.

"Was thinking," Vince said, "maybe it might be…maybe I'd like to…stay."

"With Duncan?"

"Yes. No. Here. Stay here, in the village. For good. Do you think Robin would… Would he…"

"He'll be thrilled. Really. Absolutely thrilled."

"Well," Vince said, squirming slightly where he sat, but smiling too. "Good."

Chapter Seventeen

After a drizzly morning, the sky had brightened and sunlight rippled on the empty waters of the harbour. Some people sat on the low stone walls laughing and singing as they mended nets and lobster pots.

Duncan had finally found work for Vince. The belfry builders needed someone to operate a pulley to carry heavy stonework up from the ground. They could have rigged a clockwork system but it would have been time-consuming and expensive. Vince was given a chair where he could sit and rest his injured leg. When called upon, he heaved a rope with the arm on his good side, to avoid aggravating his ribs. This hoisted a platform of materials up to the roof. It would have taken at least two ordinary people to operate, but he did it with ease. It wasn't the most exciting occupation in the world, but it got him out of the house and kept him busy. It also, as Duncan had planned, got him talking with the locals.

People waved to him as they passed by, and he even waved back once or twice. Peter Underton brought his dog over so Vince could pet him, and before long, the dog was running after a stick Vince would throw towards the beach. It was an enormous relief to see Vince mucking in with life in the village. He didn't know if Vince was planning to stay much longer, but his remaining time would be easier once people got used to him.

At midday, Duncan and the rest of the workers climbed down from the roof, sat in the sunshine, and passed some ale around.

"Good boy," Vince said as the dog dropped a slobbery stick at his feet.

He picked the stick up and threw it again, then wiped his hand on his trouser leg.

"Always preferred dogs to cats," Vince said.

"No wonder Bramble doesn't like you," Duncan said.

The conversation turned to the news of the day, which was Mrs. Bell's missing jewellery. Some necklaces and a bracelet had vanished in the night. Some said she'd simply misplaced them; some said her husband had sold them to pay his gambling debts. No one could countenance the idea of a thief in their midst.

"You could hunt down the burglar," Duncan said to Vince. "Be good practice for you if you ever decide to join the Port Knot Watchmen."

Vince ignored him and petted the dog which had returned with the now sand-encrusted stick.

"Doing a good job with the pulley, Mr. Knight," said Mr. Trescothick.

Vince nodded awkwardly; he even smiled a little.

"There you go," Duncan said to him. "You just had an almost completely normal moment with another person. See, you can do it."

"Had a good teacher," Vince said.

His smile broadened. The lines around his eyes deepened, his cheeks bulged. It made Duncan's pulse race a little faster.

Mr. Allister Stillpond arrived and greeted the workers. He was a fisherman by trade but had a passion for sculpture and sold his work in the Blashy Cove market whenever he had the chance. He stood gazing up at the roof, using his hand to shade his eyes from the sun. "I was thinking, Mr. Hunger," he said. "We could add some decoration to each corner of the belfry. Seahorses, maybe. Or birds, like a gull or a guillemot."

He had brought along some drawings which he passed out amongst the workers. Duncan studied each drawing carefully. One was of a hunched wolfish creature with wings and long, curved fangs.

"What's this one?" he asked, showing it to Vince.

"I thought I'd try my hand at creating a gargoyle," said Mr. Stillpond. "It's functional too. Carries rainwater away from the main building. I thought we could work them into the Moth & Moon's guttering,"

"Why's it so bleddy ugly?" asked Mr. Trescothick, scrunching up his face at the drawing.

"To ward off evil spirits!" said Mr. Stillpond. "Or so they say. And this place could use all the help it gets, don't you think, Mr. Knight?"

Duncan was surprised to hear the question aimed so squarely at Vince, who didn't react at all. He just threw the stick again. It travelled even farther than the last time.

"You don't remember me, do you?" said Mr. Stillpond.

"Should I?" Vince asked.

Duncan's stomach twisted, sweat gathered under his arms.

"A few years back," Mr Stillpond said, "I was in Port Knot trying to sell my sculptures. I wanted to be considered for a commission I'd heard was coming up. New statues for the council building. I wanted to make a name for myself over there. You got wind I was setting up on your patch. Just a little market stall was all. Just to get me started. You and your gang came round, demanded I pay you. I told you I'd already paid for my table and I couldn't possibly afford to pay you as well. It wasn't good enough for you. You had one of your blokes smash one of my little sculptures. Then another. You came back the next day and the next and the next, until you'd smashed all of them. I had no money, no stock, I had to come back here, go back to working on my father's fishing boat to earn some money so I could one day, hopefully, start over. All because I wouldn't bow to the great Vince Knight of Port Knot."

The other workers had stepped away, whether as a reflex or on purpose, Duncan didn't know. He positioned himself in front of Vince, who stood up and clenched his fists.

"Come on, Vince," Duncan said. "Time we were leaving."

He expected some jeers from the workers, from the other villagers who had gathered, but there was only a deathly silence. Vince took his cane and walked over to Mr. Stillpond, staring him down.

"Vince..." Duncan said.

Vince said nothing, he simply followed Duncan back home in silence.

Chapter Eighteen

The event to celebrate the reopening of the Frost & Thaw Tearoom was to be the highlight of the month's social calendar. Everyone who was anyone would be in attendance. Eva wasn't entirely in the mood and toyed with the idea of returning to Merryapple instead, but she wanted to support her friend.

The tearoom had been damaged the previous Midwinter, during Baxbary Mudge's mad scheme to seize control of the island by blowing up a stage holding the ruling council. He failed but did significant damage to the building. In the months since, it had been renovated and expanded. It remained a spacious, glass-walled building, though it was now essentially one large floor filled with tables set around a circular stage.

Overhead was a gallery with yet more seating. Clementine's love of automata had been taken to a new height. She still had her little clockwork songbirds but these were joined by tin flamingos who dipped their necks to catch imaginary fish, copper peacocks who splayed their gemstone-studded tail feathers, and the star of the show, a life-sized ostrich covered in real feathers, who spread its wings and bellowed out a deep, throbbing call on the hour. It was all arranged so no matter where one was seated, a view of the stage was possible. It had become less of a tearoom which sometimes held balls, to a ballroom which sometimes served tea.

Eva wore the gown Clementine had sent to her—a beautiful floor-length teal dress with laced cuffs and bronze detailing. She had already made small talk with various town business people for a good hour before a sudden cessation of the music indicated something important was about to happen. Eva could guess what it was. Clementine Frost had arrived.

The band on the centre stage struck up a dramatic tune, full of low drums and high horns. The crowd cheered and parted as Clementine made her entrance on the arm of a striking, svelte man who moved with the grace of a panther. She wore the symbol of her office, the Fox mask, and a high-collared black satin gown overlaid with layer after layer of gold florals. She smiled and laughed and enjoyed every single iota of attention lavished upon her.

"Darling!" she called out to Eva. "You're still here? I thought you'd be eager to return home to...what is it called again? Rainy Day Bay? Hurricane Harbour? Cloudy Creek?"

Eva rolled her eyes and laughed. "You know very well I was supposed to have left by now, but how could I refuse an invitation to such an occasion?"

"Why, you couldn't!" Clementine said. "I simply wouldn't allow it! Music, please! These people came to dance."

With a flourish of her wrist, the band struck up again, an allemande this time. Clementine extended her hand which Eva took and together they moved to the floor and began to dance. The scent of Clementine's jasmine perfume was subtle but alluring.

"You could smile," Clementine said. "This is not a hardship."

"I know, it's just..."

"You feel guilty for being here having fun while Iris is home alone?"

"You are so terribly astute, my dear."

"It has been said," Clementine said. "And how is our dear Dorothea now?"

"Still fuming," Eva said as they hopped side by side.

"Can you blame her?"

"She should know by now—I always know best," Eva said.

Clementine laughed as she spun beneath Eva's raised hand. The rest of the crowd had joined the dance, and the room was filled with a goodly number of spinning couples and triunes.

"While you may certainly think so," Clementine said, "and please believe me, so do I, you did put her in charge of the company."

"Your point?"

"Well, how would you feel in her shoes?"

"Dowdy."

They pressed close together then pushed apart, still clutching each other's hands.

"You know what I mean," Clementine said. "How would you feel if you were in charge yet she had the authority to overrule your every decision?"

"Oh, don't exaggerate; it's not every decision."

"Isn't it?"

"No, of course not. In this instance, she's clearly wrong. The pirates must be taught a lesson. They must be shown the C.T.C. is not a soft touch."

"And the new ship designs?" Clementine asked.

"Fine," Eva said, "in these two instances, she's clearly wrong. Lavishing money on decorating merchant vessels is a waste of funds. The money would be better spent improving the living conditions of the crew, increasing their pay, not on pretty paintwork and gold filigree."

"And would it be terribly fatal for you to explain it to her instead of simply running roughshod over her orders?"

Eva took Clementine in her arms as the song came to an end. "Let's find out," she said.

Dorothea Chase, wearing her Swan mask, sat with the rest of the ruling council of Blackrabbit, each one suitably bedecked in their mask of office. Their table was the best in the tearoom, naturally. It was the most prominent and had the best view. It was the place to sit if one wanted to be seen, which Dorothea did not. She didn't much care for attention and certainly didn't need it. Not like some other people she could mention.

To her left, poised and calm, sat the aged Ms. Agatha Samble in her Rabbit mask. Stuffing his face with almond pudding was the young new Magpie, Mr. Andrew Boon, a successful tailor from Port Knot. Easy to like and quick to laugh. The new Badger was Lord Anthony John Stamp, a middle-aged landowner who was very easy on the eye. He'd fought a hard campaign for the position against one of Baxbary Mudge's relatives and was perhaps the only current councilmember who Dorothea felt truly earned their position. The last member was Fox, Ms. Clementine Frost. Her role was to be the opposition, the contrarian, the one to find faults in any proposed legislation. A role she excelled at.

Lady Eva Wolfe-Chase approached the table and nodded. She looked radiant, as ever. The woman had an effortless elegance to her which

Dorothea had always envied. She herself found clothing a cumbersome mystery, even with advice from her maid. Had she her way, she'd never wear a stitch and indeed regularly went nude at home. Her staff didn't mind, nor did her husband, who sometimes joined in. When the weather was nice.

Eva was speaking quietly with Rabbit, the head of the council. *Finding some new way to undermine me.* Eva had been appointed to the role of Swan after the death of her father but had passed the title on to Dorothea, along with managing the family company. Such a thing to do. The power, the responsibility, dropped like it was nothing. Like she was too good for it. Despite the prestige of the position, the glamour of it, Dorothea could never truly shake the feeling she'd been handed nothing more than some scraps from Eva's table.

"Dorothea," Eva said, "may we speak privately?"

She rose from her seat and joined Eva in a less noisy corner of the great glass room. Overhead, clockwork armatures fitted with lanterns spun in mesmerizingly complex patterns, casting colour light onto mirrored tiles in the ceiling.

"What have I done to displease you today?" Dorothea asked.

She hadn't meant it to sound quite so tetchy but what's done is done.

"Clementine made me see how...brusque I must have seemed," Eva said. "It was not my intention."

"Wasn't it?" Dorothea asked. Her blood was rising and she clenched her fists.

"I merely wished to make you see—"

"Your way. You have no faith in me at all, do you, dear cousin?" Dorothea asked, quite unable to control the volume of her voice. "Why did you even bother to appoint me as head of the company?"

Eva appeared somewhere between surprised and amused. Dorothea wasn't sure which was worse.

"I couldn't stay here on Blackrabbit," Eva said, "and you were best suited to the position."

Dorothea thought she was going to laugh but instead it was anger which caught in her throat. She spat her words out. "*Best suited.* What a loaded phrase that is," she said. "Best suited, how? Don't answer, I know how. I was best suited insofar as I was the easiest for you to control. I was best suited because I would perform the day-to-day tasks but leave the important decisions to you. Do you deny it?"

Eva cocked a hip and took a sip of her wine. "I deny nothing," she said. "You're entirely correct."

Dorothea threw her glass across the room. It shattered against a black iron pillar and brought many stares from the crowd.

"You don't even have the courtesy to lie to me," she said.

"I respect you too much to do so."

"Respect? *Pah!* Are you out of your mind? What respect have you shown me? You've just admitted to installing me as your puppet."

"No, not as my puppet, as my right-hand woman."

Dorothea stepped back, uncertain how to respond. It was the last thing she expected to hear. "I beg your pardon?"

"Perhaps I was unclear," Eva said. "Allow me to explain. The Chase Trading Company is the most important business in this part of the world. It employs hundreds, if not thousands of workers, to say nothing of the satellite businesses which exist in its orbit and depend entirely upon it. I chose to build my life on Merryapple. Merryapple is too small to house a business like ours so what I needed was someone I could trust—implicitly—with keeping the business afloat here on Blackrabbit.

"It is no secret I have never warmed to you on a personal level, nor you to me, but this is business. Apart from some extravagant spending, you have done a superb job of keeping the company running. In fact I daresay it's in better shape now than it has been in years. I may — sometimes—go over your head but it is always in the greater interests of the company, of the people in its employ. There is no one I trust more with the livelihoods of our workers than you, Dorothea. Perhaps... perhaps I could have done more to make it apparent."

Dorothea knew this was as close to an apology or admission of fault as she was ever likely to receive. "Well," she said. "You certainly could have made it clearer. Though as you say, we have never gotten along as well as we should have. We are not used to the ways of one another."

"Something we should bear in mind from now on," Eva said.

Dorothea lifted another drink from a passing waiter and clinked it against Eva's glass. "To a brighter future."

Chapter Nineteen

Robin was wrapped up in his heaviest jumper, thickest scarf, and warmest gloves, but still the icy sea air stung his very bones. During the day, it was warm enough, but once the sun started to fall, so did the temperature. With the setting of the sun, he worked by the light of a striker-lantern. He sat shivering at the tiller and strapped it tightly with rope to steady his course while he slept, which he did in bursts. A couple of hours at a time—if he was lucky.

The fear of drifting off course roused him regularly. Even though he enjoyed sleeping under the stars, it was at times like this when he wished *Bucca's Call* had a deck with a cabin below. They were often found on larger luggers, but when his father commissioned *Bucca*, he clearly hadn't seen the need to include one. She was open decked and twenty-odd feet long, made for inshore fishing with the promise of a nice safe port to dock in each evening. He would be eternally glad the removable platform he'd made for her was still in place when he'd left Merryapple. He was able to sleep with his head and chest covered by it, protecting him from the rain and spray of the ocean, though it was far from comfortable.

It was the eighth night of his journey. He'd caught sight of the pirate vessel the day before, though it had remained an indistinct blob on the horizon before being swallowed by the shroud of dusk. He checked his charts again and again. He'd long since left the usual shipping lanes and as far as he could tell, his course would take him past the Azores, not directly to them as he'd expected. He stared bleary-eyed into the blackening distance, shaking with cold and hunger. He'd run out of food the night before and his supply of fresh water was running perilously thin. His mouth was dry, and his stomach grumbled. If he didn't make landfall soon, he never would.

As he settled down for some rest, he wished, as he always did, that Edwin was there to keep him warm. He didn't know how much longer he could go on. He was so far from home, and he didn't have enough supplies to make it back. Weak from hunger, he nodded off and dreamt of his cosy bedroom at home, with its little fireplace blazing.

He woke when *Bucca's Call* lurched savagely to starboard, knocking his head against the hull. Frantically, he scrambled to his feet to find himself in the middle of a violent squall. Rain pelted him, drenching him from head to toe in seconds. Waves stretched higher than the masts of his boat, clutching at the stars themselves.

He quickly unleashed the tiller, deftly manoeuvring *Bucca* through the sea. The boat sliced along the crest of a breaking wave, the open deck awash with foam. He slid the craft down into a trough only to be picked up by another wave, taller than the last. He was taking on more and more water. He didn't dare leave the tiller long enough to start bailing out, gambling instead on *Bucca* holding out until he reached calmer waters.

"Just a bit farther, *Bucca*, please," he said.

Onwards he went, into the heart of the roaring, pitch-black night with a howling enemy desperately grasping at his clothes, eager to pull him overboard. He could wait no longer. He reached under a thwart and pulled out a long, clockwork bilge pump which he fixed into place. Grabbing the key, he turned it quickly. Too quickly. It snapped off in his hand. In anger, he flung it out into the ocean. He rummaged under the seat again and retrieved a handle, then slotted it into the pump. He carefully wound the handle round and round. The pump took up water and flushed it overboard. With one hand still on the tiller, he wound the handle again and again. Over and over he turned it, until his arm burned and his back ached.

The winds were not dying down. The sails whipped violently to and fro; the rigging rattled and shook and the lug sail...oh, the lug sail. Robin held his breath at the sight of it. The sail was ripping at the seams. A slice broke free. Robin tried to catch it but in the high wind it flapped about viciously, obscuring his vision and threatening to swaddle him. If that happened and he were to be knocked overboard, he would surely drown.

With his good hand he caught the sail and pulled with all his considerable strength. The remaining seams came undone and he cast the sheet into the ocean. Without it, he'd be unable to control his heading. The waves continued to pound against *Bucca's* hull. More than once they were accompanied by a great cracking of wood. Robin returned again to bailing out the water as best he could. His chest thumped, his stomach churned, his eyes blurred, and he bellowed defiantly into the moonless night, as if his anger and desperation were enough to quell the seas. When the first light of dawn finally touched his cheek hours later, he toppled to the deck and lay as still and quiet as the grave.

Chapter Twenty

Duncan walked carefully down the steep, sandy track leading to a secluded beach on the northwest side of the island. He steadied himself with one hand, grabbing on to tufts of grass as he went. Behind him Nick laughed as he followed.

"It's all very well for you and your long legs," Duncan said, "but I've got to be a bit more careful."

They arrived at the beach, and he wiped his hands together to clean them.

"It's the climb back up I hate," he said.

The sun was beaming down from a clear, blue sky onto Blue Eye Bay. The waves gently lapped the shore, where pristine white sands arced round to the towering, oval sea arch which gave the area its name. They were alone on the beach.

"The sunsets from here are spectacular," Duncan said.

"It's very quiet," Nick said.

"Yes, I thought there might be more people about, though most are put off by the climb. If they come here at all, it's by boat."

"I think you brought me here because you knew it would be deserted," Nick said.

"The very idea!" Duncan said. "I simply wanted to show you the sights of the island."

Nick kicked off his boots and pulled off his top shirt revealing a wide, hairy chest. Next, he ditched his breeches and darted, naked, into the water. Duncan admired the view of his sturdy legs and round bottom before they were swallowed by the waves.

"Aren't you going to join me?" Nick called back to him.

Duncan stood with his hands on his hips, an eyebrow arched. "I'll pass, if it's all the same to you," he shouted. "I don't want wet sand clinging to me."

Nick waded back towards the shore and stopped at the point where the waterline still covered his modesty. Duncan thought it a very practised manoeuvre.

"I understand if you're too embarrassed by your shortcomings," Nick said.

Duncan was being teased. He hated being teased. He hated being manipulated. He removed his clothes, slowly, deliberately, and dropped them into a pile on the sand, setting his spectacles on top before striding slowly and purposefully into the sea. It was his idea, he told himself. His and nobody else's. If he was going to go in, it was because he bleddy well wanted to.

"Shortcomings, indeed," he said as he reached where Nick was standing. The waterline was past Duncan's navel, such was the height difference between them.

"I clearly misspoke," Nick said, smiling. "You're not embarrassed by them."

"I'll have you know the sea is cold."

"It's not *that* cold," Nick said, laying back.

He floated off in the direction of the oval stone arch. Duncan followed, splashing him. Nick laughed and splashed him back. They were close now. So very close. Treading water, Nick leaned in and kissed Duncan on the lips. Duncan, with his heart beating as if to burst, wrapped his short, hairy arms around Nick's waist and held tightly as they sank beneath the waves.

Vince stood on the clifftop high above Blue Eye Bay as Duncan and the other man swam. He lost sight of them as they passed under the sea arch. With a deep breath, he buried his hands into the pockets of his claret overcoat. Not wanting to encounter anyone on his way back, he avoided the road and instead cut through the woods, past Stamp Downs and onto Loves Last, the little tree-covered track from the cemetery. From there he trudged past the orchard, breathing in its brewery's fumes, and onto Winter Walk, the lane which led to Duncan's little blue house on the hill. Remembering place names was second nature to him, and there were so few of them here compared to Port Knot, with its tangle of roads, lanes, avenues, paths, streets, and entries.

He sat by the cold, quiet fireplace stroking the smooth leather of his eyepatch. Bramble was sleeping outside on the windowsill. A stack of paper rested on a table. He leafed through it. Mostly blank pages but there was the occasional architectural drawing. Plans for the bell tower. Varying designs, most of which were extravagant in size and complexity and very different from the actual belfry. It was clear to Vince how Duncan had compromised on his vision. He took a blank sheet of paper and a piece of willow charcoal from a box. He'd watched Duncan making his own sticks of charcoal by heating willow batons in a tin on the fire. Vince sat by the window, and for the first time in many a year, he began to draw.

It was an hour or so later when a movement along the hilltop caught his eye. Duncan and his friend returning from the beach. Vince's heart began to beat louder and louder. The noise of it filled his ears. Before he knew what was happening, he'd taken his cane and walked out to meet them. He didn't feel in control of his actions. It was as though he were an observer sitting at the back of his own skull, watching it all unfurl before him. Why couldn't he leave them alone? Why was he confronting them?

Duncan looked flushed, almost embarrassed. He introduced Vince to Mr. Nick Babbage. Vince grunted in response. Duncan was talking about needing to collect items from his house, and he left them alone. Mr. Babbage was making noises about the weather or something equally inane. He was dressed like the Barley Hill prats back home. The ones who thought they were better than everyone else.

"The teacher?" Vince asked.

"I am, indeed," he said.

"Been spending a lot of time with Duncan?"

"Also correct."

Vince wiped his mouth with the back of his hand. He didn't want to say anything more, but he couldn't stop himself. Why couldn't he stop himself?

"You two courting?" he asked.

Mr. Babbage took a step back and crossed his arms.

"I'm not sure it's any of your concern, Mr. Knight," he said.

"And if it were?" Vince asked, drawing himself up to his full height. He puffed out his barrel chest and clenched his hands. He was at least a head taller than Mr. Babbage and a good deal wider, stronger, fiercer.

"In which case," Mr. Babbage said, "you should have discussed your concerns with Duncan directly. You have had ample opportunity, no?

What with you sharing his home? As his guest? While you recuperate from the injuries sustained in your vicious beating by your criminal associates?"

"Perhaps I should have asked him the other night," Vince said. "When we were in bed together."

Mr. Babbage's arms dropped by his side, and he looked Vince up and down before shaking his head and walking away.

Duncan appeared from the house a moment later with a bundle of papers in his hand. "Oh, where's Nick? I designed a display case for his coin collection, I wanted to show it to him."

"Coin collection? Do you mean his purse?"

"No, he collects coins. He finds them interesting.

Vince had never heard anything so dull. He just shrugged and leaned on his cane.

"Said he had to go."

Duncan followed him back inside and began to clear up the table, shuffling the pages of his tower plans. His attention was drawn to one sticking out. He pulled out the page. A charcoal drawing of a sleeping Bramble.

"What's...? Did you do this?" he asked.

Vince barely glanced in his direction. "Burn it," he said. "Was just frittering away my time."

"This isn't a misuse of your time, Vince," Duncan said. "This is beautiful. I didn't know you could draw."

"Not done it for years."

"Where did you learn?"

"Nowhere. Taught myself. In the orphanage. Used to steal paper from the office. Soot and charcoal from the fire. Wasn't any good, it crumbled too easily. Used to smudge it with my hands. Other children made fun of me. Big, tough Vince liked drawing animals. Flowers. The governor used to find them. She'd burn them."

"What? Why?"

"Wasn't healthy, she used to say. Soot got everywhere. More dirt to clean up."

"You could start drawing again. Here. There's no shortage of artists in the village, I'm sure they'd teach you."

"*Ho!* After yesterday?" Vince asked. "After what Mr. Stillpond told them? Be lucky they don't run me off the island."

"It won't come to that. I'll talk to them, explain. Tell them what you're really like."

"Maybe it's not worth it," Vince said, his head hanging. "Maybe it's too late to change. Thought I could start over. Just make trouble wherever I go. Made a fool of myself."

"You didn't," Duncan said.

Vince slumped onto the sofa and rested his hands on his cane. "Wanted to be...better," he said. "Wanted to be...*more*. But I'll only ever be a lout from Blackrabbit. Should have let Penhallow finish me off."

"Don't say such things. I've liked having you here."

"Whole village thinks I'm a villain. Even your cat hates me."

"I think it's the beard. And the near-constant scowling. Look, try not to let what happened yesterday get you down. Robin will be home before long, I hope. He can smooth things over with the rest of the village. They'll listen to him. Spend a bit of time with him and, who knows, you might even learn a thing or two about making friends."

Duncan bumped his shoulder against Vince in a friendly manner and smiled. Vince rubbed his own mouth again. He shouldn't have said anything to Mr. Babbage. It wasn't his place. Why did he say it? Jealousy? Spite? Both, probably. He was never any good at dealing with matters of the heart. He was used to the sort of problems one could solve by punching.

How could he explain himself to Duncan? How could be make him see he was out of his depth? He wanted to tell him, but he lacked the words, lacked the courage, even. He'd spent a lifetime building walls to protect himself. The one time, the only time, he'd ever lowered them was with Martin, and look how that ended. When Martin was killed, something within Vince died too. He was sure Duncan never had any similar issues with Robin. He was sure Robin was better equipped to deal with such matters. Perfect, flawless Robin bleddy Shipp.

"Not the same as my brother," Vince said. "Never could be. No matter what you do."

"I'm not trying to make you the same as him."

"Aren't you?"

"No, Vince, I'm not," Duncan said, pacing across the room. "And frankly I'm insulted you think I was. Robin is one of the best of men I've ever met. I see a lot of him in you. Is it such a terrible thing? Robin... He's become a yardstick for me, I freely admit it. Every man I meet gets compared to him. But is it any wonder? After so long spent with the monstrous Baxbary Mudge I met my saviour in Robin. Of course it affected me. Of course it left an impact. Robin may not be the only man I ever loved, but he's the only one who ever loved me back. Wholly, completely, honestly. The love we shared changed but connects us still. If I've learned anything from him it's the importance of having a friend who'll stick by you, no matter what happens. You said you wanted to change. You said you wanted to be better. Then let me help. Let us help. All of us."

Vince rubbed his mouth again. He shouldn't have said anything to Mr. Babbage.

Chapter Twenty-One

Robin was woken by a barking dog. No, dogs, definitely more than one—yipping and yapping somewhere in the distance. His vision was blurry, and he thought this was it—the hallucinations had begun. Too long at sea, too much sun, too little water, his mind had finally gone. The sunlight hurt his eyes. His lips were dry and cracked, his stubble caked with salt. Still drenched and shivering, he heaved himself upright and rubbed his face. He'd been lying in about a foot of seawater. *Bucca's Call* sat low in the now-calm ocean. The dogs continued to bark. Ahead of him was the port beam of a ship and a substantial one to boot. A ship of the line, in fact. The largest class of sailing vessel on the seas. Oddly, it had a deep jetty floating alongside, attached with ropes.

Frantically. Robin tried as best he could to steer *Bucca* towards it. The bilge pump had vanished, lost overboard in the squall, and there was now no way to bail the water seeping in through the cracks in her hull. As he approached the jetty, Robin cast the mooring line onto a piling and pulled in close. He leapt from his boat and landed with a wet thud. He tied the line to a mooring post, more out of habit than anything else, and stood there as *Bucca* bumped against the small pier. He was distraught. He didn't know what to do. His precious little boat was taking on more and more water.

"Please, no," he said, pawing at the mooring line, trying in vain to heave her out of the ocean.

"Please don't go, *Bucca*, please don't leave me…"

Even under the best of circumstances, he wouldn't have been able to lift the boat himself. Finally, the weight of her burden became too much. She sank lower and lower into the water, her scarlet hull catching the rays of the early morning sun for the last time. The line slipped from Robin's exhausted hands, tore the post from the jetty and down she went. Down, down, down into the cold and quiet dark, taking with her Robin's heart, his peace of mind, a sliver of his soul. The last he saw of her was the tip of her mast sliding beneath waves. And then she was gone.

He stood staring at the spot for a good long while, completely unable to accept what had happened. *Bucca's Call* had been his constant companion, his refuge from the world. When the pain became too much, he'd sail in her and be soothed. When the world became too confusing he'd sail in her and everything would become clearer. He'd been born in her and deep down he always thought he'd die in her too. He'd lost her only once before, during the hurricane. Afterwards, the whole village had come together to repair her, but this time there could be no restoration. She was gone forever. He felt a terrific emptiness inside. A hollowing of his spirit.

He craned his neck to see the weather deck of the mighty vessel behind him but there wasn't one. No gunwale, no bowsprit, no masts, and no open space at all. The side of the ship kept going up, and up, and up, as one huge, wooden wall. In his stupor, it took Robin a few moments to understand what he was seeing. He was standing inside the walls of a giant, floating castle. It would have been perfectly hexagonal in shape but one side was missing, open to the ocean and flanked by two tall lighthouses. Were it a castle on land, the gap would be the main gate, and home to a portcullis to stop intruders from coming inside. Without one, there had been nothing to stop him drifting through while unconscious.

There was no keep, no central structure which the walls protected; rather the walls were themselves the keep. They were made from ships of the line, stacked up like toys in Duncan's shop. Each stack was connected to the next by round towers, identical to the lighthouses but without the glass lantern rooms on top. The "courtyard" was ocean, like an immense tidal pool trapped by the structure, on which floated the jetties where he now stood.

The ships had been fitted with covered balconies and open hatches. The distinctive bay windows of captain's quarters remained, bulging outwards from the otherwise smooth surfaces. The whole affair was strung with moving, clockwork-powered gangways bridging one round tower to the next, or one balcony to another. And then came the sails. Lots and lots of sails. They ringed the top the floating citadel like clean washing on a line. Each mast twitched and turned in competition with the next.

"It's heavin' to," Robin said.

The sails were constantly moving across the wind. Robin guessed the outer walls must contain rudders operating in unison to keep the entire structure more or less in place. He couldn't begin to imagine how large they must be. Large flags billowed in the breeze atop the two lighthouse-cum-guard towers at the entrance. They featured a white skull wearing a tricorne, its jaws set with gears, lying upon a field of black.

"Pirates..." Robin said.

The jetty on which he stood ran along the entire inner walls of the castle. A handful of ships were docked at it, including the brigantine with the bull masthead he'd been chasing. It was flying a black flag depicting a skull in a red bandana which wove through the bones and emerged from the mouth like a tongue.

The animals weren't a hallucination, he suddenly realised. There were indeed dogs barking at him from windows and balconies. Spaniels, terriers, and other small, scruffy mongrels. Over his head, gangways extended, retracted and swung about on loud, clicking, clockwork mechanisms. There were figures moving about on them now, going from one stack to the next, whooping and hollering. In no time at all, dozens of people—dozens of pirates—were leaning over parapets, out of portholes, off gangways, all chanting and jeering at him.

His throat, already raw, ran drier still, and he was so very weary, but he drew himself up to his full height, ready to fight. A hinged doorway, cut out of the hull of the bottommost ship, opened slowly. From it emerged a solitary figure, clad in leather breeches, boots, and wearing a tricorne hat. A dark-bearded pirate with sharp eyes and a prominent chin.

"You look lost, big man!" he called out.

"I'd say I'm right where I need to be," Robin said.

The man laughed and held his hands out. "Well, in that case," he said, "welcome to Driftwood."

Robin was taken aboard and given a mug of ale which he gratefully swigged from, wiping the suds from his heavily stubbled face. Once within the structure, he had a better sense of how it was constructed. From the outside it looked as though enormous ships has been simply been shorn of their masts, stacked on top of one another and then buttressed. The vast open space he was presently confronted with indicated a greater engineering effort on the part of the pirates. For starters, Driftwood was two ships deep, a fact he hadn't been able to see from outside. The skeletons of the ships remained to hold the basic structures together while most of the hulls had been stripped away. Some decks had been removed entirely and those which remained had been cut in such a way as to make them look like rooms in a doll's house.

The masts he'd seen ran through the entirety of the structure, rising from the very bottom and towering above him until they poked through the topmost deck. They were oiled and turned in place, creaking as they moved. Huge columns had also been erected to bear the additional weight of the ships above. The original stairways of the vessels remained in place, sharing duty with rickety ladders, and long gangways stretched across the full width of the ships, connecting the oceanward side to the "courtyard." The light was dim, the air rank. Robin leaned over a railing to get a better view and it screeched under his weight.

"Careful now!" shouted one pirate with an Irish accent somewhere in the crowd above. "Wouldn't want ya fallin' over the edge, would we?"

Robin was never the most observant person but even he could tell that despite the more or less friendly welcome, the pirates were sizing him up. It had never occurred to him to bring a weapon—he didn't even own any. On the rare occasions when trouble had found him, his size and strength were enough to see him through it, but this was a different world. All around him were men and women with flintlock pistols tucked in waistbands, belts, even strapped to thighs. Black eyes and broken noses were commonplace. Some hid their faces beneath hats, behind scarves. He was being guided along with forceful smirks.

"Have you found yourself a new pet?" a woman shouted from yet farther above.

She was clad in purple, and her hard eyes made Robin flinch. The deck on which she stood was very different to the rest, draped as it was in silks and lit by curving, jewelled lanterns.

The bearded pirate in leather cupped his hands around his mouth and shouted back: "You can't have this one! I found him, he's mine!"

"Lucky for him."

They came to an arched door leading to a converted captain's quarters. Robin was gently but emphatically encouraged to sit on a chair. It groaned under his bulk.

"Now then," said the pirate, "what could possibly bring a fisherman all the way out here?"

"Who says I'm not a pirate?" Robin said, lifting his head high.

The remark prompted much laughter from the room.

"A pirate with no weapons and such a sweet, innocent face? And sailing a lugger, of all things? I don't think so. I know another pirate when I see one. My name is Captain James Trewin, but you can call me Red Jim."

"Quite a name."

"It's well earned, I can assure you," he said. "And what do they call you?"

"My name's Robin Shipp. I'm 'ere to find a man named Bill Barrow. Do you know 'im?"

Red Jim beamed, his eyes sparkled. "*That's* who you remind me of. Is he a relation of yours?"

The blood drained from Robin's face. He was trying to be subtle, but he'd never been good at masking his emotions. "Maybe," he said. "No. I dunno. 'E's 'ere, then?"

Red Jim shot a look at two men standing beside Robin—one long and clean-shaven, the other earthy and sprouting a bushy black beard. The pirates he'd encountered at the asylum. They squirmed under Red Jim's glare.

"Oh yes, he's here," Red Jim said. "He arrived not long before you, actually. I'll send for him."

He waved at the men who appeared grateful for the chance to leave as they bundled themselves out of the cabin. Robin didn't know what to think. His mind had seized up. Nothing felt real any more.

"Could it be you followed Barrow here?" Red Jim asked. "In such a little boat? You must be very brave. Or very desperate."

"Can't I be both?"

Red Jim laughed and sat back, a little more at ease. A little more natural. "You're lucky, you know. Usually any ship that approaches without flying the black is sunk with our cannons."

"Why didn't you attack me then?"

"Well, you weren't exactly threatening," Red Jim said.

He smiled again, but Robin wasn't sure if he was being complimented or insulted.

"So, what is it?" Red Jim asked. "Does he owe you money? Because you don't strike me as a magistrate or a pirate hunter of any kind."

"Like you said, I'm a fisherman. Nothin' more. I just need to talk to 'im, is all."

"I'm glad to hear it, because if you came here to cause trouble, I'd be forced to take action."

For a bloodthirsty pirate, he was really quite dashing. He had a strong jaw, sharp nose, and heavy, expressive brow. He was husky, too, and his white shirt opened to a hairy chest. But it was his smile which disarmed Robin so, as it could dance from friendly to fiendish in the blink of an eye.

"Are you in charge round 'ere?" Robin asked.

"Oh, no, Captain Gulabahaar is. You met her earlier. No, I was fortunate enough to spot you before they did. Who knows what these other degenerates would have done if they'd gotten to you first. Especially Gulabahaar. She doesn't like visitors, and she rarely gives them a quick death."

Robin swallowed hard at the thought. Red Jim laughed and waved his hand. The remaining pirates behind Robin left the cabin. He took it as a good sign.

"You've come a long way to find our Captain Barrow," Red Jim said.

"A very long way," Robin said softly.

"Well. I'd best be going before he arrives," Red Jim said. "He and I don't exactly get along."

He hesitated before rising from his chair.

"A word of advice from a new friend," he said. "Captain Barrow isn't what he seems. Tread carefully."

Robin didn't turn to watch Red Jim leave; instead, his attention remained fixed on the wall in front of him. He could barely move. His stomach was in knots. Presently, floorboards creaked under the weight of a newcomer and a hand came to rest on his shoulder. A gravelly, grumbling voice accompanied it.

"*Robin?*"

Chapter Twenty-Two

Unable to secure the use of a horse, Duncan had been forced to push a cart the whole way from his workshop, across the village and up to the top of the steep Anchor Rise. A few months ago, Edwin had likened him to a Shetland pony—squat and hardy. He'd meant it as a friendly insult, but Duncan had been secretly quite pleased with the comparison. Nonetheless, the task would have been taxing for anyone, and so he stood at the door of Wolfe-Chase Lodge, panting for breath.

The largest home on the island, the lodge lay nestled in a plot surrounded by a low stone wall mottled with moss. The modest forecourt contained a shed for the family carriage and stables where a young girl was brushing down one of the speckled horses while another girl shovelled hay. Duncan stood on the doorstep and dabbed his forehead with a handkerchief before ringing the bell. The door was opened by Drake, the footman.

"Hullo," Duncan said. "I'm here to—"

"Tradesmen use the back entrance," Drake said and slammed the door closed.

Duncan's face flushed and blood pounded in his ears. He moved to bang on the door with his fist but thought better of it as Iris might be resting and he didn't want to disturb her. Instead, he took several deep breaths to calm himself then heaved the cradle he'd made out of the cart. He regretted making it so heavy. He considered asking the stable girls for help but they were hard at work. Sighing, he lifted the cradle and waddled with it down the narrow passageway at the side of the lodge and around to the rear. He was compelled to stop more than once for a rest, each time gently setting the wooden crib on the flagstone path and muttering under his breath.

"If the legs get scuffed...make him wish he'd never left...slam the bleddy door in my face again and see what happens..."

It often made him feel better to make threats out loud, even if no one was around to hear them. He knocked rapidly on the rear door and was left standing for several minutes before Drake opened it.

"Ah, Mr. Hunger, how delightful; please, do come in."

It took all of Duncan's self-control not to shout at him. Drake made no effort to help with the heavy crib.

"I'm here to see Iris, if she's not busy?"

Drake said nothing but beckoned him in with an indifferent wave of his hand before striding off, heels clacking on the expensive parquet floor and leaving Duncan to linger in the well-appointed kitchen. He'd been to the lodge many times but always felt out of place when Eva or Iris weren't around. It was a grand house, no doubt about it, but it had always left him a little cold. Some furious tutting drew his attention to an alcove where he found the cook shaking her head.

"Whatever's the matter, Mrs. Roscrow?" Duncan asked.

"This!" she said, pointing to the table in front of her. "This is the problem, Mr. Hunger."

The bloodied bodies of three chickens lay in a pile. An unruly mass of red feathers and meat.

"What happened to them?" Duncan asked.

"A dog happened to them," she said. "Someone's mangy, savage dog got into our gardens last night."

"How awful," Duncan said.

He couldn't think of anyone who had an animal capable of such an act. There were some dogs on the island, including young Peter Underton's, but they were all very well trained. Iris greeted him and beckoned him through to the drawing room.

"I've brought the cradle," Duncan said.

"How marvellous!" Iris said. "Drake, bring it in here, if you would?"

Drake gave Duncan a side-eye glare intense enough to melt iron. Duncan grinned as broadly as he possibly could.

"And please do be careful with it, Drake," he said. "Lady Eva would be so dreadfully disappointed if it were to be damaged."

Duncan followed Iris into the lodge's main drawing room where she poured him some brandy and bade him to sit. The room was lined entirely with dark wood and decorated with taxidermy and some lavish seascapes. He recognised one or two as being the work of Barnabas Whitewater, husband to Robin's mother. Drake arrived with the cradle which he set in the middle of the room with an exaggerated sigh.

"Thank you, Drake," Iris said. "You can go."

He turned and left, uttering a barely audible tut in Duncan's direction as he passed.

"What is his problem?" Duncan asked.

"Oh, he doesn't like it here," Iris said. "Not as glamourous as life in Port Knot. I can't blame him, I suppose. He's a young man; he craves excitement."

"He doesn't have to be such a tuss about it."

"I'm sure it was the same for you when you first arrived here. But then, you soon had Robin to play with."

Iris giggled a little, then winced and laid a hand on her stomach.

"When does Eva get back?" Duncan asked.

"She was supposed to have returned already, but she wrote to say she's been invited to a do at Ms. Clementine Frost's tearoom."

Duncan took a sip of brandy and grinned. "She's over there having the time of her life, leaving you all alone. And in your condition."

"I'm sure she's only staying out of duty," Iris said, smiling. "Besides, she could do with some entertainment."

"She has been very anxious of late," he said.

"And overprotective," she said. "I'll be honest, since she's been away I'm more rested than I've been in weeks."

Iris examined the cradle, running her hands across the end piece engraved with a wolf standing on its hind legs, wearing a high cocked hat and working a ship's wheel. "This is beautiful work. So clever how you've weaved our family emblems together."

Duncan blushed a little. He usually cared little for the opinion of others but he took pride in his work, and praise from a friend meant a great deal to him.

"It's terribly good to see you, Duncan," she said. "How are things going with you and Mr. Knight?"

"As well as can be expected, I suppose."

"Is he behaving himself? And more to the point, are you?"

"There's a very loaded question," he said, sipping his drink.

"I've heard all sorts of gossip about you two," she said. "All alone in your little house, huddling together for warmth."

She laughed again, and Duncan's cheeks flushed.

"We have huddled, and it was warm," he said.

"Sounds serious."

"It isn't. Just some fun between friends. You know how it is."

"Are you sure you're not looking at Vince as a second chance with Robin?" she asked.

"I beg your pardon?" The question had come entirely out of the blue and left him slightly stunned.

"Oh, I know, you don't see the very obvious physical resemblance, but I'll wager you see something of Robin in Vince's nature." She crossed the room and rested on a settee by the window. "You're more perceptive than you let on. And no, you're not in love with Robin any more but wouldn't it be nice to find someone who had all of his best qualities? His good heart, his barrel chest, his big, strong arms? Certainly, Mr. Knight must be possessed of some of Robin's less tangible qualities, or you wouldn't waste your time with him. You've never been one to suffer fools. Quite what those qualities are is a mystery, I must say. He keeps them well hidden, you must admit."

Duncan swirled the brandy in his glass.

"He's not as bad as everyone thinks," he said.

"He makes you feel safe, I'll wager. The powerful man who'll protect you the way Robin did?"

"You're quite mistaken, I assure you."

"Am I?"

"I like Vince for who he is, not for who he reminds me of. Anyway, this is all neither here nor there. I'm not pursuing him, not in the way you mean."

"You could have fooled me."

"You're in fine form today," he said, slouching.

He knew she was joking, for the most part, but it still felt like being picked on. He wondered why it was. Perhaps, if he were being honest with himself, he'd admit it was because there was some truth in what she was saying?

"Duncan!" Iris said. She doubled over, her eyes wide. She huffed and puffed as she steadied herself and held her stomach. Sweat gathered on her brow. "*Duncan!*"

"What's wrong?" he asked.

"Nothing, sorry, simply a bit of discomfort, took me quite by surprise. Would you be a dear and please help me up to bed?" She was doubled over as he took her hand and began to guide her to the door.

"Iris," he said, "are you sure it's not more serious?"

"Oh, please don't start," she said. "I've had it up to here with Eva's worrying, I don't need you to—"

"The carpet is wet," Duncan said. "So are your legs."

The colour drained from Iris's face, and she spoke with a barely contained panic. "Send for Mrs. Whitewater," she said.

Chapter Twenty-Three

It can't be him, Robin told himself. *It can't be.*

He stood, slowly, and turned. The man standing before him was almost as tall as Robin himself. He wore a gaudy lime-green waistcoat, a scruffy white shirt open almost to the navel of his round belly, tatty cream breeches and a thick leather belt. He was unshaven and thickset, with long, snowy white hair pulled back into a tail and a bushy white moustache, curled up at the ends. Like Robin, he had small, jug ears, but also a bulbous nose and deeply wrinkled sky-blue eyes beneath a stern, heavy, frowning brow.

"You need to leave," he said. "Now."

"Dad?"

"It's not safe here."

"*It is you!*" Robin said, entirely unable to control the volume of his voice.

Weak though he was from his journey, he flung his arms around his father and hugged him tightly.

"Steady! You'll crush the life from me!"

"I thought it were a trick," Robin said. "Or a mistake. When 'e said you were 'ere, I thought 'e must be wrong. But 'e weren't. You're 'ere. You're alive."

"I'm here," his father said. "I'm alive."

Composing himself, Robin stepped back.

"Robin, my boy," his father said. "I never thought I'd see your face again."

If someone had told Robin that one day he'd be reunited with his father yet neither would shed a single tear, he'd have called them a heartless fool. Nevertheless, there they both stood, cheeks dry and eyes unmisted. Imposing as he was, his father was smaller than Robin remembered, half a head or more shorter than Robin himself. Age, he thought, had diminished him but then Robin had been a boy when last he set eyes upon him. A boy's perspective of his father will always be skewed, he supposed.

"You're grown, in more ways than one," his father said, patting him on the stomach. "And you're still wearin' my cap, I see."

His father led him out of the cabin and up some very shoddy stairs. Around them, pirates shouted and laughed with each other, mostly ignoring them. One group was playing cards in a large common area, others were counting coins in vestibules. They went outside to a small balcony overlooking the inner ring of the structure—the courtyard as Robin had come to think of it. He was glad to be out of the relative gloom and stifling smell of unwashed bodies, lantern oil, and rum.

"How did you get here?" his father asked.

His voice wasn't quite how Robin remembered it. Rather, it was deeper, raspier, with only a little hint of the once-thick Merryapple accent remaining.

"The only way I know 'ow," Robin said. "In *Bucca*."

His father slapped the rail in delight. "You still have her!"

"I did," Robin said quietly. "Until this morning. The journey here was rougher than I expected. She didn't survive."

His father's face dropped, his eyebrows gathering a knot in his brow. "She had a good run."

"She always took good care of me," Robin said. "It's like I've lost a piece of my 'istory. A piece of myself."

The great floating castle threw deep shadows on the vessels docked within her embrace. Driftwood hugged the ships like a mother guarding her young. Without warning, his father darted back inside and Robin struggled to keep pace. He was weak from his journey and found the cramped arteries of Driftwood difficult to navigate. Both he and his father were much too big for the place and were forced to duck in spots.

He passed by two pirates engaged in a bare-knuckle brawl. Their blood-splattered fists crunched into each other's bodies while a handful of onlookers jeered and cajoled. He expected money to change hands, wagers to be placed on the outcome, but saw none. Instead of money, the fight was for honour, perhaps, or the settling of a score. Or maybe it was just for the sheer fun of it.

He followed his father into one of the thin towers which joined each stack to the next. His father flicked a switch and a clockwork-powered gangway rose up from the bottom of the next tower and clicked into place at the big open portal in front of him. His father sprinted along it, bypassing an entire stack, but Robin took his time, fearful the ramp would give way under their combined weight.

He was outside now, walking along a thin bridge, high above the jetties. These gangways could be moved up and down, and they connected one tower to another. The tower portals were irregularly placed, so permanent bridges wouldn't have been possible. Still, Robin felt there must have been an easier solution and wondered if the pirates weren't simply showing off their presumably pilfered technology. He found his father inside the next stack, standing on a wide footbridge with handrails made of rope. It was one of many, and they all ran across Driftwood from port to starboard. The space formed by the hollowing of the ships was cavernous, and the noise of the pirates going about their day was extraordinary. Above them, the doll's-house decks. Far below, row after row of long tables and benches.

"You can't stay here," his father said.

"Can't leave, neither," Robin said. "Not without a boat. Anyway, I just found you again. I'm not leavin'." He leaned against a pillar and took off his cap, fussing with the little tuft of hair on his forehead. "Looks like I'm the only one in the family who went bald. Vince still has 'is 'air. 'E's your other son, by the way. From Blackrabbit. 'E's a lot more like you than I am."

Robin waited for a moment or two. "Well?" he asked.

"Well what?"

"Aren't you going to ask about 'im?"

"Who?"

"Vince!" Robin said.

"Oh yes, the Blackrabbit boy. What was his mother's name again? Glory? Honesty?"

"'Er name is 'Onor! 'Ow can you not remember?"

"Be fair, Robin; it were a dalliance fifty years ago."

"So, you didn't recognise her in the asylum?"

His father turned away and fussed with a splinter.

"You did!" Robin said. "You're unbelievable."

"Thank you."

"I didn't mean it in a good way! Why didn't you say anythin' to 'er?"

"What were I supposed to say, exactly? *Hello, my dear, remember me? We used to roll around together in the taverns of Port Knot until you got pregnant; then I ran off and pretended to be dead.*"

"Mum is going to be furious when she finds out you're still alive," he said.

"I daren't face her!" his father said with a laugh.

Robin didn't see what was so funny. "She never really recovered from the night you— I nearly said died. Disappeared, I suppose I should say."

His father turned away from him again.

"She lost 'er brothers to the sea," Robin said. "Losin' you the same way—it were devastatin' for 'er."

His father said nothing. The woman he was meant to have loved suffered because of his actions, yet he gave no indication whatsoever that he cared.

"She doesn't talk about them much," Robin said. "Nor you, besides."

"I suppose Barnabas's work is still stuffing the Painted Mermaid?"

Taken aback by the shift in topic, Robin struggled to respond. The Painted Mermaid Museum had been one of the jewels of Blashy Cove and had housed artwork from villagers stretching back generations.

"No," he said. "The Mermaid's gone, taken by the 'urricane."

"And his paintin's?"

"Scattered to the four winds, for the most part. We recovered as many as we could. Mum still has a few."

"A shame," his father said. "I always told him they'd be worth money someday. He never appreciated his own talent. Ah, well, another unfortunate casualty of the Great Leveller."

"The what?"

"The hurricane, my lad, the hurricane."

"Why do you call it the Leveller?"

"Because it took away the Chase Tradin' Company's great advantage over us—numbers. For years, we couldn't move too far north without runnin' afoul of their pirate hunters. Then the hurricane blew in. It sank dozens of ships but it cleared a path for us over to the Caribbean and right up the channel to Denmark and beyond. It's been nearly a year and they still haven't recovered. We've not had it so good in years! Well, I spent most of the time in gaol, but I'm told the rest of us have been makin' the best of it."

"They say a thousand people drowned when the 'urricane struck," Robin said, shaking his head. "And I don't know 'ow many more died on Blackrabbit, or on the mainland. And you celebrate it."

"It's an ill wind that blows no one any good."

"And no pirate ships were sunk by it?"

"Some. Not many. I lost the ship I were servin' on and most of the crew in it."

"And do you celebrate those losses too?"

His father held his hands open. "Such is life at sea," he said calmly.

Robin had never heard anything so callous in all his life.

Chapter Twenty-Four

Morwenna Whitewater was in her usual spot next to the main fireplace of the Moth & Moon, discussing the latest events with her inner circle. The quorum of older villagers kept a close eye on all the island's comings and goings from their round table. Someone had to, they argued.

Mr. Vince Knight was the issue of the day, as he had been since he arrived, though some concerns were raised about the new schoolmaster, Mr. Nick Babbage, and his apparent bachelorhood. He could turn out to be like Mr. George Reed, who was happiest in his own company, but until it could be proven either way, it was to be assumed he was in dire need of a spouse. If there was one thing the Tweed Knights found difficult to stomach, it was a lonely person in their village.

They had no actual proof of Mr. Babbage's loneliness, of course, but they weren't about to stand on ceremony in such matters. Early days it may well have been but if he showed no obvious signs of taking a partner, steps would have to be taken. They were well into the deliberations over what might be done about him when a stable girl from Wolfe-Chase Lodge arrived, panting.

"Please, Mrs. Whitewater, come quickly!" she said. "It's Lady Wolfe-Chase—she's having the baby!"

"Don't be silly, girl," Morwenna said, rising to her feet. "It's much too early. I daresay her wife is panicking needlessly again, but I will come along and have a look at her."

Mrs. Hanniti Kind also stood, gathering her knitting needles.

"No need for you to accompany us, I'm sure," Morwenna said.

"Better safe than sorry," came the reply.

The stable girl had the foresight to bring a carriage, and Morwenna bundled herself in as quickly as her rickety hips would allow, followed by Mrs. Kind. After a swift dash up Anchor Rise, they were met at the door of the lodge by the worried-looking footman who guided them up to the master bedroom suite. There they found Lady Iris Wolfe-Chase in bed, panting and squirming while Duncan held her hand and fretted. Morwenna took one look at Iris and straightened up.

"It's time," she said.

"But it's too early!" Iris said. "Doctor Cranch isn't even here yet; she's still on Blackrabbit!"

"Send for Doctor Greenaway," Hanniti said.

"There's no need," Morwenna said, removing her red shawl. "I've delivered countless babies and plenty of early ones."

Hanniti put a hand on Morwenna's shoulder and leaned in close. Her voice was low.

"Morwenna, it's *very* early," she said. "Better safe than sorry."

Duncan hurried out of Wolfe-Chase Lodge and rushed up Hill Road towards the bakery, where he found Edwin teaching his young apprentice, May Bell, some of the finer points of sourdough. Edwin's face dropped when he heard the news. He tore off his apron and bolted out the door.

Edwin may not have been the athlete he was in his youth but he was still a good deal faster than Duncan ever was. With his stubby legs, Duncan found it impossible to keep up, and he paused on the cobbled road to catch his breath. A flash of scarlet silk at the harbour caught his eye. He waved, yelled, and started to hurry down to where Eva was disembarking from a longboat.

"Duncan! How lovely, this is quite a welcome home. I hardly expected—"

"Go home!" Duncan said, doubled over and fighting for air. "Iris! Baby! *Now!*"

He pointed in the direction of the lodge, as though Eva had forgotten where she lived. She took up her dress and dashed towards Anchor Rise. It was some minutes before Duncan felt able to tackle the steep road, and he was wheezing by the time he reached the lodge. He sank onto a lemon-yellow chaise lounge to regain his composure. Edwin walked slowly down the staircase, looking back over his shoulder.

"Any word?" Duncan asked.

"I was politely shooed away," Edwin said. "But they insisted they had things well in hand."

"Well, there's a relief," Duncan said with his hand on his chest.

Edwin stood in the hallway, rubbing the back of his own head with his hand. Duncan had been surprised—shocked, really—when he found out Edwin was going to father a child with Iris. He understood why they chose Edwin to be the father, though. He was a good man. Quiet, decent, reliable. While he wasn't nearly meaty enough for Duncan's tastes, it wasn't hard to see what attracted Robin to him.

Edwin and Iris had been friends for years, and both had lain with men and women in the past, but this was a huge leap for them. Duncan naturally assumed the child would be conceived the usual way but Doctor Cranch had a less awkward suggestion. She had been taking care of Eva's father in his final days and chose to stay on when Eva converted the family home into an asylum. A brilliant doctor in multiple fields, Cranch had studied a technique called "Romantic Medicine" which involved Edwin's seed and syringes. Duncan didn't totally understand the specifics and had no particular desire to. What mattered was, it had worked. He knew what Edwin needed right then but Robin wasn't around to provide it, and so Duncan got up from his seat, crossed the hall to where Edwin was standing and hugged him.

"I'm sure everything will be fine," he said. "She's in good hands."

Edwin smiled weakly. "I wish Robin were here."

"So do I," Duncan said, hugging him tighter.

From the bedside, Eva brushed the hair from Iris's eyes. She felt every pang as if it were her own, her stomach had turned to lead, and her head throbbed as if caught in a vice. Iris was screaming now, and with teeth clenched, she huffed and puffed and roared, gripping the sheets, twisting them as if to wring the pain from her own body.

Mrs. Whitewater was coughing again. Her body shook with the force of it. She was a hearty sort but the illness was taking its toll. She'd lost some weight in the past week, Eva noticed. Mrs. Kind gave her some water. Once she regained her composure, she addressed Iris from a footstool at the end of the bed.

"This is the worst part, dear," she said. "But once it's done you won't remember how much it hurt, you'll only remember the joy that came after."

Eva was lost; she didn't know what to do, so she started talking, saying something, anything. She knew she was blathering. She never blathered.

"I'm so sorry, darling," she said, over and over. "I'm so sorry. I didn't mean to stay away so long. I didn't know this would happen. I thought we had weeks. I should have been here. I'm so sorry..."

"Enough now, Lady Wolfe-Chase," said Mrs. Kind. "Why don't you get some air?"

Eva left the room and paced the carpeted hallway, turning hither and thither. She slammed her fists against her legs. What was wrong with her? Why couldn't she think clearly? Every now and then she heard Iris scream and thought the sound would burst her heart.

She sat in a chair and closed her eyes, trying to regain some composure, but all she could think was how Iris needed her, how scared she must be. On the wall in front of her was a painting she'd brought from Chase Manor of herself, her dear sister, Daisy, and their parents. Her father looked severe, as he usually did. Daisy's mother, Sada, stood with her hand on his shoulder, smiling happily. It was a lie. It had been painted a few months before Sada left her father, disappearing into thin air and taking Daisy with her. The artist had originally captured her melancholic expression, but her father had insisted it be altered to something more "appropriate."

Beside it hung a portrait of the Wolfe clan—Iris and her three parents—one mother, two fathers. Having one father was more than enough for Eva: What must life have been like with two? She and Iris had both been around the same age when the paintings were made. Eight or nine years old. Iris's red hair was unmistakable, as was the grin she wore.

Eva often felt heartsick at the thought of Iris losing all three of her parents in the same night. They'd drowned out in the cove in bad weather. So close to home yet they were never to reach it. How alone Iris must have felt after that. How aware of the fragility of life, the transience of it. Eva wondered if it explained why Iris was always so cheerful. She'd been through bad times and survived. She tried to let nothing unnecessary in her head, nothing needlessly dark or sinister. She avoided stories of bloodthirsty pirates and sensational murders. She maintained a kind of balancing act between adulthood responsibility and childhood innocence. To some, she occasionally came across as a little dim, but Eva knew better. Iris was smart enough to keep the darkness out.

Another scream brought Eva to her senses and she ran to the bedroom.

"You came back," Iris said through tears and sweat. "You came back."

"I'd never abandon you," Eva said, kissing her hand. "Never."

Doctor Greenaway arrived a short time later, red-faced and out of breath. He bumbled about in his usual manner, occasionally twirling one end of his bushy moustache. Things between him and Eva had been a little tense in recent months. His nose had been put out of joint by their reliance on a doctor from Blackrabbit, but the simple fact was Iris was a special case. This was the first time Doctor Cranch had put the theory into practise. Doctor Greenaway acted as though he'd been relegated to a secondary position in the matter, there to keep things ticking along until the real doctor arrived. He was a proud man, and it rankled him, but despite the looks and occasional muttering, he never gave any less than his best. Nonetheless, Eva couldn't help but wish Doctor Cranch were there and wondered if the process was the reason for the premature birth.

"I can see the head!" Mrs. Whitewater said suddenly.

Iris squeezed Eva's hand even more tightly. She pushed and pushed until she was delivered of a baby boy. Mrs. Whitewater handed him over to Mrs. Kind who took him to a table to be washed and dried. Eva waited. And waited. She turned to Mrs. Whitewater who was shaking. There was no sound. No crying. Nothing. Eva couldn't face Iris. She couldn't look into her eyes. Not now.

"Eva!" Iris said. "What's happening? Why isn't anyone saying anything? Why—"

She screamed again, clutching her stomach.

"Keep going," said Mrs. Whitewater.

Eva's head was swimming; she thought she was going to be sick. The world was sliding out from beneath her feet. Spots formed in front of her eyes.

"Keep going, keep going," Mrs Whitewater said to Iris. "Don't stop now."

A baby's cry rang out as Mrs. Whitewater held up a second infant. A girl this time. Mrs. Kind took the baby to the table, as before. She lay the child next to her brother, gently wiping and drying her. The baby girl's wailing filled the room and echoed back. No. Not an echo. Two cries, in unison. Eva ran to the table where both children were bawling at the top of their tiny lungs. Overcome, she wept, touching both of their tiny, perfect faces.

"Twins!" said Mrs. Whitewater. "How marvellous."

"One of my fathers was a twin," Iris said. "Are they both healthy?"

"Perfectly so, it seems," said Mrs. Kind. "Apparently your son was simply waiting for his sister."

She carried both babies to Iris. Exhausted, Iris kissed their foreheads softly.

"We're going to have to decide on names," she said. "We hadn't planned on two. What will we call them?"

Chapter Twenty-Five

"Oi, Barrow! Barrow!"

A young lad of about fourteen pushed his way through the crowd. He had a prominent gap between his front teeth, and he wore a brown woollen Monmouth cap over his black hair, an apricot kerchief with white spots which was a touch too big for his scrawny neck and linen slops to the knee. Robin's father took him to one side. The lad rustled in his pocket and produced from it a scarlet gemstone.

"I heard you were back, Captain Barrow! What'll you give me for this, eh?"

Robin's father took the jewel and held it up to the light. The stone flashed red.

"What do you want for it?" he asked.

"My usual, I suppose," the young man said.

"Your usual! For this little pebble?" Robin's father said. "I'll give you half."

"Half! Get out of it, it's worth more than half!"

"What am I supposed to do with a ruby? You think there are a lot of fancy lords or ladies passin' through here? I have to pass it on to someone else, who has to take it to a port and try to find a trader who won't ask a lot of questions. That's a big risk for them and a financial risk for me. So, half. And this is me being generous because I like you, Fausto. You're young and you're keen and you'll make a fine captain one day."

Fausto huffed and puffed but eventually he shook hands on the deal. Robin's father pulled out some coins, the exchange was made, and Fausto went on his way.

"This is what you do 'ere?" Robin asked. "Trade in the spoils of piracy?"

"Amongst other things. Every now and then I grace a crew with my presence, offer them advice on how to better their craft. For a fee, of course. I may not be the force of nature I were in my youth, but I've accumulated quite a lot of skills over the years. And I've got contacts in ports all over the world. Traders who don't mind so much where their goods come from."

"But you told the boy you'd have to find a buyer?"

"Right."

"I thought you said you already knew traders who'd take it off your 'ands?"

"I do," his father said, "but Fausto didn't need to know. And those traders will give me a little somethin' for sendin' goods their way next time I see them."

"You're makin' money on both ends of the deal?" Robin asked.

His father winked and laughed. "Gotta make a livin' somehow! And I've been out of the game for a while; got a lot of lost time to make up for." He flicked the gem upwards and snatched it out of the air, depositing it in his shirt pocket.

"So, this is what, a floatin' pirate market?"

"Oh, Driftwood is far more than just a market. It's a sanctuary—the last pirate-friendly port in the western world. It's also a home."

"People actually live 'ere?"

"Nowhere else will have us. In my day, port governors were only too happy to turn a blind eye in exchange for a little coin. We had free run of most of the Caribbean. It all ended with the King's Pardon, long time ago now. Most of our kind took the chance to be absolved of any crimes, settle down to a *normal life,* whatever that is. We're tryin' to keep our way of life alive, you see?"

Robin had never thought of pirates as an embattled minority, struggling to retain their identity. And he still didn't.

"Way of life?" he asked. "What way of life? Pillagin' and murderin'?"

"Ah, we're not murders, boy!" his father said. "Most of the time a crew will give up at the mere sight of a black flag. It's the fear that gets them, you see. The stories they've heard of us."

"And all them stories are entirely made up, are they?"

"Well, not all of them, I grant you..."

"Aren't you worried he'll find out you're dupin' 'im? Fausto, I mean?"

His father drew himself up to his full height and lifted his fists. "If he tries anythin', I'll beat him senseless and feed him to the sharks."

A cold look in his eye suggested he'd done it before. He dropped his fists and smiled his slick, easy smile. "But it won't come to that. Poor Fausto over there won't last long in this line of work. He'll be lucky if he's not swingin' from the end of a rope in Antigua by Midwinter."

"'Ow come?"

"He doesn't like it here; he wants to strike out on his own. He's not captain material, and even if he were, he won't make it without this place. The hurricane was a setback for the Chase Tradin' Company, but eventually they'll recover and then their pirate hunters will be back out in force. Even back in my day, most of us only got a handful of years before our luck ran out."

"Is that why you came back to Merryapple all them years ago?"

His father shrugged. "I were never one to push my luck. Driftwood was founded a few years ago as the last bastion of piracy. Our last hope for a truly free life. If Fausto thinks he can do without it, he's in for a nasty shock."

"About the name he called you, the one you used in the asylum. *Barrow*. Why do you use it?"

"Yeah, Bill Barrow, pleased to meet you," his father said, doffing his tricorne cap. "Or, if you don't like Bill Barrow, I could be Francis Byrne, or Robert West. Oh, Eddie Sparks! Always liked that one, haven't used it in ages."

Robin's brow furrowed.

"You remember the last time I left you with Morwenna and Barnabas," his father said, "when I went back to sea?"

Robin nodded. He'd been around eight years old at the time. His father was gone for an entire summer.

"I were needed on my old ship, the *Fledglin' Crow*. Now, I didn't want a fuss made, and I had your safety to think about, so I started usin' the name Bill Barrow. There were only a handful of my original crew left, and they understood the need for a bit of discretion. And then, after I "died" I couldn't keep usin' my real name; I didn't know if there were anyone lookin' for me. Someone from Chase Tradin', or...whoever. I needed an alias. Or two. Or three dozen. It were safer all round if the world thought Erasmus Shipp were lyin' on the seabed."

"Your accent's softened," Robin said.

"Yours hasn't. I needed to lose it as much as I could. Look at the size of me. I can't exactly blend in, can I? So, a new name and a different accent made me a touch harder to find."

"So, even if I 'ad suspected you were alive..."

"You never would have found me," his father said. "Because I didn't want to be found."

They had come to a throng of pirates gathered in an area open to the air but shaded by striped, frayed awnings. Fausto waved to them as he pushed his way through, carrying a crate filled with angry, squawking chickens.

Red Jim sauntered past, deep in conversation with the two pirates from the asylum raid. "So I said to her, I said Gulabahaar, my dear and fair captain, if you'd just put me in charge, like I suggested from the start, none of this would have—"

"*Jim!*" his father shouted. "I've been wantin' a word with you!"

His voice was a deep growl, much like Vince's. It rumbled and roared out from the depths of his barrel chest. He grabbed Red Jim by the collar and flung him against the hull. Jim laughed and held his hands up.

"Barrow!" he said. "So good to see you abroad in the world once more!"

"You left me to rot for months!"

He snarled the words out with such ferocity Robin feared he would dig his teeth into Jim's neck and tear off a chunk of flesh. He stood ready to intervene.

"Now, it wasn't my fault," Red Jim said. "By the time we handed over the gunpowder in Port Knot, the watchmen were closing in, and you were nowhere to be seen. Besides, I reasoned you were big and ugly enough to look after yourself and would rendezvous with us later on."

The two nervous-looking pirates shuffled about uneasily. They muttered to each other but Robin was unable to hear all of what was being said. They seemed to disagree with Red Jim's assessment of events.

"Once we heard you'd been incarcerated, there was nothing we could do," Red Jim said. "We couldn't very well sail up to Blackrabbit Gaol to spring you, now could we? Be reasonable, Captain Barrow—" Robin's father let go of Jim's shirt and took a step back. "—We kept abreast of your situation, and once we heard you'd been moved to the asylum, we knew you'd be easier to free."

"And yet," his father said, "I don't recall seein' your face among the rescue party, nor on board ship on the journey back here."

Red Jim shot a look at his associates, causing them to squirm. "Ah, well, I had duties here, didn't I? Trusted my best people though. Gave them the use of the *Pride of Ithaca*. Now, if there's nothing else?"

Robin had never witnessed a sarcastic bow before, but Red Jim performed one like a seasoned pro before leaving with his anxious lieutenants in tow. Robin did his best to keep up as his father led him through the narrow passages of Driftwood. His father was obviously well used to the layout, but more than once Robin banged his head or his arm or his leg on various corners and beams. He squeezed himself through tight doorways, one aspect of life on board ship which he'd always disliked. They simply weren't built for men like him.

"That's 'ow you ended up in gaol?" Robin asked. "You were deliverin' gunpowder to Port Knot last winter?"

"Sort of. Gulabahaar heard there were people in Port Knot lookin' for a quantity of gunpowder, no questions asked. As it happens, I'd earlier acquired a supply from a Spanish vessel, more than I had any use for. She ordered Jim to take it, and me, to Blackrabbit. Jim contacted the buyer, who arranged a boxin' match in the harbour as a distraction while we slipped ashore and unloaded the barrels. I... I thought I recognised one of the pugilists. He were big, like me. Like you."

"It were Vince," Robin said.

His father avoided eye contact and hung his head low. "I weren't in the mood for any awkward conversations so I slipped away. As the match were endin', a patrol of watchmen appeared. The crew scarpered and I couldn't reach them without bein' seen so I hid. I spotted an empty rowboat and hopped in, intendin' at the very least to move away from shore and have the crew collect me. Unfortunately for me, I were spotted before I'd even cast off."

"We Shipp men don't exactly blend in," Robin said.

"Precisely. The alarm were raised and the watchmen set upon me before I had a chance to run. Or row. I were taken in but I refused to speak, I just scribbled the name *Bill Barrow* on their book. I were in front of the magistrate before I knew it. Right quick, I thought. I soon found out why. Turns out the rowboat belonged to a friend of his, so to make an example, he sent me to Blackrabbit Gaol. Horrible place, it is. Damp and dark, the air thick and putrid. I were locked up with all sorts. I started scratchin' symbols on the stone walls. Winding snakes, and ropes, and anchors, and masts. Anythin', really, just to keep me sane. To keep me from panickin'. I don't... I don't like being cooped up. It brings back...memories."

His voice quivered, betraying his advancing years, but only for a moment, and then the rolling growl returned. "I never spoke one word, tried to look simple, hopin' they'd take pity on an old man. After a while

I were moved to the asylum for proper care, as they put it. Then Red Jim's crew came to get me. What's the look for?"

"I were thinkin' about 'ow you must 'ave been in the gaol'ouse when I brought Lady Eva there last winter. She asked me if I wanted to go inside, but I refused. If I'd gone in, I might 'ave seen you. I might 'ave..."

His father put his hand on his shoulder. "It doesn't matter now," he said. "Don't waste time thinkin' about what might have been."

A thunderous roar startled Robin. It was as if every pirate in the place was shouting at once.

"Sounds like Captain Thorne is back," his father said.

Robin followed him again through the gloomy, narrow walkways to a railing at the great central cavity of Driftwood, the towering doll's house. All about him, people whooped and hollered as they welcomed back their fellow freebooters. Below, a crew was carrying in box after box filled with silks and spices. One man, well dressed in a banded robe and with spectacles perched on the end of his nose, took note of everything as it went past, rummaging through each box in turn and making a list.

"Nasir is taking stock," his father said, pointing. "It's his job to make sure everyone gets their fair share."

Robin wasn't sure what he meant. Surely the spoils belonged to the crew who raided it?

"The plunder is divvied up amongst the crew first, then some goes to coffers for maintainin' this place, and the rest gets split between the remainin' citizens of Driftwood."

"'Ow very charitable," Robin said.

His father squinted at him. "It's not charity. It's community. Gulabahaar wants us to see each other as part of one big crew and to treat each other as such."

"And she's, what, the King Arthur of this floatin' castle, this shinin' example of fairness, this Camelot at sail?"

"I don't think I like your tone, boy."

He didn't like it either, because it wasn't his tone, it was Duncan's. He could practically hear Duncan's voice coming from his own mouth. This cynicism wasn't like him at all, but he couldn't just stand there listening to his father proclaiming these wonderful, idyllic things and not say something. These were pirates. *Pirates.* This wasn't Avalon; this wasn't Arcadia; it was a hive of outlaws, brigands and cutthroats. It was his father who was dragging this side of Robin to the surface. He didn't care for it one bit.

She was there now. Gulabahaar, the pirate queen herself, congratulating Captain Thorne on his success. She lifted a scarf from a box and wrapped it round her neck, laughing as she modelled it for her subjects. How many people died on the raid, Robin wondered? How many lost their lives so his father and the rest of them could laugh and cheer and carry on as if the outside world couldn't touch them?

"And it works, does it?" Robin asked. "This dividin' of wealth? No one skims off the top? Keeps somethin' back for themselves?"

"Of course they do; it's human nature. But unlike on land, where everyone is expected to behave themselves and be open and honest about their activities at all times, we expect people to be a bit greedy sometimes. A bit weak of spirit."

"If everyone gets a share regardless, then why does anyone risk their neck by goin' on raids?"

"For the adventure," his father said, grabbing Robin's shoulder and shaking it. "For the thrill. Besides, if you don't lift a finger to help, you'll be made to, sooner or later. We all have to pull our weight. Do our bit. And think about it, if you know you can make a little extra by goin' on a raid, you'll try harder to make it successful."

His father begrudgingly accepted the fact Robin would have to stay, and told him he could sleep on the floor of his untidy cabin. Formerly the captain's quarters of one of the vessels Driftwood was made from, it now resembled a scatter-brained bookmaker's workshop. Every surface, and most of the floor, held a leaf, or a stack, or an entire box of paper scribbled upon in a jittering hand. His father's script had deteriorated in his later years, Robin supposed. Three of the walls held bay windows set with small, square panes of glass. Only one frame remained uncovered and it overlooked the inner docks of Driftwood. A small writing desk was wedged beneath, covered in ink stains and littered with paper. The wall behind him was covered with a large, black flag.

"What is this?" Robin said, pointing.

The flag bore the bone-white image of a bear's head in front of a sunburst, a dagger clasped in its jaws. Over one eye sat a patch decorated with a paw print. His father stood beside it, hands on hips and chest puffed out.

"My very own flag," he said. "My first crew used to say I were like an angry bear at sea, so they made me this. I used to fly it from my ships in my heyday."

"It certainly makes an impact," Robin said. "It reminds me of someone..."

He cleared a space on the floor and unfurled a blanket.

"You'd think a place this size would 'ave a spare 'ammock or cabin. It must be made of, what, fifty ships?"

"You're safer here with me. Besides, a lot of the ships were hollowed out to make storage areas. Food, munitions and the like. Plus the galleys. Feedin' this many people requires a lot of space. You could ask Gulabahaar but I doubt she'd let you stay on her deck."

"What's so special about 'er? Why's she in charge?"

"She's the last of the Pirates Three, the founders of Driftwood. That whole starboard deck is her territory. Plenty of space in it for her crew, and more, but none of us dare say anythin'. She's ferocious. And I suppose bein' Pirate Queen has to come with some perks. Anyway, it's not always so crowded, usually some crews are away for weeks or months at a time, but business is good at the moment. We don't have to go too far to find plunder. The Great Leveller opened up a lot of opportunities for us."

"And what, they bring it all back 'ere for you to sell on?"

"No, no, I only run small pieces like this," he said, tapping the gemstone in his pocket. "Little extras, is all. Anyway, you must be used to cramped conditions, workin' with a crew on *Bucca?*"

"I never 'ad a crew."

"What, *never?* You must have done! I designed her to be crewed by one but even I had to have help when I fished in high season!"

Robin took off his cap and overcoat and sat on a blanket on the floor. His knees popped and clicked the whole way down. "No one in the village would work with me," he said. "After all, I were the son of a murderer, or so they thought. They'd 'ardly even talk to me for the longest time. I didn't need anyone else to 'elp me with oyster dredgin'. I got used to workin' alone. I 'ad no other choice."

His words made no appreciable impact on his father.

"Well, you'll always have crewmates here!" his father said.

"I'm not a pirate."

"Not yet."

"Get that idea out o' your 'ead," Robin said, pointing at him. "I'm not followin' in the family business."

"Oh, think about it, son! You and me! On the high seas together! The way it always should have been. Don't answer yet, just think about it. And if not, maybe your brother would be more open to the idea…"

"Oi, you leave Vince alone, you 'orrible old man. 'E's tryin' to put all that stuff behind him."

Robin immediately regretted saying anything. His father's eyes lit up.

"What stuff?" he asked, leaning forward. "Wait, is he already a pirate?"

"No, not a pirate…"

"But he's used to workin' outside the law! Ah hah, Shipp blood runs thick! He'll follow in his dear old dad's footsteps."

"You're assumin' 'e won't just knock you out cold for abandonin' 'is mother."

"Oh," his father said, tugging on his own earlobe. "Fair point."

While Robin could never countenance being a pirate, his father's offer struck a chord deep down inside him. He'd often dreamed of them sailing together, father and son, side by side against the elements, against the world. There was a time, not so very long ago, when he would have jumped at the chance.

"You're not merely passin' through, are you?" Robin asked. "You live 'ere."

"Have done for years. It's gettin' harder and harder to keep this way of life goin'. It's why the Leveller were such a boon for us. I got no taste for runnin' a crew any more and no vessel to call my own. Kept my rank, mind you. Means I get perks like this cabin. Anyway, I like it here. It's a fine place to see out my remainin' years."

Robin thought about broaching the subject of returning with him to Blashy Cove but couldn't find the words. Not yet.

"Why white sails instead of red? On *Bucca*?" he asked. "She's a lugger, she should 'ave 'ad red sails."

"I made them white so I'd stand out. Women won't notice you unless you stand out," his father said, pulling out the creases of his hideous lime-green waistcoat. "You turned out big and strong. I'd wager your love life is long and storied!"

"Not really," Robin said.

"Oh? You might not dazzle the girls with your intellect, or your looks, but you've got plenty of confidence. Chasin' me across the sea, comin' into a place like this—it takes guts."

"I might 'ave nowadays. It's what comes from 'avin' the love of a good man."

"I always thought you'd end up likin' women like I do."

"I think you like 'em enough for the both of us."

Robin turned under the threadbare blankets, trying to get comfortable. The whole of Driftwood swayed and creaked but it was otherwise quiet. In the weak glow of lantern light, he had to admit it wasn't the conditions keeping him awake.

"Why did you stay away, Dad?" he asked.

He was met with silence for a minute or two. He thought perhaps his father had fallen asleep.

"When Barnabas died all those years ago," his father said, sitting up, "and I were captured by the Chase Tradin' Company. I were free in a funny way. Free of the island, of my responsibility. I were glad I had the chance to leave you the letter in my journal."

"I saw it for the first time last year," he said.

"Only last year?" his father asked, turning to face him. "Why?"

"Morwenner took your journal the night you disappeared. She 'id it from me."

"Whatever for?"

"She were grievin'. She weren't in 'er right mind. In the same night, both of the men she loved were gone forever, or so she thought. She never believed you killed her 'usband, but she couldn't bear to face any more upset."

"Wait, so when did she tell you?"

"That she were my mother? Not till last summer."

"And you never had an inklin' before then?"

"No," Robin said. "She were one of the only people in the village who cared about me. I knew she were close with you, but I never even suspected. A smarter man might've, but I've never been very bright. When the 'urricane struck, it took the roof off 'er cottage, spilled its contents. I found your journal in 'er garden. Then it all came out."

His father's voice turned lower. It was almost a whisper. "Then who raised you?" he asked. "When I was gone?"

"I looked after myself as best I could. Morwenner looked in on me as well, whenever she could. Not often enough to raise suspicion."

"You were alone? All them years?"

"All them years," Robin said.

"Well. I didn't think that would happen."

"Did you think about me? At all?"

"I thought I'd left you in good hands. I left you money. You had a roof over your head. You had your mother, or so I thought... Well, it doesn't matter now."

"It doesn't matter?"

"No, it's done," his father said, rolling over once more. "Can't change what's done, can we?"

"No," Robin said. "I suppose not."

Chapter Twenty-Six

Robin left the cabin before dawn and stood on a long balcony overlooking the jetties lining the inner courtyard of Driftwood. The curve of pontoons where the pirates docked their vessels was mostly deserted. Only three ships were present, fewer than when Robin arrived. The knock of boots on deck announced the arrival of two men, the pirates from the asylum.

"Why ain't we going on the big raid?" asked the heavily bearded pirate.

"Captain does not think it worthwhile," said the other. "Says he has something better lined up."

"He better had, the crew won't like missing out."

The bearded pirate was a fighter, fat-lipped and bruised. The other was thin as a rake, with long limbs and a studious brow. Robin approached them, smiling broadly. They hadn't noticed him and their hands moved to the hilts of their cutlasses.

"Mornin'," he said. "No need for swords. Name's Robin, I believe you know my dad."

"Barrow?" said the bearded pirate, eyeing Robin up and down. "You wouldn't half know you're related. Giant buggers, you are. I'm sorry about before. Y'know, the punch."

Robin instinctively touched his own nose. "It's fine; it didn't 'urt. Sorry about your arm."

"That definitely did hurt," he said, rubbing his forearm where Robin had grabbed it in the asylum.

"You're part of Red Jim's crew, aren't you?" Robin asked. "I saw you with 'im yesterday."

"S'right. I'm William Longbeard, this lanky Dutchman here is Sam Pro. Not to be confused with Rotterdam Sam."

"I don't know who 'e is," Robin said.

"He's part of Captain Nolan's crew."

"I don't really know who 'e is, either. But speakin' of captains, you didn't seem to agree with yours. All that business about rescuin' my dad from the asylum?"

The two pirates exchanged glances.

"Was there more to it?" Robin asked.

"Well," William Longbeard said. "The captain neglected to mention how we tried to get him to wait for Barrow but he wouldn't. It was almost as if—"

"Steady, William," said Sam.

"As if what?" Robin asked.

"As if he wanted to leave Barrow behind," William said.

"But he sent you to rescue him from the asylum?"

Again the loaded glance between the two pirates. Sam Pro, slim and twitchy, was becoming more uneasy. His hand flexed on the hilt of his sword.

"Not exactly," William said. "We paid a couple of contacts in Port Knot to watch out for chances to liberate Barrow."

"The same contacts you sold the gunpowder to last Midwinter?"

"Local louts named Penhallow and Palk," he said.

"I've met 'em," Robin said. "Nasty pieces of work, they are. They attacked me and my brother last Midwinter."

"They got word to us that Barrow was being moved from gaol to an asylum, so we went to Red Jim and told him."

"And?"

"And he refused to help. Gulabahaar got wind of it and ordered Red Jim to go and rescue Barrow. Again, he refused."

"Why did he say no?" Robin asked.

"You'd have to ask him," Sam said.

"In the end, Gulabahaar ordered us to take *Pride of Ithaca* and the rest of the crew to Blackrabbit."

"The captain stayed behind," Sam said. "He was *not* pleased."

"I'm sure 'e weren't," Robin said. "Sendin' a ship off without 'er captain?"

"What's all this about?" Robin's father asked, as he appeared from the doorway.

"Nothing," said William. "Just talking with your son, here."

"You shouldn't go wanderin'," his father said, eyeing William up and down. "It isn't safe."

"I'm not a child any more, Dad. I can look after myself."

"I'm hungry. Let's go get somethin' to eat."

Fausto, the young lad with the apricot-and-white-spots kerchief, walked past carrying two cages. A chicken pecked at his hand through the wire, causing him to drop first one cage, then the other. They clattered to the floor, the lids opened, and several birds dashed out.

"Stop, stop, get back here!" he called after them.

"We should 'elp 'im," Robin said. He took off his overcoat and hung it on a nearby post. "Come on, Dad, give us an 'and."

"Not likely," his father said. "He can look after himself just as much as you can. See you down below." Without another word he descended a staircase and was out of sight.

"Yes, thank you, Captain Barrow!" said Fausto. "Helpful as ever."

Annoyed at his father's disregard, Robin pointed at William and Sam. "You two, come on, grab those birds."

They hesitated and looked at each other uneasily.

"*I weren't askin'!*" Robin said.

He immediately felt bad for shouting as they nearly jumped out of their skin. They ran ahead of Robin, chasing after the errant chickens. He wasn't mad at them, of course, nor at the chickens. It was his father. Such a simple thing to do, stop and help someone in need, but his father didn't even consider it. Shaking his head, he set to chasing after one of the chickens—a plump red specimen with a mean look in her eye. The next five minutes were spent hunched over and chasing after the birds.

Finally, Robin caught one and held it up. "Got you, *ow!*"

The chicken pecked at his hand, over and over. He rushed to the cage and shoved the bird inside before closing the lid. He sucked on his nipped finger. Fausto returned the other chicken to its cage. William and Sam followed soon after.

"Sorry about the pecking," Fausto said. "They can be a bit... temperamental at times. Thank you for your help."

He slapped Robin on the back before picking up the crates and carrying on his way.

"We'd best be going," Sam Pro said. "Lots to do. Lots to prepare before...well, as I said, lots to do."

Robin retrieved his overcoat and found his father standing at the bottom of the staircase. His hand was pressed against a wall, and he was talking to a woman in a mottled bandana. They were laughing a little too loudly, in the way some people do when they want everyone to know they're having a better time than them. Robin cleared his throat as he approached. The woman lightly touched his father's arm, whispered in his ear, and left them to it.

"Who's she?" Robin asked.

"Just a friend," his father said. "Part of Captain Nolan's crew. She was helpin' me fill in some details about a raid of his a while back."

"I see. And is—"

Robin trailed off as he began frantically patting down his pockets and searching the floor around him. He rushed back up the stairs, still scanning the floorboards.

"What's wrong?" his father asked.

"My coin 'older, the one Edwin gave me as a Midwinter present—it's gone!"

"Someone probably pinched it from your coat while you were helpin' catch the chickens," his father said. "Which is odd, considering you said you could look after yourself."

Robin just glared at him.

"It's why we wear our gold as rings or earrings instead of keepin' them in pockets. Makes them a lot harder to steal."

"I'm goin' to get it back," Robin said.

"How? You don't even know who took it. Are you goin' to march in there, start accusin' people? Pick a fight?"

"I can't let 'em away with it!"

"Look, Robin. This is Driftwood. We don't have watchmen or judges. You let your guard down and someone took advantage. It's just the way it is. If you're goin' to stay here, you need to keep your wits about you. This life doesn't suffer fools gladly."

"I thought you were all in it together, one big pirate society? But you'll steal from each other?"

"The important word there is *pirate*," his father said. "You took your coat off and left it hangin' in a den of thieves. You're too trustin'. This is a community, but not the kind you're used to. Now, if you're lucky, you might be able to buy it back, or even steal it back."

"Buy it back with what? My money were in the 'older, and I'm no thief."

"Then I suppose that's the end of it," his father said, slapping him on the shoulder as he walked by.

Robin stood alone, his ears burning, his stomach churning. He desperately missed Edwin, more than any time since he'd arrived. He wanted to hug him, to hide in his arms, hide from the world, just for a little while. Edwin wouldn't have let him hang his coat up, wouldn't have let him be so stupid as to trust these people. He stomped about, frustrated at being taken advantage of and feeling like a massive, inept fool.

Chapter Twenty-Seven

Edwin stood at the door to Iris's bedroom, trying to compose himself. He'd been given the nod from Mrs. Whitewater on her way past, letting him know it was safe to go in. He ran his hand over the back of his neck and was certain the floor beneath his feet had begun to tilt.

"Are you coming in or not?" Iris called.

He politely knocked on the door and let himself in. Iris was in bed, holding both babies in her arms. How tiny they were. She was beaming. Edwin wobbled his way across the room and sat as softly as he could on the bed. Iris leaned forward and he took the sleeping children from her. Not a single sound escaped from them, or from the world at large, as far as Edwin could tell. It was as if the universe held its breath so as not to spoil the moment. Both of his children had hair like a warm autumn day and he kissed them on the forehead. *His children*. He started to laugh.

"I can't believe it," he said.

He was whispering to the fullest extent his excitement and bewilderment would allow.

"I'm actually holding them. We actually did it. They're so beautiful. They're amazing. You're amazing. Doctor Cranch is amazing…"

Iris laughed. "You're blathering, Edwin. Seems to be the day for it."

"Am I? I can't help it. And you, are you…well?" He wasn't entirely sure if it was a stupid question or not. He suspected it probably was.

"As well as can be expected," Iris said. "I have been confined to my bed for the foreseeable future though."

"You scared us," he said. "For a second, I feared the worst."

"I knew all would be well," Iris said.

"Truly?"

"Not a doubt in my mind. Well, perhaps there was a mote of a doubt in there. Somewhere. At the back."

"I wish my Dad had lived long enough to meet them," Edwin said.

His late brother, Ambrose, had two children. After his death, Ambrose's wife had taken them with her to live on Blackrabbit. Edwin knew his father missed them terribly, even if he never admitted it. It would have meant so much to have his father there. He sniffed away some tears. Iris lightly rubbed his arm, then lay her head against it.

"I hoped Robin would be back by now," she said. "Fighting those pirates in the asylum, chasing after them, it all seems so dangerous."

"He thought it was the right thing to do, so whatever the outcome, he had to do it. If he didn't, he wouldn't really be Robin."

"You're correct, of course. Still..."

"Don't worry," Edwin said. "There's no finer sailor on the sea. He'll be back safe and sound before we know it. He'll be fine."

Iris laid her hand on his arm and looked him in the eye. "I wonder how many more times you'll have to say that before you start to believe it," she said.

Edwin had stayed with the babies for hours before Eva insisted he get some rest. She had offered him a room at the lodge, one which had been made up especially for him.

"We thought you might appreciate a place to stay, closer to the children," she'd said.

He'd been moved by the thoughtfulness of the gesture but thought it best to return home. However, he'd been entirely unable to sleep and decided a walk would help.

He sauntered down the cobblestones of Hill Road in the pale moonlight. It was so late, even the Moth & Moon was closed. The only sign of life was a single lantern in the window of an upper floor. George Reed's quarters. Edwin worried about him, all alone up there. He still hadn't told him about Robin's refusal of his offer to take over the running of the inn. Every time he tried to broach the subject, George would cough and look so frail as to cause Edwin to lose his nerve. He promised himself he'd try again. Tomorrow, maybe. He would hand over Robin's father's journal and then gently break the news to him.

Before he knew it, he'd opened the sky-blue front door of Robin's house. It was usually full of noise, from the clanging of pipes, to his singing, to the bellowing of his laughter, but it stood deathly still. Edwin picked his way upstairs, past the imposing portrait of Robin's father and up again to Robin's bedroom. The bed was unmade, as usual.

He stripped off his clothes and let them fall to the floor; then he climbed under the bedcovers. He pulled the blankets tightly around himself and buried his face in them, losing himself in the lingering traces of Robin's scent. He felt he was losing control. He'd been telling everyone how Robin was the best sailor on the island, how he could take care of himself at sea and how nobody needed to worry about him, which was all true, so why didn't he believe it? Why did he have the gnawing certainty that something was going to go horribly wrong?

Iris had seen right through him, of course. She knew he was fooling himself. Or trying to, at any rate. He didn't know why, but that night he felt every aching mile of the distance between him and Robin. Was it the children? He'd dreamed about the day so often. The look on Robin's face. A moment they'd share and never, ever forget.

His stomach was lead, his mind a fog. What would he do if Robin never came back? He hadn't allowed himself to think that way before now. He'd always been very independent, but he felt Robin's absence keenly, as if an entire portion of his mind, an entire chamber of his heart, were missing. There were times when he was distracted by work, blissfully lost in the mundane, but then he'd snap back to himself, and the pain would return, stabbing him like an unsharpened blade in his belly. In the past, when times were tough, he'd turn to drink, lose himself in a bottle, but he'd given it up for good the previous Midwinter. Whatever happened, he was determined not to slip back into bad habits.

There came a fluttering at the balcony doors. A shimmering blue moth was banging against the glass, seeking escape. He crossed the room and opened the door. The moth hesitated, clinging to the white frame before an encouraging nudge from Edwin's finger sent it on its way. He stood there, the night air cool against his bare flesh, as the moth flew silently down towards the harbour. Waves crashed, trees rustled, and the tang of salt on his lips was the first Edwin knew of his tears.

"Come home, Robin," he said. "Please, come home."

Chapter Twenty-Eight

George Reed put out a hand to steady himself against a wall as a clatter of coughs ripped out of his throat. His head pounded with the force of it, and he swayed from side to side. He'd gotten little sleep and was well and truly fed up with it.

The coughing sickness was still moving through the village, and every night the Moth & Moon was assaulted with a barrage of hacks and barks from the villagers. He and Morwenna Whitewater were the worse afflicted. He chalked it up to their advancing years, though she had almost a decade on him. Wiping his mouth with his handkerchief, he picked up some empty tankards and began to wash them behind the bar. Arminell Kind's husband and local popinjay, Mr. Archibald Kind, sat with their infant son on his lap, rocking him gently from side to side.

"You're spending a lot of time with the boy," Mr. Penny said.

"A father should spend time with his son," Mr. Kind said. "And he loves to see his uncle as well, doesn't he? Doesn't he?"

He leaned in and made a noise like a horse. His son burbled and laughed. Mr. Kind and Mr. Penny weren't actually related by blood but they might as well have been, so close was their bond. There had been some question as to what Mr. Penny's first name actually was and it hadn't been until the naming ceremony some months earlier that the question was finally put to rest. Mr. and Mrs. Kind had stood before the community and declared their baby would be named Jago after Mr. Jago Penny.

"Did you hear about the burglary?" Mr. Kind asked. "Apparently someone sneaked into the Bounsell's home during the night and took a sizeable amount from the kitchen cupboard."

"Giss'on!" Mr. Penny said. "Who'd do a thing like that?"

"And Mr. Trease still hasn't found his missing statuette."

"Sounds like there's a thief about," Mr. Penny said, squaring his shoulders and pulling at the scruffy lapels of his shabby overcoat. "Well, he better not come near me, is all I'll say."

"Why would he?" Mr. Kind asked with a grin. "You've got nothing worth stealing."

"A more cynical man might point out none of this happened until a certain brute from Blackrabbit arrived."

"But of course, you would never say it."

"Of course not. Besides, there's still the matter of the sailboat on Porthsophie beach."

"What of it? It was just a visitor stopping off for a break."

"Then why is the boat still there? I tell you, something's afoot, Mr. Kind. Something is definitely afoot."

May Bell stood nearby, looking lost. She was holding her elbow, patiently waiting for the grown-ups to notice her.

"Something wrong, Ms. Bell?" asked George.

"I was wondering if anyone has spoken to Mr. Farriner today?" she asked. "I went to the bakery this morning but it was closed."

Edwin hadn't been seen around the tavern in recent nights either.

"I think he's pining for Mr. Shipp," said Mr. Kind.

"Robin's been at sea for, what, a week now?" George asked.

"It's strange not seeing *Bucca's Call* moored at the pier every night," said Mr. Penny. "The harbour looks empty without her."

May twirled her hair in the way George had come to know so well. She was about to ask a question.

"Why is it named *Bucca's Call?*" she asked.

"Mr. Shipp's father named her after the tale," Mr. Penny said.

"Have you never heard it?" George asked.

May shook her head, clambered onto the bar and settled into her favourite spot against the pillar. Whenever she did so, George knew she was expecting a story.

"A long time ago," he said, "long before the village had spread much beyond the harbour, before the Trease farm was more than a single field, there lived a great hulking, ruddy-faced youth named Barker —a distant ancestor of the Shipp family. This lad was big and strong and very, very lazy. He'd do anything to get out of an honest day's work, from feigning injury to hiding in the upper floors here in the Moth & Moon. Back then, the world was always in strife. Soldiers and warships passed by regularly, often stopping for days at a time in the cove. One day, the sound of a soldier's trumpet came blaring from over the hills. The villagers, fearful a battle was breaking out, hid in their homes.

"For three days and three nights the people of the village busied themselves in their houses, never daring to go outside. Every morning and every evening, the terrible sound could be heard. Finally, Barker took his father's musket and set out to find the true cause of the sound. Given his reputation, the villagers said he was only doing it to get out of the household chores."

"He definitely was," May said.

"Barker climbed the hills and travelled past the woodland to the old well from where the trumpet call was said to emanate. Fearful of being caught in a battle, he hid himself in the trees and watched. As night fell, he heard the sound of laughter and a clang of tin on stone. From out of the well came a horde of tiny creatures carrying pickaxes and shovels and hammers.

"Barker knew at once he was looking at a troupe of bucca, the busy little creatures who live in damp caves and mines and wells. They were hauling up with ropes a shiny trumpet which they sat on the edge of well. Then they all gathered behind it and, pressing their lips to the mouthpiece, they blew. A terrible call issued forth, the bucca's call, the very same call the villagers had been hearing for the past three days.

"The bucca, full of merriment at their mischief, fell around laughing so hard Barker thought their little hearts would pop. He watched them stow their tools around the well, then they lowered the trumpet back down and followed it into the darkness. Barker settled down to sleep, as the thought of walking back to the village sounded like too much work."

"I don't blame him," May said. "The well is ever so far away."

"Indeed it is!" George said. "Anyway, the following morning he woke to the chatter and laughter of the bucca as they emerged to reclaim their tools. Once they retreated back into the well, Barker crept from his hiding place and lay hiding in the long grass, basking in the bright sunshine. He pressed his ear to the ground and heard from deep below the banging and clanging of the bucca at work. In time, he discerned the words of the bucca and came to understand them. He heard them laughing at the great joke they'd played and how scared the people of the village were. When night began to fall, the bucca came out of the well, carrying the trumpet, intent on blowing their call again. First though, they hid their mining tools.

"'I shall hide my axe under this rock!' said one.

"'I shall hide my shovel under the ferns!' said another.

"'And I shall hide my bucket on Barker's knee!' said a third.

"Barker, being most frightened at hearing his name on their tiny lips, ran away but fell to the ground when he felt a heavy weight upon his knee. He roared out in pain while the bucca laughed and told him off for spying on them. Barker, fearful of what else the bucca might do to him, pulled out his father's musket and took aim. *Bang!* A shot rang out across the field, the trumpet was struck and a hole punched right through.

"The bucca, frightened for their lives, scarpered back down the well, never daring to return to bother the people of the village again. Barker took the trumpet home and told everyone what happened, but no one believed him. No one thought the lazy boy capable of such an act of bravery. They said the soldiers must have had their battle and departed and the boy simply found the trumpet lying in a field. Barker knew otherwise, and he kept the trumpet, passing it down to his children, who passed it to their children and so on."

"It's a fine story," said May, tilting her head and frowning. "But it's simply not true, Mr. Reed."

"You're probably right," George said, as he reached up to the wall behind him.

He lifted an old, battered trumpet and set it on the bar in front of May. She picked it up and poked her fingers through the musket hole in the side. George wiggled his eyebrows and returned to serving his customers.

"Good afternoon, Nick," Duncan said.

He had let himself into the schoolhouse, and he carried with him a long plank of wood fitted with a row of coat hooks.

"I was thinking this might be useful," he said. "Maybe along the back wall? Somewhere for all the children to hang their coats and scarves and whatnot?"

"Yes, very good," Nick said.

He barely looked up from his book. Duncan walked to the back of the classroom and started work. Not another word was spoken between them. After a few minutes, the tension became unbearable.

"Did I do something wrong?" Duncan asked.

"Not at all," Nick said, flicking a page. "From what I hear, you did it just right."

"And what is that supposed to mean?"

"Nothing, it doesn't matter."

Duncan stood up and paced forward. "Don't do that. I hate that. It obviously bleddy well does matter or you wouldn't have said it."

Nick slammed his book shut. "What happened to you being apprehensive? You weren't apprehensive with Mr. Knight."

Duncan's stomach lurched. "According to whom?"

"Mr. Knight himself. He said as much to me after our trip to Blue Eye Bay."

Duncan returned to hammering nails. He battered one so hard it bent in two. "He had no right to say anything."

"Clearly, he feels differently."

"It was one drunken night."

He grabbed one of the hooks and shook it vigorously to make sure it was stable. "I told you I was nervous about starting a relationship," Duncan said. "I wasn't planning on starting one with Vince."

"Does he know as much?"

Duncan dropped his hammer, grabbed his coat, and all but ran out of the schoolhouse. Outside, he paused at the dull thud of Nick's book striking a wall.

Chapter Twenty-Nine

Driftwood was a living colony, a floating pirate castle that was, in essence, one immense ship, with all the accompanying problems. It was cold, for one thing, murky, and damp, in the main. Seawater dripped through seams. Rats were an issue whenever a new ship arrived, but the company of dogs on board soon took care of them. Ratters all, small and swift, they darted after the vermin before they could take a foothold. The constant wear and tear required continuous maintenance, and regardless of whether one was a visitor or resident, everyone was expected to pitch in when needed. This meant swabbing decks, keeping watch or tending to any repairs.

"Here," Fausto said.

Robin took the pot of tar and followed him up a series of stairs and ladders, some woefully unsuited to someone his size, until they reached an overhead hatch. Climbing out, he held tightly to his cap as a sea wind threatened to snatch it off.

On the deck of the galley, which formed the topmost part of Driftwood, huge masts with vast sails automatically twisted and turned into the wind, ensuring the fortress remained broadly in the same place. He marvelled at the ingenuity on display. Clockwork powered devices were common, of course. From the strikers used to start fires, to the sign above the door of the Moth & Moon, they were everywhere, but never before had he seen them used on such a scale. For the first time, he became aware of a line of figures along the outfacing gunwales, and he went to examine them, taking great care in his steps.

"Careful," Fausto called after him. "It's a long way down."

While the bulwarks were tall enough to prevent the average person from slipping overboard, Robin wasn't certain they were up to the task of protecting him. He'd never in all his life been so high off the ground or off the sea. Not when he was in the Merryapple lighthouse, not even when he climbed to the crow's nest of a ship. He peered over the edge to the frothing white foam of the Atlantic far below. It was as though the ocean itself was salivating at the thought of swallowing him whole, as a fall from up there would mean certain death.

Leaning out over the water was a woman wearing nothing but a Greek helm. Next to her, a naked man clutched his obscenely long member to his chest. Then came a unicorn ridden by two children, then a shark, a winged wolf, a maiden clad in a diaphanous gown clutching a harp and a dozen others, each one unique. Made of wood and covered with chipped paint and even some gold leaf, Robin realised these trophies must be the figureheads from the captured ships which made up Driftwood. At least, he assumed they'd been captured. He rather doubted anyone would have donated their vessel out of the goodness of their hearts.

The great sails overhead looked like any one might find on a seafaring vessel and they required the same care and attention. Dozens of pirates were clambering across the rigging, singing as they went. An old, sorrowful shanty full of yearning to return to the comforts of home. Robin had heard it back in the days when he himself had served aboard a sailing ship. Songs helped the crew work in unison, helped them maintain the rhythm necessary for the smooth running of a ship. A single loud voice sang out the first line of each verse and was met with a chorus of replies, a chorus Robin joined in with.

Where have ye been all day?

Workin' aft and doused in spray.

Where have ye been all night?

Head kept low and out of sight.

Where has your lover been?

Not in my bed; my ardour's lean.

Where will you go when snow does fall?

Under tree and over wall.

Where will that take you to?

Home, dear Mum, and back to you.

Come home, Harry, now it's late.

I will, dear Mum, if tis my fate.

"A fine voice, sir," Fauto said. "But we're here to work, not sing."

Robin sat on the deck and got to work with the tar. He took a brush and dipped it into the pot before swabbing it across the wood.

"It's important to waterproof it as much as possible," Fausto said. "This place will have to stand the test of time. It might be the last place most of these wretches ever get to call home."

"I 'eard you were all for strikin' out on your own," Robin said.

The fumes from the tar were powerful but at least up there they wouldn't have a chance to give him a headache.

"I will someday," Fausto said. "I'll have a ship of my own, a crew of my own. I'll sail past here with my hold full of coin, and I'll wave, and I'll doff my cap, but I'll never have to set foot here again."

Suddenly, a horn was sounded. Then another and then another.

"What's goin' on?"

"We're under attack," Fausto said.

They hurried back down through the hatch where they caught up with Robin's father. People began rushing around, closing shutters and arming themselves. His father grasped one of the many great levers Robin had noticed protruding from the walls and pulled it down until it clicked. Then the whole structure started to shake, and a great rumbling echoed throughout Driftwood. Robin turned to his father, who smiled.

"Defences, my boy," his father said. "Defences."

Massive, thick, metal shields began sliding up from below the waterline, slotting into place over the outer walls of Driftwood. Robin and his father stood by a window and watched the attack, such as it was. A single-masted boat, not much bigger than *Bucca's Call*, with a solitary occupant. A bony figure with a ragged grey beard and round shoulders. He was shouting indistinctly, raving, almost. He crouched behind a small cannon and struggled with the fuse. A loud boom and a cloud of smoke accompanied a little shot which dinged pathetically against Driftwood's fortifications. Robin's father laughed.

"You'll have to do better than that, Tommy!" he bellowed.

"You know 'im?" Robin said.

His father, still laughing, waved to the other pirates. "False alarm. It's only Tommy, back again and drunk as usual."

"The Driftwood Bard himself," the Irish pirate said. "Back to stick his nose into our business."

"That's enough of that, Nolan," his father said. "He's one of us, always has been."

"This is the last time," Captain Gulabahaar shouted from below. "His last chance! If he causes any more trouble, I will slash him to pieces!"

She brandished a sword with a long, flexible blade which she whipped above her head. It crackled viciously. Robin had never seen a weapon like it. The horns sounded again, double blasts this time. His father pulled another lever and chains sitting in recesses sprang to life, suddenly racing upwards and downwards. A loud clicking began, turning to a mighty clunking. The receding shields allowed sunlight to pour in, starting at the topmost deck and moving downward.

"Come round to the docks, you old fool!" Robin's father shouted from between cupped hands.

Tommy screamed something ribald in response. Robin and his father made their way towards the docks on the inner courtyard of the castle, for though it was on the high seas, that is truly how Robin thought of it, especially with its shielding in place and cannons armed.

"Those barriers…" Robin said.

"Clever, aren't they?" his father said. "Heavy things, damn near impenetrable. Counterweights stop us toppling over when we deploy them. Anyone can activate them with these levers. They're all controlled from that room up there and only captains have a key."

He pointed to a locked shed-like room suspended high up in the main cavity, between the doll's-house decks. It was the meeting point of two footbridges, dozens of pipes, and was in full view of everyone. An extra security feature, Robin assumed. If everyone could see it, no one would be tempted to tamper with it.

"Why don't you leave them up all the time?"

"It's gloomy enough in here without them, don't you think?"

After Robin helped his father secure the mooring lines of his small sloop, Tommy wobbled down the gangplank, clearly drunk, and fell into the arms of Robin's father.

"'Rasmus!" he said, slurring his words. "I heard they were going to get you out! I wanted to come along but they said no. They said no, 'Rasmus! To me!"

Tommy was almost as old as Robin's father, but rake thin and gangly, with wild, dull, grey hair and bulging, yellowed eyes. He reached out with hands long and thin, like December branches. He wore the drawn expression of a man who has seen too much of life.

"Hullo, Tommy," his father said. "Let's get you inside and out of harm's way before Gulabahaar sees you."

"Did she miss me?" he said, with wide-eyed excitement.
"She did not."

Robin followed his father to his higgledy-piggledy cabin. It took some effort to guide Tommy inside, as he kept grabbing the door and singing. His father heaved some boxes from a shelf onto the floor. At least, Robin had thought it was a *shelf*.

"There's a *spare bed?*"

"No," his father said, quite calmly. "There's just Tommy's bed."

Robin shook his head. His back still ached from sleeping on the floor. "What was it the Irishman called him?" he asked. "The Bard?"

His father set Tommy onto the edge of the bed. Robin couldn't tell which was the more pungent—Tommy or the surroundings.

"A daft and grandiose title," his father said. "He's spent years writin' down all our stories. Our history. Some folk, like Captain Nolan back there, don't much like havin' a detailed account of their exploits written down. Others love it, mind you. Your average pirate loves a bit of notoriety. Adds to their mystique, you know? Their legend. Gulabhaar encourages it. She says it'll be good for us in the long run. Help people understand us."

"It's the only reason she puts up with me," Tommy said. "And without me, you'd be out on your ear, 'Rasmus."

"Rubbish," said Robin's father, setting his jaw and fixing his shirt collar. "She can't get enough of this handsome mug o' mine." He laughed then but it was clear he believed what he'd said.

"But he'll not be writin' about me, I can tell you that much. Isn't that right, Tommy?"

He lightly slapped Tommy's face as he spoke. Tommy giggled like a child.

Robin lifted a sheet of paper with a list of pirate names on it. Clearly, then, this was all Tommy's work. "Don't you want a bit of immortality?" he asked.

His father scoffed at the notion. "I didn't last this long by shoutin' about my deeds. He can write it all down after I'm dead, and not a minute sooner."

Tommy was on his hands and knees now, clawing at the floorboards. With cracked and filthy nails he dug into the grooves and pulled up a small piece of board. "I kept them safe, 'Rasmus, I did."

He lifted from the secret compartment a wooden box. Robin's father took from it several rings which he slid onto his knobbly, sausage-like fingers. One of the rings, a chunky gold piece, was lovingly engraved with the same bear head adorning the flag on the wall.

"Gave this to Tommy for safekeepin' before I set off for Blackrabbit," his father said. "Can't trust those Blackrabbit reprobates. Thieves, the lot of 'em. They can't help themselves. Must be somethin' in the water."

"You're a big one," Tommy said, looking Robin up and down.

"Nothin' wrong with your eyesight," Robin said.

"Wait. You remind me of someone," he said, his tone suddenly very serious. He leaned in and squinted, looking Robin up and down.

"This is my son Robin," his father said.

"Ah! This your son Robin!" Tommy shouted, extending his bony hand outwards for Robin to shake.

"Tommy Oughterlauney, a pleasure!"

Robin stood back and clenched his fists. "Oughterlauney? Captain *Thomas* Oughterlauney?"

"Captain of nothing, these days," Tommy said.

"What's the matter?" his father asked.

"The matter? *The matter!*" Robin shouted. "'E's Captain Thomas Oughterlauney! The man who 'unted you across the seas! 'E attacked the village! 'E... 'E tried to kill you!"

"And I tried to kill him," his father said with a shrug. "Lots of times."

"'E's the reason you died! Or disappeared I mean!" Robin said, shaking his head. "'E's your mortal enemy!"

"You're bein' a bit dramatic, Robin," his father said. "Yes, we've had our differences in the past—"

"*Differences?*" Robin bellowed, startling Tommy.

"Yes, differences. But we've put all that behind us."

"Literally!" Tommy said, laughing, though Robin didn't know why it was supposed to be funny.

"We've been through a lot since then. We escaped the estate together, crewed together, came here, started over..."

"Estate? What estate?" Robin asked.

His father turned away. "Nothin', forget I said it."

"You and 'e aren't...you know..." Robin said.

"Hah, no! No. Why would I want a hairy-arsed pirate in my bed when I could have the sweet bosom of a maiden?"

"You'd be lucky to have me, 'Rasmus!" Tommy said, puckering his lips and laughing.

"He's also the only person alive who still calls me by my proper name, even though I've told him time and time again not to."

"Ha-ha! It was 'Rasmus Shipp who stole my heart," Tommy said, clasping his hands to his breast, "and it's 'Rasmus Shipp who'll always have it!"

He doubled over laughing, dotting his bedraggled grey beard in spit. Robin didn't think Tommy's mind was entirely intact.

"Don't listen to him; he's had more women than I have. He even got three of them to marry him, though not all at the same time, mind you."

"So, you're no longer enemies?"

"We've been enemies, friends, business partners, crewmates, love rivals, brothers, and everythin' else in-between. I've known him longer than anyone. Isn't there anyone in your life you have a complicated relationship with?"

"Not *this* complicated."

"You won't get far in life by holdin' on to grudges," his father said. "Piracy is a dirty business. You make friends, you live longer. Sometimes you just have to...move on, you know? Get past it all. We all want the same thing, after all."

"Which is?"

"Freedom, my lad, freedom!" his father said.

"From what?"

"From rules! From laws! From society! From expectation and struggle and work. Freedom from the politicians, the banks, the wealthy landowners!"

"Like the Chases?"

"Exactly! Like the Chases. Bunch of no-good toffs."

"My lover, Edwin, is 'avin' a baby with one of them."

"*What?*" his father shouted.

A chill ran down Robin's spine, and he was cast back to his childhood in an instant. His father had rarely lost his temper around Robin, but when he did it was truly frightening to behold. As he grew older, Robin wondered if his youth had coloured the immensity of his father's rage, skewed his mild anger into a fury. It hadn't. His father's wide, round face flushed red, his teeth were bared, his eyes wild. He looked ready and able to tear Robin limb from limb.

"Iris Wolfe-Chase and 'er wife, Eva, asked my Edwin to father a child with them," Robin said. "You probably knew Iris's parents, the Wolfes. The blacksmith family? They own the forge. Eva is part of the Chase family from Blackrabbit."

"I wouldn't mention as much round here," Tommy said, checking their surroundings. "The only thing pirates hate more than the navy is the Chase Trading Company."

"*No, no, no,*" his father said, pacing the room. "Your betrothed cannot father a Chase child, Robin. I forbid it."

"It's a bit late in the day for you to be forbiddin' anythin' in my life, Dad," Robin said. "Anyway, it's already done. And it won't be a Chase child, they're the Wolfe-Chases now. Besides, Eva's very nice. Well, not *nice*, exactly, but she's decent and honourable."

"Honourable? A Chase! Her father held the shippin' lanes around Blackrabbit in an iron grip, squashin' any competition, no matter how small."

"Thought he was Poseidon of old," Tommy said, holding up a grimy fork. "Ruler of all the seven seas!"

"She's not like him. She's changin' things. For the better."

"Bah!" his father said. "She gave away her lands, did she? Her ships? Her…"

"Were you going to say 'er 'ome?" Robin asked. "You know, the one you were bein' cared for in until very recently?"

That put his father on the back foot and took the wind out of his sails. Robin was grateful for it.

"You were already free, Dad. Before all this. You didn't need to run away and play pirate."

"I don't want to live a small life, Robin. And you've benefitted, don't forget. You think I would have made all that money I left you by fishin'?"

"I suppose not."

"You suppose right."

Robin would be lying if he said the money his father had left hadn't been an enormous help. It wasn't a fortune by any means, but it meant he never had to worry when his catch was light. He didn't fear the winter months the way other fishermen did. He always had a nest egg to fall back on. The greatest comfort in any life is knowing no matter what happens, you'll always have enough to keep a roof over your head and food in your belly. There were a good many people who could do neither. He perched himself on the edge of his father's bed.

"Let me ask you, what happened after I left?" his father asked. "What happened when everyone thought I killed poor Barnabas? Did the community rally around you? Support you? Comfort you?"

"You know they didn't," Robin said quietly. "I told you as much."

"They took my actions out on you. Because that's what people do, Robin. The *person* is good but the *people* are bad. People are petty and spiteful and ready to do anythin' to stop themselves from thinkin' about how meanin'less their lives are."

"The village is different now."

"Is it really."

"The 'urricane," Robin said. "It frightened people. It made them see what was important."

"Did it."

They weren't actually questions but Robin answered, regardless. "Yes!" he said. "In the face of nature, in the full blown, unstoppable force of it, all we 'ad were each other, all we 'ad to protect ourselves were each other. All we 'ad to turn to in our time of greatest need were each other. And we were up to the challenge. We rallied, we supported, we *cared*, Dad. We could 'ave all been swept away into the sea in an 'eartbeat. Nature doesn't care about us. The weather, the seas, none of it. The only thing standin' against it, the only protection from it, is us. And if people are so bad, 'ow do you explain this place?"

"Hah! We're not like ordinary people, my boy. You can't rely on ordinary people, you can only rely on those who've stood by your side in battle."

His father slapped Tommy's arm as he spoke.

"Does a battle against the elements not count?"

His father snorted a laugh. "Hardly."

"You're just anarchists," Robin said.

"We take a broader view."

"You don't care about anybody but yourselves."

"At last, we agree. Oh, stay here for a while, boy, see what it's like to be truly free. Free from—"

"Responsibility."

"If you like. I were never one to settle down, Robin. It never suited me. I were never any good at it. I realised you would all think me dead and saw no reason to dissuade you of that belief."

"No reason?" Robin said, sitting bolt upright. "No reason! I were a reason! Morwenner were a reason! You left us both in agony!"

"Oh, don't exaggerate."

"I'm not exaggeratin'! We loved you, Dad. We mourned you for years. I don't... I don't think I ever stopped mournin' you. The night you vanished became an...an anchor for my whole life. No matter how far I tried to move away from it, it pulled me back, kept me in place, in my 'ead, in my 'eart."

"You're ramblin', son," his father said in a condescending tone which made Tommy smirk.

"I'm tryin' to explain! I missed you, every minute of every day. The portrait of you Barnabas painted, I talk to it, talk to you, every time I pass it."

His father sniffed and adjusted his belt, hooking his thumbs into it. "You should have let me go," he said. "You should have moved on with your life."

"I couldn't let you go! That's the whole point! You disappeared under a cloud; the entire village thought you were a murderer and took it out on me for my whole life."

"They shouldn't have."

"They wouldn't 'ave if you'd come back and explained what really 'appened! I were your responsibility. Did you even think twice about leavin' me alone?"

"You were a man."

"I were a boy. Barely ten years old."

"Didn't I teach you how to fish? How to feed yourself? How to cook and clean? Didn't I leave you money? What more did you need?"

"You! I needed you! I needed my father!"

"You did fine without me."

Robin's shoulders slumped. "You 'ave no idea what I went through after you left. And what's worse is you don't even care."

"Sorry to disappoint you but seems as though I've been doin' little else since you got here."

Robin looked at him. Truly, honestly looked. The man before him was not the man in his memory. It was not the man in the painting on his landing. It was not the man in the blood-red journal.

"You're not what I expected," Robin said.

"What did you expect, then?"

"I expected my father. The one I remembered from when I were a boy. Instead I found..."

"What?"

"A man," Robin said. "Just a man."

"It's all I've ever been."

"Not to me. Not in my 'ead. Not in my memories."

"The memories of a child," his father said. "The ideas of a child. Who could possibly ever live up to them?"

His tone had shifted, it had become mean, vicious even. It cut Robin like a knife. This isn't how it was supposed to be. His reunion with his father was meant to be a joyous affair, the fulfilment of a lifetime's wish. Not this.

"Did you ever want to be at 'ome?" Robin asked. "Did you ever want to be my dad?"

His father shuffled about where he stood. "I loved you, didn't I? Provided for you?"

"That's not what I asked. Despite what everyone told me about you, I used to think you were a good father, but now—"

"Well if you thought I were a good father, then what difference does it make if I were or not?"

"But..."

"Look, boy, you built up some idea of me in your head, but it were never the real me. It were a child's idea of what a father should be. Don't blame me because I'm a real person." He spat the words out like they were no more than pieces of gristle.

"Can I blame you for abandonin' me?" Robin asked.

"Yes," his father said. "It's only fair."

Without another word, Robin rose from the bed and walked out. The wooden floor creaked under his gait.

Chapter Thirty

A loud thumping at his front door alerted Edwin to Duncan's arrival.

"I do have a perfectly functional knocker, you know."

"I know," Duncan said, "but listen." He lifted the knocker with his finger and let it fall. It made a feeble tap on the brass plate. "See? It's rubbish. You'll never hear it all the way up there."

"Better than having you bash the door down with your hairy gorilla paws."

He invited Duncan up the narrow stairs to his living quarters above the bakery. Duncan closed his eyes and took a deep breath. "It always smells of fresh bread here. It's wonderful."

"I don't really notice any more." He bade Duncan to sit at his table in one of the room's two bay windows overlooking Hill Road. "What's this about? I've made tea if you want some?"

"Nick is upset."

"Why? What did you do?"

"What makes you think I did anything?"

Edwin put his hand on his hip and tilted his head. Duncan rubbed his own face with his hands, drawing his cheeks down.

"Fine. Remember when you said Vince not only looked a lot like Robin, he was Robin's brother and doing anything with him would be a terrible idea?"

"I was wondering when you'd tell me," he said.

Duncan's face dropped. "You already knew? *How?*"

"Vince and I spoke the day after it happened; he told me then."

If Edwin didn't know better, he'd swear Duncan was actually blushing. "Did you think—at all—about what would happen?"

Duncan poured some milk into his cup and arched an eyebrow.

"Afterwards, I meant!" Edwin said with a laugh. "You are incorrigible."

"It's true," Duncan said, sipping his tea. "I cannot be corriged. Oh, Edwin, I've made a right mess of things."

"Yes, you have."

"You're meant to be helping! How is this helping?" Duncan asked with his hands spread wide open. "Tell me what he said."

"He said it was the most magical night of his life."

"Stop."

"He said he never knew it could be so good."

"Stop!"

"He wanted to know how he should propose."

"*Stop it!*" Duncan said, laughing. "What did he actually say?"

"He said it was something you both needed to get out of your systems," Edwin said, wiping away a tear.

Crying for a good reason was a nice change of pace. Duncan leaned back, and for a moment Edwin thought he saw a flicker of disappointment. "Did...did you want it to mean more?" he asked.

Duncan removed his spectacles and cleaned them with a handkerchief from his waistcoat pocket. "No, of course not. If anything, it's good to know. Nick and I have been spending some time together recently. He's an...interesting person."

"My word, it's getting so the village isn't safe for any man! I hope Robin comes home soon to protect me from your wanton desires."

"You should be so lucky," Duncan said. "Look, this is a small place and my options are limited. When someone new arrives, it behoves me to investigate."

"And what a thorough investigation it was," Edwin said, sipping his tea. "You know how you said you didn't see the resemblance between Vince and Robin?"

"Yes," Duncan said.

Edwin smirked and raised his eyebrows. "Is that still the case?"

"Moving along," Duncan said. "Nick was upset when he found out."

"You told him about it?"

"Vince did," Duncan said, shaking his head. "Apparently he couldn't wait to let everyone know."

"Clearly you have talents worth shouting about. I'll have to ask Robin for some details when he gets back."

"Don't you dare," Duncan said, laughing again. "We haven't seen you in the Moth for a while. You've been hiding away up here for days."

Edwin put his cup down and turned away. "I've been busy, clearing out Dad's house, the babies... I haven't had much time for socialising."

"How are you getting along without Robin?"

Edwin toyed with his cup, turning it in its saucer. "It's probably good for us, actually."

"What is?"

"A bit of distance. Some time spent apart. We've been in each other's pockets for months now. So to speak." Edwin gazed at the ground, at the window, at his hands—anywhere but at Duncan.

"What's going on?" Duncan asked. "You're being odd."

"Am I?"

"Exceedingly so."

Edwin sat back and rubbed his own neck. "I've been thinking a lot in the past few days and I just... I worry about Robin getting bored of me."

"What's brought this on?"

"It's something Vince said."

Duncan slammed his cup onto the saucer. Some drops of tea splashed over the edge. "The horrid, spiteful old— Don't listen to him, he's only—"

"No, no," Edwin said, "not directly. He didn't say anything cruel to me. I'm not like you and Robin. I haven't lived the way you two have. I haven't sailed the world like he has. I haven't started my life twice over, as you have. I've hardly ever left the island. I was born in this bakery, and I'll die here. I've lived such a small life compared to you both. I know where I've been, and I know where I'm going. I know the shape of my future."

"Is that such a bad thing?" Duncan asked. "Believe me, there's little comfort in chaos. There's nothing at all wrong with knowing where your life is headed. There was a time I'd have given anything for such certainty. And believe me, I know Robin better than anyone; he thinks the sun and moon rise and set in your eyes. If he said he cares for you, he meant it wholly. Completely. Robin Shipp doesn't love in degrees."

Edwin grabbed Duncan's knee and smiled. He should have talked to him sooner. For all his caustic remarks, Duncan was the best friend anyone could ask for.

"Now, if we're done talking about you," Duncan said, "can we get back to what's truly important?"

"You mean you, of course."

"Naturally."

"I'm not going to sugar-coat it," Edwin said. "You made two men unhappy; you have to fix it."

"How?"

"You know how."

Duncan groaned and threw his head back. "Open and honest discussion about my feelings?"

"That's the one," Edwin said.

"Why is that always the answer?" Duncan asked with a groan. "Why is the answer never... I don't know...hiding in a wardrobe until the problem goes away?"

Edwin took a mouthful of cake and stopped, mid-chew. "I don't actually have to answer that, do I?"

Eva stood by the arched window in what had until recently been her study. The plan had been to convert the large attic room into a nursery but Ms. Popplestone had thought it too musty and dark. She suggested the study as a far more suitable location, being as it was bright, airy, and located close to the master bedroom. Eva wondered if perhaps Iris had planted the idea in Ms. Popplestone's head. At any other time, Eva would have put up more of a fight, but given the fact Iris had been more or less confined to bed since the birth, she wasn't inclined to add to her burden unduly.

She left the nursery and paced along the plush carpet to the master bedroom where she found Edwin sitting by Iris' bedside. Iris had been frightfully pale and weak for days but had of late seen the colour return to her cheeks.

"Edwin, delightful to see you," Eva said. "Ms. Popplestone is tending to the children; she'll bring them in presently. Are you quite well? You seem distracted."

While Edwin was possessed of a very pleasant face, it could be frightfully difficult to read at times. Eva always liked to know what everyone was thinking, even if they weren't saying it. Especially so.

"I'm fine," he said. "I only came round for a bit of company, if I'm honest."

"Still no word from Robin?" Iris asked.

"None. I saw Duncan this afternoon, but he's mostly busy with his men."

"Plural?" Eva asked.

"Vince and Mr. Babbage have both taken a shine to him, it seems."

"Well, well!" said Iris. "Lucky old Duncan. It seems his dry spell is over."

Drake arrived with a tray laden with cups and a silver teapot. He began pouring.

"I'm told you've started clearing out your parents' house," Eva said.

Edwin ran his hand over the back of his head. "Yes, but"—his eyes darted towards Drake—"I had to stop. It was all too overwhelming."

He blew on his tea to cool it, obviously playing for time until Drake departed. Unlike Eva, he hadn't been raised in a great house, surrounded by servants, and wasn't used to speaking openly in front of the help.

"My father left so little behind," he said. "His clothes I gave to his neighbours in need, his furniture too. Some of it was too old to be of use. He had no books, no jewellery, no heirlooms. It's like he simply...disappeared from the world. It's as if he wasn't even here." He set his cup down without tasting a sip.

Iris leaned forward to speak. "He made his mark," she said. "There's the bakery, for one. And you, most importantly."

Edwin forced a little smile. It wasn't very convincing. "I wish he'd lived long enough to see the children," he said. "I wish they'd gotten a chance to know him, at least then...at least then he'd be remembered."

Iris shot a look at Eva, her eyes wide and sparkling. Eve knew it meant an idea had occurred to her, but it would have to wait until they were alone to be voiced. It was good to see. It was her Iris come back to life. She cocked an eyebrow in response.

"I found some paintings in the loft," Edwin said. "Mum's work."

"I didn't know she was a painter," said Iris.

"Nor did I until last winter, when I saw a diptych she did of myself and my late brother, Ambrose. She was very talented, but she'd hidden her work away. Come to think of it, I remember she often took herself up over the hills with a bag. I never knew why. She must have found somewhere quiet to paint."

"What were they of? Landscapes? Seascapes?"

Edwin pursed his lips and sat back. "Portraits," he said. "Nude portraits. Of my father as a young man."

"Oh, my," Iris said.

"How wonderful!" Eva said. "I didn't know Nathaniel was so game!"

"I suspect he wasn't given much choice," Edwin said. "There were some self-portraits too. And one or two of Barnabas Whitewater."

"Of course. He was her great obsession," Iris said. "Are they any good?"

"I don't know much about art, but I think so, yes."

"What will you do with them?" Iris asked.

"I left them in the garden at the back of the house with some other rubbish to be burned."

"Why?" asked Eva.

"What else should I do with them? Hang them on the wall as a celebration of a woman who tormented my dad for most of his life? Pretend she hadn't been in love with another man?"

"Art isn't always a celebration," Eva said. "Sometimes it's an explanation."

"You think they explain why Mum tormented Dad? Why she lied about Robin's dad being a murderer?"

"They might. At least in part."

Edwin ran his hand across his head again, and Eva knew she'd lost the argument. "No, no, I have no room for them anyway. Best they're gotten rid of. Then I can forget about them."

Ms. Popplestone arrived with the babies in her arms, and Edwin took both of them. He sat by the window, cooing and laughing with them. Eva hadn't given much thought to how his family was now part of hers, how they'd been linked by blood. They'd been talking about Edwin's mother, but wasn't she also the children's grandmother? The last time Eva had seen Sylvia Farriner, she'd been so frail and lost in her own mind. Committed to the asylum the previous winter, she would never leave its walls; of that much Eva was certain. It saddened her to think how Sylvia was the children's only living grandparent, and they would likely never meet.

Although, come to think of it, should Edwin and Robin wed, Morwenna Whitewater would make a fine grandmother. Did they have any intentions of marriage? Eva didn't know. Edwin kept much close to his chest. More so in recent days. He'd become more withdrawn, smiled less readily. He must be missing Robin terribly. They all were. His presence had become a part of their daily lives, his warmth and good nature a welcome balm. Eva had given orders to her company's captains to keep their eyes and ears open for any word of him. So far none had been reported. Edwin stayed for an hour or so, and once he left, Eva took Drake to one side.

"I should like you to pop down to the garden at the back of Nathaniel Farriner's house on Fisherman's Run," she said. "And recover the items therein."

"What am I looking for, ma'am?" Drake asked.

"You'll know when you see them," Eva said with a grin.

Chapter Thirty-One

Robin stomped through the decks of Driftwood in a foul mood. All about him were pirates going about their daily routine—checking for leaks in the walls, moving food and drink around in barrels. Some were even cleaning up, though the pervasive stench of the place would suggest that particular activity didn't happen as often as it should.

He wasn't paying much attention to where he was going or what he was doing. He'd stormed out of his father's cabin like a petulant child. His face was hot and his ears burned with embarrassment. He batted at a length of silk which billowed into his face and obscured his vision. It tangled about him and he spun on his heels, trying to free himself. A metallic crackle popped by his ears and the silk fell from his head. Before him stood an Indian woman in purple silk: The Pirate Queen of Driftwood.

She had wide, intelligent eyes and the bearing of someone who was utterly convinced of their physical and mental superiority. She wore a bandana, as many pirates did, and a finely embroidered doublet. She was dripping with gold chains, rings, necklaces and earrings. About her neck hung beads of pearl and obsidian.

The thing he noticed most about her was how much cleaner she was than anyone else he'd met there. Her skin was unmarked, her hair lightly perfumed. How she managed such a feat under those conditions, he'd never know. Her bucket boots were black and shiny, and her plain breeches showed no signs of the wear and tear displayed by others. She whipped her flexible sword around her waist and wore it like a belt. The hilt was a moulded stingray, its golden wings curling round to form a cross guard, its tail the grip. When she moved, it was deliberate and measured.

"James Trewin should keep a tighter leash on his pets," she said.

"I'm not 'is pet," Robin said.

It came out grumpier than he'd intended, and the fiery look in her eyes made him instantly regret it.

"Nor are you a pirate," she said, "so why are you here?"

"I came to find my dad. Now I'm wonderin' why I bothered…"

She moved closer to him and he blanched. She was willowy and athletic and she oozed menace. Big as he was, Robin doubted he could best her and her whiplike sword. Other pirates began to draw near. Members of her crew, Robin assumed.

"Allow me to guess," she said. "Your father is Captain Barrow?"

Robin nodded, his gaze darting around at the gathering horde.

"Of course," she said, eyeing him up and down. "Who else but that randy elephant could produce something like you?"

Her crew laughed and Robin felt almost certain he was being insulted. "Now 'ang on a minute…"

"You are not welcome here, son of Barrow," she said.

"I didn't mean to come to your deck," Robin said. "I weren't sure where I were goin'. Anyway, I thought all you pirates were meant to be equal. I don't see anyone else markin' their territory like this." He batted at another piece of silk hanging beside him.

"I am no ordinary pirate," she said as she lounged on a divan, arms outstretched. "I am Captain Gulabahaar of the *Mortal Grace*."

"She built this place," said one of her crew, a craggy-faced man with a wispy beard. "She gave us somewhere safe to live, to thrive. We're besieged on all sides—from the Chase Trading Company, to the navy, the governments, the people. We have enemies all about us. Each one seeking to tear down what she built."

"What we all have built," Captain Gulabahaar said. "Driftwood is nothing without its people. But you are not one of us. You are from the outside world, and so you are the enemy."

"I'm not your enemy," Robin said, flustered. "I'm only—"

"The outside world wants to eradicate us," she said. "They think us relics; they say our time has passed. The modern world does not want us, but we will fight to keep our place in it. I do not know you, son of Barrow."

"I'm—"

She held her hand up. "Nor do I want to know you," she said. "It is only my respect for Captain Barrow which keeps me from hanging you from the highest yardarm. I suggest you make your time here as brief as possible."

"Don't worry," Robin said. "I won't be 'ere a moment longer than necessary."

"Not good enough for you, is it?" said the crewman. "Doesn't meet the high standards of a lowly Pell Isle fisherman?"

Robin was taken aback. The crewman had a high forehead, large chin, and curly hair. He spoke with a distinct upper-class clip, like someone used to giving orders to the poor. A lord, perhaps, or a duke. "I don't believe I caught your name?"

"Harry Vosper," the man said, keeping his thumbs firmly tucked in his waistband. "Quartermaster of the *Mortal Grace*. I used to have land in Devon. I'd know your accent anywhere."

"Well, Mr. Vosper," Robin said, "You've done a fine job with it, you all 'ave, but even you must admit it's a bit creaky, a bit cold. A bit damp."

He chuckled as he spoke. And then he stopped. The pirates simply stared at him. Robin had honestly thought they would agree with him but suddenly felt very vulnerable. Whatever Driftwood meant to them, it *was* cold and it *was* damp. As if to illustrate his point, a drop of water fell from the beams overhead and splashed on the deck by his feet.

"You are very brave, coming to our home and insulting it," Captain Gulabahaar said as she rose to her feet.

"It weren't my intention..." Robin said.

She was in front of him again, staring up at him with her piercing brown eyes. She smiled, catching him off guard. "You are correct, of course," she said. "Blunt, but correct. I cannot speak for my crew, but I know I would rather have a stately house in the countryside. Somewhere with bountiful gardens and trees. But this leaky old tub will have to do for now, I suppose."

"Why's a pirate want an 'ouse in the country?" Robin asked. "Wouldn't you rather live by the coast?"

"I do not enjoy the cold of the sea."

"Well," Robin said, "I can certainly understand that. I were in a nice country 'ouse recently, as it 'appens. Much nicer than bein' on any boat. Servants and fireplaces and a weird, glass dinin' room. Bit fancy for my tastes, mind, but—"

Captain Gulabahaar's smile vanished, and Robin flinched again. Her eyes were like steel. "Get him out," she said to her crew.

Three foul-mannered louts joined Harry Vosper in drawing their cutlasses and forcing Robin back the way he'd come. He tripped over his own feet as he tried to avoid being stabbed. He stumbled through a thick curtain and found himself amid rows of chairs on a dimly lit balcony overlooking a stage, of all things. About him were pirates drinking and laughing and shouting at the players who tread the boards. Nasir, the robed man who counted Captain Throne's bounty, recited some incredibly foul passages about what the royal navy got up to when their admirals weren't looking. Robin sat, grateful for the relative darkness of the playhouse. Although with the way the seats were arranged in a curve, the lighting rigged overhead and the approximation of a royal box to one side, it honestly felt more like a ramshackle opera house.

On stage, men dressed as women pranced about in a grotesquely exaggerated manner. Women dressed as men strutted across the boards, some passing through the audience itself, stopping only to spit on, or thrust their crotches into, the faces of the patrons. Somewhere in the shadows a violin was being thrown down a flight of stairs. Either that or someone was trying to play a hurdy-gurdy. Robin couldn't be sure either way.

The scenery shifted, turning blue and green. The backdrop was coral and fish. The sea bed, Robin supposed. A large and entirely nude hairy-chested gentleman carrying a trident and wearing a crown walked out from the wings. In his unexpected state of undress, it took Robin a moment to realise it was Red Jim. He proclaimed himself to be Poseidon in a booming voice which filled the room. Behind him, three naked women writhed inside a colossal oyster. Poseidon tried to stop them, only to end up joining in and giving a performance so convincing Robin was no longer sure if there was any acting going on at all.

The crowd cheered all the way through with many offering to join in. Indeed, a handful tried, climbing onstage with trousers round their knees only to be shooed away by the tips of Poseidon's trident. Robin guessed the interaction to be all part of the show, but the whole affair was so unruly he couldn't be certain. As a gift to the triune of women, Poseidon gave to them an enchanted shell and sent them on their way.

The scene shifted again, to a sunken ship. This was accompanied by a truly wretched song screeched by a man with lank hair and no understanding of musicality whatsoever. A chorus of booing erupted from the crowd. One rotund pirate, sitting in what passed for a royal box, showed his particular displeasure by undoing his breeches and urinating onto the stage. Robin had heard of similar occurrences in even the most reputable playhouses on Blackrabbit and on the mainland, though not being one for the theatre he'd never witnessed it himself.

As the play went on, Robin began to understand what he was watching. The actors came and went, some far too timid, others far too exuberant, but the story they told was clear enough. It was the history of Driftwood itself. How it had been founded by an all-female band of pirates. How numerous wrecks had been raised from the ocean floor by Poseidon's magic conch shell and filled with only the most noble, the most worthy seafarers to become a beacon of freedom.

"A bunch of claptrap, of course," said the voice beside him.

He hadn't noticed his father sitting down.

"Gulabahaar, Brigid Bonny, and Elizabeth Chalk built Driftwood to escape the noose or the gaolhouse. The world has become increasin'ly hostile for pirates. With no safe ports left, we built our own, somewhere we could band together. Safety in numbers, as they say." He handed Robin a tankard of rum.

"I'd prefer whiskey."

"Add it to the list of times I've disappointed you, and drink up."

Robin took a swig. The rum was dark, spiced and not entirely unpleasant. He thought it might be something George Reed would like to sell in the Moth & Moon. He imagined bringing a barrel of it home and telling George all about the pirates who'd made it. Or stole it, most likely. He'd tell him about Driftwood, about the people he'd met, and George would write it all down in his book, probably. He might even start using the pirates in his ghost stories. There was so much Robin wanted to tell him.

"They based this farce on Tommy's writin', if you can believe it," his father said, pointing at the stage. "He wrote a true and honest account but it weren't excitin' enough. A few tweaks, they said. A little spice to keep it interestin'." He shook his head and tutted again. "Tommy is sleepin' the rum off. Enjoy the peace and quiet while you can; he'll be up and about in no time."

The play was nearing its end. Fausto ran on to change the backdrop to a crudely rendered painting of Driftwood bathed in golden sunshine. Red Jim returned to the stage, dressed now in striped breeches and a fine doublet.

"How many crews are 'ere?" Robin asked.

"Ten," his father said. "The last ten pirate crews in the western world and they all call this place home."

"So few? I 'ad no idea."

"Just how we like it. If people knew how few of us were left, they might put up more of a fight, might be more likely to attack us here."

"I thought Tommy were writin' about the pirates? Is 'e not mentionin' numbers?"

"Oh, he is, but by the time anyone reads his work, it'll be too late. As much as I'd like to believe otherwise, the truth is we're on the way out, my boy. We've had our time. Gulabahaar thinks she can use his writin' as a sort of promotion in the wider world. A way to bolster our numbers. She wants Driftwood to be a beacon for those of a like mind, and be somethin' for the rest of the world to fear. I hope it works—don't get me wrong—but as long as it's all in my cabin, no one is ever goin' to read it."

"I'll wager Eva knows someone who can publish it for 'im. If you can bear to 'ave a Chase 'elp, of course."

His father raised his eyebrows and said nothing

"What will you do when it's over for good?" Robin asked.

"I know what you're gettin' at," his father said, "but I can't go back to Merryapple. I tried to settle down, I did. But it were never goin' to work. Even if Morwenna and me could have been together. I had too much of a wanderin' eye."

"It weren't only your eye doin' the wanderin'. Those other times you left me with Morwenner and Barnabas to go off who-knows-where. *Unfinished business*, you said in your letter."

"It weren't always business. Most of the time, it were rather more pleasurable, in fact."

"'Ow pleasurable?"

"Let's just say I'm surprised you and Vince are my only children."

"Oh, Dad. Wait. Oh, no."

Robin's blood turned to ice, his belly heaved as a terrifying thought occurred to him. "Please," he said, "please tell me you didn't bed Sylvia Farriner."

"Oh, no, never. She was too wild, even for me. She only had eyes for Barnabas, anyway."

Robin tipped back his cap and rubbed his forehead. "Well, that's a relief."

"Why?"

"I'm engaged to 'er son."

"Ah. Ah! Yes, I see what you mean," his father said with a chuckle. "What a horrible revelation that would have been. So, you're still talkin' to me, then?"

Robin looked him in the eye. "I suppose so."

"I'm glad," his father said, turning his attention to the stage. "I haven't always been a disappointment, have I? Remember when I used to take you to the Moth & Moon on Midwinter's night? You used to love it. The place all decorated in evergreen boughs and sea glass and candles. Toastin' bread by the fire, singin' songs, eatin' cake..."

"Then you'd carry me 'ome on your shoulders and put me to bed," Robin said.

"And I'd sneak back to the Moth for another few."

Robin had clung to the memory of moments like those after he was abandoned. For it was an abandonment, however he looked at it.

"A while after you...disappeared, I were in the woods," he said. "I met a boy there, round my own age. We played by the graveyard, chased through the trees. We laughed. It felt good. For a while I were normal. I were like every other boy. The lad's family worked on the Trease farm, they lived in the outbuildin's. They were new to the island. After a week or so, someone, probably Sylvia Farriner, told them about you and the lad weren't allowed to play with me any more. That were it. I were alone again. They left the island in the wintertime. The work had dried up or didn't suit them. I don't know. I didn't even get to say goodbye to 'im."

His father didn't speak. He took another drink.

"I remember you and Morwenner and Barnabas gettin' drunk in our front room when you thought I were asleep," Robin said. "I used to sneak out of bed to sit on the stairs and listen."

"You did not!"

"I did," Robin said, grinning. "Learned all sort of swearwords."

"And a lot more besides, I'd wager."

His father thumped Robin's shoulder and laughed. "I missed you, boy," he said.

"I missed you too, Dad." It was, to be fair, something of an understatement.

"Stay with me then," his father said.

"I didn't come all this way to play pirate!" Robin said.

"Then why did you come?"

"To find you!"

"And here I am," his father said.

"Come back with me—"

"No."

"—to Blashy Cove —"

"No, no I can't, Robin, I can't," his father said, holding up his hands. "That part of my life was over a long time ago."

Robin sighed and tugged his own earlobe. "I suppose it doesn't matter," he said. "Without *Bucca*, I'm stuck 'ere, anyway."

"Look," his father said, "for what it's worth, I... I'm sorry for leavin' you to fend for yourself. I'm sorry I didn't come back. But you were better off without me."

"'Ow can you say that?"

"Because if I'd stayed any longer, you might have turned out like me."

Robin slumped forward and crossed his hands. "Would it 'ave been so bad? At least I might 'ave turned out bright instead of...*like this.*"

"What do you mean?"

"There's a special torment in bein' just clever enough to know 'ow simple you are." Out of nowhere, his eyes started to sting. He tried to rub some tears away. He had no idea why he was feeling so emotional; it felt as if a floodgate were opening in his heart. "When I were a boy I used to go to the Wishin' Tree on the 'eadland and wish for you to come 'ome. There were nights when I felt completely and totally alone, and scared, and too witless to understand the world, to understand why everyone 'ated me. Nights when all I wanted were for you to come back and 'elp me." He sniffed the tears away and rubbed his nose with the back of his hand.

"When we cry, we cry the sea," his father said.

"What's that supposed to mean?"

"It's somethin' your grandfather used to say. He believed we all came from the sea and carried a piece of it inside us. It's why our tears taste of salt. He said we should never cry because the more sea we had within us, the better sailors we'd be. The sea would recognise us and be more forgivin'. Treat us as kin." He stopped to take a drink. His expression was pained, sorrowful. "He'd get so angry when I'd cry as a child. He'd shout at me whenever I did it. Real, proper fury. '*Don't you understand, boy, when we cry, we cry the sea!*' He didn't like any displays, any fuss. He needed everyone around him to be like him, quiet and cold."

"You were never like 'im," Robin said. " You were never cold. Not with me."

"I tried to be better than him. Be a better father, at least. You keep sayin' you're stupid. Why?"

"Because I am," Robin said, slouching back in his seat. "I'm dim. I've always been dim. I don't understand...things. People. The world. I weren't smart enough to realise Morwenner were really my mother. I weren't smart enough to realise how un'appy Duncan were with me. I weren't smart enough to realise Edwin 'ad been in love with me for years. I let my coin 'older get stolen... I know my own place in the world but nothin' outside of it. And Edwin is so bright, Dad, so clever. I wonder if sometimes 'e feels like 'e can't talk to me the way he talks with Duncan. That 'e thinks I wouldn't understand."

"Duncan is his friend? And your former lover?"

Robin nodded.

"Huh," his father said. "Well, I mean, it's a good thing, isn't it? Means he has someone he can talk to? You can't be expected to fulfil every need your partner has. Otherwise, what are friends for?"

"'E's not only a friend," Robin said. "Duncan is family to me."

"Even better. Do the best you can. It's all anyone can ask." He stopped to take a drink and consider his words. "And you're not stupid. You never have been. You've always been innocent. Open. Trustin'. There's nothin' wrong with seein' the best in people. Hopin' for the best. It does my heart good to see you never lost that. I wish I could be more like you."

The actors on stage were nude again, but Robin had no idea why. He hadn't heard a word they'd been saying. He wasn't even sure if they were all part of the play or simply drunk and joining in for the fun of it.

"The night I left..." his father said, "I saw my closest friend die right in front of me. I were grievin'. I weren't in my right mind. And by the time I were in a position to come back, you were a grown man. I thought by then you'd either made your way in the world or you were..."

"Dead?"

"Dead. Either way, my comin' back wouldn't have made any difference."

"If you'd come back you could 'ave told them what really 'appened with Barnabas. Cleared your name. My name. What did 'appen the night 'e died? You two were arguin'? Iris reckons you must 'ave left the village to stop Tommy from attacking us."

His father nodded and slid back in his seat. "She's very perceptive," he said. "Barnabas didn't want me to go, he said I had you to think of now, I couldn't leave you behind. I told him I had no choice. Told him I didn't want to leave you, or Morwenna, but I had to put an end to it." He took another drink, avoiding Robin's gaze.

"So you did tell him then," Robin said. "About you and Morwenner."

"It was out of me before I knew what I'd said. He was heartbroken. I could see it in his face. He turned away, slipped on the wet grass, I grabbed his jacket but he tumbled out of it and down onto the rocks. It were like the whole world stopped. The waves, the rain, all frozen in place. My life as I knew it were over. I took a rowboat out to Tommy's ship; we sailed off, and before we even got as far as Blackrabbit, we were attacked by Chase Tradin' Company pirate hunters. But it all worked out in the end, didn't it? Eventually."

"Eventually," Robin said. "Eventually."

"You need to stop lookin' for answers to questions that no longer matter, Robin. You said your lover is about to become a father. So, why didn't you stay there with him? Why aren't you lookin' to the future instead of bein' here with me, wallowin' in the past?"

Chapter Thirty-Two

The air in Duncan's house was thick with smoke from the fireplace. He attempted to read a book while Vince puffed on a clay pipe. Bramble sat outside, looking in through the window. Duncan had tried to coax him in, but he'd looked at Vince and refused to budge. Finally, Duncan could stand it no more and slammed his book closed. Well, he wanted it to slam but it was quite a thin volume and thus didn't produce the effect he'd hoped for.

"What did you say to Nick?" he asked.

He'd spent all evening trying to get past his embarrassment and work up the courage to ask. Vince made it a hundred times more awkward for him by remaining silent. A dark cloud drifted from the bowl of his pipe.

"Actually, never mind," Duncan said. "I know what you said. I want to know why you said it."

"Don't know."

"You don't know. Marvellous. Really, just excellent, Vince. Are you trying to sabotage my chances with him?"

"No."

"Then, what, you wanted to put him in his place? Let him see how you were in charge, how you'd bedded me first?"

Vince fixed him with an icy glare.

Without knowing why, Duncan stood and moved by the window. "Because if that's the case," he said, "if you think it so vital for Nick to know where he stands in the pecking order, I find it odd how you haven't once spoken to me about our night together, and you certainly haven't tried to repeat it. Do you regret it? Do you feel as though I coerced you?"

Vince set his pipe down. "'Course not," he said. "You didn't make me do anything. Did what I wanted, like always."

"So you don't regret it, and you don't want to repeat it. Fine. Then why tell Nick? You said it didn't mean anything; you told Edwin as much."

"Thought it didn't. Then I saw you and the teacher together in the bay."

Duncan didn't know he'd been seen and for a split second felt quite exposed. Not in a physical sense, Vince would have seen nothing he hadn't seen around the house in the past week or so, but Duncan had thought it a private moment shared between Nick and himself. "And?" he asked.

Vince lowered his gaze.

"*And?*"

"And it hurt," Vince said. "More than I thought it would."

Duncan swayed where he stood. He'd expected shouting, maybe throwing furniture, but not this.

Vince's shoulders were slumped, his hands clasped on his lap. "You were having fun with him. Playing. Laughing. Didn't do that with me. Made me feel worthless. All my life I've only ever been good for manual labour—lifting, fighting or...the other thing. Seeing how you were with him brought it all home to me. Reminded me I'm nothing more than a lump of meat."

"I never wanted to make you feel this way," Duncan said. "Why didn't you say anything?" He tried to take the ire from his tone. No matter how big or how intimidating Vince was on the surface, Duncan couldn't help but see underneath, to the abandoned boy drawing pictures with soot from the fireplace.

"Spent a lifetime building walls," Vince said. "Can't..."

"Can't what?"

"Can't let them down again. Not after Martin. Never felt as...vulnerable as I did back then. Let the world see my heart and it got stabbed. Showed weakness and the world exploited it."

"It's not weakness—"

"*It is.*"

Duncan jumped at the force of Vince's interruption. His voice was gruff at the best of times but when barked it was truly frightening.

"It is weakness," Vince said. "Have to be strong. Have to be on guard. When I'm not..." He touched his eyepatch. "When I'm not, this happens. Can't just go around wearing my heart on my sleeve. Not easy for me, all this."

"It's not easy for me either, Vince! It's not easy for anyone. I'm not blasé about affairs of the heart. I know there's always a chance of pain; I know there's always risk. And the worst part—the absolute very worst part—is this means Edwin was right!"

Vince sat wide-eyed before he laughed. Duncan sank heavily onto a chair and laughed as well.

"What're we doing?" Vince asked. "We're grown men, behaving like children."

"If only we'd been honest," Duncan said, "everything would have been fine. I like you, Vince, a great deal. You're not simply a lump of meat—you're a good man deep down. Yes, I have fun with Nick—we flirt and gallivant, because it's a side of me he brings to the fore. You and I, we're both a bit too similar. We have Blackrabbit, we have Baxbary bleddy Mudge, we have a shared history, and I think... I think we bring out the darker sides of each other. We need someone to find the light. I enjoyed our time in bed together. I would happily do it again, but I don't believe pursuing anything romantic would be in either of our best interests. And I honestly thought you felt the same way."

Vince took a deep breath and closed his eyes. At least, Duncan assumed the one behind the patch was closed too. "Like you too," Vince said. "Think we could have something, but you're right, it would be difficult, us being together. We'd end up at each other's throats. Don't think either of us needs that in our lives."

Duncan moved to the sofa and sat with his arm around Vince's shoulder. "Who knows," he said. "If I'd never left Blackrabbit, never come here, maybe you and I would have ended up together."

"In another life," Vince said.

"Yes," said Duncan. "In another life."

After an hour or two of shifting tea crates filled with old clothes and chests full of bent silverware, George rested on a creaky chair with chewed legs. He and Arminell had come up with a system for setting aside what was to be kept and what was to be thrown away. Beside him sat the crate which was to be filled with items he wanted to keep. It was overflowing. As were the other four crates next to it.

"You know, Mr. Reed, we're never going to make any space if you insist on hanging on to everything I find."

Arminell stood by the crate that had been set aside for rubbish. It was almost empty.

"It's not everything," George said. "Just some things. Important things."

"What about this?" she asked, holding up a small brass object set with a long chain.

"The bosun's whistle from the *Tall Clarke*—the ship that ran aground on the rocks and prompted the building of the lighthouse. The poor bosun blew and blew on it, trying to warn the crew but it was too late. Most of them perished. He swam ashore with the whistle around his neck."

"And this? Is this from the wreck too?" She held an old spyglass, its lens clouded over.

"No, it belonged to my grandmother. She was a sailor her whole life. Her father gave it to her on the day she became a captain."

"Fine, we'll keep these."

In front of her sat a little ammunition box. Unremarkable in every way. She thumbed it open and found a document within.

"Surely we can at least throw away this one, tiny scrap of paper?" she asked.

George took it and unfolded it close to a lantern for a better look. When he saw what it was, he smiled from ear to ear.

"Oh, no," he said. "This is special. Very special indeed."

Arminell sighed and threw her hands up into the air. "Of course it is."

"I can't help it if we're surrounded by history. The Moth has been at the centre of life here since before there was a village. It's only natural it would hold a lot of memories."

"But memories take up room, Mr. Reed," Arminell said. "Room I thought you needed."

"Well," George said, rubbing his bead, "I don't *need* these rooms, exactly."

"Pardon me?"

"I wanted to clear out any rubbish, yes, but it's not as if I'm short on space." He held his hands out as he spoke. Arminell's face was like thunder.

"So this is what, pointless busy work?" she asked. "Because I do have actual work I could be getting on with."

George lifted the whistle and let the long chain pour through his fingers. "I wouldn't say it was pointless. I'd forgotten about these things. I need to write them down, so they won't be forgotten again."

His voice cracked as he spoke. He hoped she'd chalk it up to the coughing sickness and not realise he was holding back tears. She knelt in front of him, and when she spoke it was with genuine tenderness.

"Mr. Reed, don't worry. I was just feeling a bit frustrated. I didn't mean it. We can keep going. I understand the importance of these things. I really do. It's just...by the end of her life, my mother was keeping everything. And I mean everything. Broken dishes, rags, spoiled food. It piled up everywhere. There was hardly any room to move in our home. She'd grown up very poor, and I think she was terrified of ending up with nothing again. So when I see you hoarding things, I worry about you. I don't want you to end up like her."

"Kitty Pinch," he said. "Now there was a force to be reckoned with. She was a good woman, your mother. There was a time when I couldn't imagine the Moth without her. I really thought she'd take over this place one day."

"She loved working here. She told me so many stories about this place, it made me want to be part of it."

He smiled, unable to keep his eyes dry any longer. For many years, Kitty had been his right-hand woman and had kept the inn ticking over when he'd been unable to cope. She had been a sailor at heart and often left for extended trips to sea, much to his consternation. Arminell had practically been raised in the tavern so it was no surprise to him when she became a fully paid employee. After she'd fallen pregnant and could no longer work, George had told her there would always be a place for her at the Moth. Now here she was, looking at him with her mother's eyes. He patted the friendly hand on his knee and he dabbed away his tears.

Arminell stood and flicked through a box of paintings, stopping to pull out a seascape of the Merryapple lighthouse besieged by waves. "Clearly we can't get rid of stuff like this. We might as well just..." she trailed off, lost in thought. Then she turned to George and grinned. "I've got an idea," she said.

Chapter Thirty-Three

Robin had poked his head out of one of the many gunports on the ocean-facing side of Driftwood. "Those are the rudders, yes?"

Fausto was leaning against a wall and eating an apple. He'd been asked by Robin's father to show Robin around, and he wasn't very happy about it. "Right," he said between noisy, wet chomps. "They work with the masts to keep us in place."

"Why aren't we floodin'?"

"Each stack has a clockwork-powered pump in the base going all day and night to keep the seawater at bay."

Robin leaned against one of the cold iron cannons held in place with a thick rope. "And the only way into Driftwood is to sail between those lighthouses? The ones on either side of the gap?"

Fausto crunched his apple. "You'd have slammed against the oceanward wall when you arrived, if Red Jim hadn't ordered us to come about and let you in," he said. "You're lucky, you know. We don't let just anyone on board."

"Oh, I know," Robin said. It had been made abundantly clear to him that the pirates didn't approve of visitors. He'd smiled and been polite and done his best not to make waves, but they still didn't like him. "I can't get my 'ead around 'ow this all works."

Fausto rolled his eyes. "Think of it this way, yeah? There are five stacks. The first stack, it's like a marketplace. It's where goods change hands, deals get made, raids get planned, all the fun stuff, right? It's also got all our food stored in it. The stack farthest from it is the living quarters. The largest cabins are for captains, of course, and the rest is a free-for-all of hammocks, bunks, tents, shelters, whatever we can squeeze in to make life a bit more comfortable. The middle stacks had most of their inner decks removed, yeah? They're open from the bottommost ships all the way up to the weather deck of the topmost ships."

"They're the ones that look like a tower of doll's houses? The ones with all the footbridges stretchin' from port to starboard?"

"The lowest part of the centre stack is the drinking hall," Fausto said, finishing his apple. He wiped his mouth with the apricot-coloured kerchief around his neck. "High above it is the control room for Driftwood's defences."

"I need a map..." Robin said.

"You need a drink," Fausto said, as he threw the apple core out of a gunport and into the ocean.

The noise in the drinking hall was like nothing Robin had ever experienced before. Not even the Moth & Moon on its busiest day could have compared. Being so open, the sounds reverberated up through the stack of hollowed ships and came bouncing back down again. His ears rang with the echoing clang of tankards being slammed on tables, bad singing, hoarse laughter, boots stamping, extravagant swearwords and the occasional retching of a vomiting pirate.

He met his father and they travelled from table to table, talking at length to a dozen pirates, if not more. Everyone knew his father, though each one called him Barrow. With them, his father was slick, friendly, charming to a fault. Even the most stoic buccaneer eventually opened up to him. It took a while before Robin realised what his father was actually doing was interviewing them. With a careful cocktail of ale, camaraderie, and compliments, he coaxed out detail after detail from the pirates of Driftwood. He'd been doing it the entire time Robin had been on board, he realised. Every once in a while they'd encounter a pirate who refused to speak. Some even turned their faces away or left their seats when they spotted Robin and his father approaching. Robin supposed people like these would have a lot of rivalries, a lot of grudges.

"It's for Tommy," his father said when they were alone. "He loves to hear their stories but he's...not popular. So, I get the stories, tell them to him, and he writes them down."

Fausto strolled past on the arm of a girl around his own age. She was laden with pistols and wore a wide-brimmed hat.

"Tsuta has fallen for his charms!" his father said. "The poor girl. She can do better."

"What's 'is story then?" Robin asked. "Fausto?"

"A couple of years ago, I were on a raid with Gulabahaar," his father said. "We captured an Italian sloop. Fausto were on board with his parents. We spent a day or two lootin' it and the passengers, takin' our time, you know how it is. All the while, Fausto were pesterin' us to join the crew. Over and over, he'd ask and ask. Never seen the like of it. Anyway, we were preparin' to leave when he grabbed a knife and held it to his own mother's throat! Threatened to kill her if we didn't take him with us. Gulabahaar just laughed and agreed. He took the apricot kerchief from his mother, wrapped it round his neck and jumped onto Gulabahaar's ship. He's been with us ever since."

"'E sounds eager."

"He's reckless. He'll come to a bad end, that one. Mark my words."

It was hours later when they were joined by an apparently sober Tommy. A mighty groan erupted from the throng as he descended into the drinking pit.

"Not him!" shouted one pirate.

"I thought we banned him?" said another.

"I thought we killed him!" said a third.

"Not at all, I'm alive and well, as you can see!" Tommy said in his sing-song accent, which Robin struggled to place.

Tommy joined Robin and his father at their table, pouring himself a mug of ale. He either didn't notice or didn't mind the sediment floating at the top of it. It took only a few mouthfuls for him to strike up a shanty, one rather more bawdy than any Robin had heard since his arrival. Tommy sang the first line as best he could, and a dozen other pirates, including Robin's father, lent their voices in response.

Stormy sea or blashy sky!

None can stay my wanderin' eye!

Drink your whiskey, drink your beer!

Then come try my obligin' rear!

Girl or boy, young or old!

My skill in bed's worth more than gold!

Fret not, my dear, keep thine heart true

For someday I'll get round to you!

Robin blushed a little at the song, leading to much jeering from the company. After a couple of drinks, during which Tommy suffered quite horrendous verbal abuse from the other pirates, he suddenly stopped dead mid-sentence, stared at Robin and pointed at his head. "Been meaning to ask you," he said. "Who said you could wear that?"

"My cap?"

"Not the cap, the anchor!" Tommy said.

"Dad did, I suppose," Robin said. "'E gave me this cap when I were a lad."

"'Rasmus!" Tommy said, feigning woe. "How could you?"

"What's the problem?" Robin said.

Tommy jumped out of his chair, turned around and dropped his breeches. Robin's father followed suit and Robin found himself faced with two hairy rear ends, both tattooed with the same image of an anchor with a spindle of rope in its crown. The two men were laughing gleefully.

"It's our emblem!" Tommy shouted, slapping his cheeks. "Our special branding! The sign of our bond!"

Robin leaned back in his chair. "So, all my life I've been wearin' on my cap the same thing you two 'ave 'ad inked on your arses?"

The men pulled up their breeches, still howling with laughter.

"Oh, smile, son!" his father said. "It's just a bit of fun!"

"Vince has a similar tattoo. On 'is arm, mind. Where did it come from?"

"I saw the design when I were sailin' in the Orient. A papersmith had these little charms on the journals he crafted. We both bought a journal each, didn't we?"

"And when I was sleeping, your dad took the pendant from mine and sewed it to that cap!" Tommy said.

"I told you I liked it. I used the sigil on all my letters and charts."

"A foppish affectation," Tommy said. "If you don't mind me saying."

Robin's father slapped him on the side of the head. "I bleddy well do mind. It added an air of mystery to me. Women bleddy love a man with a bit of mystery about him."

"What 'appened to the other journal?" Robin asked.

His father and Tommy exchanged a loaded glance.

"Your dear old dad stole it!" Tommy said.

"I borrowed it!"

"Then why haven't you ever given it back?" Tommy asked.

"I haven't had the chance to go home and get it!" his father said.

"Home? It's in Blashy Cove?"

"In the Moth & Moon," his father said. "You know the paintin' Barnabas did? The one of our ships fightin'? I hid it behind there, in a recess. Didn't want it fallin' into the wrong hands. Or anyone's hands, really. Anyway, it's probably long gone by now."

"The paintin' 'angs over my favourite seat," Robin said.

"Hang on," Tommy said. "What do you mean '*our ships fighting*'? Whose ships?"

"Yours and mine," his father said. "The *Mercury* and the *Fledglin' Crow*. Barnabas Whitewater painted our fight. He called it the *Battle in the Bay*."

Tommy slapped Erasmus on the arm. "You never told me that!"

"Because I knew you'd be insufferable about it. Bein' immortalised in paint. Anyway, Barnabas never knew I were on one of those ships when he painted it."

"Why is it called the *Battle in the Bay* when it happened in a cove?" Tommy asked.

"You'd have to ask Barnabas," his father said. "Maybe he thought it sounded better than *Kerfuffle in the Cove?*"

"*Conflagration in the Cove*," Tommy said. "Ooh, no, *Clash in the Cove!*"

"Oh, that is better, actually."

"Tommy, what 'appened to you on the deserted island?" Robin asked. "'Ow did you escape?"

"The what now?" his father asked.

"Remember when you stranded me on a remote island with nothing but the clothes on my back and musket loaded with a single shot?" Tommy asked.

"Oh!" his father said. "Yes. You deserved it."

"Debateable," Tommy said.

"Not really—you killed a crewmember. Anthony Cook. A good man, he were."

"He had it coming. He was an overbearing, arrogant fool. Anyway, I was rescued a few days later when a navy vessel passed by. I fed them a sob story about being framed for murder by an unscrupulous captain, and they took me to the nearest port. I slipped away from them as soon as I could, before they had time to look too closely into my story. I managed to get hired on board another ship, the *Mercury*. The captain was a pitiful wretch. Within a month, I was quartermaster and within six months I'd convinced the crew to make me the captain."

"You organised a mutiny?" Robin said.

"No!" Tommy said. "Well, maybe a bit. Look, on pirate ships, the crew elects their captain. It's all very democratic, you know."

"But you weren't on a pirate ship at the time..." Robin said.

"A mere technicality," Tommy said with a shrug of his bony shoulders. "I wanted revenge on your no-good dad, but I knew if I wanted my new crew to go along with it, I'd need to offer them something to keep them happy. So, we ambushed a Spanish treasure fleet and took their entire horde of silver. I kept it locked up in my cabin and promised to share it out, once 'Rasmus was dead."

Tommy's cavalier retelling of his plans made Robin feel sick. What kind of person was he? And what kind of person was his father to call this man his friend?

"We headed for the Pell Isles. 'Rasmus had talked about his home once or twice, and I thought even if he wasn't there, I could do some damage. Unbeknownst to me, one of my crewmen was spying for 'Rasmus and got word to him what we were planning, so when we got to Merryapple, the *Fledgling Crow* was waiting."

"Along with two Chase Tradin' Company pirate hunters I lured there," his father said.

"This is the *Battle in the Bay?*" Robin asked.

"Right," his father said. "Tommy sank one of the C.T.C. ships and while the other rescued her crew, I filled the *Mercury* full of holes and chased it out of the bay."

"We were faster, but we only got as far as the coast of France before we took on too much water to continue," Tommy said.

"We finished the *Mercury* off and watched her sink beneath the waves."

"Taking all my lovely Spanish silver with her," Tommy said. "I hid under a piece of floating wreckage, treading water until I was sure 'Rasmus had departed. You hung around long enough!"

"Ho ho! I wanted to make sure you were dead, you scrawny good-for-nothin'." His father's booming laugh cut right through Robin. What made it worse was the laugh sounded exactly like his own.

"I floated for hours before some other ships arrived to see if there was anything they could salvage," Tommy said. "All they found was me. I was exhausted, bleeding and furious. I didn't even have the satisfaction of knowing the spy had drowned!"

"She jumped overboard in the cove," his father said. "We scooped her up on our way past."

"How did you get a spy on Tommy's crew?" Robin asked.

"Poor Vyvyan Scantaberie," his father said. "She were a nice woman, in all honesty. Served on the *Fledglin' Crow* for a summer and then somehow ended up servin' under this pillock. I asked her to pass on any information I might find useful. She were only too happy to help."

"Why?" asked Robin.

"She were hopelessly in love with me. And who could blame her?" his father said, stroking his creamy-white moustache. "I were quite the dashin' gent in my day."

"You were a giant, coarse brute with a face like a granite bluff," Tommy said. "'Rasmus knew about the silver, and there was no way he'd just let it disappear, so I reasoned he would have noted the position of the shipwreck in the journal. I was disorientated and had drifted for hours; I'd no idea where the *Mercury* had gone down by then."

"I mostly kept Tommy's journal for ship's business and used my own for more personal use. I meant to go back and search for the silver someday, but before I got a chance, you were born and I got sidetracked."

"There I was," Tommy said, "shipless, crewless, hopeless. Eventually I ended up in Blackrabbit and was hired by Chase Trading as captain of the *Caldera*."

"Wait," Robin said. "Why would they 'ire you? You sank one of their ships."

"I may have forged some papers," Tommy said. "And they were desperate. They were going through a difficult period, finding it hard to get captains willing to sail in pirate-infested waters. It wasn't long before I'd replaced the crew of the *Caldera* with my own men and women. Pirates I'd sailed with before. We were able to plunder the seas right under the noses of the authorities, all because of the oh-so-respectable name of the Chase Trading Company."

"Lord Chase were no better than a pirate himself," his father said. "Only he had official papers and a fancy title and we didn't."

It wasn't remotely the same thing, but Robin didn't think it was worth arguing the point.

"The night Tommy came back to Merryapple were the night Barnabas Whitewater died," his father said.

"I know," Robin said. "'E were goin' to level the village with cannon fire if you didn't surrender to 'im."

Tommy furrowed his brow. "Who told you that?"

"Dad did," Robin said. "Earlier on."

Tommy sat back and smiled, slapping Robin's father on the back.

"Actually," his father said, "you said it. I simply didn't disagree."

"Well, well!" Tommy said. "He thinks you're some great hero, sacrificing yourself to save your village!"

"Tommy, leave it," his father said.

"Wait, you lied to me?" Robin asked. "Dad?"

"Go on, 'Rasmus, tell the boy!" Tommy said.

His father stood up, knocking some tankards over. His face was like thunder. "*I said leave it!*"

His father's voice thundered across the hall, causing more than one head to turn. He clenched and relaxed his massive fists, over and over. He huffed and puffed and appeared torn over what action to take, finally deciding to storm off. Robin jumped to his feet, knocking over a tankard. He quickly grabbed his father by the arm and held fast, locking eyes with him.

"*Dad,*" he shouted, surprised by the steel in his own voice, "I've waited forty years for an explanation. Now you sit back down, and you tell me the truth about the night you vanished. You owe me that much."

Chapter Thirty-Four

The drinking hall had fallen silent. All eyes were on Robin and his father. Robin wiped up the spilled ale with a cloth while his father sat and regained his composure. Tommy signalled for more drink to be brought to the table.

"You ever heard tell of a husband and wife pirate duo named Eric Cobham and Maria Lindsey?" his father asked.

Robin shook his head.

"Nasty pair, they were. Cruel. Used to kill the crew of every ship they raided. Tommy and I both ran afoul of them a handful of times. A few weeks before the night Barnabas died, Tommy sent me a letter. In it, he said he'd gotten word Cobham and Lindsey were sellin' their fleet and assets and moving to France. A nice little retirement for them both."

"Couldn't have that," Tommy said.

"Quite right. Tommy was goin' to settle the score and, well, he asked me to put aside our differences and join him."

"I said I needed help, and your dad was the only man for the job," Tommy said.

"I knew it would be dangerous, knew I couldn't trust Tommy, so I started writin' my letter to you, in my own journal. In case anythin' happened, I... I wanted you to know somethin' about me, of who I were."

"You never said nothin' about these other pirates in your letter," Robin said.

"There's a lot I didn't put in the letter."

He stared into his father's eyes. After finding the blood-red journal, after he and his friends had pieced together what happened the night Barnabas Whitewater died, Robin thought he'd uncovered the single shred of nobility that proved his father wasn't the terrible person everyone said he was. Since then, he'd clung to that notion, grateful beyond measure for its comfort after a lifetime of uncertainty. But he'd been wrong. The disappointment he felt in that moment made him sick to his stomach, but it was nothing compared to the embarrassment.

"So, you didn't give yourself up to save the village. You left on a mission of revenge and it went badly wrong for you. You're no 'ero."

"I never said I were. On the night Tommy arrived in the *Caldera*, I told Barnabas what I were plannin'. He objected, as I told you. He tried to talk me out of it. We argued and he fell to his death."

His father took another drink. Robin was certain this part was true. The pain on his father's face was unmistakable. "After Barnabas fell, I rowed out to the *Caldera* and we got underway. In the waters between Merryapple and Blackrabbit, we encountered two Chase Tradin' ships."

"Pirate hunters out on patrol," Robin said.

"Yes and no," Tommy said.

"They were pirate hunters, but they weren't on patrol," his father said. "They were waitin' for us. Because they knew where we'd be."

"'Ow did they know?" Robin asked.

His father glared at Tommy, who seemed to shrink under his gaze.

"I told them," Tommy said. "Lord Marley Chase found out I'd been using one of his C.T.C. ships for piracy. He told me he wouldn't have me thrown in gaol if I agreed to help him capture one pirate who'd been a particular thorn in his side. One Captain Erasmus Shipp."

Robin's father was seething. Some wounds, it seemed, never fully heal.

"I told Lord Chase I could get 'Rasmus for him," Tommy said, "and where we'd be. So, that night we were both taken aboard one of the pirate hunters. I expected to hand over 'Rasmus and be done with it. Instead..."

"Instead the pirate hunters opened fire on the *Caldera* and sank her with all hands on board," his father said, taking a swig from a tankard of ale.

"Why didn't they do away with the both of you?"

"Respect for rank, we were told," Tommy said. "Though I suspect it had more to do with Marley Chase wanting to punish us. They sold us."

"Like animals," his father said.

"They sent us to a remote estate. A place where political prisoners and troublesome members of wealthy families can disappear to, out of the public eye."

"In one fell swoop," his father said, "Lord Chase got rid of a ship with a bad reputation, a crew full of pirates and two captains who'd raided his company vessels on and off for years."

Robin tugged at his earlobe as he tried to understand everything he'd just been told. "Wait, wait," he said. "Let me try to follow this. Tommy, you lied to Dad about goin' out for revenge. The lie led to Barnabas Whitewater dyin', your whole crew dyin', and both of you bein' held captive on some estate?"

Tommy rocked his head from side to side. "Mmm, yes, sounds about right."

Robin couldn't believe what he was hearing. The dismissive way in which Tommy regaled his past misdeeds made them sound no more serious than a child stealing apples from an orchard. His father, unbearably quiet, was clearly stewing over the finer details.

"And now it's all forgiven?" Robin asked him.

"We've all made mistakes," his father said, fixing him with a cold stare. "You can't live in the past, Robin. It will drown you."

"So, where was this estate you mentioned?"

Tommy visibly bristled at the mention of it.

"The Spanish coast," his father said. "We were put to work on the land with dozens of other captives."

"Ten years we spent there," Tommy said. "Ten long, hard years." His eyes were unfocused, his voice soft.

"We worked, we fought, we laughed, we plotted," his father said. "We suffered the torments of the cruel family who owned the land. We mourned the loss of other captives. We formed our own factions. We fought off others. Somewhere along the way, I won his respect and he won mine. Somewhere along the way, we became friends."

"Despite everything?" Robin asked.

"Despite it or maybe because of it," his father said. "Who knows?"

"How did you get out?" Robin asked.

"We hatched a plan," his father said. "Overpowered the guards and escaped."

"Not quite the whole story, though, is it?" Robin said.

"Obviously not," his father said. "Don't get the wrong idea, we didn't sneak away in the dead of night. We took care of our captors before we left. Made sure they wouldn't harm anyone else."

"Who were they?"

"A horrible family," Tommy said. "A couple and their four children."

"Children?" Robin said, his heart sinking.

"They weren't infants, they were grown men and women who delighted in tormentin' and torturin' us. Whippin' us under a hot sun or beatin' us in the middle of the night with belts. One of his daughters had a penchant for breakin' fingers and toes. On a whim. No rhyme nor reason. She broke three of my fingers over the course of a week. Got her guards to weigh me down on the ground with my arms out, grabbed a finger and pulled it back, then snap! She giggled while she did it too. She said she liked the sound.

"Then when I were put back to work, the rest of her family would whip me for not workin' as hard as the others. They had a box, a metal box, they used to punish us. They'd put one of us in there, leave us all day in the hot sun. It were...uniquely horrible. I still don't like being cooped up. Does somethin' to my head. This went on for years, Robin. Years. Sometimes, captives would just disappear overnight, and you daren't ask why. Do you know what that's like? The threat that hangs over you? Never knowin' when or where it will strike? The toll it takes on you? Others had it worse than me, mind you. The things they did to Tommy..."

Tommy was staring at the floor. He started to rock slowly back and forth.

"We only had each other to rely on," his father said. "If it weren't for him, I never would have survived. Those people were sick, twisted monsters. We did the world a favour by doing away with them. We organised the other captives. One night, we broke out. Killed the guards first. Trapped the family in their house. Little Miss Fingersnapper were the first to go. Musket shot to the side of the head. Made her daddy watch. You'd think he'd beg for her life, or his own, but he didn't."

"He knew it was going to happen, sooner or later," Tommy said. "He knew they deserved it."

"We tied the rest of them to their beds. Set the house on fire. Watched it burn to the ground with them still inside."

"We sang while they screamed," Tommy said, shaking his fist.

"I weren't goin' to mention that bit," his father said.

Robin felt sick. The details, the cold look in his father's eyes—it all painted a picture of a man he didn't want to know. More though, he was struck by the change in his father's voice. The drop in tone, the iciness, the clipped manner. He sounded like Vince. And then there was Tommy. Clearly not in his right mind, he was like a lapdog, the way he followed his father around. Since first learning about the man through his father's journal, Robin had built Captain Thomas Oughterlauney into a figure of fear. A bloodthirsty monster who had snatched his father away from him in the middle of the night. Yet before him sat the reality—a scrawny, funny-looking old man with yellow teeth and straggly ashen hair who'd been his father's companion longer than he'd been his enemy.

"I suppose I should thank you," Robin said, "for bein' a friend to Dad. For lookin' after 'im."

Tommy laughed his cackling, shrill laugh. "Someone had to!" he said.

"What did you do after you escaped?" Robin asked.

"We walked until we found a port," his father said. "Talked our way onto a ship, eventually found some pirates we knew and joined up with them. I went back to captainin' the *Fledglin' Crow* as Bill Barrow for a while, but my heart weren't in it. We were both a bit long in the tooth, and the estate had taken the wind out of our sails. I still dream about it..."

"So do I," Tommy said.

His father's gaze was fixed on the floor, and he flexed his thick, calloused fingers around the mug of ale. He hadn't touched a drop since the estate was mentioned. "Afterwards, we flitted around various pirate ships and offered our expertise to any crew who needed it."

"Spent time in Port Royal, Tortuga, Nassau, the Azores," Tommy said. "Lots of places. But it wasn't always vengeance and horror! Hey, 'Rasmus, remember Amsterdam?"

"And Oslo?" his father said with a wink. "We spent years together and years apart, but somehow always ended up back in each other's company. Then, what, about five years ago?"

"Six, I think."

"Six years ago, we got wind of a floatin' pirate haven and set out to find it. We've been here ever since."

"Barring the odd stint in gaol," Tommy said.

"Anyway, after we escaped the estate, we decided we needed a tattoo to commemorate the occasion. I hadn't had much chance to use my anchor for a while, so I suggested it. And it became..."

"A symbol," Tommy said, raising his mug, "of a lifelong friendship. Well, friend-and-enemy-ship."

His father clinked his mug against Tommy's. "Let's get you one!" his father said.

"Oh, no, no thank you," Robin said, waving his hand. "I don't need no drawin's on my skin."

"You're not tattooed and you call yourself a sailor?"

"I call myself a fisherman."

"You're not tattooed and you call yourself a fisherman?"

"Dad..."

"Come on, Robin, live a little!" his father said, grabbing Robin by the arm and pulling him out of his chair.

"I'm not gettin' a tattoo on my arse!" Robin said.

"But there's so much room for one back there!"

"You're one to talk!" Robin said. "I didn't get my fat behind from Morwenner!"

"Oh, I'm only teasin'," his father said. "It doesn't have to be there!"

"I don't want the anchor either. Not now."

"Fine, fine," his father said, ushering him towards the ale barrels. "We'll find you somethin' else. A sea serpent, maybe. Or a nice mermaid with lovely round...er, well, maybe not. But we'll find you the perfect one!"

His father filled a large tankard and thrust it into Robin's hand.

"I don't know about this, Dad. I don't think Edwin would like it."

"You're not even married and he's already controllin' you!"

"It's not like that..."

His father lifted Robin's arm, practically forcing the drink down Robin's throat.

"If I do," Robin said, "and I'm not sayin' I will, you 'ave to do somethin' as well."

"Anythin', name it."

"Get rid of that stupid long 'air; it doesn't suit you at all."

"Just drink up, my boy," his father said, laughing.

The next few hours were a haze for Robin. He remembered a lot more ale, plenty of rabblerousing and at one point he was certain he ended up on a table singing with his shirt off. Pirate ale might be grainy but it was strong stuff. He woke the following morning, dizzy, naked and lying on the floor of his father's quarters. A bandage round his neck held some cloth in place over his chest. He poked at it and winced.

"Don't, it's not healed yet," his father said from across the room. He was running his hands through his short, ruffled hair and over his neat, white moustache. He curled the ends of it between thumb and forefinger, smiling broadly as he did so.

"What isn't?" Robin asked as he sat up and groped around for something to wear. He found his topshirt tossed in a corner under some empty bottles.

"Your tattoo, of course," his father said.

"Oh, no, tell me I didn't. Tell me you didn't make me—"

"I didn't make you do anythin'!" his father said. "You insisted."

"When?"

"Sometime around the ninth ale? Maybe the tenth."

"What is it?" Robin asked.

"What else? The first great love of your life!"

"Edwin?" Robin said. "No, you said the first... Oh no, please tell me it's not Duncan..."

He carefully peeled back the bloody bandage to reveal a red raw yet surprisingly adept inking of a lugger slicing through rough waves.

"It's *Bucca's Call!*"

"Told you you'd like it. You made me get rid of my hair afterwards."

"Did I? I can't remember much."

He slapped Robin on the shoulder as he walked past, laughing. "I'm not surprised, the amount you put away! You didn't stop at nine or ten ales, either. You take after your old man! It takes a lot to sink a Shipp!"

Chapter Thirty-Five

Nick was in the middle of a history lesson which likely went over the heads of some of the younger pupils.

"And so, with the perfection of the Tattet Double Mainspring, the Swiss watchmakers launched an entire industry and are today one of the richest nations in the world. Clockworkings can be found everywhere in daily life. Even in damp, windswept, remote places, so far off the beaten track most people have never heard of them. Everything uses them. From sanitation, heating..."

"Mr. Farriner uses clockwork mixing bowls in the bakery," May Bell said.

"And they're in the sign above the Moth & Moon," said Peter Underton.

"And in Mr. Hunger's toys," said May.

"Mr. Beuguet took the mainspring and created elegant timepieces such as the world had never seen. And he charged a pretty penny for them. This, of course, went against the spirit of the Tattet company, who wanted the technology to remain within reach of the common man. Beugeut and his supporters, aristocrats all, argued if the technology was available to everyone, then there was no problem. Supporters of the Tattets countered by saying the precedent was a dangerous one. If prices could be raised by Beuguet, they would be raised by others. At the time, you were either a Tattetist or a Beuguetist and never both. Indeed the rivalry between the two groups led to violent clashes on the streets of Versailles."

"But I don't understand," said May. "Why did it matter so much, people had to get hurt for it?"

"It is human nature to crave a tribe, Ms. Bell, an identity. Something to define ourselves by, something to belong to. It can be anything— family, for example. Or one's country, one's town, one's profession, even a set of principles. It's what we point to and say here! Look! This is what we are! This is where we belong! It's a good thing for the most part. But an attack on the ideals can feel like an attack on the self and personally I'm certain it's how most wars start. Turning a deaf ear to the vexed has led to the downfall of many a civilisation, but never mind that for now. The point I'm trying to make is this—community is primal, essential, but you ignore disgruntled and marginalised voices at your peril."

"You mean one bad apple can spoil the barrel?" May asked.

Nick was slightly miffed at her summing up his point much more neatly than he had done. "Precisely," he said.

There came a knock at the front of the schoolhouse. Peter Underton jumped out of his seat and ran to the window. "It's Mr. Hunger!"

Every pair of eyes turned to Nick, leading him to deduce they all knew what had transpired between him and Duncan. He muttered under his breath as he left the room. "Small communities... No privacy..."

He stood at the door, composing himself. He thought about ignoring it, letting Duncan stand there all day, but it wouldn't have been very practical. And it would have certainly been a bad example to the children. He clicked open the door. A gull screeched overhead. Duncan removed his tricorne cap and tried to speak.

"Nick," he said. The word squeaked out. "Nick," he repeated in a deeper voice. "I know you're upset, but I'd like to talk."

Nick said nothing but stepped out, closing the door behind him. He beckoned Duncan into the yard.

"I feel like I'm a truant child being scolded," Duncan said, then hung his head low, his cheeks flushing red. "I truly wish I hadn't said that. It was ferociously stupid."

Nick didn't disagree. He was going to ask why Duncan had come during the day, why he hadn't waited until the school day had finished, but he suspected he knew the answer. Duncan wasn't one for calm, measured responses. He gave in to impulses.

"I brought you something," Duncan said. "A peace offering." He unwrapped a large object leaning against the school gate. It was an exquisite, glass-topped, wooden display case.

"You can prop your coins up between those slats on the inside," Duncan said. "And there's space for title cards too. I thought it might be, you know, useful."

It was quite the most thoughtful gift Nick had ever received. He had absolutely no idea what to say.

"I bedded Vince because I wanted to," Duncan said, quite suddenly. "That's all there is to it."

Nick was surprised by the admission but not half as much as Duncan appeared to be. He stood, wide-eyed, as if he hadn't known what he was going to say before the words came out of his mouth. Nick became aware they were being watched intently. A dozen little heads had appeared at the windows behind him.

"*Back in your seats!*" he said, and all the little heads vanished.

"We'd been drinking," Duncan said. "I felt an attraction to him and acted upon it. It happened once and won't happen again."

Nick was silent. He studied Duncan's face, his stupid, handsome face, with its adorable fat, button nose and hypnotic brown eyes and bushy black muttonchops. Did he have to be quite so good-looking? It made it so wretchedly difficult to stay mad at him.

"He cares about you," Nick said.

"He does. In his way. But we've spoken, cleared the air."

"There's nothing between you?"

"Not a thing."

"You're quite sure? Because I don't like wasting my time, Duncan, and I'm not interested in sharing you with anyone."

Duncan held his hands up. "I promise. It's done."

Nick's shoulders slumped, and he exhaled loudly. "Why did he make such a point of telling me?"

"Because while deep down he is a decent man, on the surface he can be a bit of a mean old tuss. It's not his fault, really. He's had a difficult life."

"Haven't we all?" Nick asked.

"Well, yes, but Blackrabbit isn't an easy place to grow up."

He'd been told tales of the island by his uncle and the children. The island of thieves and cutthroats, with its warren-like towns and ruthless gangs. He could easily see how a place like that could produce someone like Vince. Huge, mean, tough. He found it hard to picture Duncan living there, this short, squat man in the funny spectacles. Though on the other hand, he could easily imagine Duncan giving a thorough tongue-lashing to anyone who crossed him. Even a terrier may bark at a mastiff.

"Thanks for my gift," Nick said. "It's beautiful. Really."

"Why did you leave London?" Duncan asked. "To come here, of all places?"

"I fancied a change of scenery," Nick said. "I thought the sea air might be good for me."

"Fine, don't tell me."

"I'm being serious."

"No, you're not," Duncan said. "You didn't give up your entire life in London for some sea air."

Nick set the display case on the ground, passed through the gate, and walked towards the laneway. "You're right. I'm sorry," he said. "I was born to a fairly well-off family. When I was very young, my parents married me off to a much older man. Someone my father knew and owed many favours to. I wasn't happy about it, and it caused a rift in the family which remains to this day. My uncle Mark still won't speak to my father. The man I was married to, Ellery Babbage was his name, was wealthy and not very attentive, thankfully. He was content to have a young man on his arm at society events and at the theatre."

Nick reached into his pocket and withdrew a small item from it. "For our first Midwinter together," he said, "he gave me this silver snuff box. It had been in his family for a few generations. He wanted me to have it because...well, I suppose it was his way of telling me how much my companionship meant to him. I never loved him, nor him me, but we grew fond of each other. I always carry it with me now."

He rubbed his thumb over the tarnished surface of the box as he spoke. His eyes grew distant, his voice, quiet. "Ellery passed away after only a few years," Nick said, "and left me a lot of money. After some time, playing the part of the grieving widow for the sake of appearances, for the sake of my parents, I met someone else. A businessman in London.

"We were madly in love. Or so I thought. He bought and sold clockworks from the continent, was part of the horological revolution in plumbing. Made a fortune, or so he claimed. He swindled me out of most of my money. Played me for a fool. Afterwards, everywhere was spoiled. Every street corner held a biting memory. Every building was a monument to failure and pain. Then my uncle Mark contacted me about the position here, and I jumped at the chance to get away."

"I was in love with a monster, once," Duncan said. "Before I came here. Baxbary Mudge was his name. He was...not kind. I escaped him, came here and fell in love again. With Robin."

"Did it feel the same?"

Duncan shook his head. "Love is never the same twice. Like a favourite song sung by a new voice. The words are the same, the tune, the melody, but it's different."

"You're still close, the two of you. You talk about Robin a lot."

"Yes, we're very close, but don't worry, there's nothing romantic between us. He called me family last year. At Midwinter."

"Well, people drink a lot at that time of year, say all sorts of things," Nick said with a little grin.

Duncan's entire posture changed. He'd been holding himself taut, his short arms tensed, fists clenched, but when Nick smiled he relaxed. "He wasn't drinking," Duncan said.

"Oh," Nick said, scrunching up his face. "Bit of an odd thing to say, then, isn't it? About someone he used to court?"

Duncan took off his spectacles and cleaned them with his shirt sleeve. "We've been through a lot together," he said. "Robin, Edwin, and I. We're family in the ways that matter. And anyone who is interested in courting me would have to understand as much."

Nick tilted his head, studying Duncan once again. He noticed the little dents on his nose caused by the spectacles. Was there a name for them? Surely there was, he should look it up later. If there wasn't, he could coin a term. Duncan Dots, maybe? Hunger Dents?

"So, will I have to get Robin's approval?" he asked.

Duncan smiled broadly. He put his spectacles back on, fixing the ends behind his ears. "Don't worry, he'll like you. He likes everyone."

"Does he? How bizarre."

"I know, I don't understand it at all. Will you let me make it up to you this evening? Come with me to the Moth. George Reed has some important announcement to make."

At sunset, Edwin met up with Duncan, Nick, Eva, and the rest of the crowd gathered in the twisting first floor hallways of the Moth & Moon. Most people held drinks in their hands; all were chattering about the announcement George Reed was to make. Some had heard rumours of a new automated bathing machine he'd had installed. Others talked of a great brass telescope which could poke out of the newly uncovered windows. Whatever the secret about to be unveiled, the villagers were on tenterhooks.

George and Arminell Kind stood by an arched double doorway. George was coughing into his handkerchief. He took a sip of brandy and composed himself before addressing the crowd.

"I'd like to thank you all for coming," he said. "I'm sure I'm not alone in saying how much I miss our beloved Painted Mermaid."

"It was flattened by the hurricane," Duncan whispered to Nick. "The owners started to rebuild but a death in the family forced them to leave the island not long after."

"Art is important," George said. "Art shows us who we are, who we were, and who we could be. We're fortunate to have so many talented artists in our little village, and they deserve a place where their work can be appreciated. Moreover, the village is changing. Our history could easily slip away, unnoticed. We should preserve it. We must preserve it. Arminell Kind came up with the most marvellous suggestion as to how we might best do so."

"We mustn't squander our heritage," she said to the crowd. "Our traditions matter."

"And so this evening," George said, "we'd like to welcome you all to the opening of the Moth & Moon's very own museum."

He and Arminell both opened the double doors behind them, beckoning the crowd inside to two spacious adjoining rooms. Every wall was covered with paintings and sketches, large and small. Portrayals of villagers past and present, of buildings long since turned to rubble, of dramatic seascapes and the peaceful countryside.

In the middle of the rooms, plinths held sculptures depicting fantastical creatures like mermaids, piskies, and buccas. People gasped and pointed when they spotted images of relatives long passed. Artists proudly picked out their work and directed friends and family towards them. One small section held a number of glass-fronted boxes. Carefully pinned inside, their beautiful wings splayed, were samples of every kind of butterfly and moth to be found on the island. George had a lifelong interest in lepidopterology and spent every spare moment in fields and amongst hedgerows, net in hand, searching for rare specimens for his collection.

One entire wall was devoted to the work of the late Barnabas Whitewater. Morwenna spoke of how she had donated much of her collection, fearing for its safety in her cottage. She welled up at the sight of it all displayed so beautifully and the little plaque bearing his name.

It was to another wall Edwin's attention was drawn. There upon it hung a dozen or so unframed paintings. Some were nudes of Edwin's father, Nathaniel, painted when he was still an athletic young man. Some were portraits of Barnabas Whitewater. Several were striking images of a red-haired woman with her face partially obscured, a haunted look in her eyes. They were full of movement and energy but had a savageness to them. Each painting of her was darker, more sinister than the last.

"That's Sylvia Farriner, isn't it?" asked one villager.

"So it is," said another. "I didn't know she was a painter."

Hamilton Bounsell, the village butcher, stood tilting his head at them, like a confused puppy.

"They make me feel all funny inside," he said. "Like I'm being churned up. Chewed by an animal."

Edwin's face flushed, his heartbeat pounding in his ears. He charged out of the museum. Duncan and Eva followed him.

"*How could you do this, Eva?*" Edwin said. "How could you go behind my back?"

"What's wrong?" Duncan asked. "Are you upset because now everyone has seen your father in the altogether? Because I think he'd be fine with being remembered as a strapping, handsome, young man with a generous—"

"That's not it," Edwin said, throwing his hands in the air.

He understood what Duncan was trying to do, but in the moment he had no patience for levity. Eva stood before him, hand on hip and eyebrow cocked. She was doing the thing she did where she patiently waited for someone to finish speaking before completely destroying what they'd said. He slapped a wall in frustration.

"Is it Barnabas Whitewater then?" Duncan asked. "Seeing how delicately she painted him when we know she was in love with him?"

"No, it's not him... I just..."

Edwin slumped against the wall and slid to the floor, his head swaying. He covered his face with his hands. Duncan sat on the floor next to him.

"Edwin," he said, "what is this? It isn't like you."

Edwin found it hard to catch his breath. Eva was shooing away some of the nosier people who followed them out of the museum. When he spoke, his voice was hoarse and low. He found it so hard to get the words out. "I don't like this," he said. "I don't like being so...weak. I'm supposed to be strong. I'm supposed to be dependable."

"Says who?"

"Everyone. For my whole life. I'm the one who put his drunken past behind him and took over the family business, kept it going. I'm the one people are supposed to be able to rely on. I'm not supposed to be the one who falls to pieces in a tavern hallway."

"You're allowed to fall, Edwin," Eva said. "Everyone is."

"No, I'm not, I'm not. This, this feeling, this helplessness, this was meant to be the drink's doing. Don't you see? It's why I gave it up for good last winter, after I had too much and lost control. I thought giving up would be the end of it, and I haven't touched a drop since. I haven't. But here I am, feeling like I'm losing control again. It wasn't the drink. It was me. It was the animal inside me all along."

"So, you occasionally fall to pieces when you're stressed," Duncan said. "Who doesn't? You're not our dad, Edwin. You don't have to take care of everyone, all the time. You're allowed to lean on us now and again."

Edwin rubbed his face in his hands. Duncan was right, of course. He just needed to hear it said out loud.

"I thought he'd be forgotten," Edwin said. "Dad, I mean. This isn't how I'd have chosen to honour his memory, mind you. I...between clearing out Mum and Dad's house, the twins and now this. I... I need Robin back. I miss him so much. I just need to know he's safe."

"Finally," Duncan said, squeezing Edwin's knee. "I thought you'd never admit it. You didn't really think you had us fooled with all that 'He'll be fine' stuff, did you? We know you're worried about him; we all are. But you weren't wrong. There's no better sailor out there."

"I know but what if something's happened to him? I'll never know. He'll simply...vanish."

"I must say, I'm surprised at you," Eva said, crossing her arms. "The one thing I never thought you lacked was faith in our Mr. Shipp."

"I have faith in him," Edwin said quietly.

"And so you bleddy well should," Eva said. "I think we all know him well enough to know there's no force in this world which could keep him from coming back to you. Don't lose hope, Edwin. Don't give up on him."

To his knowledge, Eva had never said anything she didn't mean.

"Do you want us to take down the paintings?" Duncan asked.

Edwin leaned his head against the wall and inhaled, deeply. "Mum hid them for a reason," he said. "Showing them without her knowledge; it feels so...personal. It's like we took her mind, her heart, and hung them on the wall for anyone to gawp at."

"Don't you think it's good for the village to see them?" asked Eva. "When people here think of your mother, they think only of her last days with us. The spite and vitriol. The lies. When we all found out she knew all along Captain Erasmus Shipp wasn't responsible for Barnabas Whitewater's death. Don't you think this could go some way to restoring her reputation? This way you have a chance to change how people think of her."

"Does she deserve as much?"

"Whatever she did, she's still a person in her own right. People should know there's more than one aspect to her."

"Mum made Robin's life a misery for years," Edwin said. "He could have been angry at me for what she did, but he wasn't. I doubt it even crossed his mind to be. He's been on the other side of it. He even defended her after she and I had a falling-out last Midwinter. Can you imagine? Standing up for the person responsible for turning your whole community against you?"

"He did it because it was the right thing to do. That's the kind of man Robin is," Duncan said, rising to his feet.

"Just one of the reasons why I love him," Edwin said.

Duncan held out his hand and helped Edwin up.

"Your mother is more than her actions," Eva said. "More than her illness. She was a wife, an artist, a woman. You said before you were worried about how your father would be remembered. Don't you want to have some say over how your mother is?"

Chapter Thirty-Six

Robin fiddled with the buttons of his rough linen trousers. His square, meaty fingers always made the job a little tricky. From the moment they had woken, his father had been doing his best to convince him to join him on a raid.

"Oh, come with us, boy—see what it's like to live a truly free life!"

"I'll do no such thing," Robin said, crossing his arms. "I told you, I'm no pirate."

His father was standing shirtless in front of a mirror, shaving with a discoloured straight razor which he washed in a bowl of water. He had more tattoos than just the one on his behind. His broad back was slathered with sea serpents, ships and exotic symbols Robin had never seen before.

"Do you want this when I'm done?" his father asked. "You're lookin' a little unkempt."

"Says the scruffy freebooter," Robin said.

Nonetheless, he looked in the mirror and ran his hand across his chin. It had been almost two weeks since his last shave and his normally smooth skin was covered with dense, snowy hair.

"It weren't so white last time I grew it. I think I'll leave it, though," he said, eyeing the partially rusted razor. "No tellin' what damage I might do with that thing."

"Suit yourself," his father said. "But the beard ages you."

"Thanks, Dad."

Robin had worn a beard for most of his life, right up until his relationship with Duncan ended, though it had been more straw-coloured back then. At the time, he'd felt the need for a change. He couldn't express why, exactly, but it had resulted in him taking off his beard late one night in a fit of pique. It was as though he couldn't bear to be that person any more—the one whose love had been rejected, the one whose pride had been crushed. He donned his cap while his father rummaged under the bed and lifted out a box. Inside were two muskets.

"Now 'ang on," Robin said. "What are those for?"

His father held up a pistol and checked the flint. "Thought I might get some grouse shootin' in this afternoon," he said. "What do you think they're for?"

"I'm not goin' to let you shoot anyone."

"Then you'll have to come along and keep an eye on me, won't you?" his father said, grabbing a coarse linen shirt and his lime waistcoat. "Come on, we're late."

Robin followed his father and Tommy to the floating jetties along the inner circle of Driftwood. A chill ran down his spine when he thought about poor *Bucca's Call*, lying fathoms below on the sea bed. He'd dreamt about her sinking more than once and each time he'd woken up drenched in sweat. Reluctantly, he joined his father aboard the *Mortal Grace*.

The anchors were raised and the pirate fleet was underway. The *Mortal Grace* and her two usual consorts—the *Prospero In Exile* and the *Ivy*—led the way, with the *Skinless Hand*, the *Courteous Victory* and the *Storm Over Snow* following. Six vessels in all, with Red Jim's *Pride of Ithaca* remaining behind with the three other ships. Captain Gulabahaar strode the deck of her ship, barking orders. Crew climbed rigging and tended to cannons. Everything had to be ready.

In her cabin, Captain Gulabahaar went over the plan again. The gold they were after would be held on the most heavily armed ship. The plan was to approach under the Spanish flag, then when they were close enough, they'd raise the black. It had been many years since Robin had been on a ship that size and he helped where he could.

The crew were wary, at first, but he quickly proved his worth. While he had at least ten years on the youngest of them, he was the strongest by far. He heaved ropes with ease, fetched barrels as if they weighed no more than pillows and stacked shot for the cannons. Sadly, it was there his clumsy hands let him down. He spent as much time chasing an errant ball rolling across the deck as he did actually stacking them. He'd like to have blamed his scarred left hand but the simple fact was he was no better coordinated before it had been injured.

It was hours before they reached their destination, whereupon crewmen scanned the horizon through spyglasses. Captain Gulabahaar's brow was knotted, her eyes sharp. In the north, the skies darkened.

"There's a storm coming," she said.

"Captain! Sails!" A crewman in the rigging waved frantically to her, pointing to the horizon. She turned her glass to the target ships.

"Take us towards them, nice and steady," she said. "We don't want to panic them yet."

As the fleet drew closer, they noticed something odd. Rather than the heavily armed vessels they had expected, the targets looked like nothing more than typical merchant ships.

"It's a trick," Robin's father said. "Sometimes they'll use less obvious craft so they're not as much of a mark."

"This is it!" Captain Gulabahaar said, springing into action. "Trim the sails! Signal the fleet! Fly the black!"

The whole crew raced to their positions and hoisted the Skull and Cogs. The black flag with its white, clockwork skull flapped furiously in the winds, straining to be free, like an angry dog on a leash. Within moments the entire pirate fleet was bearing down on their target—three schooners, two of which were sitting low in the water.

"They're the ones we want," Captain Gulabahaar said. "Fire the warning shots."

From the gun ports below, the *Mortal Grace's* cannons fired high over the other ships.

"Signal them to surrender," Captain Gulabahaar said.

A crewwoman lifted some small flags and made the signal. Either they'd return fire or they'd come to a stop. Everyone on deck held their breath. Everyone except the captain. Robin was certain she knew what the outcome would be before even their targets did. The sails of all three ships dropped.

"Bring us in," she said.

The *Mortal Grace* pulled up close to the lead ship. Hooks were thrown to stop them from sailing away. Planks were drawn out and set in place, and the boarding began. Hollering at the tops of their voices and with cutlasses drawn, the pirates of Driftwood swarmed onto the deck of the captured vessel. Robin remained behind. His father thrust one of his muskets into his hand.

"Absolutely not," Robin said.

"I told you already," his father said, "sooner or later, everyone has to do their bit. Even you."

"And I will. But not like this."

Robin set the musket on a barrel. Whatever happened, he would never shoot at someone. The very idea made his blood run cold. His father squared up to him, face red, eyes narrow. Robin braced himself for a dressing-down, but instead his father just shook his head and boarded the other vessel.

The captain of the captured vessel stood, his hands raised. His crew followed suit. Robin took a spyglass and checked the other ships. Sure enough, all had surrendered peaceably. The plank wobbled under his weight as he carefully crossed to the captured ship. One of the captured crew stared at him, wide-eyed, before dropping to his knees and begging not to be harmed. Before Robin could answer, his father shouted at him.

"With me. Now."

The deck below was dark and cramped, and both men had to duck. Robin found a striker-lantern and turned the key to spark it into life. He held it up as they walked.

"I thought the skull and cogs were the flag of Driftwood," Robin said.

"It were hers first. You don't look pleased," his father said.

"You've turned me into a pirate," Robin said. "But I won't stand by and let you 'urt anyone."

"Look around you," he said, laughing. "We are a pirate fleet! Armed to the teeth and with experience beyond measure! Did you think anyone were goin' to give us trouble? And you're forgettin', we sail with Captain Gulabahaar! She's known in these waters. Feared. More often than not, the mere sight of the skull and cogs flappin' in the breeze is enough to quell any resistance."

Robin had heard plenty of stories of ships surrendering at the sight of a pirate flag, though he'd never really believed it.

"It's not in our interest to go in, all guns blazin'," his father said. "Fewer battles means fewer crew lost, so fewer to be replaced."

"What's she done to earn such notoriety?"

"It's not what she's done," his father said. "It's what people think she's done. Out here actions fade, but stories? Stories get passed from crew to crew, from ship to ship, port to port. Stories take on a life of their own. Stories last forever. Tell enough tales of a fearsome Indian captain slicin' off noses and ears with her magical ribbon sword and soon you don't have to do so much as load a musket to take a ship."

Without warning, there came a scrape of boots on wood and a flash of metal as two merchant crewmen jumped out from behind a crate at them, knives in hand. Robin balled his fist and struck one on the jaw while his father took aim at the other and fired. In the cramped conditions below deck, the noise was a deafening thunderclap. The man fell dead.

"Dad! No!"

The look on his father's face was ferocious. His teeth were bared, his breathing heavy as he quickly took the stock of his musket to the other man's head and sent him tumbling to the deck. He went to strike him again, but Robin grabbed his arm.

"Enough, Dad. He's down."

After a moment, his father calmed and took a pouch of gunpowder from his belt to refill his musket. "There are always exceptions."

The crewman lay insensible. Other pirates, drawn by the gunfire, came and took him up to the rest of his crew. Robin and his father continued downwards into the hold, meeting no more resistance. They soon found themselves faced with stacks upon stacks of crates. Robin's father rubbed his hands with glee before tearing the lid off the nearest box. His excitement was short lived. He opened the next crate, and the next.

"Gulabahaar isn't going to like this," he said.

Back on the weather deck, his father took Captain Gulabahaar aside and whispered to her. Robin could see the growing unease on her face. Her pirates were becoming anxious. They held the crew of the ship at gunpoint. A wrong move now could spark further violence. She drew her ribbon sword and marched over to the merchant captain.

"Where is the gold?" she asked. "Tell me before my urumi blade claims your head!" She cracked the sword by his side.

The captain swallowed hard and began to sweat. "What gold?"

The next hour was spent unloading the contents of all three captured ships. Crate upon crate of iron goods. The ships weren't coming from the colonies, laden with gold, they were coming from an ironworks with holds full of gates, railings, stoves and various other items destined for the continent. Captain Gulabahaar was furious but couldn't return empty-handed.

As the last of the crates was being loaded, a cry went up from a spotter. "Sails! Looks like pirate hunters!"

The pirates scrambled to be away from the merchant ships and got underway before the hunters approached but they were closing fast.

"Why didn't we spot them sooner?" Robin's father asked.

"The storm," Captain Gulabahaar said. "It hid them from view."

The pirates were underway and it wasn't long before they were under fire. Cannonballs whirred overhead. Robin ducked for cover. The *Courteous Victory* was already aflame and put up almost no resistance. The hunters made short work of it.

"No!" Captain Gulabahaar shouted. "I will not let you take us!"

"Get below!" his father said. "Help with the cannons!"

Robin did as he was ordered but he wasn't built for the confined spaces below decks and he stooped as he walked. He found a space in a corner where he wasn't causing too much of an obstruction though he still took up entirely too much room. It was already stiflingly hot and difficult to breathe and the deck was filling up with smoke. He quickly fell into a pattern of helping the nearest cannon crew. Time after time, he lifted shot and passed it to the nearest gunner.

After the battle had raged for an hour or more, he lifted a shot which slipped from his grasp and rolled away across the deck. "Ah, stupid, useless 'ands," he said.

He chased after it, ducking as he went but still bumping his head off the beams above him. His cap stopped him from doing any damage to the bald skin of his scalp. In a flash and with a thunderous boom, the hull where he had been sitting exploded inwards, knocking Robin off his feet. The cannon crew he'd been helping were blown clear across the deck. The cannon itself slid backwards, knocking into a crewwoman.

His ears ringing, Robin checked on his crewmates. Only one survived. He dragged her to one side, to a relatively safe corner, then he returned to his cannon. The previously small gun port was now a gaping hole in the hull. In the distance, hunter cannons shredded the hull of the *Storm Over Snow*. She was taking on water and sinking fast. The *Mortal Grace* could easily be next.

He heaved the heavy cannon back into position, lifted another cannonball and dropped it into the muzzle. He aimed at the lead ship and paused. He was about to fire on another vessel. And not just any vessel, but a Chase Trading Company one. Could he actually do it? Had he slipped so far? How could he ever face Eva again, knowing he'd attacked one of her ships?

But then what choice was there? He couldn't exactly swim over there and explain his situation. He was fighting for his life, the life of his crewmates, the life of his father. He'd been manipulated into joining the venture, he realised. He doubted his father knew what was going to happen, but he nonetheless ensured Robin would be on board the *Mortal Grace* for the raid.

Cursing his father's name, Robin touched the linstock to the priming hole and fired. The ball whirred through the air and plopped harmlessly into the ocean, well short of its target. He reloaded the cannon with chain shot, adjusted his aim and fired again. The cannonballs, joined together with a thick chain, whirled through the air, spinning viciously until they connected with the mainmast of the attacking ship, slicing straight through it. The mast split in two and toppled into the sea. A great cheer went up from the pirates and the firing gradually tapered off. Apparently the other pirate hunters were less confident about their chances without their lead ship.

Robin, his ears still ringing from the cannon fire, emerged onto the top deck with stiff neck, burning joints, and a face covered with soot. He carried the injured gunner who had survived the attack on the cannon port and brought her to some pirates who were tending to the crew's wounds. He received a few slaps on the back from other gunners, congratulating him on his skilful shot. Word spread quickly on a ship, even in the heat of battle. He staggered around the weather deck until he found his father sprawled motionless against a barrel, and for a moment Robin's heart stopped.

"We got away," his father said. His eyes were barely open and he was breathing heavily.

Robin slumped beside him, drinking grog from a small cask. Not for the first time, he wished he were aboard *Bucca's Call*. He could still feel his hand on her mast, the wood smooth under his touch. Every line, every curve, was etched into his memory. He could have sailed her with his eyes closed. Aboard *Bucca* was the one place in all the world where Robin had never felt out of place. Where he wasn't knocking something over or dropping something. Where he wasn't in the way. He missed that. He missed her. Losing her was the end of an era. When he returned to Blashy Cove, he'd be starting a new life, with new responsibilities. A new future beckoned.

He closed his eyes and breathed deeply. The air was briny and fresh, it filled his lungs, his entire being. For a time it even made him forget the pain in his hand.

"Penny for your thoughts, cap'n," his father said.

"I'm no captain," Robin said. "Never were."

"You were the skipper of *Bucca*, weren't you?"

"I suppose so, but I could never quite bring myself to use the title. There's only one Captain Shipp."

His father smiled and budged up against Robin's shoulder.

"I'm goin' to see if any of the Driftwood ships are plannin' to head north soon," Robin said. "Maybe they'll take me with them."

"Oh."

"It's time, Dad. I've been away too long as it is. I've been thinkin' about what you said, about 'ow I oughta be lookin' to the future. You were absolutely right. I should be 'ome, with Edwin. I needed to see you, one last time, to finally get some answers. I 'ave everythin' I need to be 'appy. And, *Bucca*, well, she'll always be close to my 'eart." Robin tapped his chest and winced. The tattoo still hadn't fully healed.

"What will you do without her?"

"George offered me the Moth & Moon. To take over runnin' it when 'e, you know, passes."

"Who? Oh, little Georgie Reed? Why'd he offer it to you?"

"'E's a good friend. And 'e never 'ad a family of 'is own."

"Has he thought this through?"

"What do you mean?"

"Well, look at you, Robin," his father said, patting Robin's belly and laughing. "Will you even fit behind the bar?"

"Just about..." Robin said as he slapped his father's hand away.

"Well, well. I can't believe it. The Moth & Moon in the Shipp family."

Robin rubbed the palm of his scarred hand. It helped ease the pain. "Don't get too excited, I turned him down. I'd probably smash every glass in the place within a month, but maybe whoever 'e gave it to instead will take me on. There's always work needs doin' around the place. I could be, I dunno, an odd-job man or somethin'. I need to make a change. Is there any point in tryin' to convince you to come back with me?"

His father sighed. "I've been away from the island for far longer than I ever lived there. What would I even do in Blashy Cove? Sit around tellin' stories of the high seas? Another withered old fisherman without a purpose, gatherin' dust in a corner of the Moth?"

"Would it be so bad?" Robin asked. "A roof over your head, a full belly, a warm bed?"

"After today, it does sound nice, I must admit," his father said.

He was quiet for a spell. About them, the crew took stock of the damage, assessed their loses.

"Can you forgive me?" he asked. "You know, for not comin' back? For leavin' you alone?"

Robin tipped his cap back and tugged on his little earlobe. "I've been givin' it a lot of thought, actually. I wish you'd come 'ome back then, but I know why you didn't. I don't know if you did the right thing, but we can't change the past, can we? It's done. For better or worse, it made me the man I am."

"I'm takin' that as a yes. Oh, before I forget, I have somethin' for you." He reached into the pocket of his tattered lime-green waistcoat and drew out a silver object. Robin turned it over in his hands. It flashed where it caught the sunlight.

"My coin 'older!" Robin said. "'Ow'd you get it back?"

"Pinched it, of course," his father said. "It's empty, but I can promise you, it's the way I found it."

He held his hands up to demonstrate his innocence. Robin didn't entirely believe him. "Who took it?"

"Fausto."

"Giss'on! The bloomin' cheek of 'im. After I 'elped 'im with 'is chickens too."

"I know it's been tough," his father said, "but I'm glad you came here. I'm...proud of how you turned out, of how you survived. I..."

"I love you, too, Dad."

"Ah, you soppy old tuss, who said anything about love? I'm only tryin' to—"

Robin hugged him tightly. "Come on, old man, just say it."

"Ah, gerroff me!" his father said, laughing. "You know I love you, you big oaf."

"I know," Robin said without letting go. "I know. So, what happens now?"

"We can't go straight back to Driftwood in case we're followed," his father said. "But once we're back, I'll make arrangements and come back to the island with you."

"You were so eager this mornin', full o' talk about livin' free. What's changed?"

"All of this, it can't go on forever, I suppose. We nearly didn't make it this time. The world is getting smaller every day. The navy, the C.T.C.: they're growing larger, stronger— Oh, we can bring Tommy with us! He'd love to see the island properly. Not just from the deck of a ship."

"Might be best if we don't tell people who he is," Robin said. "The time he came to attack the village is a bit of a local legend now. George Reed is goin' to dive 'eadfirst into Tommy's writin's. A whole 'istory of pirates? All them stories and legends? We'll not see 'im for weeks! I can't believe it. My dad's goin' to be at my 'andfastin'.'"

"Assumin' I approve of this Edwin, of course. Assumin' he's good enough for you."

"And assumin' Morwenner doesn't strangle you first."

His father laughed and nudged against his shoulder. Robin's heart lifted at the notion of returning home with him, of reuniting his parents after forty years apart. His mum would be angry at first, of course, but in time she'd come round—he was sure of it. Only a year or so ago Robin had thought himself an orphan, all alone in the world. Soon, he'd have his parents, a husband, and a family of his own. He closed his eyes and became engulfed in a great calm.

"I am told you landed the shot that broke their mast," Captain Gulabahaar said.

She had approached from behind, looking weary. She leaned against a barrel, took the cask from Robin, and drank deep.

"You slowed them down enough for us to escape. If you had not been here..."

Robin's sense of calm was quickly shattered. "What if I 'urt someone on the mast?" he asked. "What if I—"

"You did not," Captain Gulabahaar said. "The mast was unmanned. They had every able body operating the guns. I saw it all. Do not worry, son of Barrow. You are not a killer today."

Robin leaned his head back and breathed a sigh of relief. He wanted nothing more than to have Edwin's arms wrapped round him in bed. Every bone in his body ached, every joint was ablaze.

"We lost some good people today," Captain Gulabahaar said.

Robin had seen a somewhat callous attitude towards death at sea from his father and a cavalier attitude from other pirates, but he believed Captain Gulabahaar truly regretted the loss of her crewmembers.

"We knew it were only a matter of time before the Chase Tradin' Company replenished the forces it lost to the Great Leveller," his father said. "Like it or not, the C.T.C. is the future of these waters. They will come for us. Sooner or later, they'll come for us all."

"And we will fight them," Captain Gulabahaar said. "To our last breath."

"You're howlin' into the wind," his father said. "Our time is endin'. The future is comin' and its teeth are so sharp."

"Before," she said to Robin, "you spoke of a country house with a great glass dining room. I knew of such a house once. I grew up in one, in Goa. Do you know where that is?"

"Um, it's in India, isn't it?"

"I can barely recall it," she said. "My mother left my father when I was very young, but I do remember it was so very warm in the summer. The sunlight would stream through the glass wall, through the ceiling. It had a pattern in the ironwork that would cast a shadow on the floor, across the table. In my mind, it looks like the symbol of the C.T.C.: a ship's wheel with a letter C inside. I suppose over time I have gotten it mixed up with the memory of the real thing. I see their hateful mark everywhere. It is on the goods we take, on the vessels that hunt us, even in my dreams..."

"It really were a ship's wheel," Robin said. "In the glass wall."

His father frowned at him.

"How could you possibly know?" Captain Gulabahaar asked.

"Because I've been in the 'ouse you're talkin' about," Robin said quietly. "Last winter. But it weren't in India; it were on Blackrabbit Island. It were called Chase Manor then, and it's the Wolfe-Chase Asylum now. The glass dinin' room is called Moonwatch. I 'ad dinner there. There's a portrait hangin' in it of a little Indian girl. Eva's sister, she told me. She were named after a flower. Let me think...Primrose? No. Lily? Daisy! That were it. Daisy."

Captain Gulabahaar drank some more watered-down rum before fixing him with a stare. "Son of Barrow," she said, "do you know what my name means in English?"

Chapter Thirty-Seven

It was Nick's first experience of market day, and he found the hustle and bustle somewhat reminiscent of home. He turned the collar up on his apricot-coloured velvet overcoat and adjusted his cap. He didn't care much for wet weather, though no one around him seemed to mind it too much. Possibly because none of them owned any clothes which could be ruined by the rain, except for Mr. Kind, who appeared to take particular care in his appearance.

Nick was standing with Duncan outside the Moth & Moon as the workers put the finishing touches to the bell tower. Four small sculptures had been installed, one looking in each cardinal direction. A seahorse, a pilchard, a gull, and a moth. Duncan pressed his lips together and sighed.

"It's off centre!" he said, pointing to the belfry.

"So?" Nick said. "It still works, doesn't it?"

"Well, I don't like it!"

Nick just laughed.

"What's so bleddy funny?" Duncan asked.

"You are," Nick said. "Look at you, all puffed up and red in the face." He put his hands on his hips and frowned. "*Well, I don't like it. Grr.*"

"I don't sound like that," Duncan said.

"You need to relax," Nick said, slipping his arm around Duncan's shoulders and kissing him on the forehead. "They did their best. It's not about being absolutely flawless—it's about the community working together for the greater good."

Mr. Henry Bell, May's father, climbed down a ladder and approached, scratching his arm and avoiding eye contact.

"Well, Mr. Hunger," he said, "what do you think?"

Duncan chewed the inside of his cheek and crossed his arms.

"It's perfect, Mr. Bell," he said. "Just perfect."

"See?" Nick said softly as he held open the door of the inn. "It didn't kill you to be nice, did it?"

Duncan sighed again and held his stomach. "It's too early to tell."

Inside the Moth & Moon was a chorus of barking coughs. The infection had passed quickly from the younger and healthier villagers though it had lingered in others. Morwenna Whitewater sat by the fireplace wheezing and hacking most ferociously. Duncan had been growing ever more concerned for her, but Doctor Greenaway had assured him she was in no danger. It did little to assuage Duncan's fears, as the village doctor had been wrong before. Nick was charmed by the concern Duncan showed towards the old woman. It proved Duncan did have a softer side, no matter how much he liked to hide it.

He and Duncan were meeting Vince for lunch, and he steeled himself for the ordeal. After their last encounter, he was a bit more wary of Vince, a bit less trusting. Duncan had sung his praises but there was still a niggling feeling in the back of Nick's mind, an unquiet doubt. He wondered if this Robin person would be the same, if he too had the same innate air of menace about him. He wondered what attracted Duncan to men of their ilk. Nick didn't consider himself to be threatening at all. Schoolchildren were often frightened of him, but they had reason. A child was wont to be afeared of their teacher.

They found Vince lurking under a cobwebbed stairwell and sought out a place to sit. With so many new faces about, their usual booth was occupied so instead they opted for stools at the bar. Duncan chatted to a man with a deep scar running down his face. Mr. Penny, Nick seemed to remember his name was. Now there was a frightening-looking person. At least Vince had the good grace to cover up his injured eye, Mr. Penny's was on show for all to see. The fetching grey-bearded innkeeper, Mr. Reed, coughed and spluttered a little into his sleeve as he brought them their drinks.

"You're sounding much better, George," Duncan said.

"I think the worst of it has passed," he said. "I can finally get back to work properly."

"To your health," Nick said, slamming his tankard against Duncan's. "Will Edwin be joining us?"

"No, he can't get away," Duncan said. "It's his busiest day today."

The crowd ebbed and flowed as patrons brushed past, ordering drinks and being generally a bit rowdy. They ordered food and made small talk about the schoolhouse and the bell tower. Vince hardly spoke at all, just grunting whenever the conversation turned to him. Nick tried desperately to think of something to say to Vince but kept drawing a blank. It was like trying to converse with a statue.

"Should have brought more money with me," Vince said to Duncan. "Going to owe you a fortune soon."

"Did you know we call it money because ancient Romans minted their coins at a temple to the goddess Juno Moneta? Moneta. Monetary. Money," Nick said.

Vince just stared at him, confused. Nick politely excused himself and set off to find the nearest water closet. He took his time, hoping the ground would open up and swallow him before he made it back. It didn't, although he did get lost a couple of times.

"I've been trying to find my way back for about fifteen minutes," he said. "I swear every door in this tavern leads to at least two more..."

"You get used to it," Mr. Reed said from behind the bar.

"You bleddy well don't," Duncan said. "I still get lost if I don't keep my wits about me. We're going to have to find a bell for the tower sooner or later."

"I don't understand why the village won't take Lady Eva up on her offer to pay for one," Nick said.

Duncan was lifting a glass to his lips, and he stopped halfway. "A Blackrabbit bell in the village?"

"On top of the Moth & Moon?" Mr. Reed asked.

"Are you out of your mind?" Mr. Penny asked, even though he wasn't part of the conversation.

Nick felt suddenly surrounded and decided not to pursue the idea any further. Clearly, this was one aspect of village life which was never going to change. "What about the forge, then? Surely they can make one?"

"They're not set up for something so big," Duncan said. "It would cost a fortune. What are you looking for, George?"

"Has anyone seen my pocket watch?" he asked. "I'm sure I left it here."

Assuming the worst, Nick glanced at Vince, then reached into his pocket for his snuff box while Duncan made a joke about Mr. Reed getting absent-minded. His heart dropped. He checked the pocket again, then every other pocket, patting himself all over.

"Fleas?" Duncan said.

"No, it's gone!" Nick said.

"What is?"

"My snuff box! The one Ellery gave me! It's gone!"

"Are you sure you had it?"

"Yes! I always have it!"

"It can't have gone far. I'll help you look," Duncan said, hopping off his stool. "Vince, step back, let me check."

Vince moved his claret overcoat out of the way and a glint of metal caught Duncan's eye.

"What's that?" he asked, pointing.

"What's what?" Vince asked.

"In your coat pocket, what is it?"

Vince reached in and pulled out a small snuff box.

"What are you doing with that?" Duncan asked.

Vince said nothing; he merely frowned. Mr. Penny grabbed Vince's coat before he could stop him. He rummaged through the pockets, pulling out Mr. Reed's pocket watch.

"Vince?" Duncan asked.

Vince was practically snarling. His wolflike eye was wide and fierce, his meat-pie hands clenched tightly and held ready to pummel. Nick backed away. The look on Vince's face was like nothing he'd ever seen before.

"*Didn't take those things,*" Vince roared, causing Nick to jump. "Never seen them before."

He slammed his fist on the counter, and the tavern fell silent.

"What about all the other things that have gone missing lately?" asked Mr. Penny. "Mrs. Bell's jewellery? Mr. Trease's statuette? The money from the Bounsell's house? Do you have them too?"

"No idea what you're talking about. Wasn't me," Vince said.

Duncan's eyes darted around the room, assessing who was likely to make the first move. Vince was like a cornered animal, ready to strike. It was Mr. Reed who put his hands up and spoke first.

"Calm down, everyone, please," he said. "I'm sure there's an explanation."

"Search him!" came a voice from the crowd.

Jeers of approval followed. Nick didn't know Vince very well, but he suspected he wouldn't be too pleased about being inspected.

"Try it," Vince said, his voice low, like thunder. "See what happens."

"I think," Mr. Reed said, "in order to allay concerns, it would be best if we checked your possessions, Mr. Knight. Will you consent?"

"He will," Duncan said. "Won't you, Vince? Won't you do your best to cooperate and alleviate the concerns of the village folk?"

Vince bristled under the glare of the public.

Vince barged through the doors and stormed out of the tavern, pursued by a gang of villagers. He stood there, leaning on his cane, spittle shooting from his mouth as he roared his innocence.

"*Damn you all!*" he bellowed at the top of his voice.

"They were right about you all along!" Duncan shouted after him. "We never should have trusted you!"

In a fury, he charged through the village's narrow cobbled streets, making for the headland. The storm clouds, so heavy all day, broke once more and rain fell in wide sheets. He marched along World's End Walk until he reached the partially uprooted tree standing alone on the grassy promontory. He slammed his fists into the trunk of the Wishing Tree and roared.

"Well, isn't this a picture," came a voice from behind.

Vince would know the nasally voice anywhere, and he spun on his heels to face his tormentor.

"Penhallow," he said.

"The great Invincible Knight," Penhallow said, "reduced to this. No friends. No family. No gang. No nothing."

Penhallow was pasty and wiry, in want of half a finger on one hand. Rain dripped from his shabby woollen tricorn. He moved closer, his attack dog snarling and straining against his leash. Palk—hulking, youthful, dark-haired and dark-eyed—was beside him now, flexing his muscles, popping his joints. Penhallow pointed his knife towards Vince's face.

"Been on the island the whole time, haven't you?" Vince asked. "Stole those things. Planted them in my pockets. Your dog savaged those chickens."

"We followed you," Palk said. "After we went and picked up Crabmeat, here." He bent to scratch the dog behind the ear. The animal licked its foaming mouth and barked.

"You remember Crabmeat, don't you?" Penhallow asked. "He remembers you. Remembers how you treated him. Always kicking at him."

"Because you kept trying to set him on me."

"We've been watching you the whole time. Waiting. You don't know how my heart sang when I spotted that eyepatch," Penhallow said, pointing. "I didn't know we'd done so much damage when we jumped you in the cottage at the asylum. We've taken your peace of mind, your friends... We've taken everything from you, Vince," Penhallow said. "Well, almost everything. Let's see what we can do about relieving you of your other eye, yeah?"

"Welcome to try," Vince said. "Just the two of you this time, is it? Where are the rest? Still recovering from your last attempt on my life? Nursing broken bones? Come closer. You can join them."

Crabmeat furiously pawed at the soft ground.

"Gonna make you wish you'd left me alone," Vince said, dropping his cane and adopting his boxing pose.

"And why should we leave you alone, exactly?" Penhallow said. "Why should you know the peace and acceptance of a life in this village? What right have you, after all you've done?"

"What right have you to stop me? Who appointed you as my tormentors?"

"Someone has to make sure you get what you deserve. What right has a traitor to such a life?"

"A traitor, am I? For wanting a different life?"

"For turning your back on us!" Palk said. "On Mr. Mudge."

"Even if he hadn't ended up in gaol, Mudge would never have repaid your loyalty."

"Of course he bleddy wouldn't; we're not fools!" Penhallow said. "We know we had to take what we wanted. He used us and we used him, but at least we didn't turn on him like you did!"

"For years, you two tried to get rid of me," Vince said. "Well, you got your wish. Port Knot is free of me. So why aren't you there taking over where I left off? The rest of the gangs are still there. Why aren't you in charge? Tell you why. Because you're weak. The gangs will no more listen to you than a dog in the street."

Crabmeat barked louder, straining his leash and Penhallow's arm.

"You left everything in tatters!" Palk said.

"Mudge did that," Vince said. "Got greedy. Tried to use us to help him take over the whole island. But his failure created opportunity. With him and me out of the picture, the town was yours. If you were half the men you think you are, you'd have tightened your grip over the gangs. Kept them in line. But you ran. You hid. Like cowards. Now you're here, sneaking around a fishing village. Like frightened little mice. Hiding in bushes when Port Knot is being ripped in half by warring factions who used to be under my thumb. Not Mudge's. Mine. Now all you have left is me. You're obsessed. Both of you. You might be the quiet one, Palk. You might like to think of yourself as the deep thinker. But you're every bit as bad as him. Look at you. Strong as an ox. And don't you love how scared you make people? Don't you love the power you have over weaker folk?"

"Are you so different?" Palk asked. "Don't you use your size to intimidate?"

"You're educated," Vince said. "From a good family. You had chances the rest of us never did. Chances we could only dream of. Chances you squandered. You've got intelligence, more than him. Certainly more than me. You've done nothing with it. What was this to you? A game? See how far you could get in the underworld? Well, you could be at the top right now. Instead you're here. Standing in the mud. About to have the life beaten out of you. Here, because you're afraid to do anything without his say-so. He's pathetic but you. *Tsk*. You're a disgrace, Hickory Palk."

"The joy of a game isn't solely in the win," Palk said. "It's in *how* you win."

The hatred on Palk's face was plain to see. It was all true, of course. Palk was from a good family—he could have been anything but he had a penchant for violence. He revelled in it and in the freedom of servitude to Penhallow. He didn't have to think for himself, and it was exactly how Palk liked it. It had suited Vince in the past, as well. He'd gladly used Palk's talents for his own gain. He knew he'd feel guilty later but he couldn't afford to be distracted now.

"Thought about what happens once you do away with me?" Vince asked. "Going back to Port Knot, are you? Going to enter the fray? The watchmen will be waiting for you as well, let's not forget. Brave enough to face them this time, are you? Or will you hide again?"

"And how was it we came to be wanted men?" Penhallow asked. "How was it the watchmen knew of our involvement in Mr. Mudge's plans?"

"The council asked questions. I answered."

"And there it is," Penhallow said. "You won't even try to hide your treachery. You only cared about yourself. You've no loyalty, Vince. You turned your back on all of us. It's fitting you should die here, alone."

"Who said I was alone?"

A sharp crack of wood split the night air as Palk tumbled to the ground with a heavy thud. Penhallow turned to see a gang of villagers standing over him, holding daggers, various metal tools and substantial planks of wood. One of which had been broken over Palk's head.

"Drop the knife," Edwin said.

Penhallow looked at the knife in his right hand and the leash in the left. He opened his left hand.

"Oops," he said.

Crabmeat ran full tilt towards Vince, teeth bared, foamy saliva flicking through the air. His paws kicked up mud as he ran. Lightning flashed. The rain made it difficult to see. The dog leapt at Vince's chest. Vince clicked his fingers twice and pointed at the ground.

"Sit," he said.

Crabmeat obeyed, sitting on the mucky grass with his tail wagging as Vince scratched behind his ears and pet his head. Penhallow was apoplectic. He shouted over and over again to Crabmeat, but the dog refused to obey him.

"Got tired of you trying to set him on me," Vince said. "Every chance I got, I fed him scraps of meat. Trained him when you weren't about. No wonder he's excited to see me. Planned to have him rip your throat out one day. You wanted to run the gangs? You can't even keep the loyalty of a dog."

Penhallow yelled, driving forward with his knife. Vince took his cane, pulled at the octopus-shaped handle and drew the blade hidden within. He blocked Penhallow's thrust, then swiped hard at him. The blade swished through the air, flicking raindrops as it went. He swiped again and again, missing his mark every time. He'd never been much of a swordsman, even before he'd lost an eye.

Penhallow ducked and dodged, using his long dagger to fend off Vince's attack. With one last, powerful jab, Vince lunged forward, slipping in the mud. Penhallow turned his dagger upwards, aiming directly for Vince's heart. Vince knocked the knife easily from his hand and grabbed Penhallow's thin neck, digging his thumbnail into the skin.

He shoved him against the trunk of the tree. Hot blood trickled over Penhallow's throat and inside his shirt.

"Not the first time I've had you by the neck," he said, "but it'll be the last."

"You're a monster, Vince. You always have been, and you always will be."

"How right you are," Vince said as he held up his blade and aimed it at Penhallow's eye.

"Vince!" Duncan said, his voice was barely audible above the storm. "Don't. Don't hurt him. He's beaten. He's done."

Vince leaned in close, tightening his grip. "What's one more?"

"Everything you said about changing will have been a lie," Duncan said. "You'll be a killer. Nothing more. It'll be who you are. You really will be ruined."

"Doesn't matter what you do to us," Penhallow said. "There'll be others. You made plenty of enemies over the years. You'll never know peace."

Vince jabbed his dagger deep into the trunk beside Penhallow's head, then he placed both hands around the man's throat.

"I know what he's done," Duncan said. "I know what he is. But you wanted to change. You wanted to be better than you were. This is your chance."

Vince leaned in so close Penhallow must have thought he was going to bite his nose off, so he tried to turn away, shrieking. Instead, Vince gave him a mighty slap in the face and dropped him to the muddy ground.

"Oww! Dammit..." Penhallow said as he rubbed his clicking jaw.

Penhallow and Palk were marched down to the inn, where some thick rope was used to tie them to chairs. Crabmeat lay by the fireplace, messily slurping water from a bowl.

"So, what happens now?" Penhallow asked. "A sham trial and imprisonment? There's no gaol we can't escape from."

"Doesn't matter," George Reed said. "We don't have any prisons here."

Palk's face dropped.

"Not...*hanging*..." he said.

"I know we're only simple island folk," Mr. Penny said. "But we're not savages."

"Leave it to me," Vince said. "They'll be taken care of."

"You're not... You're not going to kill them?" asked Nick.

"Course not," Vince said. "They're wanted men on Blackrabbit. Going to hand them over to Port Knot's watchmen."

"Oh. Good."

"Really thought I was going to do away with them?" Vince asked.

"I mean, you do have a reputation..." Nick said.

"That was before," he said, turning to Duncan. "When I came here, I was...broken. In more ways than one."

"Wait, stop," Penhallow said. "This is... Weren't you all shouting at him for stealing your belongings not ten minutes ago?"

"Oh, no," Duncan said. "It was all a ruse."

"Knew something was up when they found those things on me," Vince said. "Duncan believed me. So did Mr. Reed."

"I told them about the sailboat on Porthsophie beach," Mr. Penny said. "And the dog prints in the sand. I knew something was afoot."

"Put two and two together," Vince said. "Realised you pair must have followed me here."

"I have to say, sneaking around the island? Stealing things? Planting them on Vince without anyone noticing? I didn't think you had it in you," Duncan said.

"Palk's idea, no doubt," Vince said. "The only one with brains. Penhallow was a master pickpocket in his day."

"With market day being so busy, you could have moved about the inn without drawing any attention," Duncan said. "I'll wager you had plenty of opportunities to drop the things into Vince's pockets."

"Duncan suggested everyone play along," Vince said. "Pretend to be mad at me. To see what you'd do next."

"I didn't think you'd show yourselves so quickly, mind," Duncan said. "I'm glad you did though. I'm not sure how long we could have kept the pretence up. Where are the rest of the things you stole? Mr. Trease's bucca statuette? The Bounsell's money?"

"I put them under Vince's bedding in your house," Penhallow said.

"Why?"

"Extra insurance," Palk said. "We couldn't be certain you'd find the things Penallow put in Vince's pockets. We wanted to make absolutely certain you'd turn on him."

"Very thorough," Vince said.

Palk fixed him with a stare. "All part of the game," he said.

A few hours later, Vince sat with a glass of whiskey in his hand.

"It's your brother's drink of choice, too, you know," said Morwenna Whitewater.

She lowered herself carefully onto a chair next to him and adjusted her red shawl about her shoulders. Vince was unsure of what to say. She was Robin's mother but he had hardly spoken to her during his time in the village. They shared no real connection. More than once she'd looked at him funny, those sharp eyes of hers cutting right through him.

"It hasn't been easy for me, having you here these past few weeks," she said. "You're a lot more like your father than Robin is. But you're not a bad sort, honestly. You just need someone in your life who will help you keep a level head. Someone who'll stop you being too much of a Shipp."

The unsolicited advice surprised him. She wasn't wrong, mind you. He couldn't honestly say what he would have done to Penhallow if Duncan hadn't been there.

"Dad was like me?" he asked.

"Very much so. Quick to anger, quick with his fists. Sad inside." Her voice was weak and wheezing slightly.

Vince's heavy brow knotted. "What makes you think I'm sad inside?"

"Oh, Vince," she said with a soft, kind laugh. "It's written in your eyes. Well, eye."

She was a lot like his own mother in some ways. Not just in appearance but something in the way she spoke, in the way she saw through to the core of a person. George Reed arrived with a tray of empty tankards and glasses. He wiped the table in front of them.

"Wanted to say, um, thank you, Mr. Reed," Vince said. "For before. Thought you all would turn on me. Didn't think you'd listen. Wouldn't have happened like that back home in Port Knot."

"There was a time when we probably wouldn't have," said Mr. Reed. "But that was before. When we all found out your father had nothing to do with the death of Barnabas Whitewater, it shook the village to its core.

I'm sure you've heard about the way Robin used to be treated round here. It's a source of communal embarrassment. It wasn't right, and it wasn't fair, and nobody wants to make the same mistake again."

"You should be resting," Mrs. Whitewater said to him.

"I could say the same to you."

"It will take more than a tickle in the throat to stop me. You've been overdoing it. Clearing out those rooms for the museum must have been a lot of effort."

"I didn't do it alone. And it was all worth it," he said. "In the end."

Vince downed the glass of whiskey and made his way to the pier. Penhallow and Palk sat in Mr. Penny's boat with their hands tied. Mr. Penny and Mr. Kind sat behind them, hands clasped tightly to their swords. Crabmeat sat facing the prisoners and barked when he saw Vince. Penhallow sighed and shook his head.

"Are you sure I can't change your mind?" Duncan asked.

"It's for the best," Vince said. "Trouble follows me wherever I go. Got lucky this time. But I'll keep in touch. And I'll visit. Thank you. For everything."

"Robin will be so disappointed. I really thought you'd stay."

He turned to take one last look at the village. "Truthfully? So did I."

Chapter Thirty-Eight

The four remaining pirate ships, battered and broken, spent hours following a twisting course back to Driftwood. On board the *Mortal Grace*, Robin went to the hold where he found Captain Gulabahaar examining the spoils of the raid. Iron railings, gates, stoves and other commercial items, all freshly forged and destined for the continent.

"Quite the collection," he said.

"I have no idea how Nasir is going to divvy this up amongst all the crews. Who wants a share of pots and pans?" Captain Gulabahaar asked. "Not quite the gold coins we had been hoping for."

"No, just goods belongin' to a small company."

The words came out more harshly than he'd intended, and he regretted saying them. Though he towered over her, she was the pirate queen for good reason. Her hand rarely wandered far from the stingray-shaped hilt of her sword.

"Judgement, son of Barrow?" she asked. "I am sure the company was insured; they will suffer no hardship for its loss."

"And the crew of the ships carryin' it?"

"Unharmed," she said, "for the most part. They should have known better than to put up a fight."

He'd never forget the look of shock on the crewman's face as his father's musket fired. She squinted at him, as if trying to see inside his heart.

"Are you trying to assuage your guilt for having been part of the raid?" she asked.

Robin thrust his hands into his pockets and shrugged. "Maybe," he said. "I just stood by and watched. I didn't even try to stop you."

She laughed, a little too enthusiastically for the good of his pride. "You think you would have been able to?"

"No," he said with a sigh, "but I still should 'ave tried."

She smiled at him then, a warm, genuine smile. "You were coerced and vastly outnumbered. You are a good man, son of Barrow. Do not worry: on this occasion, your hands are clean."

He was rummaging around in the boxes, turning over items, examining the craftsmanship. "Fine work, mind you," he said.

"I do not know what I will do with it all," she said with a sigh. "Especially that." She pointed to a large item in the corner of the hold, easily three or four feet high.

Robin ran his hand across its smooth, cold surface. "Actually," he said, grinning. "I might 'ave an idea."

There came then a frantic scrape of boots and a panicked call from the quartermaster, Mr. Vosper. "Captain," he said. "We're getting close but you need to see this."

Robin followed them up to the weather deck. Driftwood sat in the distance, silent, monolithic, like a bluff thrust from the seafloor.

His father was frowning. "The defences are up," he said.

A cannonball whirred overhead. Robin ducked, reflexively. He was the only one to do so.

"A warning shot from Driftwood," Harry Vosper said. "Have they been overrun?"

Robin's father took his spyglass and inspected the castle. He breathed in sharply, before dropping the glass to the deck. It rolled and became lodged in a scupper. He gripped the gunwale with both hands to steady himself.

"Dad?" Robin asked, picking up the spyglass. "What is it?"

Robin held the glass to his eye. On the battlements of Driftwood a number of pirates had gathered below a mast. Above them, four bodies hung by their necks, hands tied behind their backs. The three pirate captains who had stayed behind and Tommy Oughterlauney, who had pages sticking out from his mouth. Some of his writings. His work detailing the life of the pirates. Robin's stomach lurched.

"Dad, I'm so sorry..." Robin said.

Captain Gulabahaar was watching from a spyglass of her own as one of the pirates stood waving semaphore flags.

"Red Jim is demanding we surrender," she said.

Robin thought his father would explode. He'd never seen him so furious. The veins in his temples throbbed, his face flushed, and he roared so loudly it caused Robin to flinch.

"How *dare* he! The murderin' little... I'll wring his bleddy neck!"

"He's demanding you and I take a longboat over to him," she said.

"I'm comin' too," Robin said. "Don't argue, Dad."

Harry Vosper strenuously objected, but Captain Gulabahaar insisted on going. They were in no position to object to Red Jim's demands. The fleet was exhausted from battle and low on supplies. They could reach land, but what then? Leave Driftwood to Jim? Hardly.

The longboat was lowered, and Robin and his father rowed Captain Gulabahaar through the great gap between the lighthouses and into the floating castle's courtyard. Robin felt tremendously exposed. He kept looking over his shoulder, expecting to see a cloud of gun smoke or hear the booming of a cannon. Instead, they were received at the jetty by a squad of armed pirates, headed by William Longbeard and Sam Pro.

"Don't try anything," Longbeard said. "Please."

Sam Pro took their weapons and they were marched at swordpoint up to Captain Gulabahaar's deck where they found Red Jim lounging on some cushions and playing with a crooked dagger.

"You have already made yourself at home, I see," Captain Gulabahaar said.

"I thought I might as well, since you won't be needing it any longer." He pointed his dagger at Robin. "I don't remember asking for this oaf to come aboard."

Robin's father was eyeing every pirate in the vicinity. "These people, they're not your usual crew, are they?" he asked.

"For the past month or so, I've been replacing my dear old crewmates with pirates a little more amenable to my ideals," Red Jim said. "I told them to keep their heads down; didn't want anyone to recognise them."

Almost every pirate had their hair shaved tight or their face half covered with a scarf. In the vast throng of a busy Driftwood, it didn't seem strange, but when they were all together it was highly suspicious. An entire crew had altered their appearance in order to hide in plain sight. His father flicked the scarf away from one pirate's face.

"I know you," he said. "Maggie Troke. You were part of old Chalke's crew, the one who mutinied against her." He turned to another pirate, a man this time. "And you! Tyrrell! You used to have long hair and a wild beard. You were banished from here a couple of years ago."

"The funny thing about exiling people from a place like this," Red Jim said, "is that it isn't so hard to sneak back in after a while. Especially with a new look and a captain to vouch for you. Just wait a year or two, and half the pirates who were here are dead or imprisoned and a whole new batch has arrived."

He climbed on a table and addressed the crowd. "But it's not all mutineers and exiles!" he said. "Every man and woman here is tired of suffering under Gulabahaar's yoke. And we all think it's time for a change."

A chorus of cheers erupted from the pirates. Robin's skin tingled and he clenched his fists, ready to fight, if need be.

"Suffering," Captain Gulabahaar said. "You call getting an equal share suffering?"

"We don't want the same as everyone else," Red Jim said. "We want more. We want to keep our spoils instead of handing it out to those too weak, too lazy, or too incompetent to get any of their own. I did try to tell you as much on many occasions. You didn't listen. You never listen."

"The lead on the shipment of gold—it came from you didn't it?" Captain Gulabahaar asked.

Red Jim laughed. It was cold and harsh as a winter wave. "Was it not quite what you were expecting? And did you like my little extra surprise? The Chase Trading Company pirate hunters, who may or may not have been tipped off about the raid around the time Barrow here was being sprung from the asylum? It was quite good, I thought. If they sink you, then I win. If you escape and come back here, I kill you myself, and I win."

"You think you can take on an entire pirate fleet?" Robin's father asked. "Driftwood has a lot of cannons but you can't possibly work them all."

"A fleet that's had to fight tooth and nail against hunters? A fleet exhausted from fleeing as quickly as they possibly could? I think I'll manage. And besides, you seem to be a couple of ships light, which changes the odds quite significantly, I'd say. Now, the question is what to do with the three of you?"

"Same as you did with Tommy?" Robin's father asked. "I'll kill you for what you've done to him."

The other pirates grabbed Robin's father and held him back. It took a lot of them.

"Not likely," Red Jim said. "He didn't even put up a fight, the drunken old sop. It's sad, really. Well, more pathetic, to be honest. He was legend in his time. I offered him the same choice I offered the rest. Join me or face the consequences. Such an ignoble end. Ah, well."

"What about the crews of the other ships?" Robin asked. "The ones who stayed behind?"

Red Jim drew his thumb across his own throat. "They're feeding the sharks by now," he said. "They should have pledged themselves to me."

"You spiteful fool," Captain Gulabahaar said. "How much longer do you think we can survive? Every day, the Chase Trading Company grows stronger. We should be standing together, not fighting one another!"

He ignored her and ran his dagger down Robin's chest, over his belly. It snagged in his jumper.

"Let him go," his father said. "He's not part of this."

"Hmmm, true, he's not, but he had the misfortune to be in the wrong place at the wrong time. And I don't like loose ends." He grabbed Robin by the chin and looked him dead in the eye. "You never should have come here, fisherman," he said. "Bring them up to the masts. The rest of you, man the cannons. Oh and boys? Don't forget the ropes."

Chapter Thirty-Nine

The great masts of Driftwood creaked as they turned, their huge sails flapping in the warm breeze. Robin stood close to the edge of the battlement, as he thought of it. He tried not to look down and instead kept his gaze fixed on the horizon.

To his left stood his father, to his right, Captain Gulabahaar. Their hands had been tied behind their backs. William Longbeard and Sam Pro stood with cutlasses at the ready. Three ropes dropped at their feet. Three hangman's nooses. Maggie Troke climbed down from the yard and placed the first noose around Robin's neck. His blood ran cold. He struggled at the ropes around his wrists. High above, the bodies of Tommy Oughterlauney, Captain Nolan and the other two pirate captains swung in the wind. Nearby, Red Jim was peering seaward through a spyglass.

"Signal them to surrender," he said.

Sam Pro lifted some flags and began his semaphore. He stood with arms outstretched, lifting them into different positions.

"You three, step up," Red Jim said.

They hesitated. Maggie Troke pushed Robin's father and he staggered forward. They stood on the gunwale, each between two figureheads, with nothing below them but smooth, metal shields of Driftwood and the roiling sea. Not that they'd get anywhere near it. The ropes around their necks would make sure of it.

Robin was flanked by a pouncing lion and a bearded man armed with a sword and shield. The shield was emblazoned with a crescent moon. It made him think of home, of standing beneath the sign for the Moth & Moon, where he and Edwin shared their first kiss. His stomach lurched and his blood boiled. It was all so unfair. He'd only ever tried to do the right thing and this is where it led—to a violent end a thousand miles from the love of his life, swinging from the end of a rope next to the man who had abandoned him.

His breathing became rapid, shallow. His armpits grew damp. He struggled again at the binding around his wrists. Twisting and turning them. Surely he could loosen them, snap them? Wasn't he big enough? Wasn't he strong enough? He loomed over these pirates, how had they gotten the better of him? Hadn't he always bested anyone who crossed him? It couldn't end here, now. Not like this.

"Wait!" Red Jim said. He took his crooked dagger and approached Robin. He reached up and with the tip, removed Robin's flat cap and put it on his own head.

"No sense in perfectly nice headwear going to waste," he said. "Push them off."

Maggie Troke moved fast but William Longbeard was faster. He shoved her hard against the mast while Sam Pro yanked the prisoners down from the gunwale.

"*What are you doing?*" Red Jim shouted.

Sam cut through the restraints and they quickly scrambled out of the nooses. Maggie Troke sliced at William, slashing his chest and drawing blood. He thrust his sword at her, hammering at her weapon harder and harder. She took one mighty lunge at William who dived out of the way, leaving her to barrel into the raised edge, then over it, thumping onto the wet, slanting walls of Driftwood as she fell. Her screams ended in a splash.

"This has gone far enough, Jim," William said. "You said you wanted a change—you said you wanted fairer governance but these people haven't done a thing to you."

Red Jim reached for his sword but thought better of it and ran instead. He jumped through an open hatch and disappeared into the castle. Sam rummaged in the deep pocket of his tattered overcoat and withdrew a coil of metal which he handed to Captain Gulabahaar.

"My urumi," Captain Gulabahaar said. "Go. Lower the defences."

Sam nodded and ran. Robin thought he appeared rather relieved, as if he were concerned there was a chance Captain Gulabahaar might use her blade on him. She wrapped her flexible sword around her waist, fixing it in place with the stingray-shaped hilt.

"What about you?" Robin asked.

"I am going to have a word with James," she said.

They climbed down the ladders and into Driftwood. A single crew was all it contained, not nearly enough to guard even a tenth of the massive structure. Robin's father battered one pirate viciously, then took his sword and musket.

"Look," Robin said. "The levers, they've all been broken."

Each one had been snapped off, effectively locking the defences in place. A dull boom sounded. Then another. Then another. Robin's father opened the porthole window and slid back a peephole cover in the shield wall.

"Jim is firing on the fleet," he said. "They're going to have to—" He was interrupted by a loud thud on the shield wall. "—fire back."

The whole structure reverberated with the barrage of cannon fire.

"They'll never breach the defences, will they?" Robin asked.

"I've an idea," Robin's father said. "We have to get to my cabin."

Red Jim ran along the walkways until he met a cluster of his crew. "Go up there and finish them off!" he said. "And get those traitors, Longbeard and Pro!"

The pirates dashed off, muskets loaded and cutlasses drawn. Jim found more of his crew manning a battery of cannons. He barked orders, insisting they keep up the pressure on the fleet.

"Captain! Two of the ships are breaking off."

Jim followed the vessels with his spyglass. "They mean to flank us," he said. "They're going to come in from the open side and attack the inner circle."

Driftwood's defences were only on the outer walls. The inner circle, where the ships docked, were unshielded.

"Concentrate all fire on those ships!" he shouted.

Every manned cannon diverted its attention to the sloops which were rushing away from Gulabahaar's fleet. Cannonballs ripped through the air, shredding the crafts' masts and hulls in seconds. Jim's face was red hot with the flush of victory. He was so close to doing it. Ending Gulabahaar's reign and life in the same day. Taking control of Driftwood. Red Jim—the Pirate King. It was all within reach.

The attack continued apace. Plumes of cannon smoke drifted past on the breeze. The walls rattled but held firm. The *Prospero in Exile* took a devastating hit to its hull and began to break apart. The *Skinless Hand* lost both masts in a matter of seconds. Jim's crew cheered and hollered.

Suddenly, the chains which held up the shields furiously raced through their channels. The shields slid down, crashing into the sea, back into their dormant state.

The blood drained from Jim's face. "No. *No!*"

He turned to the broken lever in the wall, then up to the control room. There, standing in the doorway was Barrow. He was smiling down at Jim, brandishing a key in one hand and an axe in the other.

"That's for Tommy, you rotten swine!" Robin's father shouted.

He and Robin had split up from William Longbeard and Sam Pro to retrieve the control room key from his cabin. They had taken an axe to the chains controlling the shields while Longbeard and Sam cleared the jetties for the fleet. The assault from the ships was redoubled. Cannon shot whirred through the hull of the fortress in a haze of splinters and sawdust, knocking pirates off their feet and disabling the main battery of cannons.

Robin followed his father as he ran through the passageways. The pirates had realised what had happened and attacked in force, swarming through decks. The fleet was targeting the fortress's cannons and one by one they fell, being either knocked backwards into the structure or falling outwards into the sea.

Robin had found a dozen or more pirates lying dead on his deck. Others attacked him and he was forced to pummel and kick them on his way past. He could have retrieved a weapon from a fallen opponent, but he'd never learned how to swordfight and there was no time to load a musket. Half the time they didn't work anyway. Seawater and gunpowder made poor bedfellows. In the melee, he'd become separated from his father. He called out to him but his shouting just drew more pirates his way.

He grabbed one man in a headlock while he kicked at another's knee. A solid punch to the jaw sent a third crashing to the deck like a sack of potatoes. He paused, panting, trying to catch his breath. A glint of light on the wall in front of him caught his eye and he spun round in time to duck away from the tip of a cutlass. A weather-beaten pirate, salivating and wild-eyed, lunged at him again.

Down in the drinking hall of Driftwood, William Longbeard and Sam Pro sat with tankards of ale. Seawater pooled around their feet, soaking through their threadbare boots. How cold it was, William couldn't say, as his toes had long since turned numb. Above, from the doll's house of decks, the screams of their former crewmates, the clash of cutlasses and the roar of muskets mingled in an horrific symphony of battle and pain. A splashing announced the arrival of six more attackers, all armed with swords. Each was a member of Red Jim's crew whom William and Sam had served beside these past few weeks.

William had expressed concerns about his captain's actions. Replacing the old crewmembers with a pack of foul-tempered cutthroats had been an odd choice, to say the least. He's been assured by Red Jim it was all part of some grand scheme he was cooking up, something to set them all up for life. Increasingly, it had felt as though he and Sam were entirely separate from the rest of the crew. Fearing the worst, they had vowed to stay together, no matter what happened. To support one another.

They'd watched in horror as their new associates slaughtered the crews of three ships that had remained behind. Ambushed while going about their duties, or drinking, even sleeping, their victims hadn't stood a chance. The looks in their eyes would haunt him. The betrayal would haunt him.

It was then he and Sam knew they had to escape. They sought to bide their time until Captain Gulabahaar returned, to play along until they saw a chance for freedom. And so they remained by one another's side, fighting against the very people they'd served with, until they'd ended up in the drinking hall in the bottommost deck of Driftwood.

He and Sam spoke not a single word to each other. Sam's arm had been broken in the skirmish on the jetties, and he held it, breathing heavily. Beside William sat the body of a pirate, still clutching the dagger he'd stuck into William's side before William's musket had fired into the pirate's face. The blood rapidly seeping into William's clothes was warm and oddly comforting. His mind briefly drifted back to the dewy green fields of his youth. To the rolling hills and the scent of harvest time. He'd had a gutful of life at sea. He wanted more than anything to go home.

The six pirates advanced from all sides until William held up one finger, causing them to pause in their tracks. He lifted his tankard to his lips and drained it entirely, covering his bushy black beard in foam. He set down the empty tankard and nodded to Sam who flicked open a striker and touched the sparking tip to the barrel of gunpowder on the chair next to him.

A fiery explosion from the drinking hall below rocked the walkways, and both Robin and the weather-beaten pirate staggered, trying to find their footing. Robin grabbed the man's wrist and squeezed as hard as he could, until he felt a pop. The pirate screamed and dropped his sword. On his cheek was a painful-looking red indentation of peculiar shape—a bear's head.

Dad's already walloped this chap, Robin thought.

Feeling bad for the poor fellow, Robin forcefully thrust the top of his bald head into his attacker's nose before knocking him out cold with a swing from his left hand. The pirate fell over the railing onto the deck below. Robin rubbed his scarred palm and tried to ignore the stinging pain.

He moved to climb down a ladder but the whir of an approaching shot made him crouch and cover his head. The wall beside him exploded in a shower of splinters. Keeping low, he raced along the walkway. In the haze of musket smoke and sawdust, it was difficult to see exactly where he was going, and he tripped over a dead woman, falling hard on his knees. He winced as pain shot through his legs.

Above him a soaking wet Maggie Troke stood and aimed her musket at Robin's head. He had no idea how she'd survived the fall or how she'd climbed back inside. He held his breath. She pulled the trigger. Nothing happened. Her powder was too wet to ignite. She growled and went for her dagger. There came then a peculiar swishing noise and Maggie Troke's nose abruptly disappeared from her face in a splash of blood. She screamed in shock. Robin screamed in surprise. The same odd sound augured the opening of deep wounds on her arms and throat. She fell gurgling to the floor as Captain Gulabahaar emerged from the smoke and kicked her out through a gaping hole in the hull.

Robin, now back on his feet, gave her a little wave, unsure of how else to show his profound gratitude for saving his life. She smirked in return and disappeared once more into the fray, swinging her lethal urumi blade as she went.

"Robin!"

He turned to find his father approaching, bloody cutlass in hand and a makeshift bandage round his arm. "What happened to you?"

"I fell in the bath, what do you think happened?"

"Dad..."

"It's only a flesh wound; its fine," his father said. "The fleet has docked. Well, what's left of it, anyway. They're takin' the fight to Red Jim's crew."

They didn't get very far before they ran into young Fausto. The boy was wide-eyed and pale. He held a dagger in his shaking hand. He saw Robin and smiled weakly before he was swallowed by a squall of wood and smoke.

"*Fausto!*" Robin shouted.

The cannon ball which had obliterated the hull next to Fausto cracked into one of the main support beams. Fausto lay on the walkway, unmoving. Robin heaved him into his arms, shielding him from a further torrent of shrapnel and splinters.

"Go!" he said. "I'll get him somewhere safe."

"My cabin," his father said, climbing down a ladder. "Get him to my cabin. And stay with him! I don't want you seein' what's about to happen."

"But—"

"Do as I say!" his father shouted.

Robin nodded and barrelled along the passageway until he reached his father's cabin. There he lay Fausto on the bed as carefully as he could. The boy moaned softly.

"Stay 'ere and keep your 'ead down," he said. "The walls are thicker in 'ere, you should be safe."

"I don't want to be here," Fausto said through tears. "Jim killed everyone I know. I hid with my chickens. I want to go home, Mr. Shipp, please." He could barely open his eyes.

"I know you do," Robin said. "You're just a boy. You should be somewhere safe, not knee-deep in this madness. You'll make it 'ome. I swear it."

Ignoring his father's orders, Robin left the cabin and closed the door behind him. The pirates of Captain Gulabahaar's fleet were fighting back against Red Jim's crew with all their strength. Robin heard his father shouting from somewhere below and sought him out.

"I told you to stay safe!" his father said as he slashed at a pirate.

"Sorry, Dad," Robin said, smashing his fist into a face. "I didn't want you disappearin' again."

About them, fires burned, swords slashed, muskets fired, and daggers sliced. Every attacker fell before their might. Some simply ran away from the sight of them. The family Shipp, striding the halls of Driftwood, smeared with blood, drenched with sweat and striking down all who opposed them. What would Robin's life have been like had his father stayed on the island and raised both himself and Vince? Would Robin have turned out like both of them? Would they all have been pirates? Imagine the havoc they'd have wrought. They'd have been unstoppable.

They found Red Jim standing over a corpse with his cutlass drawn and slick.

"*What have you done?*" Robin's father shouted as he lunged forward.

Red Jim easily dodged the attack and swung his sword. "Gotten rid of some of my competition!" he said, before running along the walkway and disappearing into the melee.

Robin and his father pursued him, clambering over bodies as they went.

"He's not gettin' out of here alive!" Robin's father shouted.

"I quite agree," said Captain Gulabahaar as she dropped from the deck overhead.

She landed in front of Red Jim, trapping him. She spun round, swinging her flexible blade around herself, becoming a hurricane of slicing steel. Red Jim roared and swung his cutlass at her, taking slashes to his forearms and legs.

Robin's father attacked Jim from behind, smacking him viciously on the head with the butt of his sword. The cap fell from Red Jim's head as he tumbled to the deck, weapon slipping from his grasp. The clash of swords and roar of muskets had begun to die away. Robin retrieved his cap from the floor and dusted it off. It felt good to have it back.

"You have doomed us, James," Captain Gulabahaar said. "All this time I was so worried about the threats from without, I ignored the ones from within."

"Yes, well, you never were much of a leader," Red Jim said. "Just because you helped build this place doesn't mean you were fit to run it."

"The people of Driftwood could have asked me to step down at any time," she said. "They elected to follow me."

"It was a poor choice. I think you'll agree," Red Jim said, gesturing around himself. "I mean, look what's come of it." He laughed again and more blood came gushing from the wound on his head. He smeared it across his face in a grotesque display of defiance.

"I saw a chance to be rid of some competitors and seize control," he said. "Would any of you have done any different?"

"Of course we bleddy would," Robin's father said. "We wouldn't have betrayed our brothers and sisters of the black. Is this why you rescued me from the asylum? So you could kill me here?"

"'E didn't know 'is men were goin' to rescue you," Robin said. "In fact 'e left you behind in Port Knot on purpose."

"*What?*"

"Longbeard and Pro talked, did they?" Red Jim asked. "Idiots. I should have gotten rid of them with the rest of my old crew, but dammit, I took pity on them. I'm simply too kind-hearted for my own good."

Robin's father scoffed and rolled his eyes.

"Last winter," Red Jim said, "you came into possession of a shipment of gunpowder, remember? I got wind of a buyer in Blackrabbit who might be interested, and so off we went. There we met two ruffians named Penhallow and Palk. They talked a good game, but it was clear they weren't the ones in charge. No, that honour belonged to the great brute lurking around in the background. A giant man named Vince, with a round face and tiny ears. Now, who did he remind me of, only dear old Barrow.

"But oh! What's this? Barrow's scarpered! Seems he didn't fancy a family reunion. Awful shame but I couldn't wait around for him. Well, I say couldn't, but to be honest the chance to abandon you was too fun to pass up. And so I did. Sailed off and never looked back.

"You were arrested and thrown in prison. I thought it fitting enough punishment, but then we heard you were being moved to an asylum and Gulabahaar ordered me to rescue you. I refused. I told her you weren't worth it. Risking a whole ship to rescue one old man? Ludicrous. But she wouldn't hear it; she kept saying how you were a vital link to our past, how your knowledge and experience were invaluable."

"I didn't know you cared," Robin's father said to Captain Gulabahaar. "I'd be only too happy to show you the full length and breadth of my experience."

"How you have survived this long is a mystery," she said. "And one worth studying. From afar, I might add."

"If I might be permitted to continue," Red Jim said. "As punishment for daring to question the great and powerful Pirate Queen, Gulabahaar ordered my crew to take my ship and rescue you without me. *My* crew. *My* ship. That would not stand. No, punishments were needed all round for such a calculated slight, I decided. Now, a bigger man wouldn't have dragged his enemy's children into it, but what can I say? I'm petty. Before they set off on the rescue mission, I ordered Maggie Troke to see about having Vince done away with. It tickled me to know while you were being rescued, your son was being cut from ear to ear."

"Sorry to tell you they failed," said Robin. "Vince is alive. 'E's the one who told me Dad was in the asylum."

"Oh? Well, how very disappointing," Jim said. "But then again, you've been away from home for a while, haven't you? Penhallow and Palk were given very strict instructions by Ms. Troke. They seemed the tenacious type, so I suspect they will have followed Vince to your home to finish the job."

Robin's blood ran cold at the thought of those two thugs running free in the village.

"Why?" Robin's father asked. "Why did you do all this?"

Red Jim's brow knotted. He almost laughed as he staggered to his feet, steadying himself with one hand on the railing behind him.

"You honestly don't remember me, do you?" he asked. "Don't remember how we first met?"

"Of course I do."

Red Jim's mouth dropped open, his bravado slipping away in an instant.

"You think I don't remember the meek little cabin boy from my last tenure as captain of the *Fledglin' Crow?*" Robin's father asked. "The scared little runt who'd flinch at every harsh word and slammed door?"

"You remembered me all along?" Red Jim asked, his voice a shadow of what it had been.

"Of course I did. I remember everyone who's ever served under me."

"But...when I met you again, years later, a captain of my own vessel...you never let on."

"What were I supposed to do, give you a hug? I expect great things of my crew. I will admit I were surprised you'd survived so long. Once you left my service, I were sure you'd be floatin' face down in the tide before long. You never showed much initiative on my ship."

"You shouted at me, demeaned me, made me feel weak and pathetic!"

"And?"

"Isn't that enough?"

"Not really, no. I did the same to all my crew. You're not special, Jim. You weren't unusually hard done by. I'm not sure if you've noticed but life at sea is hard. When you joined my crew you were weak. You'd have struggled to survive on a merchant vessel but on a pirate one? You'd have been dead in a fortnight without my trainin'."

"I wish I had been!" Globs of hot spittle erupted from the corners of Red Jim's mouth as he shouted his words.

"Oh, stop it," Robin's father said. "You wanted to be a pirate, remember? You joined us of your own free will. You ran away from home, head full of notions about a life on the open sea. I taught you how to take orders; I taught you how to fight; I taught you how to survive. If I hadn't toughened you up, you never would have made it."

"So, what, you made me what I am today?"

"Well, I don't remember makin' you a backstabbin' swine."

"You certainly didn't instil any loyalty in me. You've no idea how my heart sank when I first came here and found you swaggering around like you owned the place. The grand old pirate with all the answers. Offering your unsolicited advice to us lesser sailors, telling captains how to run their own ships!"

"If more of them had listened to me," his father said, "maybe we wouldn't be dyin' out."

Red Jim laughed a little; then he fixed Robin with his cold, hard stare again. "Remember when I said you never should have come here?"

Red Jim suddenly pulled a pistol from his belt and aimed it squarely at Robin. Robin's father yelled and leapt forward, catching Jim round the waist as the gun fired, filling the air with smoke. Robin dropped to the floor, his shin burning, his trouser leg turning red. He winced and cried out. When he opened his eyes, his father and Red Jim were gone.

Gulabahaar stood peering over the broken railing. Robin's heart stopped. His fingertips turned icy, his ears pounded, his skull grew tight as if it were fit to crush his brains.

"Dad, no!"

With every ounce of strength he had left, he hobbled over to where his father had last stood. Lying many decks below, broken over tables in the drinking hall, were the maimed and bloodied bodies of his father and Red Jim. Robin swayed and sank to the floor.

"You were comin' 'ome," he said. "It were all goin' to be over. You were goin' to see Morwenner again. You were comin' 'ome."

He wanted to cry out. He wanted to vomit. He wanted to close his eyes and never open them again. He was so close, *so close*, to getting what he'd always wanted, what he'd always dreamed of. His father alive and well, back on the island, back home. He'd imagined sailing into the harbour aboard *Bucca*—poor, lost *Bucca*—and bringing his father to his mother's door, seeing them embrace, introducing him to Edwin... Edwin, who was waiting for him. Edwin, who loved him. Edwin, who'd never stop looking to the horizon, wondering what had happened to him.

The thought shocked Robin to his senses, and he scrambled to his feet. Captain Gulabahaar was still staring, unmoving. The waters far below were rising, and they quickly swallowed the bodies.

"Are we in danger of sinkin'?" Robin asked.

"No," Gulabahaar said. "Our ships concentrated their attack on the upper decks."

There came then a deep rumbling from somewhere in the depths of the fortress, followed by a crunching and grinding that sounded like a forest being ripped up by the roots. The drinking hall had been completely immersed. Water was gushing in from the sides while above them, flames licked the hull, casting embers all about. Another splintering crack brought a forceful spout of water cascading in and suddenly the entire fortress began to list. Robin grabbed the railing to steady himself.

"You were sayin'?"

"They did more damage than I realised."

"We need to abandon ship," he said. "Quickly."

"*No!*" Captain Gulabhaar screamed. "We cannot lose our home!"

He looked her in the eye and spoke with an unfamiliar power in his voice. "It's already lost!" he said. "Please, Captain, you 'ave to let it go. We can't lose anyone else."

"But...everything we have worked for," she said. "Everything we have built..."

"Dad said this way of life couldn't last forever. He said the future were comin', remember? Well it's 'ere. It's arrived."

Captain Gulabahaar stood very still. "Yes," she said. "It is here. And I have no place in it. I have failed them. All of them. I wanted to protect them, to shield them from the world. All I wanted was a place we could call home. Tell my sister I am so very sorry."

"What are you talkin' about, you can tell 'er yourself. Come on, we 'ave to go!"

As he spoke, a thick, burning beam fell between them, smashing the deck on which they stood. Robin was thrown backwards and fell hard on his injured leg. Through the acrid smoke, Captain Gulabahaar called to him.

"You are the only one who knows what happened here," she said. "At the end. At the very end."

With those words, she was swallowed by smoke and fire. Robin scrambled to his feet. Unable to reach her, he turned and ran as quickly as he could for the jetties in the inner circle of Driftwood. His leg begged for rest. He daren't look, but he knew the damage was severe.

A whirl of flame erupted from below deck, blocking his path. He pulled his cap low to shield his eyes from the blaze and barrelled through a tower door to avoid it. Unable to see clearly, he stumbled head first through a portal. Where everything had been wood and fire, suddenly it was cloud and sky. Frantically, he grabbed on to a post with one hand as his momentum swung him out over the rushing waters far below.

He gasped for breath as he scrambled at the hull, pulling himself back inside the tower. He panted fiercely. Behind him, the inferno raged. In front of him, only air and a dive into an unforgiving ocean. Within the tower, he spotted a switch and flicked it. In moments, a clanking, jerking gangway rose into view and slotted into place in the open wall. He dashed along it as quickly as he dared. It took him across the hull of Driftwood, by-passing the fire, and bounced disconcertingly underfoot. If the simple rope handrail was meant to prevent him from falling off, he placed no particular faith in its function. The gangway connected to the next tower and Robin stood inside, catching his breath and silently thanking whoever it was who had created those bizarre mechanisms.

He carried on until he reached the jetties. The *Mortal Grace* and the *Ivy* had docked and their crewmembers were returning, carrying the wounded and the dead. The other ships remained quiet, their captains hanging from the masts of Driftwood, their crews fed to the sea life of the Atlantic.

Robin followed the crew on board the *Mortal Grace*. A small brown and white terrier ran past him and cowered by the wheel. The ship's Quartermaster, Harry Vosper, was the last to board, his hand pressed against a wounded ear.

"Captain Gulabhaar?" he asked.

Robin shook his head slowly. He didn't know what to say. He didn't know why she'd stayed behind, why she'd chosen to sink with Driftwood. Harry Vosper gave orders to cast off.

"Wait," Robin said. "Did you see Fausto? I left 'im in Dad's cabin. 'E were injured..."

"He's probably dead," Vosper said. "Like we will be if we don't get away from here before it sinks!"

"We can't just leave 'im, what if 'e's trapped?"

"I'm not risking my life for some stupid, cowardly boy," Vosper said.

"Wait for me as long as you can," Robin said.

He took a deep breath and rushed back across the gangplank, into the sinking Driftwood, which was rocking now from side to side. The mechanisms managing the great sails had ceased to be and the fortress was no longer heaving to, it was sailing. It drifted slowly westward, buckling in places. Robin steadied himself against railings, against walls, against anything he could.

Suddenly, the entire starboard side slumped into the waves. Bodies of pirates fell from the balconies, from the damaged hull, from the now-exposed walkways and splashed into the ocean. Robin yelled out for Fausto. His leg clenched as if gripped in the jaws of a shark, and he cried out in pain. He stopped, paralysed with indecision. He couldn't bring himself to simply abandon Fausto, but what of Edwin? What of the children? He couldn't give them up. He didn't know Fausto, didn't even know if he was still alive. Every time he'd tried to do the right thing during his time on Driftwood, the thing his conscience compelled him to do, he'd been punished. But what choice did he have?

Cursing himself, he took a deep breath and carried on. The waters continued to rise. He stepped over fallen bodies and avoided being thrown out of the lurching fortress until finally he reached the door of his father's cabin. Smoke billowed from beneath it. He rattled the handle but the door remained closed. He called out to Fausto again, warning him to stand back. With one mighty shove of his shoulder, the door cracked open, bursting inwards.

A wall of bitter smoke rushed towards him, filling his lungs, stinging his eyes. He coughed and coughed. Flames crept up the walls. Fausto lay still on the bed. Robin bent down to check he was still breathing. Tongues of fire lashed out, licking Tommy's writings alight. The painstakingly documented history of the pirates, every single tome, every scribbled word of it was burning. Desperate to protect Fausto from the fire, Robin searched for something to keep him safe. He grabbed a wad of black cloth, drenched it in water from a large jug and wrapped it round the boy. Then he heaved the lad on his shoulder and ran as quickly as he could back to the jetties.

He stumbled along the gangplank and slung Fausto onto the weather deck of the *Mortal Grace* before falling down beside him. He lay there on his back, panting for breath. The order was given and the ship was underway. Robin unfurled the cloth and gently tapped Fausto on the cheek, who stirred and opened his eyes.

Fausto grabbed the soaking wet cloth and flung it away from his legs. "What...what is this?" he asked.

In the chaos of the cabin, Robin didn't know what he'd used to protect Fausto from the flames, but now he found himself staring at the eyepatch of the Sea Bear. His father's flag.

"Mr. Shipp," he said, his breathing fast and shallow, "I took your coin-holder, but I lost it again..."

Robin just patted him gently on the shoulder. It was raining, he suddenly realised. The storm which had hidden the pirate hunters during the raid had finally reached them. The only other remaining pirate ship—the *Ivy*—had already left and waited for them some distance away.

The survivors all gathered on deck to watch the final moments of the great floating pirate castle. One of its stacks cracked and began to separate from the rest, spilling its contents into the ocean. From afar, it looked even more like a doll's house. Plates, books, chairs, weapons, bodies, all came tumbling out. Great sections of the outer hull slid away, revealing the constituent ships before they too broke apart and came crashing down.

The four crewless vessels, tethered to the jetties, were dragged beneath the waves. Robin thought of them sinking slowly, coming to rest next to *Bucca's Call*. Perhaps one day, drawn to the place by tales of sunken pirate treasure, someone would dive down and find her waiting patiently on the ocean floor. Her scarlet hull covered with silt and home to generations of fish.

The great masts, still strung with the bodies of Tommy Oughterlauney and the three pirate captains toppled to the water with a tremendous boom. Last to go were the great flags of Driftwood, the skull and cogs, flapping proudly in the wind, defiant until the very end when they too were swallowed by the ocean.

The battle had taken a devastating toll. The *Ivy* had picked up the survivors of the abandoned *Skinless Hand*, but most of the pirates of Driftwood were dead. An enormous amount of plunder now lay on the seabed, forever out of reach. Wounds were attended to, limbs bandaged, and losses mourned. A good night's sleep was needed.

Harry Vosper was now in command, and he ordered Robin to bed, there to be examined by the ship's physician. Once he was lying down and devoid of distractions, the pain came to him in dizzying, nauseating waves. He swigged from a bottle of brandy. The doctor carefully cut away the blood-soaked leg of Robin's trousers, all the while making tutting noises and frowning. She muttered with Mr. Vosper just out of earshot.

"What is it?" Robin asked.

Mr. Vosper stood by his side. "You shouldn't have put any weight on your leg once you'd been injured," he said. "The shot has worked its way deeper into your bone. The doctor says she can remove it, but it will be...unpleasant."

Robin's breathing grew faster. "Can it wait until we get 'ome?" he asked. "This doesn't seem like the best place for surgery. Doctor Greenaway can tend to it once I'm back in the village."

Mr. Vosper turned to the doctor who shook her head.

"The longer you wait, the more damage will be done," she said. "The wound will turn. The pain will increase. Your life will end."

Robin nodded, quickly.

Mr. Vosper signalled to some men hovering behind him. "They will hold you down during the procedure, should you need them to. And you might want this to bite on."

He handed Robin a wooden spoon. Robin, wide-eyed and frightened, took another drink of brandy, then clenched the spoon handle between his teeth as the doctor prepared her knife.

The following morning, everyone who could do so gathered on the weather deck of the *Mortal Grace*. Row after row of cream-coloured linen bundles lay side by side—the bodies taken during the evacuation of Driftwood and those who had passed away from their injuries during the night. A crew would never leave anyone behind, if they could help it. The pirates were sombre, some wept unashamedly. Harry Vosper stepped forward to speak. He recited the names of those who lay by his feet.

"We return our brothers and sisters to the sea," he said. "Do not forget them. Do not deny them. Let them sail forever in our hearts."

After a moment's reflection, the bundles were pushed overboard to sink beneath the waves.

.

Chapter Forty

There are times when books can be an escape from the world, when a well-chosen metaphor can send one on a journey of a thousand miles in the blink of an eye. But then there are times when even the most carefully crafted sentence cannot tear one away from the crushing monotony of the real world. Iris lay in her four-poster bed reading the same page for the fifth time. Or was it the sixth? Not one word of it was going in. She was so bored, she thought she'd scream. A rap at the door heralded the arrival of Drake, the footman, carrying a bowl of soup on a silver tray.

"Let me guess," Iris said.

"Lady Eva's orders," she and Drake said in unison.

He set the tray on her lap and she sighed heavily. She couldn't complain about fussing this time. Childbirth had indeed left her quite weak, and the onion soup smelled delicious.

"Perhaps once you've recovered some strength, ma'am, I could ask Ms. Popplestone to bring the children in to see you?"

"Mmm, yes please, Drake," she said between spoonfuls. "I do hope Eva has been coping without me."

"The children could use their mother's touch, if you don't mind me saying, ma'am."

She was mildly irked and had expected better from Drake. She set her spoon down forcefully into the bowl, causing some soup to splatter. She knew Eva could appear aloof to some people, but for Drake to even insinuate Eva might be anything other than a loving mother was too much.

"Eva is their mother," Iris said.

"And yet..." Drake said, as he plumped some pillows.

"Yes?" Iris asked. "And yet?"

"Well, haven't you noticed, ma'am?" said Drake.

"Noticed what?"

"Nothing, ma'am. It's not my place to say."

"And yet here you stand, saying it anyway. Spit it out."

Drake stood sharply with his eyes fixed on the far wall. "I'm given to understand Lady Eva won't hold the children."

"Ridiculous. I'm sure she's held them."

"Have you actually seen her do so, ma'am?" he asked.

Iris fidgeted with her blankets, brushing some droplets of soup from them. "That will be all, Drake."

Iris wrapped herself up in a striped, pea green banyan and walked carefully along the hallway. She was still a touch delicate and stopped every few dozen paces to rest. In the nursery, Ms. Popplestone was attending to the children in their cribs. Eva was standing by the arched window, her shoulders slumped. A rain-dappled window framed the cold, grey sky. She didn't move, didn't blink. She gave no indication as to her thoughts, her mood.

"Would you excuse us, please?" she asked.

Ms. Popplestone nodded and left.

"Come here," Iris said, holding out her hand.

Eva walked slowly towards her.

"You're behaving oddly."

"You know I'm not very maternal," Eva said, her hands clasped tightly.

"You still won't hold them? It seems so odd to me," Iris said, "given how…vigilant you were during the pregnancy. At times you were almost distressed. Uncharacteristically so, I would say."

"I just wanted you and the babies to be safe," Eva said.

"I know, of course I do, but why were you so obsessive? It wasn't like you."

Eva took a deep breath, avoiding Iris's gaze. "When I was young," she said, "Sada, my father's second wife, fell pregnant with their second child. She was so happy. I couldn't have been more than six or seven years old and I watched her belly grow with fascination. Daisy and I would sing to her almost every day. The expectation was almost more than I could bear. We helped prepare the nursery for the new baby; we picked names for them; we talked for hours and hours about all the games we'd play together.

"One day, Sada slipped on the stairs. No one's fault—it was an accident. She lost the baby. Afterwards, it was as if a dark cloud had descended over the entire household. All the hopes and dreams I had for my sibling, the lives I imagined we'd all lead together, all gone. I found

Sada crying many times but she always tried to pretend she wasn't. My father was never the most loving man and offered her little support.

"About a year or so later, she left him and took Daisy with her. I never saw either of them again. It was like losing the baby for a second time. An entire future snatched away in an instant. So, yes, I might have been overprotective, and it might be for selfish reasons, but I simply... I couldn't go through that all again, Iris. I just couldn't."

Tears welled in her eyes, and Iris hugged her tightly.

"It's fine," Iris said. "The children are safe, healthy. You don't need to worry any more. Why don't you hold them? Just for a little while?"

"I think its best I don't," Eva said.

"But whyever not?"

"Please, Iris, I don't..." She turned and dashed from the nursery. Iris followed as quickly as she could.

"Eva! Eva, wait!" she said. "I recently gave birth to twins; do not make me run after you!"

Iris caught up with her as she was steadying herself against a wall, breathing heavily. "Eva... What is this?" she asked as gently as she could.

"What if..." Eva said, trying and failing to hold back tears. "What if I hold them, and I don't feel anything?"

She kept looking at the portrait on the wall, the one of her father, Lord Marley Chase. Her eyes were wide, almost panic-stricken, her voice cracked. Iris had never seen her in such a state.

"What if I can't... What if I can't love them?"

"What do you mean 'can't love them'?"

"My father was so cold towards me. At the end, he told me he loved me, but I don't think I ever felt it. What if I'm the same? What if I do to them what he did to me? Keep them at arm's length, unable to show them affection?"

"You're nothing like him."

Eva barked a laugh, making Iris jump.

"Iris, my dear, sweet Iris, I am all too similar to him. What if I damage the children, as he did me?"

"You're not damaged."

"Oh, I am, I am. I keep the world outside, let them see the armour I wear and nothing else. It took your love, your fire, to weld the pieces of my heart together, but even now I feel the seams."

Iris took Eva's hand and clasped it tightly to her own chest. "You don't spurn the whole world," she said. "Edwin, Duncan, Robin—you let them in. You made room in your life for them and you're all the better for it, no? So what if you're a touch guarded? So what if you don't welcome strangers with open arms? Let me do it. Let me be your vanguard in the world. If they're worthy of you, I'll let them through."

Eva covered her eyes, and Iris took her in her arms once again. It felt so strange. Eva had always seemed carved from ice, always calm, always capable.

"I know you're not like him," Iris said. "I guarantee he never, not even once, felt the way you do right now. I guarantee he never stopped and questioned how he treated you when you were a child. You've already surpassed him because you've shown you do care. You already love our children so much you're terrified of breaking them!"

Eva laughed a little. She took a handkerchief from her sleeve and wiped her eyes and nose. "Whatever would I do without you?"

"You would fall to pieces," Iris said. "Honestly, you wouldn't last a day. I'm irreplaceable."

Iris kissed her on the lips. Those soft, safe, lips.

"You told me once you weren't going to make the same mistakes your father made," she said. "Instead, you were going to make entirely new ones. Start here. Today. Start by loving your children too much. Smother them with kisses and hugs. Lay all your affection on them. And if they grow up to be unbearably coddled and unable to leave your side, well, so be it."

Eva laughed through her tears. "I love you," she said.

"I should bleddy well think so. And I love you too."

That evening, Edwin went round to the lodge for supper, after which he was led to the closed door of the nursery. "Good of you to give up your study."

Eva arched an eyebrow. "I'd still be using it if Ms. Popplestone hadn't decided otherwise. Now I have to work from the attic."

"Oh, stop," Iris said. "There's more space for your papers up there; you should have been using it all along."

"I would still have preferred to have been involved in the decision," Eva said.

"True of every decision, everywhere," Iris said.

"Anyway, stop right there," Eva said, handing over a silk scarf. "Tie this over your eyes."

"Whatever for?" Edwin said.

"Because we have a surprise," Iris said.

Edwin closed his eyes and did as he was told. Iris clicked open the door as Eva took his hand and guided him into the middle of the nursery. She undid the blindfold, and Edwin squinted in the glare of lantern right in front of him. The babies lay gurgling happily in their cribs. He leaned down and tickled their bellies.

It took him a second to realise what the surprise was. On the wall facing the cribs was painted a huge tree. It had little boxes on the long, winding branches, boxes with names like "Humfrie Chase", "Allyne Weamouth" and "Angela Wolfe". Beside some of the boxes were painted small, oval portraits. He recognised Eva's parents, Iris's too. He traced one branch which led to "Edwin Farriner" and a subtle painting of himself. Above it, two names with two more images. "Sylvia Finnegan" and "Nathaniel Farriner." He ran his fingers lightly across the artwork of his father's face.

"We know it's only a small gesture," Iris said. "But it's our way of keeping his memory alive."

Edwin's eyes swelled and he steadied himself against the wall for a minute or two. "I'm glad the paint has dried," he said with a laugh. "Thank you for this. Truly, it's beautiful."

Eva lifted both of the babies from their cribs, laid them on the carpet, and sat next to them. Iris perched herself on the edge of a seat as the last light of the setting sun streamed in from the arched window behind her. Her curls seemed to shine in the amber glow. Eva laughed as the babies reached up to her, their tiny fingers grasping air. She tenderly lifted both of them into her arms, rubbing her cheek against the tops of their heads. He smiled and for a simple, perfect moment, his mind was clear, his heart still.

On the wall, the two boxes below both his and the ladies' names were left blank.

"We're going to have to fill in these spaces eventually, you know," he said.

"Actually," Eva said. "We've had some thoughts on the subject."

Nick scribbled some numbers on the great slate chalkboard Duncan had erected. He hadn't been able to stop smiling all morning. Even the prospect of yet another rainy day couldn't dampen his spirits. He turned to face the class.

"Now, who can—"

May Bell was sitting with her hand in the air as high as it could go.

"Yes, Ms. Bell?"

"I'm told you and Mr. Hunger are lovers now," she said.

Nick's grin widened. "And who told you that, Ms. Bell?"

"Mr. Farriner. I'm glad. Mr. Hunger only has a cat for company. It's good he has you now too."

Nick laughed and adjusted his cravat.

"Thank you for your support, Ms. Bell. As you can see, today's lesson is arithmetic..."

Chapter Forty-One

On a bright, cold October morning Edwin stood in the harbour, peering up at the roof of the Moth & Moon. The belfry had been completed, but it still stood empty. The gull known as the Admiral had won his battle with his long-time rival, Captain Tom, and strode around the top of the belfry in a victory lap.

No one had yet come up with a way to find a bell. There had been talk again of procuring one from the forges of Blackrabbit though everyone balked at the idea. Eva had argued the point was surely to have a bell, no matter where it came from, but island pride had overruled her. The mainland, then, was the next logical choice. The villagers had all agreed to contribute towards the cost of making and transporting a bell, though the price was expected to be astronomical. It would probably have to wait a few years.

Eva and Iris had offered to pay the full amount but the village had politely declined. Some did so out of determination not to be reliant upon the upper classes—but some did so out of an unwillingness to be indebted to the Blackrabbit-born Lady Eva. Some things about village life, Edwin mused, would likely never change. Merryapple was a beautiful island, filled with wonderful people, but they could be quite inward-looking. Insular. The rivalry with nearby Blackrabbit was, Edwin had always asserted, a joke that had gotten out of hand. It was fine for sporting events, such as the annual boat race, but it had seeped into the bones of everyday life. People rattled off their dislike for Blackrabbit and its people simply because their parents and grandparents had done the same.

Some crew from the large ships docked in the cove arrived by longboat and scrambled up the beach. They would surely add some coin to the village's coffers. They shouted to one another in a language Edwin couldn't quite place. Of late, more and more foreign sailors were stopping at the island. Down to the expanding Dutch merchant fleet, Mr. Penny had explained. Edwin welcomed the new faces and new voices. If anything was going to shake Merryapple from its often provincial attitudes, it was foreign money.

Another launch was approaching the harbour. This one filled with some particularly rough-looking people who sat around a bulky item covered in cloth. He squinted in the early morning sun, trying to get a better look. On board, a figure with a snowy-white beard stood up, resting on a crutch. Tall and square shouldered, he adjusted his flat cap and waved.

Edwin bolted to the beach as fast as he could. The launch came close to shore and some of its occupants leaped out, splashing into the shallow water. They grabbed the boat and slid it ashore. Robin sat on the edge and swung himself out. He embraced Edwin and kissed him passionately.

"You're home," Edwin said.

"I told you I'd come back to you," Robin whispered into his ear.

The sensation of Robin's hot breath on Edwin's skin made him quiver. "What about your dad? Did you find him? And where's *Bucca?*"

"There'll be time enough for all that soon," Robin said, cupping the side of Edwin's face in his massive, strong hand. "I missed you so much."

Others had noticed Robin's arrival, and a crowd began to gather to welcome him home. Duncan pushed his way through and gave Robin's arm a friendly squeeze. "You smell interesting," he said. He pointed to the covered object still in the launch. "And you brought me a present! You really shouldn't have."

"You'll 'ave to share it, I'm afraid," Robin said. "I 'ope you 'aven't already got one." He grabbed the cloth and pulled it off, revealing a large iron bell.

"Where did you find it?" Edwin asked.

"Bit of a long story, actually," Robin said. "I'll tell you over a bowl of stew."

Robin held open the door of the Moth & Moon and ushered the band of pirates inside. None of them had ever been to Merryapple before. At first, the locals balked at the assembly of cutthroats and thieves in his company, but a few words from Robin put them at ease. Many were drawn to the fine silk garments of Harry Vosper. He smiled and nodded a greeting as he passed by. Robin couldn't shake the feeling he'd love nothing more than to pull out a musket and rob every last one of them. He appreciated him being on his best behaviour.

"You're limping a bit," Edwin said.

"Ah, yes, I were 'it with musket fire. The doctor removed the shot, thankfully. She thought I might lose the leg, but it's just another scar."

"Mr. Shipp!" May Bell shouted as she ran to him. "Welcome home!"

He scooped her up in his arm, and she hugged his wide neck.

"Mum said you'd probably drown, out there all alone, but I knew better!

"Ho ho! Well you can tell your mum I'm alive and well," Robin said. "Can you do me a favour? Can you run to Wolfe-Chase Lodge and fetch Ladies Eva and Iris for me?"

"Of course!" May said.

He set her down and she dashed off in the direction of Anchor Rise. Before he could enter the tavern, Edwin beckoned to him.

"Robin, can I talk to you alone?" Edwin said.

"Course, my darlin'!" Robin said.

He took Edwin by the hand, and they walked round the corner of the inn to a deserted spot in the shade.

"I...I have some bad news," Edwin said. "You'd better sit down."

Robin plonked down heavily onto a bench and rubbed his leg.

"It's not Mum, is she—?"

"She's fine, she's fine," Edwin said, laying his hand on Robin's knee. "It's George."

"What about him? Wait. You don't... 'E's not..."

"I'm afraid so," Edwin said softly.

Robin couldn't believe it. Tears burned their way from his eyes, and he held a hand over his mouth.

"When?"

"A few days ago."

"But 'e said 'e 'ad years left..."

"That's what Doctor Greenaway thought, but you know he had a cough before you left? It never cleared up. He took a funny turn a couple of weeks ago and never recovered. I'm sorry, Robin. I know you two were close."

"'E were a good friend to me. 'E never... 'E always treated me right, always treated me proper. Even when everyone else ran me down, treated me like an outcast, I were always sure of a warm welcome 'ere."

He slapped his good hand against the uneven, white-washed wall of the inn. It was such a part of George and he of it. The two were intertwined. To have one without the other seemed impossible.

"I know, I know. I'm so sorry. I was with him at the end. Duncan too. It was peaceful. Arminell Kind was so upset. She'd been working closely with him recently. Little May took it hardest of all. When she found out she just kept saying *I'm cold, Mummy, I'm cold.* She cried for days. George was like a grandfather to her. He left her his pocket watch, and she won't go anywhere without it now."

Edwin put his arms around Robin's shoulders and held him close.

"When we cry, we cry the sea," Robin said, drying his eyes.

"I don't understand."

"It's just somethin' Dad told me. I 'ad so many stories to tell George. I wanted 'im to write them down for me. For them. I can't do it by myself. I've never been very good with readin' or writin'."

"I can help you," Edwin said. "There'll be time enough for it now you're home."

Robin thought of his father—Erasmus Shipp, Bill Barrow—standing facing his enemy one moment and gone the next. In the blink of an eye.

"There's not, you know," Robin said. "There's never enough time. Everythin' can change in an instant. Captain Gulaba'aar—she were the Pirate Queen—she tried so 'ard to 'ang on to the past, to fight against the future, but it came anyway and it swept 'er away. And 'er whole way of life too. She were a bit like I used to be, fightin' against the tide."

"Things'll change," Edwin said. "They'll always change. But not always for the worse."

"Suppose we 'ave to learn to embrace it, or we'll be brushed aside."

"All we can do is try to ride the wave as best we can. Remember the past but look to the future," Edwin said, his voice like honey, hearth, and home. "Speaking of which, there's something else I should probably tell you. I hope you won't be angry but remember what you said before you left? How I should tell George you didn't want the Moth? Well, I never actually told him. At first, I could never find the right time, but then I thought maybe you only said it because, I don't know, because it freed your mind to deal with finding your father. Freed up some space in your heart. Took some weight off your shoulders."

Robin sat up straight and wiped the teardrops from his cheeks. He didn't say anything for a good long while.

"A day or two before he died," Edwin said. "George made the official announcement in front of everyone. I think he was worried he might not last till you returned."

"Poor George," Robin said. "So, The Moth & Moon is..."

"Yours," Edwin said.

Robin took Edwin's hand in his and squeezed gently. "Ours," he said.

After he'd composed himself, Robin joined the pirates at a table. He couldn't help but picture George Reed welcoming him, handing over a glass of whiskey. The place felt different without him. Bigger, somehow. Emptier. Colder. And of course, it was all Robin's. The weight of the notion had seemed unendurable when it had first been suggested, but without George it felt almost hollow, as if its heart had been scooped out. He thought about how he'd missed his chance to say goodbye to a true friend and was almost brought to tears again.

Food and drink were bought and stories were told. The villagers rejoiced at the gift of the bell and a heated discussion began amongst Duncan and the other craftspeople as to how best to get it up to the tower. Lady Eva and Iris arrived, carrying their newborn children, calling out joyfully to Robin who dashed over as quickly as he could to see the infants.

"Aren't they beautiful!" he said, rubbing their chubby rosy cheeks with his finger. "But then, 'ow could they not be?"

He was left speechless when Eva hugged him tightly round the waist and buried her face in his jumper. He gently laid his massive hand on her shoulder. She took a moment to regain her composure, fixing her dark hair in place.

"A month is entirely too long for you to be away. Never leave again, Mr. Shipp," she said. "If you please."

"I'll try not to," Robin said, smiling.

"It's funny you should arrive here with a bell," she said with a cocked eyebrow.

Robin's mouth ran dry, and he tugged on one of his earlobes. "It is?"

"Yes," she said. "Some pirates raided my company's ships a few weeks ago and stole a bell not unlike it."

"Ah, yes," he said. "About that, you see—"

"The insurers said it was probably melted down by now, or lying at the bottom of the sea. Either way, it's gone and never to be seen again," she said.

"A man were killed in the raid," he said. "Shot by my father."

"I see. And is he...?"

"Gone."

"Then I suppose justice, such as it is, has been served. And let's not forget many pirates were killed by my ships in return. Life at sea is...difficult. Brutal. And often short."

Edwin lifted the babies and handed them both to Robin. They rested comfortably in his huge arms, and he immediately made purring and bubbling noises, as some instinctively do with infants.

"What are their names?" he asked.

"Our daughter is named Allegra," Iris said. "Allegra Ivy, for our mothers."

"And our son," Edwin said, "is named George."

Robin's eyes stung again but this time he had no free hand with which to wipe them.

"George Reed was a kind man and a noble soul," Eva said. "Edwin suggested you might want to honour him in some way."

Robin sniffed and laughed and blinked away his tears, embarrassed but moved beyond measure. "You know me too well. But didn't you want to name 'im after your father?" he asked Edwin. "Or yours, Eva?"

"His full name is George Marley Nathaniel. I think we've been sufficiently thorough," Eva said. "Besides, I have a beloved uncle named George. There's nothing to say a name cannot honour two people at once."

"George and Allegra Wolfe-Chase," Robin said. "That sounds right, doesn't it? That sounds proper."

He handed the children back to Edwin, and his heart swelled at the pride on Edwin's face. It was like a beacon. Love positively radiated from the man. How had he ever stayed away from him all these weeks? How had he been able to bear being denied the sight of him? He didn't know. All he could say for certain was it would never happen again.

"Eva, I need to talk to you. In private," Robin said.

He led her down a hallway to a small room filled with taxidermy of every animal on the islands and some from much farther afield. He closed the door behind them and they sat beneath a shelf adorned with a large stuffed hare. Robin's ears were burning, and he rubbed his hands over his belly several times as he struggled to find the right words.

"Does this have anything to do with why you sailed into the cove with the *Ivy*? It was my father's favourite ship, named for my mother," Eva said, fixing the line of her dress.

"I suppose it were the spoils of a raid against the Chase Tradin' Company," Robin said. "When I were away, I met a woman, an Indian woman, by the name of Captain Gulaba'aar. Fierce, she were, strong. Leader of a whole colony of pirates on Driftwood."

"Driftwood is real? Well, well. I owe Clementine a bottle of champagne."

"But she died, Eva. She died when Driftwood sank. It were like... It were as if the light went out from 'er eyes. She saw 'er life's work ruined, and she just couldn't go on."

"Frightfully sad," Eva said, "but why are you telling me this?"

"After the raid on your company ships, the raid where we found the bell—"

"Stole the bell," Eva said.

"Um, right. Well, after it, we got talkin', the Captain and me, of 'er past, 'er childhood. She remembered an 'ouse, you see. With gardens. And a strange dinin' room with a glass wall and ceilin'."

Eva's brow knitted.

"'Er mother told 'er it were the 'ouse she were born in, somewhere in Goa. 'Er mother's name, she said, were Sada. And in English, she told me, Gulaba'aar means *Daisy*."

Eva sobbed and held her hands up to her face. Her whole body shook.

"She didn't remember anythin' of her life on Blackrabbit, save for a vague memory of the 'ouse. She didn't even remember ever bein' called Daisy. She grew up in a place called Calicut. She said 'er mother were killed by soldiers of the crown when she were eleven years old. Soldiers came to their 'ome to evict them. They wanted to clear the land for some wealthy family to build more factories. Sada refused and so they shot 'er. Gulaba'aar—Daisy—ran away and 'id on a ship. A pirate ship, as it turned out. She made 'erself useful on board, and in return they trained 'er in their ways. When she were old enough, she returned 'ome and took 'er revenge."

Eva held her own stomach and swayed in her chair. The words had landed like a punch.

"I never knew what happened to her," she said, dabbing her eyes with her handkerchief. "I could never find her. Her mother took her and vanished. Sada never used her title or her last name. She took nothing with her. By the time I was old enough to search for her myself, I had no way to find her. I asked all of the Chase Trading Company captains to keep their eyes and ears open for any word of Sada or Daisy, but there was nothing. I even travelled to India myself, searched official records, tried to find some clue."

"I'm sorry," Robin said. "She wanted to come 'ere, to meet you."

"She did?"

"Oh yes, I told 'er all about you, I did! Told 'er about you and Iris, about your life 'ere. She were lookin' forward to meetin' you."

Eva sat back and wiped her eyes again.

"She knew about me then?" she asked. "In the end? She knew about me."

"I told 'er you kept 'er close to your 'eart. Your *dear sister Daisy*, you called 'er. She knew you loved 'er still."

Eva grabbed his hand and squeezed as tightly as she could, and they sat together that way for a good long while.

Nick had been keeping his distance, watching Duncan and his friends from afar. Clearly, Duncan had missed Robin terribly. It was interesting, Nick thought, how few people Duncan trusted. How few of them he allowed to see the more tender side of himself. With Edwin and Robin, however, he was as unguarded as Nick had ever seen. He laughed and smiled and joked and even touched them—on the hand, the shoulder, the arm. A jovial familiarity born of countless hours spent in each other's company. It was good to see how much Duncan was loved.

"Nick!" Duncan said, bidding him sit by his side. "I wondered where you'd gotten to. I wanted to introduce you. Nick Babbage, this is Robin Shipp."

Nick held his hand out and grunted slightly when the mountainous Mr. Shipp clasped it and squeezed.

"A pleasure, Mr. Babbage! You must call me Robin. Any friend of Duncan's, and all that," he said, beaming.

He was quite a jolly sort with a friendly, sweet smile. A jarring contrast to his brother, Vince. Everything about Robin was softer; he even seemed to have smoother edges. His white beard looked like silk compared to the spikey bristles adorning Vince's jaw.

"You two are together?" Robin asked.

"For now," Duncan said. "We'll see. He's very clingy, and he won't shut up about coins."

"He's already completely smitten with me," Nick said. "It's almost embarrassing."

"I'm having second thoughts, to be honest," Duncan said with a grin.

Nick poked his thumb into Duncan's side, causing Duncan to giggle and blush. Robin threw his frankly enormous arms around Duncan and hugged him.

"I'm 'appy for you," he said in what he probably thought was a whisper. "Don't ruin it."

"Hah! I'll try not to," Duncan said.

"Looks like you both coped well enough without me."

"I kept Edwin's spirits up, kept his mind off of worrying about you."

"Is that what you thought you were doing?" Edwin asked. "You did a terrible job of it."

"What? No, I didn't," Duncan said. "I talked about myself a lot, didn't I?"

"You would have done that anyway."

"Well, there's gratitude for you. Oh, I almost forgot..." He took from his pocket a package wrapped in linen and string which he handed to Robin. "George left a little gift for you. His way of saying good luck with running this place."

Robin pawed at the string, snapping it in twain. He pulled off the linen to reveal a small, willow picture frame. Inside was a rough drawing of a two-masted lugger, complete with measurements. He went very quiet for a moment. His brow furrowed, and he seemed a thousand miles away.

Nick studied him carefully. He really was like Vince in some ways, yet his polar opposite in others. Where Vince emanated menace, Robin radiated a sort of peace, a calmness. A warmth of spirit. Combined with his beautiful sky-blue eyes and powerful frame, it wasn't at all difficult to see why Duncan had fallen in love with him all those years ago.

"Is this what I think it is?" Robin asked.

"The original plan for *Bucca's Call*," Duncan said. "Drawn by your father's very own hand. Would you believe George found it when he was clearing out the rooms for his new museum?"

"His new *what?*"

"You missed quite a bit while you were away," Edwin said. "Arminell Kind decided it should be named the *George Reed Museum*. She had a plaque made up and everything."

"I'm not sure it was strictly necessary—this whole place is a museum," Nick said.

"He turned up a lot of stuff," Duncan said. "Apparently neither he nor his parents before him ever threw away anything left behind at the inn. He found drawings of the village from a hundred years ago, plans for the houses on Anchor Rise, the schoolhouse, all sorts. It's all on display up there."

Robin touched the glass of the frame with a wide, thick finger.

"So, *Bucca's* really gone?" Edwin said.

"I couldn't save 'er, just like I couldn't save Dad," he said, his eyes closed and wet.

Edwin held him tightly. "Listen to me," he said, his voice soft as sea foam. "*Bucca* kept you safe and sane all these years, until she could take you back to your dad. And as for him, what's the passage in his journal you keep going back to? *There has been much turmoil and strife. Much suffering and loss, but it will all have been worth it for it was all for my son.* He gave his life to save yours, as any father would for his child. As I would for mine."

Robin kissed the top of Edwin's head. Edwin was different now, too. Since Nick had known him, he'd been withdrawn, guarded, but with Robin back he smiled wider, stood straighter. He was, quite simply, happy.

"You could always build a new boat," Duncan said, tapping the frame. "You have the plans. She'd be identical."

"But not the same," Robin said. "It sounds daft to say it, a man of my age, but I were never goin' to grow up while *Bucca* were still 'ere. She kept me tied to 'im—to Dad, I mean. Tied to the past. I miss 'er, of course I do. But to be truthful, I feel...lighter."

"You don't look it..." Duncan said.

"Freer, I mean," Robin said, giving him a friendly jab on the shoulder. "Ready to start again. As your 'usband if the offer still stands?"

Edwin took his hand and kissed it. "Of course it does."

"You two are getting married?" Duncan said, wide-eyed and smiling.

"Looks that way," Robin said. "Only leaves the question of when?"

"As soon as possible," Edwin said. "Before something else happens."

"Not before you lose the beard, I hope," Duncan said.

"Why?" asked Robin, admiring his reflection in a nearby lantern. "I think I look quite distinguished."

"It ages you terribly," Duncan said.

"I like it," Edwin said, rubbing his hand across the soft, white hair. "It suits you. You look more like...yourself, if you follow me? As though it were a part of you that's been missing all this time."

Chapter Forty-Two

Robin couldn't sleep. It was too warm for nightwear, too warm even for bedclothes, and he kicked them off with his feet. Yet it wasn't just the unseasonably hot October weather keeping him awake, it was excitement. He and Edwin had decided to follow the old tradition of not seeing each other before the handfasting ceremony. He ached from the separation so soon after his time at sea but knew it would make the day all the sweeter.

He hauled himself out of bed, grabbed his cap from the bedpost, and headed downstairs. By lantern light, he sat and clumsily drew a moth on a sheet of paper. The simplest lines, the crudest of shapes, for he possessed no skill in illustration. It mattered little, for no eyes would ever fall upon it save his own. He placed the sketch inside an old whiskey bottle and sealed it with wax.

He pulled on his trousers and boots, grabbed his lantern and marched out of his house. He walked down Anchor Rise, past the Moth & Moon, past the forge, and up Hill Road. All was quiet, and dark, and still. He continued along Ridge Street and down Fisherman's Run before turning on to Wolfe Ditch. Now surrounded by trees, he followed the track called Loves Last. Such a sorrowful name, he'd always thought, but fitting seeing as it was a tree tunnel which led to the cemetery in the woods. It was the path everyone on the island would take, sooner or later.

It was the custom to leave a token for the departed on the tall yew tree in the centre of the cemetery meadow, and it was strewn with items going back generations. Not all of them were still in one piece, having fallen victim to both weather and time. Colourful beads of sea glass strung across branches like dew on a spider's web. Threads of bright wool wrapped round the trunk. Coins, buttons, caps, even shoes had been stuck in or strapped to various spots. Each one had been left by a mourner and commemorated someone buried in the meadow. Throughout the years, the tributes would jangle in the breeze, glint in the sunlight, catch raindrops, or sparkle with frost. The yew tree was the island's living monument to love and loss. Robin stretched up to the highest branch he could reach and tied the whiskey bottle firmly to it. It gleamed in the fierce pink light of dawn.

He found George's grave marker. A simple block of stone engraved with a moth at each corner. It read:

George Albert Reed

5th August 1715—10th October 1781

Beloved Innkeeper and Friend

~ He Kept Us Safe ~

Robin spoke some words of gratitude, talked about his time on Driftwood, and promised to take good care of the inn. He fancied he heard George's laugh on the breeze, felt his touch in the sunlight. A tad fanciful, he told himself, but if an old sailor can't be sentimental every now and then, who can?

Robin and Edwin, dressed in their finest linen suits, stood facing each other in the Moth & Moon. Robin wore his cap, of course. He wasn't going to, but Edwin said he didn't look right without it. Most of the village had gathered and every seat was occupied. Duncan and Nick sat side by side. Vince had come from Blackrabbit for the occasion and sat with Allegra asleep in his arms while beside him Iris cradled baby George. Morwenna dabbed at her eyes with a handkerchief and tried to maintain her composure as best she could. Eva wore a rose-coloured robe à l'Anglaise and she stood before the grand fireplace, addressing the crowd.

"It is a bittersweet honour to be performing this ceremony today," she said, her loud, clear voice ringing through the tavern. "I'm certain our dear George Reed would have loved nothing more than to be standing where I am now, officiating at this happiest of occasions."

She stepped forward, cupping Robin and Edwin's elbows. "Hold hands, please." She placed a piece of sea green silk over their adjoined hands and knotted it, binding them together.

"Robin Shipp, Edwin Farriner, this knot symbolises the love that holds you together. But the true bonds of your handfasting are the vows you make before your friends, your family, and your community."

"A year and a bit ago," Edwin said, "a hurricane struck our island and turned our lives upside down. For all the pain it caused, for all the hurt it dredged up, it led me here, standing before my best friend—the sweetest, kindest, most wonderful man I've ever met. It took us a long time to be together but maybe that time helped us to see what we really had in each other. I may wish it could have happened sooner, but you were worth the wait and more."

Robin stood as straight as he could and cleared his throat, trying not to let his nervousness show. His palms, now bound to Edwin's, started to sweat.

"I 'ad a whole speech written, but I forgot I wouldn't be able to get the paper out of my pocket."

The crowd laughed, which made him feel a little better, but he was still probably more nervous than he'd ever been. He hoped someone would tell him if he started to ramble on too much.

"There are people who aren't 'ere today who should be, and there are people who are 'ere who I never thought would be. I thought... I really thought I'd be alone forever," he said. "I thought this 'ere were the sort of thing that 'appened to other people, not to me. I thought the course of my life were set a long time ago and I were fated for loneliness. But you've taken me in another direction, given me 'ope, and love, and another chance at life. You're the best, smartest, most 'andsome man I know, and I promise to love you. I don't know what else I can say. I'll love you wholly, entirely, completely."

Edwin's ears burned red, his cheeks too. He shuffled about and squeezed Robin's hands tightly. Robin's eyes swelled, and he laughed the tears away as Eva stepped forward.

"Before this community, these two men do declare their love. Before this community, these two men do declare their devotion. Before this community, these two men be wed."

A thunderous applause swept through the inn as Robin and Edwin shared their first kiss as a married couple. Whoops and cheers erupted from the gallery overhead, as did dozens of small flowers. Mr. Penny called for young Peter Underton who ran to the front doors and shouted up to the roof. Within seconds, the newly installed bell chimed for the first time ever. Three joyful, sonorous peals reverberated through the entire inn, shaking the very bones of the place. Eva untied the silk and placed it into a neatly carved box. It would be a memento for the happy couple to cherish. Duncan was the first on his feet, and he hugged them both.

"Congratulations, you two," he said. "Don't ruin it."

Vince shook Robin by the hand and pulled him in close for a hug. "Well done, little brother," he said. "Got some news of my own. Guess who's been put in charge of the Port Knot Watchmen?"

"What?" Edwin asked.

"Giss'on!" Robin said.

"In recognition of capturing Penhallow and Palk," Vince said, adjusting his eyepatch. "And in light of my extensive experience with the underbelly of the town."

"I thought you weren't interested in being part of the Watch," Duncan said.

"Wasn't," Vince said. "But Edwin made a good point. If I'm going to start over, I need to start trying to make up for past mistakes." He hugged Edwin then, taking him entirely by surprise.

"Sometimes, it takes a criminal to catch a criminal, I suppose," Nick said.

Robin tipped his cap back and laughed heartily. "I never thought I'd see the day!"

"The criminals of Blackrabbit are going to be terrified," Duncan said, as he chewed his own bottom lip. "It's enough to make you feel sorry for them."

Vince snorted a short laugh and grabbed Duncan and Nick by the shoulders. "Come on," he said. "Buy me a drink to celebrate."

Morwenna was next in line to congratulate them. Robin leaned down so she could grab his face and kiss him on both cheeks. "Your father would be proud," she said.

He'd told her everything about his time on Driftwood. She'd cried, of course. For the memory of his father, for the lost chance to see him again. He'd held back no detail, there'd been enough secrets between them for one lifetime. She deserved to know everything.

Iris went to join a group of musicians setting up under an archway. Robin hadn't even noticed her harpsichord had been brought to the tavern from the lodge. She warmed up with a few notes before launching into a lilting melody. She was joined by the haunting strings of a crwth, then came the dreamy notes of a flute, and finally the steady beat of a crowdy crawn. May Bell's mother, Louisa, sang a joyous song. Vince tapped Robin on the shoulder and pointed at the eyepatch-wearing bear on the black flag above the archway.

"That supposed to be me?" he asked.

Robin laughed and grabbed Vince's arm. "Ho ho! I knew it reminded me of someone! It's the Sea Bear, our dad's flag. I thought it would look better in 'ere than gatherin' dust in my attic."

The past week had been a whirlwind. Robin's first priority had been the handfasting as he wasn't prepared to wait a second longer than was absolutely necessary. It meant leaving the day to day running of the Moth to Arminell Kind. She'd kept things ticking over since George's passing, and Robin had asked her if she intended to stay on. The last time she'd worked there, before she'd gotten pregnant, she cared little for the place. Now, though, Robin fancied he'd seen a shift in attitude. She stood more upright. She walked with purpose. Perhaps it was motherhood which had changed her outlook? Though he'd been told she and George had spent a lot of time together before the end. Maybe that was it.

"I'd like to stay, Mr. Shipp," she'd said. "Archie wants to continue to stay at home with our baby, and I've developed an...appreciation for this place. Besides, I'm sure Mr. Reed would want someone to show you the ropes."

She wasn't wrong. Robin knew plenty about drinking but little about the business. He had stormy seas ahead and was glad of her steady hand to guide him. Fausto, Harry Vosper, and the other pirates had stayed for a few days and behaved themselves for the most part. There had been some minor drunken squabbles amongst the ranks, but they'd suffered tremendous losses and were understandably upset. Robin really thought Fausto might stay on the island, so taken was he with the place, but in the end he left his apricot-coloured bandana in one of the Moth & Moon's nooks and joined his crewmates back on board the *Mortal Grace*. Robin waved them off from shore and told them they were welcome back anytime. He meant it.

He'd spent one night wandering the halls of the inn alone, trying to get used to the idea of owning the place. He'd yet to step behind the bar, into the place where George had spent most of his days. It hadn't felt like the right time. Until now. He lifted the counter flap and squeezed through. Without George there, he felt out of place, as though he were trespassing into a private, personal space. The closest sensation he'd experienced was of being in someone else's bedroom. The floor, raised to accommodate George's diminutive stature, creaked under his boots. The boards were worn smooth from the years George spent treading across them. Robin ducked his head and ran his hand along the bar. He was touching history. The Moth & Moon was older than the village itself. This very counter was the same one the first shipwrecked settlers on the island had constructed from the wreckage of their ship, the *Eclipse*. The weight of history came crashing against him like a wave.

"Are you going to stand there all day, Mr. Shipp?" Eva asked. "Or are you planning to actually serve some drinks?"

"Sorry, I were lost in my own thoughts," he said, snapping back to the present.

Standing before him at the bar were Edwin, Duncan, Morwenna, Eva, and Vince. Iris joined them, carrying the twins and slipping in beside Eva, still singing along to the music.

"What are you staring at?" Duncan asked.

"Nothin', nothin'," Robin said, tipping his cap back. "It's just... I never thought I'd be stood 'ere with my family is all. Now, who's gettin' my first official drink as landlord of the Moth & Moon?"

"I think Morwenna should have the honour," Edwin said.

"One gin, comin' up."

Robin grabbed a bottle from the shelf behind him and uncorked it. He poured it slowly into a glass.

"George would always pour me a little extra," Morwenna said.

He laughed and tipped a little more in. He poured drinks for everyone else and took a whiskey for himself.

"I think we should all raise a glass to George Reed," he said. "Innkeeper, 'istorian, and friend. We'll never forget 'im."

"You're not only the landlord, you know" Eva said. "You're the village's storyteller now. The keeper of its history."

"And its secrets," Duncan said. "The things George must have been privy to over the years..."

"I never thought of myself as a storyteller," Robin said. "I 'ope I can do 'im justice."

"Well, you've got a few good ones yourself," Edwin said. "How you got your scarred hand. How you nearly lost your leg. How you witnessed the last gasp of high seas piracy."

"All this history on your shoulders," Duncan said. "However will you bear it?"

"You'll have George's stories," Eva said. "He wrote them all down for you."

"'E wrote them for us," Robin said. "For all of us. So we would never forget where we came from."

The celebrations lasted well into the early hours of the morning. Long after most of the villagers had gone home, Robin and Edwin lounged in their favourite seat, beneath the painting of *The Battle in the Bay*. They'd been discussing their living arrangements. It would be easier for the running of the place if Robin were to move into George's quarters in the Moth & Moon, though he was reluctant to do so. It felt too soon, and he would miss his own house. Besides which, Edwin had begun moving his belongings out of his own rooms above the bakery and into Robin's home. While it was very convenient for Edwin to live above his workplace, it was hardly necessary. The same could be said for Robin. He had no intention of moving into the Moth any time soon.

"Where are the boys?" Robin asked.

"They've taken Vince up to his room," Edwin said. "He was really quite drunk. They all were, actually."

"Vince drinks even more than Dad did. It really does take a lot to sink a Shipp."

"You haven't talked much about him. Your dad, I mean. And when you do, it's...different. There's not as much sadness there."

"'E brought out a funny side of me. A side I didn't much care for. I wonder if it's what I would 'ave been like if 'e'd stayed, or if 'e'd come back. I told Dad the night 'e left were like an anchor in my life, holdin' me in place. I'm free of it now. Free to move forward, at long last. Oh, I meant to check somethin'."

He tilted up the heavy painting behind his head. It creaked on old, rusted hinges. Behind it were several cobweb-filled niches in the tavern wall. He thrust his hand into each of them in turn.

"What are you looking for?" Edwin asked.

Robin reached the last of the nooks and felt inside. "I just wondered if maybe..."

He trailed off as his fingers touched something. Leather. He withdrew his hand and clasped within it was a dusty, blood-red journal.

"It looks the same as your dad's," Edwin said. "The anchor is missing, though."

"Not missin'," Robin said, tapping the pendant on his cap. "It's right 'ere."

"Oh, this is where it came from? Hah, I never even thought about it."

Robin blew decades of dust from the cover and opened it, flicking through the pages. Inside were maps, dates, coordinates, all sorts.

"This belonged to Tommy Oughterlauney. Dad stole it and 'id it 'ere."

"Why, what's in it?"

"A treasure map," Robin said. "The location of an 'orde of Spanish silver lyin' on the seabed off the coast of France."

Robin thought about chartering a ship and heading back to sea, diving into the ice-cold water, searching for treasure among the wreck of the *Mercury*.

"I almost 'ad it, you know?" he said. "I almost got what I'd always wanted. I nearly 'ad my dad back 'ome, nearly 'ad my parents together again. I was so close to reunitin' Eva with 'er sister. I almost made everybody 'appy. I could see it all so clearly. We'd sail into the 'arbour, Mum would slap Dad across the face, and then they'd embrace and all would be forgiven. Eva would weep with joy at seein' 'er long-lost sister again. We'd all be 'appy. Whole, you know? Then it all slipped away in a flash. Everythin' changed in an 'eartbeat, like it always does. A single moment is all it takes for your whole life to change course."

He turned to Edwin and smiled. "Like you said, though, it's not always a bad thing," he said, hugging Edwin tightly.

"You did all you could," Edwin said. "At least Eva knows what happened to Daisy now. To Gulabahaar, I mean. There's comfort to be found there. And your father may not be here but he wanted to be. There's comfort in that too. And for what it's worth, you've made me happier than I ever thought I could be."

"It's worth a lot," Robin said, kissing him. "It's worth everythin'." He stuffed the old journal into his pocket. "The silver is probably long gone, anyway. And if not, someone else can risk their neck lookin' for it. I 'ave everythin' I need right 'ere."

"How are you going to cope, do you think? Being cooped up indoors all day?"

"It'll take some time to adjust, but I'll get there. Just another change to embrace."

Edwin was slumped under Robin's arm, his head laid on Robin's chest. Robin drained the last of his drink. He'd lost count of how many he'd had. Every villager in the place had bought him and Edwin one, or wanted to, anyway. Edwin hadn't touched a drop.

"I suppose we better be headin' 'ome, Mr. Farriner," Robin said, slightly slurring his words.

"I think you're right. We've got to start your project tomorrow. The history of Driftwood. We should—hang on. We haven't talked about this, have we?"

"The pirates?"

"The names. Our names. Am I keeping my last name? Are you?"

"Ah, you'll always be a Farriner, and I can only be a Shipp. I think we should keep things the way they are."

"I thought you were all for embracing change now?"

"Some things are perfect just the way they are," Robin said, kissing him.

"Charmer," Edwin said. "Come on then, Mr. Shipp, let's go home."

Epilogue

A moth with blue wings trimmed in silver clung to the porthole of the tiny, hidden writing room on the roof of the inn, fluttering its wings silently in the cool, sea air. Inside, George Reed sat before a stack of papers. He twirled a quill round and round between his fingertips. His collection of stories, his history of the island and its people, his gift to the village was in desperate need of a title. He'd mulled it over for weeks, unable to settle on the perfect one.

To set oneself up as the chronicler of a community is no easy task. There are many avenues to be explored, many facets to every fact. No matter how thorough one thinks they have been, there will always be more stories to tell. All one can do is hope to capture enough of the spirit of a place to give a sense of it, a true and honest impression. To make it real in the heart and mind of the reader.

Beside him, his lantern grew dim, its golden flame fading until it became no bigger than a firefly, leaving him bathed in the pale moonlight. There had, he realised, been one commonality in his tales, one element to which they returned again and again. One heart beating within them.

Smiling, he dipped the tip of the quill into an inkpot and quickly scratched a title onto the topmost leaf.

It read simply *The Moth & Moon*.

Acknowledgements

I would like to thank my partner, Mark Wilson, to whom this book is dedicated, for his love, his patience, and for putting up with me being in a world of my own half the time. Okay, fine, more than half. I'd also like to thank my tireless feedback team of Tony Teehan and Christian Smith for their insights. My cousin, Dan Byrne, for his architectural know-how. Praveen Kaspa, Tony Willis and Mehdi Bennani for their translation skills. My family for their encouragement, in particular my mother who never gave up pushing me to write. In a nice way, of course. And if you are ever accosted on holiday by an Irishman trying to get you to buy one of my novels, it's probably my Da.

Thanks as well to my publisher, Raevyn McCann, to my brilliant editor, BJ Toth, to Natasha Snow for the gorgeous cover, and to all the NineStar Press team.

About the Author

Glenn Quigley is an author and artist originally from Dublin and now living in Lisburn, Northern Ireland. He designs for www.themoodybear.com. When not writing or designing, he tries to improve his portraiture skills.

Email
glennquigley@gmail.com

Facebook
www.facebook.com/glennquigleyauthor

Twitter
@glennquigley

Website
www.glennquigley.com

Other books by this author

The Moth and Moon
The Lion Lies Waiting

Also Available from NineStar Press

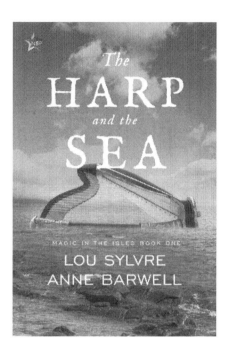

Connect with NineStar Press

Website: NineStarPress.com

Facebook: NineStarPress

Facebook Reader Group: NineStarNiche

Twitter: @ninestarpress

Tumblr: NineStarPress